SO-ABB-567

# TIGHT SHOT

# Kevin Allman

# TIGHT SHOT

## A Hollywood Mystery

St. Martin's Press   New York

TIGHT SHOT. Copyright © 1995 by Kevin Allman. All rights reserved.
Printed in the United States of America. No part of this book may be used
or reproduced in any manner whatsoever without written permission ex-
cept in the case of brief quotations embodied in critical articles or reviews.
For information, address St. Martin's Press, 175 Fifth Avenue, New York,
N.Y. 10010.

*Design by Basha Zapatka*

Library of Congress Cataloging-in-Publication Data

Allman, Kevin.
    Tight shot : a Hollywood mystery / Kevin Allman.
        p.    cm.
    ISBN 0-312-11904-6
    I. Title.
    PS3551.L462T5    1995
    813'.54—dc20                                        94-42077
                                                        CIP

First Edition: March 1995
10 9 8 7 6 5 4 3 2 1

*For Dominick Alonzo—mille grazie*

Grateful thanks to the following people:

Jeff Berry, Hope Dellon, Daphne Hart, Helen Heller, Sharen Shaw Johnson, Richard Labonte, Larry Lurin, Kelley Ragland, Jim Schmaltz, and my friends at the *Los Angeles Times*, especially Janice Mall and Jeannine Stein.

It would be a good thing to buy books if one could also buy the time in which to read them; but generally the purchase of a book is mistaken for the acquisition of its contents.

—ARTHUR SCHOPENHAUER

Everyone in Hollywood hates to think about writing. It's so uncompromisable in a sense. There's no easy way to improve it. It's so fundamental. You can't make it better with a better deal.

—TOM WOLFE

Anyone in Hollywood who knew Herman Melville from Herman Munster qualified as an intellectual.

—MARIA TANKOVICH

# ONE

# = 1 =

I WAS LYING ON MY FUTON, eating a microwaved plate of refried beans, listening to a Mekons CD for the third time in a row, rereading a two-year-old copy of *The New Republic,* and watching a rerun of a talk show when the phone rang.

"Are you busy?" my editor asked.

"Swamped. Hang on just a minute," I said, muting both Mekons and Oprah Winfrey and tapping a few computer keys in a pathetic simulation of industry.

"Sure you are. What's on 'Oprah'?"

"Former Olympic athletes undergoing gender reassignment."

"Ah, the life of a freelancer," she said. "You have time to squeeze some work into that schedule?"

"I suppose." I went to the window and peeked through the vertical blinds. Downstairs, on the Venice boardwalk, some kid was juggling chain saws for a bunch of tourists wearing fanny packs. It was a sunny Friday afternoon in February, and people were already out in shorts and tank tops, eating frozen yogurt.

"Let me look through these press releases." I heard paper rustling. "We've got a premiere at the Avco next Wednesday. Something called *Throwdown, the Rap Musical*—"

"Pass." Any movie released between New Year's Day and Oscar night was, prima facie, a piece of crap. Besides, I wasn't up for being crammed into a club with a bunch of people in clown pants and gold chains while a megawatt sound system turned my brain into kefir.

"O-kay. The Songwriter's Salute to the Songwriter is having a do at the Music Center. It's a tribute to Barry Mani—"

"Pass."

"Someone from *Blast* magazine is bugging me. They're having a party for their debut issue this weekend at someplace called the Jab-berjaw."

"What's *Blast?*"

"I was hoping you could tell me."

"Tell them we'll cover their first anniversary party, if they make it that far."

Sally shuffled papers. In the background, I could hear reporters murmuring on the phone, tapping computer keys. Doing their job, in other words.

"What about this?" she said. "Women in the Industry are honor-ing Gregory Slezak Monday night at the Beverly Hillshire. The ad-visory committee is dynamite. The guest list looks padded, but if even half of these people show up, it should be good."

"We should cover that one," I had to admit, even though put-ting on a tuxedo and sitting through four hours of speeches with a roomful of power face-lifts was the last thing I wanted to do. On the other hand, getting a check was about the *first* thing I wanted to do.

Sally cleared her throat. "Why would a women's group be honor-ing a man?"

"He directed *A Lover's Question,*" I reminded her. I'd covered the premiere a few months before and had a vague recollection of Greg-ory Slezak: wiry graying hair, aviator glasses, preternaturally tan. "It wasn't that great—typical Oscar bait—but Slezak's well-liked, and it did have four juicy parts for women. Every actress in town wanted to be in it."

"Why?" Sally was a good editor, but she freely admitted that the last movie she'd seen was *Dr. Zhivago.* She wanted to work the sports desk as bad as I wanted to work in hard news.

"Probably because (a), they weren't playing someone's girlfriend, and (b), they got to keep their clothes on."

"How novel," she said.

"Let's do it," I told her. "Oscar nominations are out Monday morning, and it's going to clean up. Slezak's a cinch for a Best Direc-tor nomination, and he'll probably win, too. Plus he and his wife produced it, and after it gets nominated for Best Picture, they're going to be the hottest production team in town."

Sally gave me the contact information, which I jotted down on

*The New Republic*'s blow-in subscription card. The only thing I hate worse than those cards are magazine ads with scent strips; the main reason I subscribed to *The New Republic* was that it didn't make my mailbox smell like a French whorehouse.

My call-waiting clicked in. I like call-waiting about as much as I like scent strips, but I don't know anyone who doesn't have it these days. There's a whole generation of eight-year-olds who probably don't even know what a busy signal is. "Hang on," I told Sally, and pressed the button.

"Hey, there." It was Claudia. "Long time no see."

"Long time no argue. Look, I've got my editor on the other line—"

"Does this mean you're getting some work, Kieran?"

"Yeah."

"How novel," she said, just like Sally. Sometimes I had grandiose, male-paranoid fantasies that Claudia and Sally got together in the evening and parsed every detail of my miserable life over margaritas.

Claudia's call-waiting clicked in with an annoying electronic crunch. "Call me back at the shop," she said, and she was gone.

"Who was that?" Sally wanted to know.

"*Vanity Fair*," I told her. "They want to fly me to South Africa tomorrow to interview Nelson Mandela."

"Be sure you're back by Monday night. Say hi to Winnie," she said, and rang off.

I dragged myself off the futon and went to the window again. The chain-saw guy had been joined by a man who had spread out a mat, covered it with shards of broken glass, and was doing a barefoot tap dance for the tourists. That's entertainment.

Two women walked past in identical string bikinis—tiny triangles in the front that disappeared into tinier pieces of butt floss in the back. I waved at them. They waved back and burst into giggles. Then I realized that I was standing in the window unshaved, in my rattiest pair of pajama bottoms, and I flicked the blinds closed.

I tried to finish the refried beans, but they'd fused themselves to the paper plate. I crumpled it up and stuck it under the coffee table for later disposal.

Women in the Industry, I thought. What the hell. A free dinner is a free dinner.

* * *

I suppose you could call me a journalist, if you define "journalist" as someone who occasionally writes something, occasionally gets it published, and even more occasionally gets paid for the effort. Hell, in a town like this, where a waitress can call herself an actress and a bookstore clerk can call himself a screenwriter, I *am* a journalist.

My specialty is a peculiar niche called event coverage. Making small talk with small people over canapés. Going to action-movie premieres, trying to extract coherent sentences out of steroid abusers. Being lectured by ninth-grade dropouts on the importance of saving the rainforest. Attending concerts, hanging around the hangers-on, and asking celebrities (or, in the argot of the business, *celebs)* what they think of Madonna. Or Spike Lee. Or the weather. Or anything. Then I go home, put it all into my computer, try to make it funny, modem it downtown, and see my name in print the next day. "Have Tux, Will Travel," by Kieran O'Connor.

As bad jobs go, it's not bad. Other people find it fascinating. And at a time when college graduates are paying off their student loans by selling sweatshirts at the Gap, I suppose I should be more thankful that I have a semi-self-supporting job doing something that I don't entirely dislike, for an editor whom I actually do like. But I've got a melancholy streak and a bottomless supply of self-pity, and I can't help but feel some slight responsibility that Bruce Willis makes more for one smarmy smile than the average teacher makes in a lifetime. It all adds up to a headful of 24–7 Irish guilt, which I secretly try to alleviate by reading a lot of obscure political journals and Victorian novels. It doesn't work.

I rolled over on the futon, stared down the Dustbuster in the corner, and decided that cleaning the apartment could wait. When my parents were my age, they were both well-established in their careers and were scrimping away in their third year into a twenty-year mortgage. I was just the opposite—living in a tatty rented apartment in the worst part of Venice, trying to make up for my substandard standard of living by splurging on a CD or a non-discounted hardback or an eight-dollar bag of French roast beans instead of the Folgers vacuum-pack.

I was born somewhere between the baby boomers and the Generation Xers, and came of age in that shallow malaise between the fall

— 6 —

of Nixon and the ascendance of MTV. I'm twenty-nine, and I freely admit that I don't understand today's young people. Nor do I trust the ones who refer to themselves proudly as old hippies. Hippies, to me, always professed to love everyone in the world, but they couldn't get along with anyone around them. They grew up denouncing phony art and capitalism and went on to create "Family Ties," the Hard Rock Cafe, and a bunch of overpriced ice creams with cutesy-poo names.

I think of myself as the diametric opposite: I'm not big on mankind as a whole, but I've met quite a few individuals I like and respect. I go out of my way to avoid humans in large groups. I've never had much truck with any organization, from the Cub Scouts to the National Writers' Union. I've never been married and I've had only one serious relationship. I hope I never become an alcoholic, because I'd never be able to stand the meetings.

I had sulked my way through the rest of "Oprah," all of "Geraldo," and was watching a particularly unexciting freeway chase on "Action News" when I remembered Claudia's call. Even though we hadn't talked in three months, she was still number one on my speed dialer. She picked up on the second ring.

"So what are you doing?" she asked. In the background, I heard a cappuccino machine hiss and k.d. lang sing about someone who left her—lock, stock, and teardrops. Do tell, k.d. Welcome to the club.

"The usual," I told her. "Right now I'm watching a car chase on the news—"

"Another one?"

"What's a day in L.A. without a car chase?"

"You and your news shows." Claudia was completely disgusted with my TV diet, which consisted entirely of bad local news, real-life cop shows, and—the socially redeeming part—all the Sunday-morning political panels.

"So what else have you been doing, Kieran?"

"I told you. I'm lying here watching Tritia Toyota and wondering how much she makes for emceeing this news-flavored game show."

"More than you'll ever make."

"Thank you for your support."

"Oh, don't be so sensitive, Kieran."

"Then let's talk about something else."

"Okay. How's your love life these days? You have a new girlfriend yet?"

I rearranged my pajamas. "No. Do you?"

There was a silence. I heard the cash register beep, and then Claudia sighed. If she was calling me and listening to k.d. lang, I figured that things weren't exactly chocolates and roses on her end either.

"Is it Cathy?"

She sighed again.

Claudia Dubuisson and I had had an on-again, off-again relationship for five years. It had been off again since September, when we'd gone to a party at her friend Pedro's house, both had too much to drink, and ended up flirting outrageously with the same woman, an independent filmmaker who'd gotten all heaty after her student film cleaned up at a few film festivals. There'd been the usual boring fight, I'd gone home alone, and she'd started an affair that had been going on for several months. The last I'd heard from her had been an aggressively cute photo Christmas card signed "C. & C." I think I was less annoyed she'd left me than I was at the fact that she'd taken up with someone in the industry.

"So what's going on?" I asked.

"Oh, Cathy's just being . . . eight twenty-five, please," she said. I heard the cash register beep again. "She's on the road all the time," she continued more quietly. "I guess I'm being jealous and stupid and *feminine*, but it pisses me off when she comes back to town and expects me to be at her beck and call. In between her lunches at the Grill and her dinners at Cormorant-at-the-Shore."

"Is she cheating on you?"

"I don't know," she said. "Well, actually I do. She's not."

"Are you cheating on her?"

"You know I don't do that," she said sharply. "But sometimes I just feel like doing it. You know that feeling? Like you just want to go out and get laid? To hell with small talk or dinner or condoms? Just shut up and do it?"

"But you haven't."

"No. Not yet."

"Well, don't," I said. "I don't care if lesbians *are* at low risk for AIDS—"

My fax machine chattered to life, sliding out a piece of paper. The guest list for the Women in the Industry dinner. Sally had drawn a smiley face with a bullet hole on the top.

"I'm *not* a lesbian," Claudia said peevishly. "I'm bisexual."

I hit the TV mute button again, turning the sound back on. "That's as may be, Claudia," I said, "but I'm not sure that it makes a hell of a lot of difference to God, the HIV virus, or the CDC." I was a strong advocate of condoms—not that I ever had the chance to use them.

"You're right," she said, sounding unconvinced.

There was another long pause. "So what do you want me to do about it?" I finally asked.

"*Nothing*," she said. "Nothing, Kieran."

"I've got to go," I told her. "An RTD bus hit a Blue Line train and 'Action News' is live on the scene with correspondent Pat Lalama."

"Kieran, you *newshound*," she said, and hung up without saying good-bye.

I rolled off the futon and went in the bathroom to take a shower. My tuxedo was still hanging on the back of the door where I'd hung it four weeks before. It was limp and gummy-looking from absorbing a month of shower steam.

Making a mental note to take it to the cleaner's sometime befor Monday, I stepped into the shower, lathered up, and got ready start my day at five-twenty in the afternoon.

# 2

I HAD SPREAD THE DINNER jacket on the kitchen counter while trying frantically to get the worst of the creases out with a steam iron I'd bought at a garage sale. It was six o'clock on Monday, and I was supposed to be at the Beverly Hillshire Hotel at seven. On the dot.

I yawned. The worst thing about the Academy Award nominations was that they were announced so early in the morning. They began in Beverly Hills at five A.M. so they could be carried live by the East Coast morning shows at eight. I couldn't stomach the thought of actually going to the Academy so early, eating complimentary crullers with a bunch of other grumpy entertainment writers, so I set my alarm for four fifty-five and watched the whole thing from my futon as the first gray drizzles of light came through my window. L.A. being L.A., the nominations were carried as a special report on several channels.

Most of the minor nominations weren't televised, so people didn't have to sit through Best Score Written Especially for a Foreign Documentary while waiting to find out if they'd won the office betting pool. There were the usual mild surprises—the obligatory nomination for a supporting actor no one had ever heard of, in a film no one had ever seen—but the most interesting moment came when one of the sleepy presenters mangled Sydney Pollack's name into an ethnic slur. As I and everybody else had predicted, Gregory Slezak was in the pack of Best Director nominees.

Last came the biggest category of all: Best Picture. The presenters alternated reading the names as the logos from the nominated films flashed on video screens behind them.

"*Beauty and the Bellboy*. Producers, Sarah Timmons and Robert Yardley."

"*Country at War*. Producer, Gemma Nicholls."

"*Femme Fatale*. Producers, Raffaelo and Luigi DeCrescenzo."

"*Final Argument*. Producer, Carl Kohut."

No surprises there. Most of the nominees were solid critical hits, and had made respectable money. *Beauty and the Bellboy* was commercial garbage—your basic bellboy-meets-girl, bellboy-loses-girl, bellboy-and-girl-live-happily-ever-after story—but it was the biggest hit of the year.

The presenter looked at the last name and waited just a beat before announcing:

"*Under the Gun*. Producer, Michael Coleman."

Whoops. Better luck next year, Mr. and Mrs. Slezak. I turned off the TV and went in the kitchen for another cup of coffee, trying to figure out what happened.

Since *A Lover's Question* was an ensemble piece for four women, everyone had assumed that the Best Actress votes would be split, leaving the field open for Meg Campbell's performance in *Final Argument*. But *A Lover's Question* seemed to be a shoo-in for Best Picture. *Final Argument* was unremarkable but solid. *Country at War* had been ubiquitous for months; I hadn't seen it, but once you'd seen the trailer every time you went to the movies, you really didn't need to. *Femme Fatale* had been lambasted for sexism, with half of the critics praising it and the other half crucifying it; and *Beauty and the Bellboy* was, well, *Beauty and the Bellboy*. By Academy algebra, the field seemed clear for *A Lover's Question* to capture both Best Director and Best Picture. It would have been one of those moments that the industry loves: a happily married team of producers delivering a forty-five-second piece of boilerplate about the value of working together both professionally and personally. Clear off the mantel. Make room for three statues. Now it looked like one statue, or none at all. Worse yet, Monica Slezak could hardly console herself with the rationalization that the Academy was threatened by women in power, because two of the nominated producers were women.

Did the members of the Academy dislike Monica Slezak for some reason? Was it Streisand all over again? From what I knew, people actually liked the Slezaks—a rare occurrence in an industry where fear and *Schadenfreude* are the dominant emotions.

I dumped a packet of Sweet 'n Low into my mug and thought about it. I'd never heard anything derogatory about Monica Slezak—only that she was tough and smart. She and her husband had been married for ten or eleven years, which counts for a golden anniversary in Hollywood. She was part of the movie industry's New Age contingent, and some people said that she was a little nuts, but if you exiled every nutcase from the streets of Beverly Hills, the reservation list at Morton's would be a blank book.

Well, I thought, sipping my coffee, tonight should be interesting.

The worst part of covering these affairs is the moment when I pull my car up to the phalanx of valets and surrender my keys. Idling in a pack of Rollses, Porsches, Lexuses, and Cadillacs, a dented and rusty '84 Buick Century tends to stand out. Most embarrassing of all, it was the special Olympic model with the five intertwined rings stuck all over the sides and the headrests. Claudia called it the Orange Countymobile. Some kid had tried to snap off the hood ornament the week before, and it dangled limply from the front of the car on a piece of sprung tension wire. Foiled, the kid had settled for breaking off the antenna instead and scrawling WASHE ME on the back with one illiterate digit. I'd never found the time to WASHE it off.

When I reached the head of the traffic jam, I could see dozens of paparazzi lining the cobblestone walk outside the entrance to the ballroom, snapping photos that they would develop that night and sell to the tabloids in the morning. Valets were pinballing through the traffic, exchanging claim checks for keys and peeling away in million-dollar machines as if they were Indy pacer cars. Tires squealed in the underground garage.

The car in front of me had its door snapped open smartly by a grinning valet. I'd seen enough James Bond movies to recognize it as a Cypriot, restored to cherry condition—probably a '64 or '65. Out of the Cypriot stepped Monica Slezak, pulling a Hermès scarf around her shoulders as if she were girding for battle. Under normal circumstances, a producer's wife wouldn't be worth wasting a flashbulb, but the paparazzi snapped one or two photos. Monica sailed through the flashes regally, head held high and an enigmatic smile on her face as she disappeared into the ballroom.

I was so caught up in watching Monica Slezak's entrance that I barely noticed when the valet opened my door. "Sir?" he said, holding out a white ticket. I took one last look at my temperature gauge, which was hovering dangerously in the red, and said a silent prayer that it would hold up long enough to get into the underground garage and get me home later.

Inside, it was the usual madhouse: people in expensive evening clothes milling around like idiots and blocking the way. Angelenos don't know how to move in a crowd. I wormed in and out of the swells, murmuring "Excuse me" to Gemma Nicholls, Dawn Steel, and Jennifer Jason Leigh. At the entrance to the reception, several women with clipboards sat behind a long table. One of the women had a placard in front of her that said PRESS.

"Kieran O'Connor," I told her. She blinked, taking in my wrinkled tux, the sloppy bow tie, and the black sneakers. I hadn't had time to find the right shoes. She pursed her lips and checked her list.

"Mr. O'Connor is already here," she said. "And I don't have him down as a plus-one. Are you his guest?"

"No, I'm Mr. O'Connor," I told Miss List. This had happened before. Despite all the security, Hollywood events are pretty easy to crash. Anyone who can read a guest list upside down can get into one of these things. All you need is the right clothes and a confident attitude. I had neither, but my name was on the list.

"Well, I'm sorry," she said, as if speaking to a retarded child, "but Mr. O'Connor is already here." She gestured toward the cocktail reception, where an inveterate party crasher was working a canapé table furtively. I could read my name on the press badge on his chest.

"You seem to have made some mistake," I said pleasantly.

"I don't think so." Miss List already was looking past me to the camera crew from "Hollywood Today!" When I didn't move, she glared and said, "Do you have any identification?"

I rolled my eyes. One of these days, I really had to make an effort to look less like a seedy undertaker, but Miss List was getting on my last nerve, so I took out my notebook and scribbled down my extension at the paper.

"If you'd be so kind as to do me this one favor," I said cheerfully. "Take this and give it to your superior. Then, when no coverage of this event appears in the paper, she can call me at this number and I can explain to her why I wasn't here. And if you'll just give me *your* name, I'll get out of your way."

She narrowed her gaze, but she was wilting. "Wait a second," she said, disappearing into the crowd.

Miss List was back within a minute, trailing behind Addie Adderley, the head of Women in the Industry. Addie's biggest assets were a brusque demeanor and a three-picture deal at Universal. "Good to see you, Kieran. Your photographer is already upstairs at the VIP reception. Gail," she added, ferociously pleasant, "take Kieran upstairs."

On the way up the grand staircase, Gail turned around and glared at me. "Sorry. It's just that you looked—"

"Like shit?" I asked her. "Happens all the time."

The VIP reception was in the Goldwyn Room on the second floor. It was the kind of luxuriously anonymous space that could host anything from a bar mitzvah to a real-estate conference: blank walls, thick sand-colored carpet, an enormous chandelier controlled by rheostat. Everyone wore the same studiedly pleasant expression that couldn't hide the fact that they'd rather be at home. I wanted to rabbit as badly as they did, but I reminded myself that while they were paying to be there, I was being paid. The thought had sustained me through many a charity-dinner snooze-athon.

Most of the women were wearing either no-nonsense business suits or slinky dresses, although it was the actresses in the suits and the executives in the dresses. The actresses hoped to be taken seriously as professional women with important projects and control over their own destinies, while the executives were just enjoying a chance to be va-va-voomy. Furs were nowhere in evidence, but there were plenty of sequins and bugle beads. One director, whose entire career seemed predicated on her ability to make action films more bloody and violent than any man's, was clad in a gold sausage casing that made her resemble an Oscar brought to life. Her chest reminded me of a Bugs Bunny short where Bugs dressed up in drag. I was so busy looking at her cartoony cleavage that I bumped into a Shirley MacLaine look-alike who turned out to be Shirley MacLaine.

I gave Gail the slip and started casing the room on my own. In the far corner, Gregory Slezak was sitting at a small table, surrounded by a pack of electronic media. He was giving an interview to the entertainment reporter from the local ABC affiliate while CBS, NBC, CNN, E!, and a bunch of less-familiar camera crews shot background footage of the crowd. As I watched, a fierce-looking publicist from Women in the Industry stepped into the shot, cutting off the interview. The ABC lights went off and the CBS lights went on. Slezak took a sip of something that could have been Evian or could have been Smirnoff. He looked drawn and exhausted.

I slinked around the room, taking notes. In one power pod, Jane Fonda and Ted Turner were talking to Whoopi Goldberg. Sandra Bernhard drifted by, looking androgynously soigné in a striped Isaac Mizrahi suit. Ogling her were the universally loathed DeCrescenzo brothers, the look-alike producers who were famous for having the same bad breath, a combination of cigars and herring. The DeCrescenzos had hired identical pneumatic rent-a-bimbos tonight.

More faces. Adam Davies, looking dandyish in a white ice-cream suit and red bow tie. Davies was the diametric opposite of the DeCrescenzos, a Brit who produced tasteful, small literary adaptations that made tasteful, small sums of money at the box office. Behind Davies, a reporter from *Women's Wear Daily* was chatting with Sharon Stone, who was doing her patented Grace Kelly–meets–Madonna vamp.

"There you are, O'Connor."

It was Marilyn Amsterdam, my favorite photographer. Most of the photographers at the paper hated Hollywood events and would rather be shooting a fire or a Kings game. So did Marilyn, but she was a good sport, hunting stars like a poacher stalks a white rhino. Right now she was aiming her Nikon at Sharon Stone. Flash. Gotcha.

"Anything decent so far?"

Marilyn stuck a lens cap in her mouth and checked her photo envelope, which was already bulging with one roll of shot film. "Our key shot is Slezak with the head of Women in the Industry. Then I got Whoopi talking to Fonda—Jane, not Bridget—and a funny setup with that guy who used to be on 'Cheers' and that woman who used to be married to Tom Cruise. Watch it," she said, pushing me out of the way. She lunged forward, held her camera above her head with one hand, and flashed.

"Quote time," I told her. "Shall we meet back here in ten minutes?"

"You got it, O'Connor." Melanie Griffith hovered into view, and Marilyn was off on celebrity safari again.

Most of the material from my stories didn't come from the official little interviews set up by publicists ("Yes, it was a challenging project, but we all got along so well, and I really think it's some of my best work"), but from cruising around the backwater shoals of these receptions, keeping my ears open and my mouth shut. My column read more like a deconstruction of a Hollywood party than the story of the party itself.

Over by a mingy little fruit-and-crackers buffet, I made a pit stop to take some notes and hang out by the only guy in the room who had more wrinkles in his jacket than I did. He wore a baggy glen-plaid suit that made him look like a combination rock star/junkie. His face was all lines and planes, with a sharp nose that had been broken a few times. He chewed a water cracker and glanced disdainfully at two agent types in Italian suits and gel-pack haircuts.

"So is Don back from Bermuda?" the first one asked.

"He was in *rehab*."

"I know that," said the first one. "I was trying to be *nice*."

I jotted the exchange down in my notebook under the category *What I Did on My Vacation*.

The DeCrescenzos' rent-a-bimbos wiggled by, drinking club soda out of tall flutes. "The guy at Disney liked my reading," one of them said. "But his secretary called and said they decided to go *taller*."

"I hate it when they do that," her friend said with real sympathy.

"That's all right. I think I'll be able to turn it into a *growthful experience*."

I jotted it down as *Notes from Silicone Valley*.

Ten minutes later, the room was packed and I was choking on dueling perfumes. If you can't be Elizabeth Taylor, at least you can smell like her. I'd downed a glass of Dom Perignon and filled up two pages in my notebook with observations that I hoped would later turn out to be mordant and incisive, if not actually funny. Gregory Slezak was still running the electronic media gauntlet. Marilyn was busy in a far corner where Streisand was making one of her famous thirty-second photo-op appearances. She stood in the middle of a bunch of photographers, face angled just so, while a publicist counted down, "Three . . . two . . . one . . . that's all, ladies and gentlemen."

Marilyn ejected her film and dropped it into another photo envelope. "Hark. Spirit speaks," she said, gesturing over my shoulder. I turned around and saw Monica Slezak deep in conversation with Suzan Morninglory.

Morninglory was a New Age writer and lecturer who was regarded as a Great Spiritual Leader among a certain crowd in the film industry. A certain stupid crowd, I thought; as far as I could tell, Suzan Morninglory was just Tammy Faye Bakker redux, with crystals where the mascara used to be. Tonight, she was earth-mother dramatic in a voluminous purple caftan and rough-cut amethysts around her neck. Her long hair, a tawny brown streaked with gray, had been piled on her head and arranged with tortoiseshell pins. She put one hand on Monica Slezak's shoulder and murmured into her ear. Monica sipped a glass of orange juice and nodded in agreement.

Up close, Monica Slezak was no Beverly Hills beauty, but she was an undeniably handsome woman. She hadn't succumbed to the vanities of an eye tuck or a boob job. In her strapless black sheath and understated diamond necklace, she looked like a real woman who was growing older naturally and gracefully. Her shoes were slingback pumps with grosgrain bows on the toes, and she carried a delicate gold scallop purse that fit in the palm of her hand. It was an aristocratic look, particularly in contrast with the reigning style in Beverly Hills, where the eighty-year-olds try to look twenty-nine. So do the twelve-year-olds, for that matter.

"That's Slezak's wife talking to her," I told Marilyn. "Get it."

"Lead the way."

As we moved toward the producer and the spiritualist, we were intercepted by an attractive blond woman. From her sensible suit, the portfolio case slung across her shoulder, and the Can-I-*help*-you look on her face, I guessed that she was Morninglory's personal assistant or publicist.

"I'm Alison Sewell," she said politely in a soft British accent. "May I help you with something?" I introduced Marilyn and myself, gave Alison Sewell our affiliation, and asked if I could talk to Monica and Morninglory for just the briefest of moments. I try to avoid the word *interview*; it makes people self-conscious and coltish.

"I'm Ms. Slezak's assistant, and I'm sorry, but Ms. Slezak is giving no interviews tonight."

"How about just a quick photograph, then," I asked her. It was a superfluous request; Marilyn had already snapped several shots. Alison gave her an unamused look.

"All right. You've got your photograph. Thank you," she said in a clipped voice that managed to be polite and proper even as it gave us the middle finger.

"Thank *you*," Marilyn said sunnily, waiting until we were out of earshot to add, "you stuck-up Limey bitch."

"I think that's it. You're done," I told Marilyn, scribbling down the names on a piece of notebook paper and handing it to her. "Thanks."

Marilyn tucked it in her photo envelope. "Great. That's my last assignment. I'll go downtown, get these developed, and be in bed by midnight for a change." She looked around the room again and shook her head. "How do you stand these things?" she wondered as she walked away.

I went back to the buffet, where I scored some artichoke puffs and another glass of champagne. As I jotted down a few notes, someone behind me laughed and said, "Hey, Kieran. Am I going to be in your article?"

It was Cathy Bates.

I don't know how I'd missed her before; she was a head taller than any of the other women and twice as striking. Plus she was the only black person in the room (besides Whoopi Goldberg) who wasn't carrying a tray. She wore a buttery silk dress in some neutral shade, topped off with a piece of kente cloth in bright stripes of red, green, and black. Her earrings were pounded African silver. I understood why Claudia had fallen in love with her. We had similar taste in women.

"Spell it right. Cathy with a C," she said in her Vassar voice. "The filmmaker, not the actress."

When Claudia and I had first met Cathy at Pedro's party, she was just another young director with a well-regarded student film that she'd financed by maxing out her credit cards. A month later, *Television Generation* won its first of a thousand film-festival awards, and Cathy Bates's stock had gone through the roof. It was hard to be jealous; I'd seen the movie, and she deserved it. I had images of her being wined and dined all over town, her life one big round of lunches with agents and executives, Cobb salad and bullshit. Cathy and I were on reasonably good terms, considering that the same woman had us tied up in knots. At least Cathy was gracious in triumph.

"Is Claudia with you?" I asked.

"Hm-mm. Is she with you?"

"No. I'm not plus-one tonight."

"I am," she said, "but Claudia's pissed off at me. You know what she can be like. Actually, I don't blame her." She toyed with her kente cloth. "I've been in town for about one week in the last six months."

"You've been cleaning up. Congratulations."

She shrugged. "Every black group, women's group, and gay group is falling all over themselves to give me a plaque. I'm covered in plaque."

"Ever considered that you might deserve it?"

"Nah. I'm just the flavor of the month."

"The flavor of the month being?"

"Chocolate," she shot back. "Chocolate with lezzie sprinkles. Hey, what table are you at?"

I checked my ticket. "One forty-eight. Up in the sky seats."

"I'm at seven. Brad Mackey's table. Agent hell. It promises to be deadly. Why don't you come down and—"

A woman with Porcelana skin and the same nose you see all over Rodeo Drive swooped down on Cathy. I recognized her as the wife of Earl Dingle, a TV producer whose big hit was a sitcom about a college fraternity from outer space.

"You're Cathy Bates! I *loved* your movie," she said, slipping her arm through Cathy's and ignoring me completely. "I'm Sharon Dingle. Earl and I screened it for a party we had last week and everyone agreed it was so real! So down-to-earth! The language was a little *rough,* but that's the way people talk these days, I suppose. . . ."

Cathy smiled at her placidly. "Shall we go downstairs?"

"Let's do!"

Cathy pointed across the room at a black waiter. "Then *ax* that *muthafucka* where the bathroom is so's we can freshen up our shit before dinner."

Sharon Dingle's arm slipped out of Cathy's. Her jaw hit the Berber carpet. There was a silence. I snorted.

All of a sudden, Cathy looked tired. "I'm just kidding. A girl's got to keep her sense of humor. Look, I'd love to talk to you." She glanced at me. "You coming, Kieran?"

"I'm waiting to talk to Slezak."

"All right. See you downstairs." As they walked off, I could hear her saying to Sharon Dingle, "Relax, honey, it was a *joke*."

# 3

I NEVER DID GET TO SPEAK to Gregory Slezak. As soon as the electronic media turned off their lights, a flack whisked him away through a back entrance, leaving me and the other print reporters to stand around and grumble. The champagne was turning sour in my empty stomach, and I was starting to feel a little lightheaded. Someone dimmed and brightened the chandelier. Dinner was about to begin.

I joined the exodus toward the staircase and ended up near the door in a traffic jam of tuxedos, rubbing elbows—literally—with the man in the wrinkled glen-plaid suit. We caught each other's eyes, and I nodded curtly.

"I see you met Alison," he said with a smirk. He stank of cigarettes and whiskey.

"Why? Is she your girlfriend or something?"

"Alison?" he said, feigning shock. He had a gravelly, nasal voice—Tom Waits by way of New Jersey. "Hey, I *need* this thing," he said, grabbing his crotch. "Whaddaya, a reporter?"

I introduced myself, which brought a brief flicker of recognition. "O'Connor, right. A good Swedish name. 'Have Tux, Will Travel,' right? I've seen your stuff." He proffered his hand—the one that had grabbed his crotch. "Drew Wilson."

"I've seen your stuff, too," I said as we jostled down the stairs. Actually, I hadn't read his work, but I'd read a lot about him.

Drew Wilson had written a jailhouse novel called *The Midnight Hour* which had gotten an inordinate amount of attention in the book-review pages. Books by cons and gang members had been a vogue in the publishing world for a while, but the ones I'd read were just as amateurish as they were gritty and explicit. Their successes had been due more to skillful publicity campaigns and spreads in

*People* magazine than to any real talent. Wilson, however, was being touted as something special; I'd read a respectful story in the Sunday *New York Times* that had been headlined NOT JUST ANOTHER FLASH IN THE PEN.

We reached the bottom of the staircase. The door to the banquet room was open, and the waiters were in full anthill scurry. "What are you doing in L.A.?" I asked.

"Rewrites on my script," he said. "We're going into production in a couple of months."

"Congratulations."

"Get it right. Not congratulations—commiserations."

"Why commiserations?" I asked.

Wilson shrugged and didn't answer. "I hate this town," he said quietly. "The only reason I came out was that I figured if I was going to get screwed, I'd rather get screwed in person."

I started to ask him what he meant, but we got caught in another tuxedo junction at the entrance to the Fairbanks Ballroom. Women in the Industry was a hot group. Through the open door, I caught a glimpse of the vast room packed with more tables than I'd ever seen before. Every woman who worked in the film business was there, it seemed, along with most of the powerful men.

Once we were inside the ballroom, the reason for the traffic jam was obvious. Everyone was stopped just inside the entrance, checking dinner tickets and looking grimly at the hundreds of tables. They should have included floor plans in the ticket envelopes. Maps to the stars' tables. The mood was festive enough, but I caught a few resigned looks among the power brokers. Even the rich and famous like to go home in the evenings, put on a bathrobe, and watch some TV. So did I, of course, but I doubted that anyone else in the room was going home to a closet-sized studio apartment with rust stains in the bathtub and three locks on the door.

"Seventy-two," said Wilson, checking his ticket. "Where you at?"

"One forty-eight. Excuse *me*," I added to a vulpine young producer who had stepped on my feet in his rush to catch up with Penny Marshall.

"Asshole," Wilson called after him cheerfully, making a couple of older women turn around and shoot us schoolmarm glares. I was embarrassed, but Wilson gave the old bats a look that was so lascivious that they reddened and hurried away. "Who was that?" he asked, amused.

"The one with the black hair was Rebecca Macnamara," I told him. "She was one of the first women directors, back in the fifties."

"A director. Why does everyone in this septic tank want to direct?" Wilson mumbled. We were still smack in the middle of the doorway getting trampled, so I moved into the ballroom, but Wilson hung back and checked his watch. "I gotta make a call before this thing starts. See you later, Swede."

He moved back through the crowd, swimming upstream in a river of sequins and bugle beads.

Onstage, the awards sat on black velvet, lit by a pinlight: silver-and-crystal obelisks. Behind them, an embalmed-looking society orchestra was massacring "Sisters Are Doing It for Themselves" at the tempo of "String of Pearls." Gregory and Monica Slezak were seated on the dais, along with Rebecca Macnamara, Suzan Morninglory, and one of the actresses from A Lover's Question. Addie Adderley was up there too, conferring with Chep Orlovsky. The agent looked naked without his cellular phone.

Looking to upgrade my seat from coach to first class, I went down front, but people were power-schmoozing, blocking all the narrow arteries between the chair backs. One waiter looked near tears. I couldn't remember Cathy's table number, and the density of humans approached gridlock as I got closer to the stage. I finally gave up and threaded my way to my table in the back. I should have brought binoculars.

I was the last one at the table. Everyone else had already started on the salad, so the introductions were perfunctory. My dinner companions were three new members of Women in the Industry, their three husbands or dates or whatever, and a bright-eyed, nervous young reporter who sat with her hands folded in her lap, as if she expected security to come by and escort her back to the children's table. No one initiated a conversation, which was just fine with me. My gut was growling from the champagne and the cummerbund.

The salad was taken away. More wine was poured. Waiters came by with the main course: baby vegetables and some kind of stuffed chicken that bulged obscenely, like a tin can swollen with botulism.

A few years ago, it would have been medallions of veal, but the film industry had gotten PC about animal rights. Nobody could eat veal anymore without thinking about some sad-eyed calf with its feet nailed to the floor of a crate. Chickens were less cuddly, so they were still okay as long as they were free-range.

Two of the Women in the Industry produced Filofaxes (one faux-lizard, one black rubber) and opened them up with big rips of Velcro. They exchanged cards. I gobbled my dinner, trying to soak up some of the Dom Perignon, and read the souvenir program. Every awards banquet had these: glossy books in which studios, agencies, and individuals could buy pages to congratulate the honorees and advertise their own connection to the event. The programs were broken up into "platinum," "gold," "silver," and plain sections, which raised even more money, as the people who bought the pages didn't want to look like cheapskates in front of the honorees they were trying to impress.

The program proper was at the front of the book. In addition to Gregory Slezak's, there were a few smaller awards. Rebecca Macnamara was receiving one called the Trailblazer, and Cathy Bates was getting the Woman of Tomorrow Award to add to her overstuffed mantel. I was surprised to see Suzan Morninglory's artfully airbrushed face in the honoree section of the program. She was getting "WII's first annual Womanspirit Award, dedicated to the woman who has done the most to introduce spiritual themes into a Hollywood production in the past year." Now, *that* was a joke. Spiritual issues and themes were verboten in Hollywood. The only time a Hollywood producer ever gave a thought to religion was after he made a pile of money and then wanted to reassure himself that being filthy rich was okey-dokey with God.

The waiters finally cleared the main course and brought out individual chocolate terrines trimmed with raspberry sauce and mint sprigs. Eating sugar in public is anathema in Hollywood, but no banquet meal is complete without some chocolate for everyone to refuse ceremonially. To my horror, all they had was decaf, but I took a cup. When the dessert bustle was finally over, Addie Adderley made a brief welcoming speech and called for the lights to dim.

Video screens lit up at both ends of the room. It was a retrospective—a look at the lives of women in the film industry. First they showed some brief clips of women behind the scenes: agents, editors, directors, producers, costumers, and others. An image of Cathy Bates flashed past, picking up some award, and Monica Slezak was shown on the set of *A Lover's Question*, arms folded, a serious look on her face. Everyone clapped at the end. Then a second montage began, a montage that showed the images of women that had been presented on-screen in the past year.

Bare-breasted jiggle girls in a shower. A secretary. An action hero's girlfriend. Another secretary. A cheerleader getting cut up with a knife. A secretary. A secretary. A secretary. The black-tie crowd laughed and booed.

Then came the pièce de résistance, a clip from *Femme Fatale*. It was the story of a gorgeous bisexual fashion model who got her jollies by chainsawing off the private parts of any man who got close to her. Finally a tough renegade cop-who-didn't-play-by-the-rules had enough and blew her away (in close-up) with his ten inches of hard steel. It was loathsome shit, but a certain group of film critics—the kind who never had a date in high school—had hailed it as a daring breakthrough in gritty sexuality. Gay groups and women's groups had picketed outside the theaters, haranguing moviegoers, giving away the ending, and giving the film so much free publicity that it became one of the biggest hits of the year. The lights came up again during a long chorus of boos and catcalls—most of which, I imagined, were coming from the same people who *made* these movies.

The speeches began. Things had to change. Things *were* changing, slowly. Things had to change faster. The people in this room could help make that change.

I zoned out. My stomach was still roiling. I had enough in my notebook for a solid twelve-inch column. I figured I'd be able to slip out right after Gregory Slezak made his speech and I got a quote. The screens lit up again with an extended clip from *A Lover's Question*—long applause—and then Addie Adderley took the mike, gesturing good-naturedly for quiet.

"Some people might find it ironic that, this year, the best images of women on the screen were put there by a *man*," she began. Slezak grinned sheepishly and waved at the crowd. Everybody laughed. "But Gregory Slezak had help, even though *some people* seem to think that a film gets produced *all by itself*."

Hisses for the Academy. Strong applause for Monica.

"And so, who better to present Gregory Slezak with Women in the Industry's highest recognition, the Dorothy Arzner Award, than the co-producer of A *Lover's Question*. Women and gentlemen"—more laughs—"Monica Slezak."

The crowd rose and applauded. Monica stood up and acknowledged the ovation. Even from the back row, I could see the tears in her eyes. She waved at the audience and started to make her way down the long dais.

Immediately it was apparent that something was wrong. Monica stumbled once; her head lolled on her neck like my dangling hood ornament. The cheers died down and were replaced by a stunned silence, punctuated by a few concerned murmurs. By the time she finally reached the mike, where she hugged the podium for support, you could have heard an oyster fork drop. She arranged index cards on the podium for what seemed like an eternity until she finally cleared her throat and took a breath.

"Friends . . ."

Monica Slezak opened her mouth twice, like a fish that had fallen out of its bowl, and then bolted from the stage, disappearing behind the curtains on the back of the dais.

The room erupted in chatter. Addie Adderley and Gregory Slezak followed her. Suzan Morninglory followed them. Just as I was about to slip backstage and find out what happened, Addie Adderley came back to the mike, wrapped in her best toastmaster sangfroid.

"Monica Slezak is fine," she said. "She's just not feeling very well, and she said that your generous tribute was a little overwhelming. She'll be back out in a few minutes, so what we're going to do right now is move on and present the Woman of Tomorrow Award."

Without warning, my armpits went wet with cold sweat, and my bowels spasmed. I was about to throw up. I shut my throat tight against my rising gorge, pushed my chair back, and half-trotted out of the ballroom.

On the way out, I almost collided with a waiter bearing a tray of lipsticky wineglasses and crumpled linen napkins. "Did you see that?" he said.

"Yeah," I said, clenching my bowels, trying to dance around him.

"Crazy broad," he muttered.

I just made it to the stall before I threw up and my bowels exploded. I used a whole roll of toilet paper to mop up the flopsweat that kept popping up on my face. I had sweated right through both my shirt and my dinner jacket. Someone came in—footfalls, running water, a whiff of cigar smoke—and left. All was quiet. I rested my face against the cool marble divider that separated the stalls and imagined sitting there forever.

When I opened my eyes, several minutes had passed, and I felt steadier. I rose cautiously, hitched up my pants, and left the cummerbund where it was, jammed in the dispenser that held the tissue-paper toilet covers. Standing up made me queasy all over again, but I thought I'd be all right. I picked my way to the basins, where I ran cold water over my wrists and said a silent thanks that there was no attendant to observe my misery. The water was icy as vodka and I ran handfuls of it, splashing my face, smoothing my hair.

And then, through the common wall that separated the men's bathroom from the women's, I heard an explosion—a pop that reverberated off the marble and the tiles and hung in the air.

Living in Venice, where every fourteen-year-old seemed to carry a gun, I'd become familiar with the various sounds of explosions. They were just the opposite of the way they were presented in the movies. If it sounded like a gunshot, it was usually a firecracker, and nothing more would happen. If it sounded like a pop, there would be an ominous silence, and then the thin sound of a siren.

I would have bet that this was a gunshot. A real one.

My face was dripping water all over the front of the dinner jacket. I blotted it carefully, listening, but there wasn't another sound. I dried my hands, waiting to hear footsteps in the hall. Surely someone else had heard the noise. All was quiet, and then a zephyr of applause floated in from the ballroom. I opened the door tentatively and stepped out into the corridor.

There was a small vestibule separating the bathroom doors, with a bank of three fancy pay phones, the kind that takes credit cards. One of them even had a TTY and a fax. The walls were papered in florals, pretty but durable, and the carpet was a soft shade of rose. I stuck my head out into the main corridor, hoping to see a security guard, a hotel employee, another guest. Anyone.

No one. Still not a sound from the women's room.

I licked my lips and knocked at the door once. Twice. No response. Finally, I pushed the door open an inch or two, ready to slam it shut if I heard a scream.

The bathroom was empty, but the smell of gunpowder assaulted my nose. My heart started to beat fast. A better person would have gone through that door for one reason only—to provide help—but what got me over the threshold was pure reportorial curiosity. Reportorial curiosity, hell; I'm nosy.

I'd never been in a women's room before. Despite my apprehension, I couldn't help looking around. Instead of urinals, this one had a couple of soft-looking couches. A whole array of cosmetics and sundries covered the basin, with a pretty little bouquet of tampons in a pink cup. There was even a hair dryer wired next to the towel rack, and I wondered who would wash her hair in a hotel common bathroom. All the stall doors were closed except for the one for the disabled, against the far wall, which hung ajar an inch or two. I squatted down and saw feet. I approached slowly and nudged the door open.

Monica Slezak was slumped on the toilet, a bright-crimson sunburst splattering the marble behind her head. A tiny gun dangled from her right hand. Her mouth was an open O, smeared with black gunpowder. One of her eyes had prolapsed, sagging from its socket on a snarl of red optic fibers. Blood had poured out of her nose, pooling in her lap, drizzling down the porcelain, making red foam in the toilet. As I watched, a wisp of smoke came from the back of her throat.

I staggered back, hitting the sink with my hip and involuntarily barking at the shock and the pain.

As I watched, Monica's head jerked forward, and the last of the blood in her head dripped from her nose into her lap, like a shower that had just been turned off.

MY FIRST INSTINCT WAS TO RUN, but I gripped the edge of the basin and looked at Monica again. I'd never seen a dead body before. Morbid curiosity got the best of my queasy stomach. I approached the stall and went in, careful not to step in the blood that seeped around the base of the toilet and across the tile floor, making little rivers of red against the white grout.

At first, I thought someone had ambushed her while she was peeing, but Monica's clothes were still in place. The gun in her hand was cute as a toy, and the blood spattering the wall was an unreal shade of ruby, brilliant and wet as nail polish. It looked like something you'd see on the news, the edges smoothed by flat videotape lighting, sanitized for your protection. The most real thing about her was a smell I can't describe—warm and thick, marrowy.

One crimson rivulet was trickling toward my feet. I stepped back a pace and noticed something else: a piece of paper, a sheet of heavy vellum, folded once and propped neatly on top of the stainless-steel toilet-paper holder. I reached for the paper, thought twice, and picked it up with a square of toilet tissue. I stepped out of the stall to consider my next move.

The reality of the scene struck again, rope-a-doping me against the basin a second time. *What the fuck was I doing?* I went to the door and peeked out into the vestibule. Still no one. I folded the note twice, tucking it behind my back. Trying to look casual, I strolled to the pay phone and dropped in a quarter. It probably says something truly nasty about me, but I didn't even consider dialing 911.

A copy editor on the city desk picked up on the second ring. I tried to explain who I was and what had happened, but she interrupted me. "Hang on. You need to talk to Charlie Donahue."

There was a click, and then I was listening to a lush orchestral version of "Love Grows (Where My Rosemary Goes)." I bounced on the balls of my feet and looked around. The phone banks were equipped with ashtrays, matches, notepads, and teeny miniature-golf-style pencils. I checked my watch and wrote down "9:20" on the complimentary pad of Beverly Hillshire paper. The next phone over was a high-tech marvel, complete with a credit-card slot, computer ports, TTY keypad, and a public fax.

An idea hit. I unfolded Monica Slezak's suicide note, using the toilet-paper to avoid fingerprints, and stuck it into the fax.

"Kieran?" I jumped, but the voice was coming out of the receiver pressed between my ear and shoulder. "Are you there?"

"I'm here." I swiped my Visa card and punched in my home phone number.

"I'm Charlie Donahue, the nighttime city editor. What's going on down there?" He had one of those airplane-pilot voices, all Virginia smoke and honey. I sketched a few facts for him. The fax beeped seven times, let out a high-pitched whine, and the note began feeding out the bottom like homemade pasta.

"You have a photographer there?" The fax stopped, started, and stopped again. This was taking longer than I'd thought. I looked out into the corridor leading back to the ballroom, but no one was coming.

"Kieran? I say, d'you have a photographer down there?"

"No, she left after the cocktail reception."

"Who was it?"

"Marilyn Amsterdam. She's probably still in the lab."

Donahue grunted. "Right. Hold the fort. I'll have somebody down there in ten minutes." I hung up. Hot damn—a chance to get my name out of the features section and, with luck, onto the front page.

The fax machine beeped twice. Monica's note was hanging out of the bottom. I took the note and went back into the bathroom, propping it against the toilet-paper holder where I'd found it, and got the hell out of there.

The Beverly Hillshire is actually two buildings, bisected by a private cobblestone drive and porte cochere where the cars pull up. The ballrooms are in the south building, and the shops and main lobby are in front, facing Wilshire Boulevard. I went across the drive at a studied pace and walked past the restaurant, the bar, and the newsstand. The gift shop was still open; instead of postcards and T-shirts, though, it sold gold jewelry and flagons of thousand-dollar perfume. In the quiet of the evening, the hotel breathed money and quiet and respectability.

At the front desk, a bespectacled guy in a blazer was giving elaborate directions in German to a pair of Europeans in socks and Birkenstocks. I waited until they left. He looked at me and raised his eyebrows.

I hesitated, trying to think of the most tactful way to tell the night clerk at the Beverly Hillshire that one of the best-known producers in Hollywood has just blown her brains all over the inside of a toilet stall while her husband was accepting an award in the next room.

"Do you know who Monica Slezak is?" I began. His face lit up.

"Are you in casting?"

The clock on the VCR said 2:46 A.M. when I finally got home. I pulled off my tux pants, pleated shirt, and dinner jacket, opened the window, and threw the whole mess onto the boardwalk.

From the moment that the clerk-slash-actor mistook me for a casting director, nothing had gone right. The Beverly Hills PD had arrived in less than two minutes, escorted me up to the room where the VIP reception had been held earlier, closed the door, offered me a glass of water, and started asking questions. I put up with it for a few minutes, chafing to get downstairs.

Allison Sewell and Gregory Slezak were in two other corners of the room with their own policemen. Allison looked as if she was in shock, but her posture was good and she wasn't crying. Gregory Slezak looked like a photograph of himself that had been crumpled and smoothed out again. Cops, security guards, and hotel officials came and went. I saw Addie Adderley and Suzan Morninglory walk through in the company of other cops. I had no idea what was going on downstairs and it was killing me.

"So lemme see if I got this right," said my cop, who was tall and rangy and would have been described in a casting breakdown as a "David Hasselhoff type." In Beverly Hills, the cops come in one of two models: the Basic David Hasselhoff or the Deluxe Tom Selleck. Officer Hasselhoff squinted at his notes. "You got sick, went in the bathroom, took a . . . went to the bathroom, and were going back to the dinner when you heard a shot from the next room. You knocked, no answer, went into the bathroom, found her slumped in the stall . . ."

"Not slumped, exactly. I mean, her head was slumped over, but she was sitting up. I didn't touch her. She was just like you found her."

"Yeah, all right. Then you went up to Mr. Wells in the front and told him to call the police. Do you remember what time that was?"

"Don't you guys keep track of your calls?" I felt like pulling a Zsa Zsa and decking him. "Look, can I go now? I'm a reporter, and I'm supposed to be downstairs."

Big mistake; I'd let on that I was in a hurry. He looked at me and scratched his neck. "You got your press credentials with you?"

"No."

"No," he said.

"No," I told him. "Maybe if I'd known that the honoree's wife was going to shoot herself I would have brought them." Actually, I didn't have press credentials. You don't really need them in the world of celebrity journalism.

"Then you're not going anywhere. Besides, you guys already have things covered down there."

"What?"

When they'd finished asking and re-asking the same questions for the eightieth time, they let me go downstairs. They had taken Alison away by some back entrance, but Slezak was still there being grilled.

All of the guests had gone home—forced out, I imagined. The bathroom area had been blocked off with that shiny yellow tape you see on TV, and a gorilla-sized Selleck cop was standing guard. Camera crews, photographers, and print reporters were swarming around the entrance to the main ballroom, which was blocked off by more yellow tape and more Sellecks. I spotted Marilyn Amsterdam in the crowd and pushed my way over to her. She was wearing her laminated credentials around her neck like dog tags.

"Hey, there you are, O'Connor. Check it out," she said with a sweep of her hand. There were people from Channel 2 "Action News," Channel 7 "Eyewitness News," "California 9 News," Channel 13 "Real News," and a bunch of less dramatically monickered camera crews. Even CNN was there.

"Have you gotten anything good?"

"They're not giving us access to shit." She squeezed off a few shots of the cops blocking the entrance to the hotel. "I left the roll we shot during the reception back in the lab for Slasky to process. We'll have those to fall back on if we don't get anything here."

"What have you heard?"

"Not much. The cops and the security director from the hotel are going to hold a press conference in a few minutes. They told Stan she blew the back of her head clean off. Talk about a sore loser."

"Who's Stan?"

"Stan Nyman. You know Stan." She pointed at a pudgy guy in a poly-blend white shirt who was tucked in a corner, conferring with the Beverly Hills chief of police.

I gaped at her. "I'm doing the story, Marilyn."

Marilyn gaped back at me with amusement. "*Stan's* doing the story, O'Connor." She took a shot of my surprised face.

Shit. When that honey-voiced bastard Charlie Donahue said that he was sending someone down right away, he meant a reporter. This was apparently too big a story to be trusted to a puffball pansy-assed dipstick society reporter like the author of "Have Tux, Will Travel." My stomach went sour all over again, and I felt the adrenaline in my body run out of my chest and down my fingers. To add injury to insult, I had to stand in a corner with Stan Nyman, telling him what I'd seen and answering his questions while his expensive little Japanese microcassette recorded every detail. I liked it even less than I liked talking to Officer Hasselhoff. When it was over, Stan Nyman pumped my arm, thanked me for doing such a thorough job, said he'd be sure to mention to Charlie Donahue how helpful I'd been—and then asked for my notebook.

I found my claim check in one of my jacket pockets, went to the valet station, and handed it in. I was waiting for my car, stewing, when someone called, "Hey. Buddy."

It was Frank Grassley, one of the Action/Eyewitness/Real News robodudes, with his camera and sound guy right behind him. He wore a suit that would have cost me a year's rent. On TV, he was dashing and handsome, but up close it was obvious that he'd had more work done on his face than Michael Jackson. And LaToya, for that matter.

"Yeah, you, buddy," he repeated. I don't like being called buddy. "One of my friends on the force tells me that you were the one who found the body."

A camera light went on. I took a deep breath.

"One of your friends on the force tells you wrong," I said. "*Buddy.*"

The camera light went off. My car pulled up. A valet stepped out and waved inquiringly. I started toward it, but Grassley grabbed my arm and signaled to the valet to kill the motor.

"Come on," he said. "The camera's off. Be a pal. What did it look like in there? Just give me some kind of a statement."

"You want a statement? All right. Fuck you. And fuck your lousy excuse for a news show."

He smirked. Apparently Frank Grassley had heard some variation of this before. He looked around, made sure no one was in the vicinity, showed me a smile that was all gums and caps, and hissed, "Suck a dead dog's dick."

"I'll have to take a rain check, Frankie," I said. "Not that I don't find you attractive."

And I turned and walked across the cobblestones to my waiting car, leaving Frank Grassley on the sidewalk.

It would have been a satisfying exit—if only I'd been able to get the Buick started.

The valets let me call the Auto Club and wait inside the ticket booth, but by the time Triple A showed up with an auxiliary battery and jumper cables, most of the cops and all of the "Action News" and "Eyewitness News" and "Real News" vans had left. Frank Grassley smirked at me as his van pulled away.

So it was understandable why I was a little peeved when I finally got home, took a three-day NOTICE OF EVICTION FOR NONPAYMENT OF RENT off my door, got inside, turned on the lights, went to the fax machine, reached inside the slot, and found . . .

Nothing.

And it was then that I pulled off all my clothes and threw them down on the boardwalk.

Mr. Have Tux, Will Travel was going to sleep for the night.

I woke up the next morning with a coat of fur on my teeth and a crick in my neck from the damned futon. One of these days I was going to have to upgrade to a bed, or at least a convertible sofa. My stomach was still sour; I estimated it had been empty for about ten hours. I pulled on a flannel shirt, a pair of shorts, and my darkest pair of sunglasses, and went outside to find some breakfast. There was a stewbum passed out on the stoop wearing my tuxedo.

The early-morning crowd was out on Ocean Front Walk. I wove my way through the usual mix of Rollerbladers, hip-hoppers, shop-till-you-droppers, crack dealers, and tourists. A tarot reader on her coffee break was engrossed in a paperback of *Hollywood Wives*. Outside the Orthodox synagogue that was wedged incongruously between sausage and ice cream stands, men in dark hats smoked and argued, fists splatting into their palms as they made their points. A kid in a Teenage Mutant Ninja Turtles yarmulke was running a toy fire engine around and around their black shoes.

I found a nice table at the Abbot Kinney Cafe, close to the board-walk action on the other side of the railing and yet far away enough to avoid the panhandlers. On a table next to me was a messy copy of the morning paper. No one seemed to be around, so I grabbed it.

There it was on the front page, a two-column head below the fold:

## PRODUCER DIES AT CHARITY BENEFIT

"A Lover's Question" producer Monica Slezak found dead during glittery dinner honoring husband. Police are investigating.

By STANLEY R. NYMAN
Staff writer

Monica Slezak, film producer and wife of producer-director Gregory Slezak, was found dead last night at a film industry function in Beverly Hills. The cause of death appears to be suicide, according to Beverly Hills police spokesperson Janet DeLeo.

Slezak, 46, was found dead in a restroom at the Beverly Hillshire Hotel at approximately 9:15 P.M. The Slezaks were there to accept an award from Women in the Industry (WII), a support group advocating greater visibility for Hollywood women.

"This is a tragedy," WII president Elizabeth (Addie) Adderley said. "We've not only lost one of the industry's most talented producers, but one of the nicest women I've ever known. I'm devastated." Said Marc Fine, a friend of the Slezaks and past president of the Producers Guild of North America, "Our prayers and best wishes go out to Greg."

Through a spokesperson, Gregory Slezak declined comment.

A native of Nebraska and former high school English teacher, Monica Slezak began her Hollywood career ten years ago as associate producer of the film "Merengue Nights," produced and directed by her husband. Over the next decade, the two (Please see SLEZAK, A23)

## SLEZAK
(continued from A1)

made their mark in the film industry as one of Hollywood's most successful production teams. Among their best-known films were "White Ice," "The Belgium Diaries," "The Dark at the End of the Tunnel," and last year's "A Lover's Question."

It was "A Lover's Question" that brought the Slezaks their greatest critical and box-office success and paved the way for their next project: an adaptation of the acclaimed Drew Wilson novel "The Midnight Hour." That film was to have been the directorial debut of Monica Slezak.

"I find it hard to believe," said Chuck Russo, longtime columnist for the trade industry daily "Biz." "Monica was poised to make the next logical step in her career. Why something like this would happen, it's just baffling."

In Beverly Hills Superior Court last year, however, the late producer acknowledged to Judge Carmen Luz that she had battled manic depression for years. Slezak was in court after her 1966 Cypriot crashed into a divider in West Hollywood, where she testified that a combination of prescription drugs had made her fall asleep at the wheel. No charges were filed in the case.

According to Suzan Morninglory, author of the best-selling self-help book "That Which Makes Me Stronger" and a close friend of Slezak's, "Monica did have bouts of depression, but she had been doing much better in the last six months."

Morninglory and other guests at last night's event confirmed reports that Slezak's behavior had been erratic earlier in the evening. "Her speech was slurred, and she was having trouble walking," said one woman who declined to be identified. Others corroborated the account.

Investigations will continue over the next few days. Other survivors were not immediately known. Memorial services are scheduled to be announced later today.

Through a spokesman, Gregory Slezak has requested that any memorial contributions be made to the Film Futures Foundation, which administers grants to needy film students. The Slezaks created the foundation three years ago, establishing it at the University of Southern California.

And then, at the bottom, in tiny italics:

*Kieran O'Connor contributed to this story.*

I stared at it for a few seconds, crumpled it up, and picked up the section with the horoscope. If the universe had anything else planned for me today, I wanted some advance warning.

# =5=

EVEN AFTER I'D READ THE COMICS, Ann Landers, and a long, abstruse article about the inner workings of the SEC, no waitress had materialized. I gave up and decided to walk over to Claudia's. Claudia was always good for a cup of coffee. Maybe, if she was in a good mood, I could scam a free meal.

Claudia owned a coffeehouse called Cafe Canem in the other end of Venice. At least she called it a coffeehouse; I called it an excuse for her to exercise her insane imagination and undeniable talent for collage. Cafe Canem was crammed full of kitsch from every epoch in American history, all of which she had picked up cheap at thrift stores and estate sales. Everything was ostensibly for purchase, but Claudia would go ballistic every time someone would try to buy a set of burnt-orange plastic Vera dishware or her prized Eero Saarinen womb chair. Nothing she did was without irony. Her life was circumscribed by a pair of invisible quotation marks.

Claudia and I had been dating on and off for five years, though whether it was mostly on or mostly off I couldn't quite figure. She was bisexual and fiercely monogamous, or, rather, serially monogamous. After one of our not infrequent fights, she would find a new girlfriend, drop out of sight for a while, and then resurface when she got tired of Kim or Barbara or Dahlia. I was never sure whether our relationship was the real thing or just the rebound, but I didn't care. If we were lucky, we could keep this up for the rest of our lives without ever having to come to a decision. Perfect for a commitment-phobe like me.

She was in the back when I got to Cafe Canem, so I went behind the counter and tried to divine her mood from the CDs in the carousel. Today she was listening to Johnny Cash; Vivaldi's Concerto in G Major for Two Mandolins; Howard Stern's *Crucified by the FCC*;

the Dead Kennedys' *Fresh Fruit for Rotting Vegetables*; and *Julie Is Her Name*, featuring Julie London.

This was not a big clue.

I grabbed a bialy and a cup of coffee and sat down in a banana-yellow hairdresser's chair. It looked like Claudia had been building some kind of tower with a bunch of cheap cuckoo clocks, the kind with the little Dutchman who came out with an umbrella when the barometer dropped. The hanging monitors were playing an old video, *Justified and Ancient*, which made an odd counterpoint to Vivaldi. It did, however, reinforce the two rules by which Claudia lived: EVERYTHING IS PASTICHE, and IT'S ALL BEEN DONE BEFORE.

Pedro Espinosa came out of the back, wiping his hands on a dish-towel. "Oh, it's just you," he said.

Pedro was the manager of Cafe Canem and Claudia's best friend. The two of them had grown up in New Orleans, where, I gathered, they had both been considered hopelessly eccentric, even by the standards of that city. Pedro spent all of his evenings at political meetings and demonstrations, mostly to collect phone numbers from cute boy activists who invariably turned out to be already coupled. He also did a lot of performance art, a bad word in my vocabulary, but at least Pedro managed to be funny at the same time he was self-indulgent. Besides, watching him roll around nude onstage in a pile of baby dolls was strangely comforting. It reassured me to know that there was one man in this city whose body was worse than mine.

"Where's Claudia?"

"In the back, talking to Denmark." Claudia made most of her money not from her three-dollar macchiatos, but from renting out Cafe Canem to fashion photographers and video crews from "MTV Internacional." It wasn't uncommon for a busload of Japanese tourists to pull up and start snapping pictures as if they'd just arrived at Hearst Castle.

Pedro refilled my coffee and sat down. "Did you read about Monica Slezak in the paper this morning?"

"I was there." That got his attention. Pedro was fascinated with true crime, particularly mass murderers and serial killers. He had been working on a one-man performance piece about the life and death of John Wayne Gacy, which he called *A Cellarful of Boys*.

*"Really?"*

"I found the body," I said casually.

*"Really?!"*

Pedro waited, but I sipped my coffee and watched the monitor. "Make me something to eat and I'll tell you about it."

"There's no such thing as a free brunch." He ducked behind the counter as I threw a napkin at him.

Claudia came out of the back. Today she was looking postpunk in a prairie-gray World War II housedress and a pair of Pucci leggings. Two green glass earrings dripped from her left lobe. Her hair was the subtlest possible aubergine. Somehow it worked.

"No free food," she snapped.

"He found Monica Slezak's body," Pedro said, already constructing a ham-and-cheese. Claudia fiddled with the CD player, switching from Vivaldi to "Holiday in Cambodia" with a push of a button. She looked dubious.

"I swear. I swear on a ten-foot stack of Bibles piled on my mother's grave," I said.

"You're going to hell," she said.

"Claudia, I live in Los Angeles. It's kind of an empty threat."

Pedro gave me the sandwich and poured more coffee. Claudia gave up and sat beside him on the couch.

"All right," she said. "Spew."

I got the story out, emphasizing my parley with Frank Grassley and omitting the fact that my car broke down and ruined the moment. When I slowed down, Pedro set a plate of biscotti and a latte in front of me to keep me talking. Claudia listened with a serious look on her face. "Well, it's rotten that they didn't let you write the story," was her only comment.

"Do you think it was murder?" Pedro's eyes were aglitter.

"Nah," I said. "If you're going to murder someone, you don't do it in the ladies' room at the Beverly Hillshire."

"What's-er-face, the assistant, could have done it," he pointed out. "She could have been sleeping with Gregory Slezak."

"I don't think so," I told him. "Alison's not the type."

"Everybody's the type," Pedro said significantly.

"Why do you think the assistant did it?" Claudia demanded. "Her husband's a more likely suspect. That scumbag Suzan Morninglory could have done it. *Kieran* could have done it."

"Drew Wilson could have done it," I added.

"Where do I know that name?"

"He wrote that book *The Midnight Hour*. The one that Monica was going to turn into a movie. I was talking to him before the dinner, and he didn't like her very much. At all." I crunched biscotti. "But it looked like a suicide."

"She was murdered," insisted Pedro.

"Why do you say that?"

"Because it makes it more interesting."

Claudia cleared away the dishes. "I don't think she was murdered," she said slowly. "But I do think this would make a good article. The question isn't who killed her. The question is why a woman like that would kill herself."

"Because she lost her chance for an Academy Award," suggested Pedro, forgetting his earlier theory that Monica Slezak had been murdered.

"Lots of people have lost an Oscar, Pedro," Claudia said. "And she didn't lose an Oscar, she just lost a nomination, for God's sake. I mean, somebody might be that unstable, but it still doesn't make sense. There's got to be more to it. You could make some money off this one, Kieran."

I poured the dregs of the coffee into my latte bowl and swirled the whole mess around. On the video monitor, a couple of guys dressed like ice cream cones were dancing with Tammy Wynette.

"It might be a good idea. I could do some research, try to get a couple of interviews. If it works out, I could write it for *Los Angeles* or *Buzz*."

"And it's not like you have anything else to do," Claudia pointed out cheerfully.

"Who knows." I drained the latte mixture. The caffeine was kicking in. "I could even pitch *Vanity Fair* if I really come up with something."

"Why not try your own paper?" Pedro said.

"Not in a million years," I told him. "Let Stanley Nyman, staff writer, do it."

\* \* \*

When I got home, stomach full and head jaggedy from the caffeine, the phone started ringing as I put my key in the door. It was Sally.

"Oh. I thought I would get your machine."

"Sorry to disappoint you."

"You didn't. So tell me what happened last night."

"Read Nyman's story." I was still smarting.

"Stan told Charlie Donahue that you found the body."

"I did."

Sally's other phone started ringing, but she ignored it. "Well, come on, Kieran. I've got three pieces to edit before lunch."

I gave her an abridged version of the story, concentrating on the details that Stan Nyman had missed. I even made up a nifty bit about the back of Monica's head, which in my version was a gruesome mass of gore, bone, and hair, sticky with blood and stinking of gunpowder. "Well, you're making most of it up, but it's still a good story," Sally concluded.

I flopped down on the futon. "I don't think I need to tell you that I expect to be paid, even though the story didn't run."

"Of course." Sally's other phone rang again. "I've got to get that. Listen, why I was calling: some heavy-metal band is having something called a 'listening party' for their new album next week at Club Lingerie. What's a listening party?"

"You stand around and eat food while they play the album over and over. And over."

"Gee, what I miss by staying home and reading at night. Anyway, I've been trying to fax you the information, but there's something wrong with your machine. Did you forget to turn it on?"

My mood darkened again. "No, it's on. It's just broken. I'll have to take it in this afternoon."

"Did you check it first? Has it got paper in it? And ink? I know how mechanically inclined you are."

"No, I just put a whole ream of paper in it last week and changed the cartridge. I'm sure it's broken. I bought it used."

"Well, I'll drop this in the mail, then. Good luck with the fax. I hope it's not too expensive."

"Me too."

I had bought my fax a year ago from Jeff Brenner, a friend of mine who'd gotten a magazine gig and moved to New York. New, it would have been priced out of my reach. But the model had been discontinued and Jeff had taken pity on me, so I got it for the price of a really cheap new fax machine. It was a high-end model that printed on plain paper, not the slimy thermal stuff. It had a 40-station autodialer, a 24-page paper feed, a memory, and lots of other functions I didn't understand and never used. The cartridge was fine and so was the paper, but I pulled out the paper drawer anyway to check. Nearly full. I shoved the tray back in roughly.

Inside the machine, something crinkled.

I pulled the tray out again and stuck my hand in. There was a piece of paper way in the back, jammed fast in a roller. It didn't want to come out, and when I pulled, it tore off in my hand. It took a few minutes to clear out the paper path, but when I put the tray back in, the fan went on and the little button marked MEMORY was blinking at me. I pushed MEMORY.

The machine whined to life. Paper rolled. Out came . . . a fax from the Music Center. Two pages. *Three* pages. Fuck the Music Center. Then a sales leaflet—offering to sell me fax paper. This one I crumpled and threw across the room. The machine chugged to a near-halt, alarming me, until I saw that the next page was dark and smudgy. This had to be it. The original was written not on white bond, but on grave-looking gray vellum. It took a while to print eight and a half by eleven inches of gray background, and I paced the whole time. When it was done, I took a deep breath and picked it up.

There, written in a small, precise hand, was the following message:

> *This is the real dark at the end of the tunnel. The lowest night of my life. Gregory, I love you, but I don't know what to say to you. Adam, it's not your fault. I don't hate you; I don't feel anything for you.*
>
> *Suzan, you've tried, but you can't know how I feel. It's not your fault you don't understand. And it's not your fault, Drew. You were the one person I thought could understand. That was my mistake. Eric . . . you were another mistake. My mistakes could fill a book.*
>
> *I can barely see to write this. I want to tell myself that to-*

*morrow will be better, that tomorrow will make a difference,*
*but it won't. I just want to go to sleep. I suppose I should*
*feel—what? Betrayed? Angry? But I don't.*
*I don't feel anything.*

I had to laugh.

It was a shitty thing to do, but I couldn't help myself. The note was just so *Hollywood Babylon,* so community-theater. "This is the real dark at the end of the tunnel"? What a drama queen. Monica Slezak should have been one of those romance writers with dyed pink poodles and three names. Face it, lady, I thought—even losing an Oscar nomination didn't entitle you to a *Sunset Boulevard* exit.

Ashamed of myself, I read it again, remembering Monica's walk across the stage, her head dangling like a broken marionette, and this time I didn't laugh. The note may have been soapsuds and organ music, but maybe all suicide notes were by their very nature melo-dramatic.

In any case, the note didn't provide any bombshells, or even clues, other than the fact that Monica's cursive style hinted at Cath-olic-school penmanship classes. The jagged edge at the top indi-cated that it had been pulled off a pad or out of an expensive blank book, but maybe it was just a transmission problem. As for the peo-ple in the note, there was only one Suzan with a *z* in Hollywood, so I knew who that was. Gregory was self-explanatory. Adam might be Adam Davies, or it might be someone else. As to Eric, I didn't have a clue.

I took the note and went in the bathroom. Standing there, releas-ing four cups of coffee and a latte, I realized that this piece of paper could be the linchpin to a magazine sale, if I could get an article done. But could I actually do that? Reprinting a woman's suicide note might be legitimate journalism—but only if the story behind the note warranted it. A Frank Grassley could do it without a second thought, but what about me? How would I feel the morning after? Pretty scummy, I knew. But just how scummy?

I zipped up and decided to worry about it later.

BACK WHEN L.A. WAS A TWO-NEWSPAPER TOWN, I'd gotten my start at the number-two paper, the *Globe-Examiner*. It was the last tattered flagship of the Westworth newspaper empire, which had once owned a chain of number-two papers around the United States. By the 1980s, though, the days of afternoon papers were over, and the chain was reduced to a few rusty links in smaller cities. The *Globe-Ex* was one-fifth the size of its competitor and five times as scrappy; aggressive when it came to covering City Hall and sentimental when it came to eulogizing kids who got dusted in drive-by shootings. By the time I landed there, the *Globe-Ex* had been crippled by a long, bitter strike and advertiser defections. Then, one day, the paper that had published every afternoon for more than one hundred years put out a final edition, sent everyone home, padlocked the doors, and left its magnificent Julia Morgan–designed building to the feral armies that roamed downtown, who promptly left a thick snarl of spray-paint tags all over the Moorish exterior.

Physically, the *Globe-Ex* was a relic, a throwback to high ceilings, dusty tile floors, and gigantic fans built into the walls. There were still bottles of Scotch and decks of cards in some of the desks over on newsside. Every reporter's station had an old Underwood bolted to the top. Computers had arrived in the seventies, but there was only one for every three reporters, and they crashed once or twice a day. Despite all this, or because of it, there was a pride in working for the *Globe-Ex*, a sort of *Poseidon Adventure* camaraderie—until that day when the ship listed for the last time and the staff stood around in shock, crying and exchanging home phone numbers that would never be dialed.

Today the building was used mostly for a movie set.

The paper I worked for now looked like a brokerage or a particularly busy real-estate office. Reporters in crisp white shirtsleeves and suspenders worked in bullpens made of movable plastic sound baffles. The phones had cordless headsets to alleviate neck strain and specially cantilevered keyboards designed to minimize carpal tunnel syndrome. The computers had a built-in stylebook that was widely derided in the newspaper world for its slavish adherence to political correctness; type in "deaf" and the machine would beep and suggest you use "hearing-impaired." The windows didn't open and the temperature was kept at a safe seventy-two degrees all year round. It was messy and it was busy, but it was all a little sterile. Today, riding up on the elevator, I wished that I'd put on something besides an old pair of Levi's and a Nine Inch Nails tour shirt.

I got off on the fourth floor and wound my way through the bullpens until I found Sally. I sneaked up behind her and said, "Cara mia. Let me take you away from all this."

She was watching a hockey game on her tiny color TV, which was hidden in the corner of the desk, camouflaged by phone books. "Kieran. To what do I owe this unexpected pleasure?"

"Telecommuting makes me lonely. I thought that spending some time with my favorite editor might help."

"I'll just bet." She wasn't even paying attention; the puck was flying and there was blood on the ice. I sat down and swiveled around. Sally had decorated her cubicle with photos of her kid and a shot of Ivana Trump with Fabio at some party. Somebody went in the penalty box and Sally shook her head as if she was coming out of a trance. "Well, as long as you're here, you can do some work." She rummaged on her desk. Sally's fastidiousness was limited to dangling participles and misplaced modifiers; her desk looked as if she'd been playing 52-pickup with press releases. She extracted a pink flier. "Some club is opening next Friday in Hollywood—what's it called? Faboo. You ever heard of Faboo?"

"Yeah. It's going to be the next big thing. For a week or two, at least."

"What's it all about?"

"Bad-boy actors. Anorexics with boob implants. Just another Friday night for the young Hollywood set. I'll be the oldest person there."

"Sounds like a winner. Do a review, make it twelve or thirteen inches, and I'll budget it to run Monday." She held out the press release. I took it without enthusiasm. "Seriously. What brings you down?"

"I came to talk to Stan Nyman."

Sally was already fixated on the hockey game again. She waved her fingers—ta-ta. On my way back to the elevators, I heard her singing "You Don't Bring Me Flowers."

I went down to the floor where the news reporters worked: national desk, international desk, city desk. It was the size of the Pentagon and I didn't know anyone. I strolled around the bullpens, ignored, until I saw pink-faced Stan Nyman chewing on a toothbrush and reading *The Wall Street Journal.*

"Stan."

"Mr. O'Connor," he said with mock formality. He was a nice guy, but I still didn't like him, on principle.

"I came down to pick up my notebook, if you're done with it," I said stiffly. "If you're not, I could just copy it."

"No, it's all yours." His desk was clean, topped with slotted plastic dividers. He pulled a folder from one of the dividers and handed it to me. Inside was my notebook, his notes, some photocopied magazine articles, and a big sheaf of dot-matrix printouts from the electronic morgue. At the *Globe-Ex,* the morgue had been a cavernous room of file cabinets full of yellowed clippings. Here, all you did was call the library, tell them what you needed, and some supercomputer did it for you. It was thorough and efficient and no fun at all.

"Funny you should drop by," Nyman said. "I spent the day working on a follow-up story for tomorrow, but there's not much. They've ruled it a suicide. I got the coroner's report and the toxicology stuff just an hour ago."

"That was fast."

"Yeah, well, they go quick when they're taking apart a celebrity."

He hit a button on his big Coyote terminal. The cursor danced down a screen of illegible notes in some electronic shorthand.

"Here it is," he says. "Stomach reports show she'd taken Zapax and Percocil, both on prescription. Not an overdose, but enough to put your brain pan into a scramble. No alcohol, though. Not even wine. I checked with a couple of MDs at Cedars, and they said the Zapax and the Percocil was definitely enough to explain the slurred speech and the stumbling."

"Enough to send someone over the edge?"

He tapped a couple more keys. "Eh. Who knows. They won't speculate. These drugs work differently on different people. Zapax they prescribe for panic disorder, and Percocil is a fairly new drug that's had some success in combating chronic depression. There were a couple of interesting court cases last year about Percocil. I pulled a few articles on it. Remember that woman in Maryland that smothered her kids? They got her into court and her lawyer claimed Percocil as an extenuating circumstance. Got a few years shaved off her sentence."

I remembered seeing the woman on a TV newsmagazine. Nobody commits murder anymore. From watching the talk shows, you'd think that the four leading causes of homicide are satanic possession, childhood abuse, MTV, and a few extra Twinkies in your lunchbox.

"Why are you so interested in this?" Nyman asked, leaning back in his chair and fish-eyeing me.

"No particular reason."

"I'd guess you were going to try and sell an article."

I tried for a poker face and failed. Nyman was pretty sharp.

A collective wail came from the other end of the room. I craned my neck. "Did the computers crash?"

Nyman blinked at me. "That's right, you're one of the refugees from the *Globe-Ex*. Computers don't crash here, Kieran. They're watching the Kings game." He smiled and tapped a few keys. The screen went blank except for the glowing green cursor. Nyman stood, cracking his neck, and picked up the Slezak file. "Come on. I've got a few minutes. We can go upstairs and you can buy me a cup of coffee."

I have never understood how a company cafeteria that managed to include both a salad and a frozen-yogurt bar couldn't manage to make a decent cup of coffee. Claudia should set up a franchise here. Nyman and I filled skyscrapers of Styrofoam with hot brown muck, dumped in the contents of two pink envelopes and some milklike petroleum by-products to make it potable, and found a table near the window, where we could look down on the men constructing a subway that no one would ever use.

"So you're going to do an article," Nyman said. He had bought a croissant swaddled in plastic wrap.

"Maybe."

"Just say yes, Kieran. I can help you."

"All right. Yes."

He smiled at me and pushed the folder across the table. "I might need this back, but I don't think so. It's not going to be news after tomorrow, unless something unusual happens. But you've got contacts in Hollywood that I don't. You might be able to turn it into something."

I took the folder. "Can I ask you some questions?"

"Shoot," he said, and laughed at his choice of words.

"Who was her doctor?"

"Sandy Richards. A woman. In Beverly Hills. She hasn't called back."

"Have you talked to her husband?"

"No. I phoned him this morning and talked to Monica's assistant. English girl. She's fending off the press."

"Did they find out where she got the gun?"

"It was hers. Registered and everything. She belonged to the West Hollywood Armament Club. I gather that a lot of these society ladies belong."

It was true. After some young actress had been blown away by one of those tabloid-cliché troubled loners, a lot of the ladies-who-lunch had gotten guns. It had become quite a vogue for a while. Some people sneered, but I figured it was better that they spend their idle hours practicing marksmanship than going down to South Central, looking at murals, and patting underprivileged children on the head. Some of the shops on Rodeo Drive had even started selling cunning little accessories like designer holsters—and, for all I knew, jeweled bandoliers.

"As near as they could reconstruct it," he said, "she went in the bathroom, ran cold water over some paper towels—they found them in the trash can—washed her face, sat down on the tank, and blammo. Her fingerprints were on the gun, and there were powder burns on her palm. There was a suicide note. I didn't see it, but one of the investigating officers read it to me over the phone. If you want, I could give you his number and you could follow up."

I looked at my lap and debated, but vanity got the best of me. "I already have one."

Stan Nyman paused in mid-chew of his croissant and gave me a penetrating look. "Whajado, copy it down in the bathroom?"

"Something like that."

"Good work, but I wouldn't mention that to anyone else. That might be considered tampering with evidence."

"Who was the source that said her speech was slurred and she was having trouble walking?"

"That was the Morninglory woman. She didn't want to be quoted by name."

"Anything else important that didn't make it in the story?"

"Not really, other than some forensic details. That Morninglory woman is a real nutball, isn't she?"

I nodded and waited, but Nyman didn't say anything more. He puffed out his cheeks and looked around. A worker walked past with a huge stainless-steel tray of lasagna, wearing the same grim expression I'd seen on every cafeteria lady in high school. "Nine Inch Nails," Nyman finally said, gesturing to my shirt. "Is that a nightclub or something?"

"Rock band."

"I should have known." He twisted the gold band on his finger. "My stepson tries to keep me up-to-date, but it never sticks. Everything I find out about turns out to be nostalgia already."

"So that's it? One follow-up story?"

"If she was an actress, we probably would have pursued it. But it's a dead issue, Kieran. No one out in Buena Park or San Bernardino knows who Monica Slezak is. Or if they do, it's just a name they've heard on 'Entertainment Tonight.' Either way, they don't care. Which is good."

"What do you mean?"

He twisted the plastic wrap around the butt end of the croissant. "Because it doesn't bear any relation to their lives. It doesn't tell them why their taxes are going up, or why they're losing their medical coverage, or what the point is of sending their kids to college when there isn't going to be a job for them when they get out. By that standard, it's not news. And, frankly, I'm so sick of these Hollywood jackoffs squeezing real news out of the paper that I could puke. Movie stars testifying before Congress. What a joke. What a sick frigging joke. Oliver North commits treason, and no one cares. Oliver Stone lights a fart and the world stops to listen." The bitterness in his voice cut across the empty cafeteria.

"I know what you mean," I told him, and I did.

We sat there in silence for a minute while the sun slipped behind a building. Nyman puffed out his cheeks again and then laughed, a sharp sound. "Nothing against what you do, of course."

He nested our empty coffee cups together, patted me on the shoulder, and headed toward the elevators. For a chubby guy, his pants sure were baggy in the back.

It was dark when I got home. The cops had blocked off the streets around my building, a not-uncommon occurrence these days. A chopper buzzed overhead, shining a blue-white light onto roofs, poking it down alleys. I parked over on Marine and walked the half-mile to my apartment.

My message light was blinking, but I ignored it. I found an elderly Budget Gourmet in the back of the freezer, its bright box covered with permafrost. When the chicken and rice was nuked, I sprinkled some parsley flakes on the top in an attempt to make it look less depressing, cleared a month's worth of newspapers off the kitchen table, and sat down with Stan Nyman's folder.

Most of the printouts from the morgue were tidbits from the paper's industry column. A metro brief about Monica's car accident. A lawsuit over *White Ice*. The Slezaks signing a three-picture deal at an ailing studio. Setting up an honorarium at USC for "needy film students." A Q&A with Gregory Slezak after the release of *The Dark at the End of the Tunnel*. I ate the chewy chicken and read the Q&A. Nothing helpful.

The biggest printout was entitled HOLLYWOOD BIDS HIGH, a year-old article about some record-breaking bidding wars for novels. Most of the story was about Michael Crichton and John Grisham, but the computer had detected a Slezak reference, and I found it on page 8. The Slezaks had paid for the rights to "an upcoming jailhouse memoir by first-time novelist Andrew Wilson," which was then still in galleys. The movie, stated the article, would be produced under a joint pact with the Slezaks' company, GMS Productions, and Oyster Hill Productions—Adam Davies's company. I smiled. One piece snapped into the jigsaw.

I skimmed a couple of Percocil stories from my own paper: PROBLEMS WITH WONDER DRUG? and RX DEFENSE IN ANNAPOLIS COURTROOM. The defendant, one Annene Chalfant, had gone into postpartum depression after the birth of her third child. When a standard "monoamine oxidase inhibitor" drug hadn't worked, her doctor had prescribed Percocil. Within a month, said her lawyers, Chalfant had to be hospitalized for bizarre, self-destructive behavior, like digging at her wrists with a fork. Her sleep habits and her sex life changed. A week after her release from the hospital, her husband came home to find their three children smothered by their mother. Freeman/DecaPharm, makers of Percocil, denied any responsibility or connection. The jury accepted mitigating circumstances and convicted her of voluntary manslaughter. Score another one for the abuse excuse.

The magazine clips were less newsy and more personality-oriented. There was one of those at-home stories with the Slezaks: Gregory and Monica working in their office, cooking together, floating in the pool in an Annie Leibovitz photo. They looked happy and breathless and a little out of shape. Monica had her hair slicked back and wore no makeup. That was unusual; most people would have demanded a four-hour styling session for anything with the potential embarrassment of a swimming-pool shot.

Next was a Sunday-magazine piece that I remembered from a few months back: WORKING GIRLS. It was a sly story about several women producers, all of whom talked about the glass ceiling in Hollywood and told a few juicy stories of male piggery they'd encountered over the years. Monica came off as a straight shooter, one of the wittiest. The reporter hinted that Monica had her nutty traits, but put a crazy-like-a-fox spin on them. Toward the end, the story mentioned Monica's friendship with Suzan Morninglory—who was described as "the industry's answer to the Dalai Lama, a woman who's managed to work some undeniable miracles for people with breast cancer and AIDS while she's built both a formidable reputation and bank account."

I grinned. Take *that*, Ms. Morninglory.

The rest of Nyman's notes were interviews with cops, hotel management, and a medical examiner. Nothing that I didn't know and nothing important. The real treasure turned up on the back cover of his notebook: the initials G.S., followed by two seven-digit numbers, one marked "H," one marked "O": Gregory Slezak's home and office numbers. It was a logical place to start.

I stayed up all night writing a proposal. I sketched a portrait of Monica Slezak, raising questions and hinting that I had the answers. I emphasized the fact that I'd found the body and described the media scramble that ensued. At the end, I described myself as a "frequent contributor" to the newspaper, without going into a lot of unnecessary detail about the content of those contributions. Not that I called myself a crime reporter, but any potential editor could be forgiven for drawing that conclusion.

I wrapped the whole thing up on what I hoped was an ominous note, hit PRINT, brushed my teeth, took a shower, and watched Katie Couric interview Kevin Costner and the Israeli prime minister. At eight o'clock, I fed the whole thing through my fax six times, to six different magazines. I called Gregory Slezak at home, got the machine, and left a message requesting an interview. Then I put a towel and some sunscreen in a paper bag and went to sleep on the beach for the rest of the day.

After that, there was nothing to do but wait.

# =7=

AND WAIT.

Slezak never called back. When I called him again two days later, his home phone had been disconnected and there was no forwarding number. I tried the office number instead and got Alison Sewell. She was polite, but her answers came in clipped little yeses and noes, as if she was taking tiny bites of meat with her teeth.

"Can you just tell me if he got my other message?"

"Yes."

"He did?"

"Yes."

"Will he be calling back? I only need—"

"Please," she said. "Mr. Slezak's not talking to anyone. He's grieving."

I tried to sound sympathetic. "Of course he is. It must be terrible. Has the press been calling a lot?"

She didn't fall for it. "Please don't call here again," she said, and rang off.

A week went by. I heard back from one of the magazines—an intern called to say thanks, but no thanks. I finally phoned the others myself. Two of them gave me the runaround before giving me an official thumbs-down. Three of them didn't even take the call.

Another three-day notice to pay rent or quit was push-pinned to my door. I stuck it under the VCR with the first one.

"Sit up straight," Jocelyn commanded. She lit the latest in her never-ending chain of thin brown cigarettes and looked at me as if I were something she'd come upon in the very back of her refrigerator. I caught a glimpse of myself in the mirror across the room, slouchy and rumpled-looking in an old tweed jacket and a gabardine shirt.

Jocelyn Albarian was my literary agent, a title that might have carried a bit more cachet if I had actually written any books in the last few years. My sole literary output was two quickie paperback biographies of two teen stars, Corey Baxter and Lissa Cassidy. The books had taken three weeks apiece to write, which was a little bit longer than Corey's and Lissa's careers. That was three years ago, and we hadn't been able to come up with another project since. Still, we talked on the phone once a month, and she took me out to lunch whenever she was in Los Angeles.

Today we were splitting a crab-cake appetizer on the patio at Cormorant-at-the-Shore. Jocelyn had requested a restaurant that was "very L.A.," so we'd come to this pricey bistro near the Santa Monica Pier, where no one even noticed if you spent your whole lunch hour making calls from your table on your cellular phone. I sipped from a bottle of San Pellegrino and glanced across the street, where hundreds of homeless were lined up in Palisades Park for the daily mass feeding. I averted my eyes and looked down at our fifteen-dollar plate of crabmeat guiltily.

Jocelyn dipped a forkful of crab into a pool of grain-mustard sauce. "What can you do about it? Go across the street and give it to them?"

Among Jocelyn's many talents was her ability to read my mind. Others included a degree in contract law; a phone voice that brought to mind Joan Collins on a 976 line; a politely imperious manner that made the snootiest waiters roll over and play dead; and an attitude toward her clients that was half-mother, half-dominatrix. Her agency was a one-woman boutique operation that was mercilessly commercial. From a reconverted brownstone in Chelsea, she controlled a stable of writers that turned out romance novels, thrillers, and true-crime sagas by the metric ton. When a client would dare to buck Jocelyn's jugular instinct for the commercial and venture an idea for the great American novel, she could be brutal. "You're not Ethan Canin," or "You're not Toni Morrison," she would say, waving the notion away with a handful of lacquered fingers. By the end of one of our lunches, I always felt as if I was sitting on a stack of telephone books, my heels dangling over the floor.

The waiter appeared. Jocelyn ordered grilled swordfish and gazpacho for both of us and turned her laser gaze on the next table, where a woman of a certain age was sharing tiramisu and some equally gooey looks with a male bimbo.

"Older women and younger men are very hot right now," Jocelyn pronounced, making a note in her Filofax. The appointment book bulged with notes as to what was "hot right now"—notes that Jocelyn processed, melted down, and assigned to her writers like a schoolteacher hands out homework. I was still waiting to receive one of Jocelyn's ideas from her million-dollar Filofax.

Waiting for the food to arrive, we occupied ourselves with our usual conversation about Hollywood. Jocelyn was endlessly fascinated by the machinations and private lives of the people in the entertainment industry—probably because she had so little contact with it. She was the third generation of a publishing family. Both of her parents were editors, but Jocelyn had figured out at a young age that taking fifteen percent off the top was a lot more fun than unraveling syntax and unsplitting infinitives. When her husband, Gerald, an accountant whose only sin was terminal mildness, had finally had enough and moved to Seattle, Jocelyn's response was to get rid of the leather sofa in her office, replace it with a fold-out bed, and rededicate herself to selling the kind of books people buy at airport concession stands. She was the queen of the embossed foil cover.

By the time the grilled fish and cold soup arrived, we had exhausted Jocelyn's favorite subjects: which big stars had been rude to me recently, who was on drugs, who looked like hell, who was a few peaches shy a bushel, and who was queer. Once the plates had been set in front of her, she examined the fish as if she were auditioning it and said, "You've got an idea for a book."

"How could you tell?"

Jocelyn produced a vial of Mrs. Dash from her handbag and nonsalted the fish. "It's not important, peaches. Now. What's been zooming around inside that little mind of yours?"

I gave her the condensed version of the Slezak events while she ate, building up to my big finish: the proposal and the suicide note. Jocelyn put on a pair of gold-rimmed half-glasses to read them, pursing her lips. When she was done, she handed the papers back.

"What do you think, Jocelyn? I mean, I know it's unfocused, but I think there might be a good true-crime book in there somewhere.

You've got to admit the suicide was pretty dramatic. There's the Oscar angle, and Percocil is in the news—"

"You're not Dominick Dunne, Kieran," Jocelyn interrupted, taking off her half-glasses.

"Well, I am the author of *Corey! Corey! Corey!* and *The Untold Lissa,*" I reminded her. "And I seem to remember some good reviews in *Sassy* magazine."

She smiled. "All right. I didn't mean it to sound so harsh. But what you have here isn't a book, it's a magazine article."

"What do you mean?"

"You don't have a hundred thousand words here. You *might* have five thousand words. This has all the earmarks of a Sunday magazine story. It would take a lot of time and research to put together a proper book outline, and I could almost guarantee I wouldn't be able to sell it." She spooned the last of her soup and smiled. "This gazpacho is fabulous. You just can't get really good gazpacho in New York."

I dropped the subject. Jocelyn ordered sorbet and cappuccinos for both of us and lit another cigarette. When the waiter reappeared with a leatherette wallet bearing the check, he set it in front of Jocelyn automatically. Did I really look that destitute? But Jocelyn didn't even notice, deep as she was in complaint about the state of publishing.

"They're saturating the market on true crime. Look at O. J. Simpson. Look at the Menendez brothers. Dozens of books. Writers were all over those cases like flies on a diaper." She fussed with the stickpin in her scarf and sighed. "The stakes have been raised. No one cares about simple murder or suicide anymore. You've got to have exorbitant amounts of sex and scandal and outrageous behavior. And once you do, you have dozens of writers all fighting to get the contract to write the definitive book. There just aren't that many *high-quality* murders out there," she said wistfully.

"All right already," I said. "I'll forget about Monica Slezak."

Jocelyn took out her American Express platinum card and tucked it in the leatherette wallet, holding the folder in the air imperiously. Within seconds, a waiter materialized and stole it away. "No, do a little digging if you have time. See what you can find out. If you come up with anything good, maybe I can get it placed at a magazine that might earn us some money. Just don't get your hopes up."

"Don't worry. You've done pretty well at dashing them."

"Poor Kieran." She smiled. "But you do have one thing in your favor, I must say."

"And that is?"

The receipt came back. Jocelyn added a large tip and tucked her AmEx card into her purse. "You have the field to yourself. No one else will be chasing this story, because they won't see any money in it. It's a long shot, but if it pays off, it would be all yours."

We walked out to the sidewalk, where Jocelyn presented her claim check to a valet. While we waited for the rental car, she looked me up and down. A little shudder shook her shoulders at the sight of my dirty white Converse high-tops.

"You know, Gerald was about your size," she said thoughtfully. "And he left a lot of perfectly good clothes in our Connecticut house. . . ."

By the time Friday crawled into view, I was thoroughly depressed. All I wanted to do was curl up in the futon with a bag of my favorite store-brand cookies and a copy of *The Brothers Karamazov*, which is what I always read when I'm depressed. Keeping all those diminutives and patronymics straight in my head takes my mind off my own troubles, but I only do it at home, because I think reading a Russian novel in public is just too pretentious. I couldn't even take comfort in *Karamazov*, though, because Friday was the night that I'd promised Sally I'd cover the opening of Faboo.

Faboo promised to be everything I hated happening simultaneously in one place. It was the latest venture of a club owner named Jess—just Jess, like Cher or Lassie. He created new clubs more often than I washed my car. Jess's clubs always opened with a big splash, became the ultimate in-spot for about six weeks, and then started to lag as soon as the clubutantes moved somewhere else. When that happened, he'd let in the Valley crowd for a few weeks to pay off his debts, close up shop, and reopen a new club within a month. I was usually there on opening night with my notebook, feeling vaguely as if I were pimping for Jess.

I didn't think I could face Faboo alone, although I couldn't think of anyone else who deserved to be subjected to it. I called a friend at HBO and dangled my plus-one in front of her, but she didn't bite. Finally, I called Pedro, even though I knew he'd be contemptuous of the whole idea. He was.

"You know what Jess's clubs are like," I wheedled. "Free drinks. Lots of cute boys there. Young, dumb—"

"And full of *fun*," he said sarcastically. "No way. I'm going to the Sadie Benning retrospective at the NuArt. Have fun on your own. Besides," he added theatrically, "you never know who you might run into there."

"What do you mean?"

"You'll find out."

It hadn't occurred to me that Claudia might be there. Of course she would; most of the clean-and-sober types on the club scene spent a lot of time at Cafe Canem, getting their fixes from Claudia's double espressos and depth charges. She went to Jess's club openings as a business obligation. Would Cathy Bates be with her? For some reason, I wasn't up for seeing the two of them.

"Is she going with Cathy?"

"Customer," Pedro said evilly. "Gotta zoom."

"Aw, *geez*, Pedro—"

"Aw, *geez*, Kieran," Pedro said, and hung up.

I spent the next few hours trying on everything in my closet. By the time I'd given up on the stuff on the hangers and had pawed through the eddy of clothes on the floor, it was nine-thirty. Damn. Faboo was in Hollywood, a half-hour drive from Venice. I'd wanted to get there as early as possible and get out as soon as I had my story. I figured the first arrivals would get there at ten, the place would be packed by eleven, and I could be out the door by eleven-thirty. Hit-and-run.

I finally settled on a houndstooth jacket, a dark-green shirt that looked like it had been previously owned by a seedy country-western singer, and a pair of black jeans—not the dyed kind, but the authentic article, real black denim. I put it all on, pulled on a pair of boots, and stared at myself in the mirror, trying to picture myself as an understated intellectual, the kind of guy whose looks aren't flashy but get better the longer you look at him. No matter how long I looked, though, the view never improved. I'm five feet ten; not short, but definitely not tall. I have nondescript black-Irish looks that sound like something out of a police lineup—dark hair, brown eyes, average weight. My build is absolutely unremarkable. Claudia once described it as "stocky but scrawny." I don't consider myself terribly vain, but once, just once, I'd like to be the best-looking guy at a party.

What the H, I finally decided, grabbing my keys and my notebook. In a town where everybody's a work of art, somebody's got to be the wallpaper.

It was ten-thirty by the time I got to Faboo. There was already a line of more than a hundred people snaking down Cahuenga: sheep awaiting abuse and willing to pay for the privilege. At the entrance, steroid apes and an artboy or two stood behind plastic chain ropes, portable headsets on, clipboards in their hands. As I loped up the sidewalk, a vulgar ultra-stretch limo pulled up and the steroid apes pulled back the fence to admit a bony young man in a black leather jacket and his two bimbettes. Even at half a block away, I recognized him as one of the actors from "Alpha Centauri Epsilon," Earl Dingle's TV show about the frat boys from outer space.

I hung out at the ropes with everyone else who claimed they were on the list until Jess finally poked his head out of the club and waved me in. He gave me a Eurotrash peck on the cheek and handed me two orange drink tickets from a roll he wore on his wrist. I pulled back the curtain—more black leather—and staggered into a humid miasma of cigarette smoke and pounding house music.

Faboo was spread out over several rooms, both large and small. I checked them all out—big discotheque, billiard room, couch room, little discotheque. By the time I got to the very back, the "performance room," I'd recognized eight young actors, three drag queens, two other club owners, one 'zine editor, the *LA Weekly* gossip columnist, a rapper who called himself Ice-Pik, and the woman who did adult diaper commercials on TV. I imagined she'd been invited for camp value. She looked tiny and lost.

I stopped at a bar and ordered an imported beer, which ended up costing both of my drink tickets. I went back to the quietest spot in the place, the couch room, and found an empty sofa in a dark corner where I could pull at my beer and take a few notes.

A guy I'd never seen before walked over, mumbled, "Hey, David, check this out," and handed me a copy of some new 'zine. I was so engrossed in trying to make out an article printed in tiny art-damaged Helvetica that I didn't see Claudia until she plopped down on the couch next to me. I didn't bother to look up from the 'zine.

"Where's Cathy?" I said. She nodded toward the disco and pantomimed dancing. "What's going on in the performance room?"

"El Vez," she said, referring to the city's preeminent Mexican Elvis impersonator. She flipped her hair to look at my magazine, and the aubergine tint shone in the smoky light. "How's your Slezak article coming?"

"Okay, *mas o menos*. Actually, not so okay. How's tricks with Cathy?"

"Like you said, *mas o menos*. I don't want to talk about it."

"Fine by me," I said, turning a page.

"So tell me what you've found out about Monica Slezak. Have you sold your story yet?"

"I don't want to talk about it."

"Well, that's two obvious topics down the toilet." For a minute, I thought she might leave, but instead she kicked off her pumps and sprawled on the couch as if she was ready to go to sleep. "You here with anybody?"

"No."

"Oh, Kieran. You need to get out more. Have some fun—"

"Staying home on a Friday night is fun. This is work."

"Maybe we should put some effort into it. Find you a nice AMW."

"AM what?"

"AMW. Actress/model/whatever."

"Maybe we *shouldn't*," I said irritably. I refolded the 'zine and held it closer to my face, hoping she'd take the hint.

But she didn't. Claudia gave a world-weary sigh and put her bare feet in my lap. "As you can gather, things aren't great with me and Cathy. Sorry about the AMW remark. I don't mean to be passive-aggressive. I'm probably projecting."

Passive-aggressive? Projecting? When had the pod people of pop-psych gotten to her? I shot Claudia a spiky look, but she was oblivious. "This thing with Cathy is getting to me," she said. "I guess I really do need to talk to someone about it."

I looked at her feet in my lap and felt my synapses sizzle. The rules between us weren't always clear, but, even in the tangled DNA of our relationship, this was a new quirk. Was she a jerk for expecting me to listen to her problems with her girlfriend? Or was I the jerk for being so unsympathetic?

I didn't know—and, all of a sudden, I didn't give a hang.

"You know, Claude," I said, taking her feet in my hands and depositing them gently on the dirty floor, "this afternoon, I made a list of the things that matter the most to me right now, and your relationship with Cathy Bates wasn't even in the top one hundred."

Her face looked as if she'd just slipped down a flight of stairs. After a deep breath through her nose, she rearranged herself.

"Kieran," she began slowly, "I know you're going through some choppy weather right now—"

"Oh, you do?"

"—but I'm not to blame. I'm not to blame for the fact that you're broke, and I'm not to blame because you haven't been able to sell an article. I'm really not. You've got to make things start happening for yourself for a change."

" 'Make things happen for myself?'" I let out a yawp. "Who the hell are you? Mary Tyler Morninglory?"

"Look at yourself," she said, unruffled. "It wouldn't hurt you to take a little bit better care of yourself, Kieran. Put on something nice once in a while." I stared down at my jeans, my green shirt. I'd thought I actually looked half decent for a change. Something in my throat went tight. My eyes stung, and it wasn't the cigarette smoke irritating my contact lenses.

I sat there for a minute trying to think of something witty and mordant to say. "Fuck you, Claudia," was what I came up with.

I got up and threw my 'zine across the room, where it knocked over a mannequin in a gas mask and pulled down a string of Christmas lights shaped like little cows. Then I went back through the billiard room and into the big discotheque, where I grabbed the first woman I saw, dragged her out on the floor, and thrashed around for twenty minutes straight to some industrial-noise song that precluded conversation.

\* \* \*

When it was over, I felt foolish. More than that, I felt mean. It felt good. I wanted a drink, so I abandoned my partner on the dance floor and stomped my way to the back bar. People were lined up three deep trying to get the harried bartender's attention. The place was obviously overcrowded, and I fantasized about calling the fire marshal just so I could have a happy ending for my story and Jess could have an aneurysm. Someone pitched into my back, stabbing me with a sharp elbow, and I whirled around with the idea of giving whoever it was a shove.

It was Drew Wilson.

He had some bored-looking AMW hanging off his arm and two whole loops of drink tickets hanging around his neck—one orange, one purple, like paper leis. His eyes were unfocused and rheumy and looked like they'd been coated in Vaseline. He looked at me glassily for a second, and then his lips pulled back in an alcoholic smile.

" 'Have Tux, Will Travel.' McCormick, right?"

"O'Connor. Kieran O'Connor."

"Oh, yeah. The Swede." He haw-hawed at his own joke and pulled the AMW forward with one hand on her ass. "Tisha, this guy's a writer." Tisha looked at me with new interest. Reporters shouldn't judge people on first impressions, but I guessed that Tisha was dumber than a sack of hammers.

"Tisha, say hi to Swede," Wilson said. "Maybe he'll put you in your column—in *his* column."

"Hi, Steve. I'm Tisha. Just Tisha."

Didn't anybody have two names anymore? "Is that T-I-S-H-A, or T-I-C-I-A?" I asked.

"Yes," she said.

There wasn't much to say after that, so we stood there getting jostled until Wilson bit her on the neck and patted her ass dismissively, like some pederast sending his lover off to third grade. "Go find us someplace to sit," he said. "Whaddaya wanna drink?"

"Sex on the Beach," she said breathlessly. Boop-boop-a-doo.

"Whadda you want, Swede?"

"A beer is fine."

"What kinda beer?"

"Any kind."

I watched Tisha/Ticia squeeze through the lummoxes at the bar. Her body was technically perfect, like a cake that looks too good to eat and disappoints on the first bite. I don't find perfect bodies attractive, and I'm not sure why. Claudia, in her current R.D.-Laing-meets-k.d.-lang mode, would probably say that I'm rejecting them before they can reject me.

Wilson got the bartender's attention by slamming his fist down on the bar and yelling, "Four Jamesons. Five-buck tip." He pulled off four purple drink tickets. The purples must have been for the good stuff.

"I wanted a beer—"

"Whaah?"

I put my mouth right next to his ear and yelled, "I wanted a *beer*. And Tisha wanted a Sex on the—"

"You're having Jameson," he yelled back. "And screw her. I don't even know her. Let her find some other asshole to buy her drinks." He handed me two of the glasses—"Saves us from coming back"— and pushed a path back through the club to the pool room, sloshing all the way. There was a whole line of people waiting to play, and, strangely, one unused table. I couldn't figure it out until Wilson took a cue ball from his jacket pocket. "You play, Swede?" he asked. "Grab a stick."

Two hulks in tight T-shirts looked as if they were ready to kill me, but I was still in a pissy mood, so I got a cue from the rack on the wall and chalked up. Wilson packed the balls into a tight triangle, using only his hands. He drained one of the Jamesons and barked, "Break."

I did. Two-ball cantered off the pad and into the side pocket. Cue ball rolled slowly into the far right.

We shot one game without talking. Even drunk, Drew Wilson could beat the pants off me. I had four stripes still on the felt when he sank the eight-ball in a perfect bank. When it was over, he raised his other glass of Jameson. We toasted, and as I took a slug of the peaty-tasting whiskey, he said,

"Fuck Monica Slezak."

W HEN I WOKE UP THE NEXT DAY and went out to get the newspaper, there was a third three-day notice on my door. This one had a handwritten note from the landlord at the bottom, assuring me that he and the sheriff's office meant business. Great. I live in a city and a state that are both broke, in a country that should have filed for bankruptcy when Reagan toddled out of office, and still the only debts that count are the ones at the very bottom of the food chain.

I read the Saturday morning paper over three cups of coffee and listened to my upstairs neighbors argue. Eavesdropping is something of a hobby of mine. I figure if people are going to interrupt your day by broadcasting their personal problems, you've got every right to listen. They screamed at each other for twenty minutes about their various failings, and then it ended as it always did, with curses, a slamming door, and someone turning on the "Home Shopping Club" at full volume.

I had all weekend to write my Faboo story, but for once I got out my notes early and turned on the computer. I typed in a few general impressions, but I couldn't get my encounter with Drew Wilson out of my mind. Being around Wilson was a lot like listening to an argument: fascinating, unpredictable, and a bit dangerous, containing the potential for ending with either a slamming door or a gunshot.

After he'd cursed Monica Slezak, Wilson had tried to start another game of pool, but the two guys who had been waiting for the table grabbed his arm and suggested that he clear out if he didn't want it broken. He'd let loose with a string of profanities and expletives, but they'd just laughed, picked him up by the elbows, and deposited him outside the door of the billiards room. I followed him out, hoping to keep him talking about Monica Slezak, but he wasn't in the mood.

"This is fucked," he yelled over a thumping house beat. "Let's get out of here. Go someplace and have a drink where people don't have their heads up their asses."

"I've got to do a story—"

"What?"

"I've got a story to write. I can't leave yet. Let's go in the back. I'll buy you a drink."

"I'm getting out of here." He took the most direct path to the front door, which happened to be straight through the crowded, deafening dance floor. I could feel the beat in my fillings. I followed Wilson as he careered off sweaty dancers, finally catching up to him in the anteway, where a vacant girl checked innumerable black leather jackets for five dollars apiece.

"Drew. I need to talk to you some more about Monica."

Wilson turned around sharply and gave me a boozy smile. "The worms crawl in. The worms crawl out. In your stomach and out your mouth." He was really potted. "Gimme your number. We'll go out for a drink sometime."

I scribbled it down, started to hand it to him, thought better of it, and tucked it in one of his inside pockets, where he'd be less likely to lose it. Wilson giggled moronically, as if I was tickling him. He pulled away.

"Give me your number, too," I said, but he lurched through the black curtain into the night, dropping an orange curl of drink tickets on the floor. A doorman in an leather S&M hood clicked off one on his little metal counter.

After an hour of noodling on the keyboard, it was clear that my Faboo story was going nowhere. I deleted the file and opened another one, naming it SLEZAK. In it, I jotted down a few notes about Wilson, and then made a list of a few more people I wanted to talk to: Gregory Slezak. Suzan Morninglory. Adam Davies. The West Hollywood Armament Club. Addie Adderley. Eric. By now, Eric had taken on the status of a mysterious one-named figure. Like Jess. Or Tisha.

I moved the cursor around idly, wondering what to do next. I could call Suzan Morninglory and request an interview, but I wanted to do some research on her first. Davies was notoriously press-shy, and I was sure that a standard interview request would get a standard refusal. Eric was a question mark.

Slezak was the one I really wanted to talk to, of course, but I had no idea how to get to him if he wouldn't call me back. I dialed his office again, expecting to get the machine, but Alison Sewell answered. She wasn't happy to hear my voice.

"I've asked you nicely not to call here," she said. "I told you he doesn't want to talk to you. Good-bye."

"I don't want to talk to him. I want to talk to you."

She paused, torn between curiosity and duty. "Why would you want to talk to me?"

"That—that's what I want to talk to you about." There was a pause while she digested this bit of nonsense. "Can we get together?"

She sighed. "All right. If you promise to stop calling and bothering Mr. Slezak."

"I promise."

"All right. I'm working here until about three, and then I want to go to the gym."

"You mean we could talk today?"

"Why not?"

"No reason. We could have dinner if you like."

"I don't *think* so," she said. It came off pretty snotty. "I've got plans for this evening, but I could meet you around five o'clock for an hour or so."

"Shall I come up there?"

She laughed. "I don't *think* so," she repeated. "Give me your address."

I looked around. My apartment was a studio that had been none too well maintained before I moved in. I'd done nothing in the way of home improvement except add piles of books, LPs, CDs, clippings, and an enormous tottering stack of newspapers that was destined for the recycler one of these days if it didn't fall over and kill me first. My file cabinet took up most of the twelve square feet of floor space that the landlord referred to as "the kitchen." The carpet was a filthy shag that had probably once been white, and there was a seeping, nicotinous water stain that covered most of the west-facing wall. I couldn't quite picture perching on the futon and splitting a Snapple with Alison Sewell.

"I don't *think* so," I told her. A devil on my shoulder suggested Cafe Canem, but I resisted the impulse. Instead, I gave Alison the address of the Abbot Kinney Cafe. She told me not to be late, and hung up.

She was there at five on the dot, carrying a gym bag, dressed in a modest aerobics outfit and a pair of Filas that looked straight out of the box. A velveteen headband held back hanks of damp-looking strawy hair. There was a portfolio slung over her left shoulder, a mesh bag containing a bottle of Evian over the right one, and I had the same reaction that I always had when I was confronted with a woman like Alison Sewell—an urge to sniff my armpits and check the soles of my shoes for dog doo.

"I've got an hour on the meter. I hope that will be enough, because I've got to be back in Beverly Hills at six-thirty." She sat down.

"No problem."

She fussed with her belongings for a moment while she looked out at Ocean Front Walk. A Rastafarian on Rollerblades cruised by, Rita Marley blasting out of the radio balanced on his head. Two hippie chicks were doing hair wraps for some tourists, while a third danced the sun grope to music only she could hear. Down by the pavilion, a group of kids were putting on a show, skateboarding in and out of orange rubber cones, thrashing their boards on a piece of plywood they'd propped against the wall. Standard stuff for a sunny Sunday in Venice, but Alison looked at the little pageant as if she'd just stepped out of the Beverly Center and into the market at Marrakesh. "I left the car in an unattended lot," she said uneasily. "Do you think it'll be safe? It's not mine; it belongs to the Slezaks."

"It'll be fine," I told her. As long as you're out of here by sundown, I added to myself.

She finished arranging her things and got the waiter's attention with one tilt of her head, something that I'd been unable to accomplish in the ten minutes I'd been sitting there. We ordered two iced teas. Most of the people in the café were now staring at an amputee breakdancer, but Alison didn't even seem to notice. I guessed there wasn't much that distracted her.

"I don't want to be quoted," she said, accepting an iced tea from the waiter and fixing me with a flat, level gaze.

"Hmm?"

"I don't want to be quoted in your article. Agreed?"

"Agreed."

"Good." She didn't look reassured. I sipped my tea and smiled pleasantly. Sometimes an interview is like trying to tame a jumpy horse; the best thing you can do is nothing. Relax and let it come to you. Two surfers squished past the café, unzipping their wetsuits like snakes shedding their skins. I picked a spot on the horizon and stared at it blandly.

"It's all been quite difficult, as you can imagine," she said.

"How's Mr. Slezak holding up?"

"I didn't bring up the topic to have you ask that question for the eightieth time," she snapped. "I brought it up in hopes of impressing upon you that Mr. Slezak doesn't want to be bothered right now. I've done something for you, and I'd appreciate it if you could do something for me. Leave him alone."

I was cowed. "I told you I would, Alison."

"Good," she said. She took her first sip of tea and looked at me as if we'd just been introduced. "Kieran," she said, tasting the name. "Wasn't there a Saint Kieran? What did he do?"

" 'Kieran, build thou a monastery,' commanded St. Patrick."

"That's right. So where's your monastery?"

"See that brick building up the boardwalk? The one with the mural and the earthquake damage? I'm on the top floor."

"Pardon me for saying so, but it doesn't look very monastic." Alison smiled. "I've been here a year, and this is the first time I've been down to Venice. I haven't seen much of Los Angeles. I don't know if I'll ever quite get used to it."

"You don't like it?"

She gave me a puzzled look. "I love it. You've got the beach and the snow and the desert and the city all in one place. Why wouldn't I love it?"

Her chilliness was fading; the thaw was on. I knew better than to rush it. "Tell me how you came to live here."

We chatted for a few minutes. Alison had come to the United States with her husband to take some complicated graduate courses in film at a college in San Francisco, and had applied for Women in the Industry's mentor program. WII had accepted her application and matched her with Monica Slezak. I was impressed. Being paired with Monica was a coup. Most of those mentor programs just stick you in an office at some studio, doing filing and being screamed at by an executive with serious blood-pressure issues.

"You must be good at what you do."

She shrugged. "Most of the women who applied for mentorships wanted to learn how to direct. All I ever wanted to do was produce. I did a couple of ghastly little projects in school, and I know how it goes. Directors live under the delusion that they're the ones who make everything happen, but it's the producer's hand that rocks the cradle, as far as I'm concerned. Monica was looking for someone who really wanted to learn how to produce a film. And so there you are. Opportunity knocking, and all that."

"What was Monica like?"

"You never met her?"

"No." The waiter brought fresh glasses of tea. He'd added a couple of flowers to Alison's saucer in an attempt at flirtation, but she didn't seem to notice. He slunk away, crushed.

"She taught me a great deal. You know, a lot of the women I've met out here have been antagonistic toward other women, but Monica didn't have any ego problems. She was a very generous person. She was a hard worker and she demanded the same." Alison twisted her lemon slice inside out, sending microscopic dots of citrus oil skittering across the surface of her tea. "I worked as a production assistant on *A Lover's Question* as an apprentice, and when the mentorship was over, she hired me to work on pre-production for *The Midnight Hour*. I'll be getting an associate producer's credit on that one," she added.

"From production assistant to associate producer? That's pretty good. Congratulations."

She shrugged, but I could tell she was proud. "It's not a major motion picture, but it's a start."

We discussed the intricacies of the industry for a while. Alison had been working with Oyster Hill, helping Monica set up budgets and locations with Adam Davies. She had no idea what would happen to the project now that Monica was dead; without a director attached, the project was unofficially in limbo. Slezak had another directorial commitment that would take up the late spring and most of the summer, and Davies was scouting for a director who, as Alison put it, "could operate within the budget parameters of the production." I took that to mean that Oyster Hill couldn't pay much.

"Are you going to keep working for Mr. Slezak?"

"I don't know. I'd like to. Right now there's still plenty to do on *The Midnight Hour*. Loose ends and all that. But I'd like to." She twisted a lock of hair, testing it for dryness. "The Slezaks are very nice people. As you probably know, there are a lot of people in the industry who are talented but not very nice, and there are others who are nice but not very talented. I've even met a few who are both untalented and—"

"Charm-free."

"Precisely." She laughed, a genuine unguarded chuckle. I wondered if I had misjudged Alison Sewell, if my first reaction to her had just been vestigial male chauvinism. She was driven, certainly, but no more so than any young man who had climbed from movie gruntdom to the rank of associate producer. Somewhere in her story, Alison's husband had switched from present to past tense, which reminded me of the double standard in the industry: a driven man was tough, savvy, a scrapper; a driven woman was a harpy, a virago, a bitch. There were more women in the industry than ever before, but, for all of Hollywood's lip service to liberalism, a lot of the ingrained attitudes had yet to change. It was a familiar, bitter complaint among Hollywood women: *A man is a perfectionist; a woman is a bitch.* Thus the formation of groups like Women in the Industry.

We seemed to be reasonably chummy by now, so I waited for a break in the conversation to ask, as sympathetically as I could, "Did you sense that Monica had any . . . problems?"

It was like shutting off a tap; Alison balked visibly, getting a look on her face like a politician who was about to enter a verbal minefield. "Off the record, of course," I added hastily.

After a pause, she spoke again, but the warmth was gone, replaced with a glaze of British reserve and politesse. "I'm sure you've heard some of the stories of Monica's . . . *erraticism,* but I've worked with

Monica and Gregory for a whole year, and I genuinely like them both. More important, I respect them. She was a fine person." Alison sipped her iced tea and looked at me as if she expected a challenge.

I noticed Alison was referring to Monica in both the present and past tenses, as if she still hadn't quite gotten used to the fact that she was dead. Time to tread carefully. "Did you think that she could ever . . . do something like she did?"

"I am not to be quoted." It wasn't a question.

"Of course."

A shaft of dying sunlight cut across our table. Alison thought about it while she rummaged for sunglasses and put them on. "Yes and no," she said. "She had some problems, which I gather came from a chemical imbalance. In the brain, you know. Gregory says they'd been deviling her all her life. For the first few months I worked with her, she was fine. But it cropped up about—I don't know—maybe six months ago, right around the time of her auto accident. She'd be fine most of the time, and then without warning she'd go into this depression where no one could help her. Even Gregory. He said that he'd always been able to reach her before, but this was different." Alison had crumpled her straw wrapper into an accordion. She dabbed it with a dot of tea and it began to unfold, a worm waking up. "That was around the time she started to see Suzan Morninglory and all that, which seemed to help. That's why I say yes and no, because aside from that one period of time, she seemed quite happy and busy for the last six months."

I didn't know anything about acute depression except what I'd been able to glean from the Percocil articles. Apparently chemical depression responded well to the new generation of psychotropic drugs, but the hurdle was finding the right drugs, in the right dosage, in the right combination. There could be side effects, and the medication could also stop working without cause or explanation. Pharmaceutical roulette, and there was no way to attack the problem except by trial and error.

"Did she take a lot of pills?"

A rind-thin smile played across Alison's face. "That," she said, "is none of your business."

"What do you think of Suzan Morninglory?" I asked.

Alison took a long time to answer. "Monica thought Suzan helped her, and I suppose she did, in some way. At least her depression did seem to ease a bit. Monica wanted me to try her program when I was separating from my husband, but I never had the time."

"What's her program all about?"

"Lectures. Tapes. Workbooks. I don't know much about it."

"What do *you* think of Suzan Morninglory herself? As a person?"

"I only met her a few times, and I never really talked with her, so I wouldn't say. It doesn't matter." Alison couldn't hide a condescending little smile. "Americans believe in a lot of things, don't they?"

She checked her watch, and I could tell she was ready to go. Time for hardball, the questions every reporter saves for the very end of the interview.

"Did the Slezaks have a good marriage?"

She stared at me as if I'd just farted. "For your information," she said, enunciating every word, "Gregory and Monica Slezak were the happiest couple I've ever met."

Under the brittle tones, there was a flash of anger, and I pressed it. "Then who is Eric?"

Alison looked startled for a moment, and then blessed me with another condescending little smile that made me want to smack her. "You're awfully nosy, Saint Kieran."

"Who is he?"

"Schroeder," she said. "The nutritionist. He had some plan to control Monica's mood swings through diet, but it didn't work." She stood and gathered her things. "I think we're through now."

"If you say so," I said.

"I do," she said, and walked away into the lengthening shadows of the boardwalk.

"BREATHE. TAKE IN THE LIGHT," said Suzan Morninglory.

She was sitting cross-legged in a circle of other cross-legged people, all of whom had their heads thrown back and their mouths open like a hundred baby birds, sucking down air with full focus and concentration. Morninglory herself was clad in a pale-lavender caftan of some translucent material that made her look like nothing more than two hundred pounds of yogurt in a purple cheesecloth sack.

I was sitting on the floor of the West Hollywood municipal auditorium, holding hands with the AIDS patient on my left and the woman with breast cancer on my right. His thumb and index finger looked like a gnawed chicken bone, the kind you snap and make a wish. Her head was covered with a bright scarf. No hair protruded from under the scarf. She wore a large amethyst crystal around her neck. Both of them had beatific smiles on their faces that made me angry and depressed and put a big old cramp in my chakras.

Morninglory was looking right at me. My heart gave a little twitch, so I threw back my head and did the breathing exercise, squeezing my eyes shut while she intoned, "The light is love, and the light wants to love you. Let it in. Let the light love you. Let yourself be surrounded by love."

Hug away cancer. Breathe away AIDS. Apparently Monica Slezak had thought she could chase away the chemicals in her brain with a good attitude and some shiny happy chants. And probably a few fat checks, I thought, sneaking a peek at our mistress of ceremonies.

It was early on a cool, damp Sunday evening, and I had crashed the weekly meeting of Morning's Glory, the support group that I'd read about in the magazine profile of Monica Slezak. These New

Agey support groups had been mushrooming all over L.A. in recent years—in the wealthier areas of town, that is; I preferred to think that the sick and impoverished had better things to do. Louise Hay had a group like this and so did Marianne Williamson, but Suzan Morninglory's acolytes made the Hayriders and the Marianne faithful seem positively uncommitted.

For the next hour and a half, we breathed and focused and made lots of mental finger paintings designed to sustain us through the rest of the week. When it was over, Morninglory bade us all get up and hug the people around us.

"I could feel the love in your fingers. You were *there*," said the bald woman. Her name was Rae, and she wore a bouquet of colored ribbons on her breast: red, purple, yellow, peach, and another red with gold teddy bears stenciled on it.

"What's your teddy-bear ribbon?" I said.

She touched it with her index finger. "That's for children with AIDS," she said happily. Under her finger, I imagined the cancer metastasizing, malignant gray cells smothering the healthy white ones, and after that there wasn't anything I could say to Rae.

The emaciated man hugged me next. Through his polo shirt, I could feel his ribs like barrel staves. When he pulled back, he looked at me oddly.

"Kieran? It's Paul Van Ocker."

Paul Van Ocker was a publicist at Levy/Symington. The last time I'd seen him, he'd been normal weight, borderline chubby. This Paul Van Ocker was a wraith. His neck was stringy, with ugly splotches the color of that drop of blood you sometimes find in a raw egg. "Are you sick?" he asked gently, and I knew he meant AIDS. I told him no and mumbled something about a cyst, the full meaning of which wouldn't be known for another week. He nodded and glanced at the front of the room. "She's wonderful, isn't she?"

I looked. Suzan Morninglory was surrounded by her followers. She pressed her hands on their foreheads and nodded her head sagely. The people around her were beaming, as if she had relieved them from a spiritual load. A headline presented itself to me: SUZAN MOR-NINGLORY'S SPIRITUAL LOAD.

I allowed to Paul that she was something else.

Paul touched his chest, just like Rae. "I'll keep you in here, Ki-

eran. Please call me and let me know how everything comes out."
He turned to the man next to him for more hugs, leaving me alone
and feeling like a real shitheel.

I stuck to the fringes of the room, avoiding further conversation,
until most of the people had left. After half an hour, there were still
a couple of hard-core disciples hanging around Suzan Morninglory.
They showed no sign of leaving, so I screwed up my courage, went
over to her, and told her my name. She held me in a gimlet gaze, a
question mark hanging in the air between us.

"I'm working on a story about Monica Slezak," I told her, "and I'd
really like to talk to you. Could we set up an appointment?"

"For whom are you writing this story?" she asked placidly.

"Well, it's—it hasn't been sold yet."

One of the Morning's Glory disciples looked at me. "You're Kieran O'Connor?" I nodded. "That's bullshit," he said to Suzan.
"He's not a freelancer. He writes that party column for your favorite
newspaper."

Suzan Morninglory's face didn't change, but something in the air
between us slid down tight-shut, like the little window in the ATM.
"I don't think I'd be able to help you," she said. "But I'll look for
your story *in the paper.*"

I stood there for a minute, trying to think of something else to say,
but the disciples were staring with some decidedly unspiritual hostility. I lost my nerve. The man who ratted me out followed me to the
parking lot and watched as I started up the Buick. When I pulled out
on San Vicente, I caught a glimpse of him standing in the doorway,
still watching.

The voice on my machine came through a forest of crackling and
buzzing noises. It was Dr. Schroeder on his car phone, sounding
jaunty through all the static.

"I'll be in town all week, and I'd be glad to talk to you. Sure was
surprised to hear about Monica Slezak. A terrible thing." The buzz
grew louder, giving him a case of electronic hiccups. "Anyway. So
listen. I'm cutting in and out here and I'd better go. Call my secretary tomorrow morning after nine and we'll set something up. Catch
ya later, Kieran."

I'd left a message with Schroeder's service that morning, not expecting him to pick it up until Monday. Not only had he gotten it, though, he'd called me back on Sunday afternoon. I shouldn't have been surprised. Schroeder lived off publicity the way a philodendron lives off photosynthesis.

Like most people my age, I had a fair idea of what had gone on in the 1960s, even if I wasn't sure of the exact chronology. Still, one would have to be brain-dead not to know about the famous *Life* magazine cover of Schroeder at the Chicago Democratic Convention, giving a press conference in his Old Glory diaper. It was a seminal image of the sixties, like Neil Armstrong on the moon or the napalmed girl running down the road. Back then, Schroeder had been a symbol, a self-appointed, all-purpose spokesfreak for a juggernaut of a youth movement that was growing by the day, spinning out of control. He was at Woodstock, at Kent State, front and center at every Vietnam march. He'd even managed to amuse the Establishment by organizing a mass attempt to levitate Spiro Agnew through ESP. I didn't get it. It must have been funnier if you were on mushrooms.

Around the time Nixon took his big dive and the hippie movement faded away, Schroeder vanished into a self-imposed exile in Switzerland. When he reappeared again in the waning days of Reagan, it was in Beverly Hills. For several years, he'd been making a fine living in his newest incarnation as a cosmic nutritionist. I remembered seeing him on the cover of *Entertainment Weekly* under the headline $OYBOY TO THE STARS. Playing back the message, I smiled. He might have gone from hippie to yuppie, from the pages of *Life* to the pages of *People*, but Schroeder was still a media whore.

I was so encouraged that I ordered a thirty-minutes-or-less pizza from the delivery company that *didn't* support the loonies who blockade women's clinics, and spent a happy couple of hours reading the Sunday paper and eating five slices of pepperoni-and-olive pizza. I seemed to be making progress at last, and for a change I was feeling like the cat's ass.

At ten o'clock, I turned on the TV for my daily dose of local news. Local news on the weekends was always an incongruous mix of bloody drive-by shootings and fluff reports from local street fairs, but I had a vague crush on the anchor. She turned out to be "on assignment" (which probably meant sunburned) and Frank Grassley was behind the desk. Halfway through the news, the phone rang.

"It's me." Claudia sounded tired and a little bit defiant.

I swallowed pizza. "Hey."

"What are you doing?"

"I'm watching Accu-Satellite meteorologist Mark Scarborough screw around with a bunch of expensive computer equipment and tell bad jokes. I figure if I wait long enough, maybe he'll make a stab at whether it's going to rain tomorrow."

"Cloudy with a chance of drizzle." She was definitely tired, drugged-sounding.

"So what's up?"

She made an exasperated, what's-the-use noise—*ehhh.* "I was wondering if you wanted to come over. And if you don't, please don't get all analytical and peckish about it. Just say no."

"Okay," I said.

"Okay you do, or okay you don't?"

"Okay. I do."

Given the circumstances, I thought it was pretty nice of me to box up the rest of the pizza in case she wanted some. It sat beside me on the seat, smelling of congealed cheese and grease, as I drove up Pacific Avenue and into Santa Monica.

Claudia lived on a quiet tree-lined street in the north end of the city, in an enclave where developers hadn't gotten around to tearing down all the little cottages and erecting their hideous peach-and-green condomonstrosities. Her building was only four units, a nice little Streamline Moderne two-story that looked like a real Schindler, especially at night when lit by yellow phosphor lamps. Her apartment was the one in front, perched over the carport. I parked on Fourteenth and walked to the apartment under a canopy of rustling trees and a sky full of dark-gray clouds.

The door was halfway open, which I took to be an invitation. I went inside and put the pizza in the oven. The stereo was on low, one of those quiet-storm stations. Behind the bathroom door, the shower was running. It shut off with a creak of pipes as I poured a club soda and sat down on the couch, kicking off my sneakers and taking off my socks. Just like old times. There was an open bag of potato chips on the coffee table, and a dish with a few lonely M&Ms rolling around in the bottom. Claudia came out of the bathroom after a minute, dressed in a thick white robe with a bath towel wound around her head.

"There's pizza in the oven," I told her.

"How sweet." She went into the kitchen, opened the oven door, and looked at it. "Eccch."

She came over and sat down beside me, taking the club soda out of my hand and sipping it. "Well, it's over," she said. "Cathy and I are *finis*."

"What happened?"

"Oh, it's been building for a while," she said airily. "We're just different people. It's hard to get anything going when one of you is always on the road somewhere, and the other one's working eighty hours a week. We didn't have a fight or anything; we just got together for dinner last night and agreed that it wasn't working. Or it wasn't working for me, primarily. Whatever. It's done." She got up and went into the kitchen, where she took a bottle of nail polish out of the refrigerator and brought it back to the couch.

Claudia stroked some red enamel on her toenails while I sat beside her, not saying anything. She finished with one foot and started on the other. I put my arm around her back. She didn't move away. Sprinkles began to land on the roof, and it was all very comfortable.

"How's the article going?" she asked.

"I did an interview this weekend. It's kind of interesting. I think I might actually be getting somewhere."

I told Claudia about my trip to Morning's Glory and all the good vibrations there, which made her laugh, and about Paul Van Ocker, which didn't. I also told her about my iced-tea date with Alison Sewell, but I had the feeling she wasn't really listening. She picked up one of my bare feet and put a coat of polish on the craggy big toenail. I twisted it around, watching it reflect the light. We sat there quietly for a while, and then she stood up and yawned.

"I'm tired, Kieran. I'm going to sleep," she said. "You going to spend the night?"

"Sure."

She shut off the oven and locked the door, took my hand, and led me back to the bedroom. Claudia's pack rat instincts and her sense of kitsch stopped at the door of Cafe Canem; her bedroom was just as I remembered it, tidy and comfortable. The duvet was pulled up neatly over the bedclothes, and the top of the mahogany dresser was bare except for a silver bowl of dried rose petals. I opened the chest at the foot of the bed and pulled out the gym bag with all my overnight things in it: toothbrush, contact-lens equipment, an old pair of glasses, washcloth, and other essentials.

"Still there," she said, pulling the towel off her head and brushing her hair. The aubergine was gone, the hair back to its natural mink-brown tint. It was raining harder now.

I went in the bathroom and cleaned my contacts, putting them in the little cooker and plugging it into the wall. I brushed my teeth twice, spat, used mouthwash, rinsed, and spat again. Claudia's birth-control pills were on the counter, that day's tiny tablet snapped out of the foil. I shut off the light and went back in the bedroom. She'd already turned out the bedside lamp and was lying on her side of the bed, facing me. "Come here," she said.

I put my glasses stems-down on the bedside table and climbed into her arms. "You want to go to sleep?"

"Yeah," she said, but she was running her hands down my back, outlining my shoulder blades lightly with her nails. I moved to kiss her, but she pinned me against the pillows and put her mouth on mine. She smelled like lemon oil and Yardley's Lavender and clean sweat. I ran my fingers through her thick hair, touched the soft area behind her ears with my index fingers, tasted her tongue for the first time in six months. It felt good.

We kissed like that for a few minutes, she on top, she in charge, until she moved her mouth down to my chin, biting gently. I moved to her neck, sucking lightly, then harder, and ran my hands under her armpits to her breasts, putting my thumbs there, rubbing her nipples in soft but firm circles, the way she liked it. She arched her back and moaned and pushed one sharp knee between mine, and I could feel she was wet.

We disengaged. I climbed out of bed and turned on the bedside lamp.

I got out the gym bag while she opened the bedside drawer. She got out her diaphragm, squeezed jelly containing spermicide and 0.5-percent nonoxynol-9 all over it, and squatted on the bed. She put her hand inside herself and screwed up her face. I tore the foil off a condom, squirted a drop of my own water-based, nonoxynolloaded lubricant into the reservoir tip, and slipped it on. I opened a second condom, double-bagged the first one, and coated the outside with more slippery nonoxynol-9, wiping my hands on the washcloth. When I was done, I tucked everything back in the gym bag, turned off the light, and got under the covers again. Claudia was already there, waiting.

It was an old rite, something we'd done since the first night we slept together. We always performed it in silence. In bed or out, this was a thing we never discussed. Fear of disease was certainly part of it, but I think we never spoke of our ritual out of another kind of fear—a fear that, together, we might create something that we wouldn't be able to handle, something that was larger than either one of us. Something that might create obligation, responsibility. Even commitment.

# TWO

# = 10 =

AFTER CLAUDIA GOT UP AND LEFT for Cafe Canem, I stayed in bed, dozing and listening to the rain. Neither one of us was big on A.M. sex, thank God. I could laze around for hours in the morning, cuddling and talking, but when Claudia was awake, she was up. No nonsense.

At nine-thirty, I climbed out of the warm sheets and slipped into Claudia's bathrobe. It still had her scent and I sniffed at it appreciatively. She'd left half a carafe of coffee for me in the kitchen. The radio was on and Howard Stern was screaming about something or other.

Not that you'd know it from my apartment, but I like things clean and orderly and a little impersonal. Claudia's place felt like that, like a very homey hotel suite. There were thick white ceramic bowls and a box of instant oatmeal by the sink, and I sat there listening to the radio and the rain, drinking coffee, and eating oatmeal for an hour. Cars schussed by on the wet street outside. Howard Stern went off and a deejay hoarse from decades of sucking down pot smoke announced a "superset" of Jefferson Airplane.

Jefferson Airplane. That reminded me. I got the phone book from the top of the refrigerator and called Dr. Schroeder's offices, which were only a block or two from the Beverly Hillshire. He must have briefed his secretary; she set up an appointment for me for at twelve o'clock on Wednesday without asking any questions.

I pulled on the clothes I'd worn the night before, cleaned up the kitchen, and borrowed a trench coat from the hall closet. Right before I left, I went out and picked a few birds-of-paradise from the mangy bushes at the foot of the stairs. They were wet and smelled of earth and rainwater. I took them back up, cut the stems, and arranged them in a glass on top of the kitchen table. Then I got a

Ziploc bag and filled it with a pound of coffee beans from Claudia's freezer. If I was going to be evicted in the next couple of days, at least I wouldn't have to drink instant.

On Tuesday, I spent a couple of hours at the Santa Monica library, communing with the newspaper and magazine indexes. Research is the part of my job I like the most. It's soothing, and you can get a feel for anyone by reading their clippings in chronological order. The biographical history is helpful, but I like to observe how people have viewed themselves, deconstruct the ways they've tried to present themselves to the world over the years. A few hours in the cool quiet of a library can make anyone feel like a shrink, a detective, and a voyeur.

The familiar moss-green volumes of *Reader's Guide to Periodic Literature* were lined up on the shelves, but they were an anachronism. Instead, I sat down at the CD-ROM terminal and typed in Wilson's name. The gadget whirred for a second, and then the screen lit up, citing several reviews of *The Midnight Hour* and a few profiles of the author. I filled out request slips for the Sunday *New York Times* story I'd remembered and an *Esquire* profile, and then typed in the name of Suzan Morninglory.

Not surprisingly, there wasn't much. Morninglory had only been around for three or four years, and mainstream reporters are uncharacteristically timid when it comes to profiling healers, be they Oral Roberts or Suzan Morninglory. Almost all the Morninglory citations were from the sort of flossy magazines that refer to their subjects as "celebs," except one, a story from my own paper. I remembered the crack that Morninglory's assistant had made—*he writes a party column for your favorite newspaper*—so I filled out another request slip and took the little pile of slips to the reference librarian.

While he pulled the microfilm and microfiche, I went to the fiction stacks, found the Ws, and looked for a copy of *The Midnight Hour*. No luck. A check of the electronic card catalog revealed that both copies of *Midnight Hour, The*, by Wilson, Drew, were checked out. There were already holds on both of them. Wilson was hot stuff, at least on the inter-library network. The book wouldn't be out in paper yet, and I wasn't thrilled at the thought of dropping twenty dollars on a hardback novel.

I got quarters, copied the articles, and walked down to the Third Street Promenade to have lunch and read. There was a take-out stand on the outdoor mall that served "heart-smart" Mexican food, which meant that they reduced the lard and hiked the prices in equal measure. I found a bench in the shade of a topiary dinosaur and started with *The New York Times*.

Drew Wilson had been a very bad boy. Even before puberty, he was known by the police. He was all of eleven when he got dismissed from parochial school for rifling the Jesuits' quarters. By his teens, he was dealing drugs, jacking cars, even pimping his girlfriends. By his twenty-fifth birthday, he'd bounced in and out of youth authorities and jails in New Jersey, Illinois, Arizona, and California. That streak of questionable luck ended down South, when he and some other losers held up a liquor store in Sarasota. His lengthy record finally toppled over on him, and he got ten years in state prison.

The photos accompanying the article told the story. Baby-faced Drew on a pony: part choirboy, part Damien. A mug shot from the liquor-store heist showed Drew glaring at the camera, a caterpillar of stitches stretching from a fat lip to a black eye. And, finally, redemption: Drew the *littérateur* at the Manhattan book party for *The Midnight Hour*, bandbox-crisp in a seersucker suit, looking terribly serious with Michael Korda and Sonny Mehta. I spooned some salsa and studied the pictures.

It was a neat evolution. Too neat. All this redemption didn't wash with me. The article was a year old, and I'd seen the follow-up in person. Drew Wilson was a con artist, and in the light of what I'd seen at Faboo, his reincarnation as a man of letters seemed like just another scam, this one played out against the entire New York literary establishment. I didn't care how good *The Midnight Hour* was supposed to be; if Wilson's publishing company had paid him an advance against his second book, they would have done better buying ten-dollar Rolexes in Times Square.

So much for Drew. I wiped my fingers and moved on to the Dalai Diva.

Like Dr. Schroeder, Suzan Morninglory (née Susan Alcorn) was a child of the sixties. Her life seemed to have been marked by the same rootlessness, but, until recently, none of the rewards. She had lived all over California, working secretarial jobs and sampling all the trendy pop metaphysics that were the state's leading export. After a bout with cancer a few years back, she founded Morning's Glory and moved to Southern California, where she found an audience eager to hear her "empowerment theories"—which, as near as I could tell, were a curdle of Norman Vincent Peale, Zen for Toddlers, and I'm OK/You're OK. This went over big in Hollywood, where no one believes anything in particular and, thus, will believe everything.

Reading between the lines, I tried to get a picture of what the real woman was like, but the more I looked, the less I found to analyze. Morninglory seemed to have no romantic ties, now or in the past. She dispensed pop psychology and pop spirituality, but readily admitted to having no formal training in either. There were no outbursts of temper to suggest megalomania. Morning's Glory brought her a comfortable living, and there was undoubtedly a healthy bank account somewhere, but she didn't go in for conspicuous consumption. Much to my disappointment, there was nothing to nail her on. At the end of the article, though, was a tidbit that raised an interesting question.

Morninglory's own recovery from cancer was part of her myth, though she refused to speak of the matter for fear of "re-empowering" it. But the reporter had spoken to several people from her past, checked hospital records, and investigated health insurance claims, and still couldn't find any tangible proof that Morninglory had ever been sick at all. This didn't prove that she hadn't, of course; it just made an already mysterious woman even more opaque.

Why would an intelligent, successful person like Monica Slezak go in for Morningloryism? I reminded myself that articles of faith have nothing to do with intelligence or success; some people were naturally credulous, just as I was naturally skeptical. Ultimately, it didn't matter if Morninglory was a charlatan. I had to admit that if I became ill, I'd *like* to believe in a Suzan Morninglory; I'd like it if the things she said made me feel better. I just couldn't. But Monica could.

So which one of us was smarter, anyway?

I hit the brakes.

She was old enough to be a grandmother, dressed in a fluted mini like a cupcake liner. Her hair was big and red, her eyelashes mascaraed awnings, and her face had been lifted so severely that it looked as if it had been dipped in egg custard. She tottered in front of my car on spike heels, carrying shopping bags of yellow stripes and robin's-egg blue. Giorgio and Tiffany. A Rolls on my right had to screech to a halt to avoid getting Granny all over its grille. Pedestrians used to have the right of way in L.A., but the system had changed to Manhattan rules, where the car is boss. Not that anyone was purposely aiming for pedestrians; it just gets hard to remember them while you're dealing with car phones, car faxes, and console-mounted CD players. Luxury-car dashboards these days are filled with more distractions than a Fisher-Price Busy Box.

Granny reached the sidewalk at Canon and the traffic pushed on. I was driving east on Wilshire on my way to meet Dr. Schroeder. Skin-care clinics, boutiques, and decorator shops passed on the left; on the right, the stone face of the Beverly Hillshire came into view, festooned with flags.

I was grouchy, and it wasn't just the Beverly Hills noontime traffic snarl or the prospect of meeting an old hippie who had converted to capitalism that had me cross. I'd left a message for Claudia on Tuesday night, and she hadn't called me back that night, or this morning. Not that she had to, of course. Things were tenuous and uncommitted enough when we were definitely a couple, and I still didn't know whether Sunday night was just a blip in Claudia and Cathy's relationship or a whole new beginning for Claudia and me. Either way, I had no right to be upset that she hadn't called me back. But I was.

Even though South Beverly was considered déclassé compared to the tonier neighborhood one block north of Wilshire, I thought it was one of the more hospitable-looking streets in Beverly Hills. South Beverly was sedate by local standards, with neat two-story office buildings that housed psychologists, psychiatrists, family counselors, and lots of other professionals who kept the natives from going completely mental. I found a diagonal space under a shedding pepper tree and fed quarters into a high-tech meter with a digital readout.

The address that Schroeder's receptionist had given me seemed to belong to an understated white brick building in the middle of the block. It could have been a perfumerie, a furrier, or a bistro with an unlisted phone. There was nothing as vulgar as a street number outside, just a discreet gold plate in all lowercase letters: *schroederfoods international*. How very e.e. cummings, I thought. How "thirtysomething."

Inside, it was low lights, cool damp air, and plants, the sort of controlled natural environment that always makes me want a cigarette. Yanni or Raffi or whatever his name was plinked out a soothing piano solo on some invisible sound system. A tropical fish tank that seemed the size of a drive-in movie screen took up one wall. Sharks scudded the bottom, sending up soft clouds of sand with their tails.

I gave my name to an overly aerobicized receptionist. She gave me a paper cup—not coffee, but some thick green juice—and took me into a waiting room lined with couches. This room had another glass wall. Instead of sharks, though, it had all of the schroederfood products on display, lit like jewels in the window at Harry Winston. There were wheatgrass juice *(schroedergreen)*, six-packs of soy milk *(schroedersoy)*, dozens of bottles of vitamin and mineral supplements, and even freeze-dried, ready-to-nuke boxes of tofu lasagna and organic enchiladas. Perfect for the macro-on-the-go.

On a redwood-burl coffee table was a pitcher with more wheatgrass juice and a dish of green algae pellets. I put one of the pellets on my tongue and read a schroederfoods pamphlet about the benefits of algae. It had a color photo of a toddler reaching past a cookie jar to get her fat little fingers on a canister of the pellets. "Many little people instinctively reach for the natural goodness of *schroedertabs*," it lectured. "They know what's good for them."

I spat out the nasty thing. Kids put dogshit in their mouths, too, I thought. What does that prove?

"Kieran!"

Schroeder bustled in and pumped my hand with what I took to be algae-induced energy. I had worn a Greenpeace shirt from some long-ago benefit, hoping to put him at ease, but he won the style war with his doctor's smock, loose-fitting undyed cotton pants, and negative-heel sandals. His hair was thinning, with the obligatory never-

— 90 —

too-old-to-rock-and-roll gray ponytail. You are what you wear, I guess.

"Thanks for seeing me," I mumbled.

"No prob, no prob. Come on back!" I followed him into his private office, where he gave me a complimentary sample pack of schroederfood products and—*quelle surprise*—a shiny white press kit about himself with an eight-by-ten glossy clipped to the front.

I slipped the unopened press kit into my briefcase and got out my tape recorder while he rattled on about what a shock this whole thing had been. His pep was getting on my nerves. It was as bad as listening to someone on a coke rap. I turned on the tape recorder and interrupted him. "Mind if we start?"

"Fire when ready." Peppy, peppy, peppy.

"When was the last time you saw Monica Slezak?"

"Six months ago? Maybe seven. We had been working on a program to solve—to solve some problems she had."

"What problems?"

He made a spreading-hands gesture. "I don't really want to go into the precise nature of—"

"I know was suffering from panic disorder and manic depression, if that's what you're talking about."

Schroeder paused. "Those terms get thrown around a lot. I think they're vague, and I don't like them. It's really just propaganda for the AMA. You diagnose someone with manic depression, and you've got the perfect all-purpose excuse to start billing insurance companies for a lot of high-priced prescription drugs."

As opposed to a lot of high-priced algae and tofu enchiladas, I supposed. But all I said was, "Really."

"Look. Kieran." He folded his hands into some isometric position. "We live in a stressful world, don't we?"

"Don't I know it."

"My program is founded on the philosophy that, in a stressful world, *not* getting stressed out would be unnatural." He sat back in his chair and preened. "Instead of taking a lot of drugs, doesn't it make more sense to take care of your body? Fortify it. Prepare yourself to meet stress head-on without drugs. Our culture, prompted by the AMA and Madison Avenue, tells you to take an aspirin when you have a headache. I say, why not find the cause of the headache? Get rid of it. And if you can't get rid of it, use your own internal resources and learn to deal with it."

Back in the Altamont era, Schroeder hadn't looked like a poster child for Nancy Reagan and her fellow dried apricots in the Just Say No program, but I let him prattle on. When he stopped excoriating the AMA and started rhapsodizing about the lifesaving benefits of high colonics, I interrupted him again.

"What kind of therapy was Monica Slezak undergoing?"

He paused. "That's confidential information."

"You're giving me a lot of very interesting background, but what I want to know is why Monica killed herself. Tell me a little about her treatment. Was she taking supplements? Was she having colonics?"

"I'll plead the Fifth," he said coyly.

God, what a cornball. "Look," I snapped. "I'm not an insurance investigator. I'm not a cop and I'm not Magnum, P.I. I'm a writer, and I'm trying to get a picture of why losing an Academy Award nomination might lead someone to commit suicide."

"I *understand* that you're trying to *understand*. It's just that that's confidential information."

"You're talking like a tool of the AMA," I parried.

Schroeder considered that. "Touché."

"I'm not trying to trip you up or anything. I'm just trying to understand why a woman like that would kill herself."

"Why do you think I might be able to help you?"

I wasn't about to tell him about the suicide note. "Because your name came up in some of her papers. You seemed to have some importance to her."

"Does Gregory Slezak know you're here?"

"Of course he does," I lied. "Who do you think gave me access to Monica's papers?"

"Shut that off."

Schroeder was pointing at my tape recorder. I hit the pause button, but he waited until I'd turned it off completely. He cleared his throat. "Okay. This is not for attribution. Just background, okay."

He opened a drawer in his desk, pulled out a thick blue Pendaflex file, and began riffling through papers. There was a chart clipped to the outside: a chiropractor's schematic of a woman's nude body, front and back, with various meridians and trouble spots marked in ballpoint pen. Notes filled the margins. I've become skilled at reading upside down, but Schroeder's handwriting was as illegible as any doctor's. Maybe medical schools should teach a course in penmanship.

"Monica came to me about a year and a half ago. She'd been experiencing severe depression, mood swings, the whole combo platter of dysfunctional coping mechanisms. Okay. So I do a diagnostic on her, and the first thing that becomes apparent is that all these prescriptions she's been taking are ninety percent of the problem. I mean, she's so full of chemicals that there's not going to be much we can do until we purify her system. Once she's clean, then we can identify the root causes of the problem and work on eliminating them. You with me?"

"What was she taking?"

"I'm not really comfortable with—"

"Zapax? Percocil?"

He nodded. "And a couple of other things." He fiddled with his ponytail and checked his charts. "So all right. So I put her on the basic schroederfoods detox. I went over to her house, looked in her kitchen, threw out what she didn't need, and put her on a program of natural foods and some of my dietary supplements. And believe me, within two weeks, her skin was clearing up, she was full of energy, she was feeling better inside and out. She told me she felt like a pilot who was flying out of a cloud into"—he made quotation marks in the air—" 'a clear white light.' And within another month, she'd dropped eight pounds."

"She dropped eight pounds in a month?" Suddenly I knew why Schroeder had such a devoted clientele in Beverly Hills.

"We don't call it weight loss. The body always stabilizes when it's getting what it needs. Think of your body as a combustion engine . . ."

He delivered a basic Nutrition 101 speech while I nodded gravely. Rich people amaze me. They won't do a hundred situps unless they're paying some personal trainer to stand over them and harangue them all the way. They won't clean up their eating habits without paying someone like Schroeder to lace their healthy meals with a load of New Age gobbledygook. The first person in Southern

California who figures out a way to market designer air is going to make a million.

"So anyway. Once Monica's eating habits were stabilized, we started to work on other things. Hydrotherapy—"

"You mean enemas."

"No, colonic hydrotherapy. Are you familiar with it?"

"Sort of."

He got up. "Come with me."

We walked down another hall—more dim lights and George Winston music—to another room that looked like a shrink's office except for a bizarre apparatus in the corner. It had a big glass bottle of water on the top, like an office cooler, and tubes leading out the bottom. In the corner of the room, there was a leatherette couch with a paper headguard and a hole where your bottom would be. On the wall was the strangest thing of all, a complicated network of clear water-filled tubing that doubled back on itself like a glass intestine.

Schroeder tapped the bottle, which gave out a hollow sound. "We clean out the colon with this. By releasing water in and out of the colon and performing some gentle abdominal massage, we break up fecal matter and toxins that have been trapped in the body, sometimes for decades. It's really an amazing process. All sorts of problems can be cleared up. Constipation, insomnia, lethargy, back trouble, irritability, even bad breath. Depending on the patient's needs, we can have the water oxygenated, or add chlorophyll and other herbal elixirs."

Oxygen. Chlorophyll. Herbal elixirs. A regular Baskin-Robbins for the bowel. "Aren't you washing out beneficial bacteria along with the toxins?" I asked.

Schroeder paused in mid-preach and looked at me as if he'd just figured something out. "How old are you, anyway?"

"Twenty-nine."

"Ah-*hah*," he said, and let it pass. Supercilious old hippie. He probably had a Grateful Dead sticker on his BMW. "It's a lot more effective for doctors in this country to treat prostate and colon cancer than it is to prevent it," he explained condescendingly. "Did you know that colon cancer is the second leading form of cancer in men?"

"Huh."

He grinned and patted the leatherette table. "I see you're a good skeptical reporter. That's fine. Just hop up here and give me fifteen minutes—"

"I think I'll pass," I said quickly. I had an image of twenty-nine years of pizza, gyros, and Mexican food floating through the clear glass tubes, like the hair clog in the Liquid Plum-R commercial, and I wasn't sure I wanted to see it.

"Come on. It only takes a few minutes."

"Maybe some other time, okay? I've got some more questions I want to ask first."

We went back down the hall to his office. Someone had left a pile of pink WHILE YOU WERE OUT slips and a few letters on his desk, and he riffled through them. While he was distracted, I switched the tape recorder back on. He didn't seem to notice, but I couldn't be sure.

"How long was Monica a patient of yours?"

He was absorbed in the mail. "She started right after we moved from our old location on Little Santa Monica, which was about a year and a half ago."

"So she was your patient for the better part of a year. But you didn't see her any time in the last six or seven months."

"That's right."

Did he send out reminder notes, like a dentist? *Ms. Slezak, it's time for your six-month colonic?*

"You didn't see her at all?"

He paused. "Maybe once or twice at a party. You know how you run into people. Especially in this town. But not here in the office. No."

"Why did she stop coming?"

"I don't know."

The answer was a little too casual for my taste. All during the interview, I'd felt like a dentist, poking around, looking for I didn't know what. For the first time, it felt like I'd hit a nerve.

"Why do you *think* she stopped coming?"

"I don't know. People stop for a lot of reasons. Often it's financial, which is why I don't press the matter."

"You've heard of Suzan Morninglory, right?"

Schroeder nodded dismissively. I wondered if that meant he considered her a spiritual quack, or whether he thought she was siphoning off cosmic cash that rightfully belonged to him.

"Monica was a follower of Suzan Morninglory's. Do you know if she was seeing Suzan Morninglory at the same time she was seeing you?"

"No," he said definitely. "That was later."

"She also had an auto accident. That was about six months ago. Was that before or after she stopped seeing you?"

"Oh, God, Kieran, I can't remember." He had the WHILE YOU WERE OUT slips in his hand, and his voice had the light pitch that people affect when they're trying to tell you that the interview is over.

I settled back in my chair. "Try."

He looked at me for a minute. "After," he said slowly. "It had to be after, because I remember reading about the accident in the paper. I thought that she might call to get a referral to a chiropractor."

"But she didn't."

"Nope." He checked his watch, feigned surprise. "Hey, I've got a new client coming in, and I'm running late. But it's been a real pleasure."

"Thanks for your time. Can I call you if I think of any follow-up questions?"

"Sure, sure. Hey, don't forget your samples. You've got your press kit?"

He walked me to the door of his office and shook my hand. Just as he turned around to go back to his desk, I remembered something I'd seen on "Columbo," and I decided to try it.

*"Did Monica ever make a pass at you?"*

Schroeder about-faced and gaped at me. I couldn't be sure whether I'd hit another nerve or whether he was just appalled at my brass. Either way, it was immensely satisfying. He opened his mouth and closed it again, and in his eyes I saw a look that I recognized from years of interviewing actors: an internal battle between circumspection and vanity. Vanity, as is its wont, emerged triumphant.

"I'll . . . I'll have to take the Fifth on that one, too," he said, and laughed. I started out the door, but Schroeder caught me by the arm.

When I turned around, he took my cheek between two fingers and held it there as if by calipers. I tensed.

He let me go.

"You drink too much coffee," he said softly, and shut the door.

WHEN YOU'RE CONDUCTING AN INTERVIEW, people will tell you one of four things: the truth, lies, honest mistakes, and that which they believe to be the truth. The way to deal with the first two is to assume everything is a lie until it's been proven otherwise. Honest mistakes—wrong dates and the like—are a pain. They seem harmless, but they're like an error in an addition problem: you forget to carry the 2 and the whole answer ends up wrong. As you work on a story, though, honest mistakes and misrecollections begin to stand out, like a piece of a jigsaw puzzle laid down in the wrong position.

The toughest of all is when people tell you what they honestly believe is the truth, and then it doesn't matter whether it's Mother Teresa or a sociopath at the other end of the microphone. Innocent people have gone to jail over what others honestly believe is the truth. Others have gone to the gas chamber.

Schroeder had said that he hadn't seen Monica Slezak in six months, which matched what Alison Sewell had told me. What I still didn't understand, though, was why his name would crop up in her suicide note. All of the other people she mentioned were current figures in her life. It was tempting to jump to the juicy conclusion, which was an affair gone sour, but there wasn't any hard evidence. Besides, I couldn't imagine having an affair with someone who had seen you with a rubber tube up your butt and the contents of your colon floating along a wall.

I drove south on Robertson until I hit Venice Boulevard, which was the fastest way to get back to the beach. The storm had moved on, and the sky was filled with bright wet sunshine that hurt my eyes. A Volkswagen van behind me had surfboards strapped to the top. Around Culver City, I passed a warehouse outlet called Futons For Less, which made me think of my own uncomfortable futon, which made me think of the comfortable bed I'd slept in Sunday night. Which made me think of Claudia. It was Tuesday afternoon, and I still hadn't heard from her. This was vexing.

I stopped at the 7-Eleven on Sepulveda, bought a Kit Kat bar, sat in my car, and listened to an interview with a ninety-one-year-old quiltmaker on "All Things Considered." I ate the Kit Kat while I debated whether to go home and transcribe my Dr. Schroeder notes or to go over to Cafe Canem and have it out with Claudia. Finally, I made a little pact with myself. If the next person to come out of the 7-Eleven was a woman, I'd go see Claudia; if it was a man, I'd go home and do some work.

Ten seconds later, two guys and one girl came out the door at the same time, so I figured it was close enough and headed over to Cafe Canem.

Claudia's Dart was parked on Main, two blocks away. That seemed strange, until I turned the corner and saw that one whole block around the coffeehouse had been cordoned off with sawhorses and cops. Trailers lined the street. Portable dressing rooms had been pulled up on the sidewalk. Giant reflectors shone harsh light in the window of Cafe Canem, obscuring my view of what was going on inside. I slowed to watch, but a grip with a walkie-talkie and a Dr. Schroeder ponytail waved me on.

Great. First the *Globe-Ex,* and now Cafe Canem. All of Los Angeles was turning into a movie set. No one shot pictures on the backlots anymore, of course, because all the backlots were now upscale condo developments or souvenir-ridden amusement parks.

Screw it. I hit the gas and headed for home as the sun slipped behind a high-rise and the theme from "All Things Considered" pealed in my ears.

There were eight messages on my machine when I got home.

One: Someone named Shaunte who identified herself as Addie Adderley's assistant. She said that Addie was on a film location in India and wouldn't be reachable until after the Oscars. I made a note of Shaunte's number.

Two: A hang-up.

Three: My landlord. I fast-forwarded that one.

Four: Another hang-up.

Five: Schroeder. He said he wanted to "amplify and clarify" some things from our interview. He left both his home and car phone numbers. I jotted them down, but decided to let him twist for a day or two. Maybe it would teach him a lesson.

Six: Jeff Brenner in New York. Just called to say hello.

Seven: "Kieran? Me." Lots of talking in the background, and the screech of something that sounded like a power saw. "They've been shooting a movie down here for two days straight and I'm going crazy. I'll be home after eight. Come on over and I'll make some dinner. Hey, don't touch that!" she yelled. I heard glass breaking. "I swear I'm going crazy. See you tonight. Bye."

Eight: More loud noise. I thought Claudia had called back, but then Drew Wilson's voice came on the line, thick and slurry as syrup. "Swede? Are you there? . . . I'm down your way. You wanna come down here and go for a drink? . . . Are you there? Ah, shi—" Click. No location and no phone number.

A mixed bag, and, except for the landlord, not bad. It was only four-twenty, so I took a shower and sat down to transcribe my notes and tapes. Transcribing is my least favorite part of what I do, but for once there seemed to be a point to the tedium, a point other than providing some free publicity for a new film or a trendy restaurant. I tried to be observant, paying special attention to Schroeder's answers that seemed too pat or too carefully phrased. I listened several times to the section at the very end, but nothing new emerged, nothing that would give me any clue as to why Monica Slezak had so abruptly stopped her visits to Dr. Schroeder.

I took a break around six to watch the news. During a commercial, I was overcome with a rare fit of ballsiness, and I called Gregory Slezak's office again. If I had gotten Alison Sewell, I would have hung up, but I got the machine instead. I left Slezak a cryptic message, mentioning my interview with Schroeder and suggesting brusquely that he might reconsider calling me back, "just to get his side of things on the record."

In the shower, I decided to share my research with Claudia in the hope that she'd pick up some thread that I'd overlooked. At seven forty-five, I printed out the Schroeder transcript, added it to the paper I'd already generated, and stuffed the whole thing in a Pee-Chee. Pee-Chees aren't very dignified, but they're cheaper than manila folders; I'd bought a case of them at an office-supply warehouse that was going out of business. Besides, they fit the leitmotif of my daily existence, which was teenage-adult all the way.

The door to Claudia's apartment was open a crack. From the porch, I could see an army of take-out cartons from Panda Palace lined up on the coffee table. "You should just give back the money," said Pedro's voice, and then came Claudia's faint reply: "It's too late. Besides, ten thousand for four days? I don't think so."

I knock-knocked and stepped in. Pedro and Claudia were sitting on the couch, looking exhausted. He was wearing a sweat-pocked T-shirt that said I'M NOT JUST A MIND—I'M ALSO A PIECE OF MEAT. As always, I marveled at the tattoos on his arms, intricate blackwork in complicated patterns, like scrimshaw carved on flesh. He also had several exotic piercings that had led to some embarrassing scenes at airport metal detectors.

Claudia was in her robe, staring bleakly at the take-out cartons as if she wished they'd disappear. I put my Pee-Chee down on the coffee table and opened one of the boxes. Tangerine-peel beef.

"What else you got?" I said.

"One of everything they had—except rice. They forgot the rice." She gave a hollow laugh. "I'm not up to going back. I'm just not. I've been up since six this morning."

"I'll go," said Pedro, standing up.

"Sit down. You're not going anywhere. You've been up longer than I have, Pedro."

"What were they shooting there today?"

Claudia just groaned.

I went into the kitchen and got out several bowls while Pedro assured me that he wouldn't stay long. Pedro always got skittish whenever he was around Claudia and me in private, as if his presence was keeping us from getting naked and tying each other to the bedpost. I brought the dishes into the living room and the three of us ate bowlfuls of Szechuan without benefit of rice. It tasted okay, if a little heavy, and by the end of it we were all sticky and flushed. My stomach bubbled, making me think of the unappetizing apparatus in Dr. Schroeder's office.

"What's this?" Claudia wanted to know, picking up the Pee-Chee.

"Some of the background stuff for my Slezak article."

Naturally, what they wanted to see was the fax of the suicide note, which made Claudia raise her eyebrows and Pedro shake his head. "Oh, brother," he said. "All that from just losing a nomination. Imagine if she'd been nominated and *lost*. She probably would have blown her brains out on national TV."

"Watch the presenters try to ad-lib their way out of that," I added.

"Maybe it would get people to start watching the Oscars again."

"Stop it, you two." Claudia had been reading the note carefully. She looked at it as if it were a rubber check. "Are you sure she actually wrote this?"

"Yeah. The police think so. They had Slezak identify it and checked it against other samples of her handwriting. I know it reads like *Valley of the Dolls*, but she was really on the edge. I believe she wrote this."

"Her husband could have done it, too," said Pedro, the conspiracy theorist. "He knew the way she talked, and he could copy her handwriting."

The take-out boxes were leaking ominous orange fluid, so I started toting them into the kitchen. "You two are still talking like she was murdered. It was a suicide, remember? I spent two hours this afternoon talking to Schroeder, and I'm more convinced than ever that Monica killed herself."

Pedro clutched the note to his chest and affected a breathless falsetto. "Eric . . . you were another mistake. My mistakes could fill a book."

"You should have seen his face when I asked him if Monica had ever made a pass at him. 'I'll have to take the Fifth on that,' he says, like something off a cop show."

"Do you think they were having sex?" Pedro asked.

"I don't know. She might have made a pass at him, but beyond that . . . Read the note. It makes sense either way. The mistake could have been having an affair with him, or it could have been the pass itself."

"Or something completely different," Claudia pointed out. She yawned, making Pedro yawn, too. He got up and shuffled toward the door. At the jamb, he turned and grinned. " 'I just *vant* to go to *zleep,*' " he said in a Greta Garbo vamp. " 'I dun't . . . feel . . . *anyz-ing.*' "

"See you tomorrow at six. Six sharp," Claudia called after him.

She went into the kitchen and started to clean up. I followed her, put my arms around her waist, and started chewing the nape of her neck, but she just growled, "Knock it off," as if I were a kid throwing a football in the house. It was ten o'clock anyway, so I went back in the living room and watched Frank Grassley do a live remote from one of those open wells that seem to exist only to swallow up children.

An hour later, we were in bed. The condoms and the diaphragm stayed in the gym bag and the night table, by unspoken mutual consent. Claudia sat up, rubbing lotion into her legs, while I killed off the last of a Beck's and watched her. Some of her weight was settling in her rear end. When did that happen? I realized that I hadn't seen Claudia naked in the light since last summer. I sucked in my stomach. It had more problems that Claudia's butt ever would.

"I have a proposition for you," Claudia said. She took a pumice stone from the bedside table and began buffing her elbows in circular motions.

"Mm-hm?"

"I want you to work at Cafe Canem for a while."

I rolled over and looked at her. "Why?"

"You need the money. I need the help. It's the obvious solution. You wouldn't have to deal with the business end of things. What I need is someone who can make coffee and clean up between customers. Pedro's going to be taking a lot of time off in the next couple of months, and I need someone I can trust."

Pedro had been cast in some highly unauthorized genderfuck production of *Grease* out in Silverlake. He was playing the Olivia Newton-John role, and Dagny Weiss, a gorgeous butch lesbian friend of Claudia's, was playing John Travolta. It promised to be quite a sensation—if it wasn't closed down on opening night.

Claudia put down her pumice stone and took up the lotion again. "It's all changing so fast," she said quietly. "It used to be fun. Now I spend all my time in the office on the phone. Sometimes I think I should just junk the whole thing and do something else, but the money's too good. It's just that it's getting to be too much like . . . like a *job*."

I squirted some lotion on my hand and rubbed it on her shoulder blades. The arrangement did make sense. Anyone could make cappuccino; what Claudia was looking for was a certain sensibility. She wanted someone who knew when to give it away and when to charge up the nose, someone who knew the difference between a struggling artist and a con artist. Lots of people never paid a cent for their refills at Cafe Canem. Claudia made up the difference on the trust-fund poets who were willing and able to spend twenty bucks of Daddy's money on coffee and pastries.

"You could have nights off when you needed to write your column," she pointed out. "And there'd be plenty of time to work on your Slezak article in between customers."

"Yeah, I could probably sleep in the back, too," I joked.

"What are you talking about?"

I told her about my three eviction notices, trying to make it sound madcap and amusing. She listened without changing expression. When I was done, she picked up my hand gently from her shoulders and threw it with such force that I thought my arm was bidding bon voyage to its socket.

"Hey!" I yelped.

"Kieran, you idiot!"

"Hey, it's not—"

"You *imbecile!*" She was out of bed now, standing over me, shaking her finger in my face like Sister Mary The Wrath of God. "This is *serious*, Kieran!"

"Calm down, Claudia—"

"Sweet Jesus in a bucket. I cannot believe you. I cannot believe you sometimes." She paced the bedroom twice, kicked the bureau, swore, and marched into the kitchen. I heard a glass rattle and water run, and then there was nothing. Three minutes passed in ominous silence, and I ticked off every second on the clock radio while I lay in her bed feeling like a lox on a bagel. She was right. It wasn't funny or silly or even tragic. More like pathetic.

When Claudia came back, she had a glass of water in one hand

and a folded piece of paper in the other. Even before she held it out to me, I knew it was a check.

"I don't want your—"

"Take it," she snapped, and I knew she was serious.

I took the check from her and unfolded it. It would cover my back rent with a couple of hundred dollars left over.

"I really don't want this, Claudia," I said in a small voice.

Claudia sat down on the bed and balled up a pillow. The tension suddenly left her body. She sagged like a wading pool that had sprung a leak. "Just take it, Kieran. Take it so I can go to bed and get a little goddamn sleep."

"We'll call it a cash advance."

"If it makes you feel better."

She shut off the lamp and climbed over me. We lay there for a long time, side by side, not touching.

This was a direct gravitational shift in our relationship. In all our years together, neither of us had ever lent the other money—not that I'd ever been in a position to lend Claudia anything more than the change to make a phone call. We weren't the kind of couple who splits checks in restaurants or keeps a mental tab of who owes what, but to have Claudia lend me a lump sum of cash seemed an obligation that went well beyond the fiduciary. We could go out together, spend the night, even have sex in the bathtub (an experiment that lasted about fifteen seconds), but having money change hands between us made me uncomfortable. I lay there for a long time, trying to wrap my brain around the notion, and when I propped myself up to look at the clock, twenty-five minutes had passed. From her breathing, I knew Claudia wasn't asleep either.

Five minutes later, she rolled over on top of me.

"Oh, Lord," she said. "Go get the gym bag."

# === 12 ===

IT WAS THURSDAY MORNING, so I made sure I picked up a paper. Thursday meant the food section, which meant coupons. I'd seen a feature on the news about a woman who couponed her way to a whole cartful of groceries for $1.48. I'd never clipped coupons before, but I was willing to learn.

I'd started to get up with Claudia when the alarm went off at five-thirty, but she shook her head and said, "Get some sleep." Neither one of us wanted to talk about the night before. I lay there with my eyes closed until I heard the front door shut behind her. In the kitchen, there was a half-pot of coffee with a Post-It on the carafe, telling me that she wouldn't need me at Cafe Canem until the evening shift on Sunday.

Someone named LI'L CHUY 753 had been by my building and left a spray-painted scrawl on the stairs to prove it. My apartment was stuffy and smelled like damp newspapers. If I ever got out of my financial hole, I was going to have to move. My message light was blinking 3, so I hit PLAY and listened while I opened the windows.

"I haven't heard from you in a while. Are you working?" Jocelyn. "Remember that idea I had about older women and younger men? Robin Prisker did an outline, and Simon and Schuster bit. She's getting a hundred and fifty grand. I think I can push them to two. Isn't that fantastic? Call me, love."

Click.

"Kieeeeeran." Pedro. "Rehearsals are getting hairy. Can you work a few shifts for me? Call me at the shop."

Click.

"This is Gregory Slezak."

His voice wasn't angry, just tinder-dry and a little beat. "I'm calling for Kieran O'Connor. I've received several messages from him."

A pause. "If you want to talk to me, you can come up to the house Monday afternoon at one o'clock." He gave the address—a tony street in the Beverly Hills flats—and hung up. All that persistence, or pestering, had paid off. Monday sounded fine to me. I called back, got Slezak's machine, and told him I'd see him Monday. What did we do before answering machines? Talk to each other, I suppose.

Coffee and the paper kept me occupied until nine-thirty. I cut out coupons for detergent, cereal, rice, and 7-Up. At ten, I went to Claudia's bank and turned her check into a money order and some cash, then drove to West L.A. and dropped off the money order at my landlord's realty company. Home free. I felt grateful and re-lieved, but underneath I was uneasy. When one person lends an-other money, it's always the borrower who ends up feeling resentful. Perverse, but true.

That afternoon, I made a few more calls. Adam Davies's assistant, whose voice was a cool duplicate of Alison Sewell's, took my name and number. The receptionist at the West Hollywood Armament Club took my name and said that she'd have the club's "press infor-mation officer" get back to me. I also called Women in the Industry and asked for Shaunte. A pleasant-sounding woman named Ellen got on the line and told me Shaunte wouldn't be in for the rest of the week. Ellen said that she and Shaunte were both part-timers at WII, college interns from the film and television school at USC.

"Shaunte's here on Mondays, Tuesdays, and Wednesdays," she told me. "Is there something I can help you with?"

"I'm a writer working on an article about Monica Slezak. I was hoping that somebody down there would be able to give me some kind of information."

There was a silence. Monica's death had gotten WII lots of press coverage, none of it the kind the group wanted. Interns and volun-teers get nervous when it comes to performing any duty that might get them in trouble. "What kind of information?" Ellen asked hesi-tantly.

"I don't know. Addie Adderley's out of the country and I'm not sure where to start."

"Well, I can't help you with that," she said, sounding relieved that the whole thing was out of her purview. "Do you want me to leave a message for Shaunte?"

"I'll just try back. Thanks, Ellen."

"Hey, no prob," she said. Whatever happened to 'You're welcome'?

That afternoon in Vons, midway between the frozen foods and the boxed pasta, something occurred to me—a phrase from Monica Slezak's suicide note. *This is the real dark at the end of the tunnel.* The phrase fell into my mind with an almost audible click, like the first correct digit in a safecracker's combination.

I was so excited that I aborted the rest of the shopping trip, checking out in a rush (total coupon savings: $1.40) and driving over to Vidiots, the video store where I had an account. I liked Vidiots because the employees knew a staggering amount of movie trivia and the owners stocked everything: independent, cult, experimental, even homemade. Claudia often rented things there to show on the monitors at Cafe Canem. They also had a good backlog of older titles.

The counter staff was watching Divine knock over a Christmas tree in an old John Waters movie and didn't even see me come in. I went to the drama shelves and found *The Dark at the End of the Tunnel*, its empty box stuffed with Styrofoam and shrink-wrapped. I also picked up *White Ice*, an even earlier Slezak movie. I didn't know what it was about, but the front of the box showed a pile of diamonds and a black glove. On the back, some TV critic promised that it was "A Nail-Biter! . . . *White Ice* Froze My Blood and Gave Me Chills!"

The clerk stopped watching Divine long enough to get me my selections. I had never managed to find a movie that she hadn't seen. "This is a dog's lunch," she said firmly, holding up the plastic box containing *White Ice*. "You don't want it."

"I have to watch it. How's the other one?"

She handed me the rental slip and shrugged. "Something like a cross between *The Towering Inferno*, *Lord of the Flies*, and *The Taking of Pelham One Two Three*."

My last stop was a bookstore. They were sold out of *The Midnight Hour*, so I took my groceries and videos and went home. No one had called. It was getting chilly outside, and no one was out on the boardwalk. I made a mess of instant red beans and rice and started *The Dark at the End of the Tunnel*.

It was the story of a subway train that got trapped by falling debris after a massive earthquake in Manhattan. On board were a pregnant woman, a white racist construction worker, a black businessman, a newlywed couple, an insufferably brave little homeless girl, and a few other stock characters. Half the story was about how they survived for a week underground and the other half was about the efforts to rescue them. It was mediocre but not interminable. Everyone got out of the subway car except the racist and the newlywed husband, who selflessly threw himself onto the electrified third rail to alert the rescuers. The precocious little girl, unfortunately, made it too, getting adopted by the pregnant woman, who'd had a miscarriage midway through the movie. I couldn't see how the movie had any relation to Monica Slezak's suicide. When it was over, I went through the credits slowly. No familiar names cropped up.

I rewound the tape and put in *White Ice,* which turned out to be almost unwatchable. One of the world's foremost diamond cutters is found dead. Diamonds are missing, and his wife is accused of both crimes. She's innocent, of course, but no one believes her. She gets off on a technicality and finds that she's being stalked by the real killer. She doesn't know why, nor what the killer wants. At the end, she finally gets a cop to believe her, the killer is revealed—her attorney—and she and the cop live happily ever after. The end. I fast-forwarded the credits, but this time one familiar name popped out, a co-producer: Maria Tankovich.

Maria Tankovich was one of the first big women producers before she blew it all with booze and dope. She was a real product of old Hollywood, having been sired by an alcoholic producer and suckled by an alcoholic musical-comedy star. Maria had a sandpaper personality that had been widely admired when she was in power and just as reviled when she lost it. She had disappeared for a few years and then written a book called *Take a Meeting, Maria,* a scabrous memoir excoriating everyone she'd ever worked with, from studio heads to the script girls. Reviewers had called it reckless and honest. I'd thought it was an unpleasant tale about some unpleasant people, as told by the most unpleasant one of all. I made a mental note to re-read the book. Maybe she had something unpleasant to say about Monica. Or Gregory.

Friday was uneventful, except for the fact I was awakened from a deep sleep at nine o'clock by a phone call from a stiff young man who introduced himself as "Gary Gray, press information officer for the WHAC." It took me a minute to realize that he was talking about the West Hollywood Armament Club. Struggling to come up to the surface of wakefulness, I told Gary Gray that I was looking to talk to someone who had known Monica Slezak.

"I can't confirm that Monica Slezak was one of our members," he said. "We don't divulge the names of our members, sir."

"That's okay. I know she was a member. I just need to talk to—"

"I can't confirm that, sir," Gary Gray said robotically.

Gary Gray was a prime example of why I believe that violent assault on a publicist should be a misdemeanor. It's the same way that cops feel about journalists. "Look, Gary," I said slowly. "Can you connect me to one of your superiors, please?"

"Like who, sir?"

"I would imagine just about anyone would fit the description."

Gary Gray, press information officer for the WHAC, disconnected.

I had coffee and did the LA Weekly crossword puzzle while I debated how to spend my day. Tonight was the night that I told Sally I'd cover the Noble Savages, the heavy-metal band that was having its "listening party" at Club Lingerie. I decided to spend the afternoon doing research at the Academy of Motion Picture Arts and Sciences. Their Margaret Herrick Library was a vast repository of information about everything related to the movie industry. They had thousands of books, scripts, and photographs, and, most useful of all, an immense collection of clippings, cross-referenced by name, subject, and motion-picture title. The Herrick Library was in a handsome building that used to house a city waterworks. It had been renovated at private expense and actually looked better than most of the county libraries.

I checked my backpack in the lobby and went upstairs with a yellow legal pad and a couple of pens. It was cool and quiet, flushed with diffuse sunlight and a cozy sense of purposeful research. Film students were reading scripts. Researchers typed into laptop computers. In one corner, people wearing cotton gloves sorted through stiff, crumbly stills from the kinds of pictures that comprise the late show. Or, rather, *used* to comprise the late show—before it turned into a world of infomercials and "Remington Steele" reruns.

The librarian brought me a pile of files labeled SLEZAK, GREGORY; SLEZAK, MONICA; and GMS PRODUCTIONS. The personal files had the date of birth typed on the front, and it gave me a chill to see that some efficient functionary had already added Monica's date of death to the front of her envelope.

I started with Monica's file. On top, naturally, were the obituaries, Nyman's as well as the eulogies printed in *Variety, Biz,* and *The Hollywood Reporter.* Most of the information I had already read in the Nyman folder, and the rest was dusty business news—notifications that a particular film was going into pre-production or wrapping. The industry trades run these little banns the way small-town papers run wedding announcements. I did find a one-paragraph story about the premiere of *A Lover's Question* at the Directors' Guild. It had been clipped from the social section in *Le Hills,* Beverly Hills's most hilariously snobbish—and error-ridden—glossy monthly. The photo caption read, *Monica and Gregory Slezak (seen here with Erich Schroeder) celebrated the premiere of their new picture, "Love and Questions," with a screening at the DGA.* In the photo, Schroeder was holding Monica's hand, apparently saying something effusive. Gregory looked off in the other direction abstractedly. There was also a story from *Biz* about Monica's auto accident, and I set both of them aside to be photocopied.

Gregory Slezak's file was bigger than his wife's, encompassing as it did his dual career as producer and director. I found a lengthy profile of him entitled "Nice Guys Finish First"; it was three years old, but it had a lot of biographical information. I added it to the photocopy pile. Same with a gushy, self-congratulatory piece about the Slezaks setting up the Film Futures Foundation at USC. There was one recent story: Gregory and Monica had spent the week after New Year's in Washington with a cabal of other producers and directors, talking to members of Congress about colorization. I frowned. To me, Hollywood should stick to making movies, not public policy, the same way that Washington should stick to making laws, not delivering homilies on family values. But the Slezaks had gone to the East Coast several times—colorization seemed to be a pet issue of theirs—and I decided to copy one of the colorization stories as well. The library was closing when I got my photocopies back, so I grabbed a Fatburger, called it dinner, and killed a couple of hours walking up and down Melrose, looking at avant-garde couture. The price tags all had figures I associated with new cars, not new clothes. And who the hell would wear a latex jacket, anyway?

At eight, I drove over to Club Lingerie to meet Noble Savages— "not *the* Noble Savages," insisted the publicist, who surgically attached herself to my elbow the minute I came in the door. She gave me a press release that called the band "rockers for our time, metal with a conscience" and told me that the band would be cutting a special single, the proceeds of which would be going to Rock It Green, a rainforest relief organization "that the guys are really very into."

The guest list was the record-industry usual: rock critics who spent most of their time at the buffet, slicked-up music executives who kept their distance from the rockcrits, and dozens of misogynist, homophobic metalheads in Spandex and eye makeup. Noble Savages turned out to be a bunch of troglodytes with a severe case of Hair Extension Syndrome. I hoped it wasn't contagious. Or flammable. When the publicist parked me at their table, the bassist launched into a rambling, incoherent monologue about how deforestation was "fucked-up, man."

"Totally fucked-up," concurred the lead singer. "Did you know that they're tearing down rainforest at a rate of, like, twenty thousand acres every minute?"

"No, I didn't. I don't know much about it at all. I don't even know which countries the rainforest is in," I told him.

The bassist ran his fingers through his hair extensions. "Brazil," he said. "And Ghana."

"It's *Guy-ana*," interrupted the singer scornfully. "Asswipe."

I wrote it down. That's my job.

I was typing up the exchange on Saturday afternoon, labeling it *Geography Lesson*, when the phone rang. It was Drew Wilson. I could hear restaurant noise in the background: cutlery rattling, an electronic cash register.

"Just called to see how it was hanging, Swede." He didn't sound drunk, just tired and a little hung over. It occurred to me that Wilson didn't have many friends—or, probably, many friends left.

"Where are you at?"

"Hugo's. I've got a breakfast meeting." He still sounded preoccupied. "So listen. Did you still want to get together? We could meet for drinks later on tonight."

"How about dinner instead?" The earlier I could get him, the less chance he'd have to get drunk.

"I've got a meeting this afternoon, and I'm booked up for dinner. We could make it some other time if you want."

I thought about it. Trying to pin down Wilson was like putting my thumb on a piece of mercury, and I didn't want to wait until he felt like getting together again. "Tonight would be fine."

"I can meet you at ten at Bridie's of Donegal. I don't know the address, but it's on Western, between Santa Monica and the freeway. East side of the street. Bridie's of Donegal."

"I'll find it."

"Okay. Look, Swede, my food's here, and my girlfriend's waiting. I'll let you slide."

"Bye, Drew."

I went back to work. Apparently Drew Wilson was accustomed to eating breakfast at two-thirty. I just hoped he could stay sober until ten o'clock.

The area around Western and the freeway had been hit hard by the riots. Buildings had charred gaps and empty lots between them, like a landscape of rotting teeth. I was ambushed at a red light by a man with a Windex bottle and a squeegee. The knife tucked into his waistband convinced me that he deserved a dollar. A scrawny man in front of a sex shop shook his hand at his side as if he was rolling dice. Crack for sale.

I drove around twice before I spotted Bridie's of Donegal: a faded green doorway on a particularly dark block. It was an unmarked storefront, just a green door and an ancient neon shamrock fizzing in the window. Glass crunched under my feet when I stepped out of the car. There were glittering piles of shards alongside every parking place on the street. I decided to leave the Buick unlocked. What the hell. A new window would cost more than anything I had inside.

I walked to the door and hesitated, my hand on the knob. Across the street, a black transvestite hooker watched me balefully, looking like forty miles of bad road in a Dynel wig.

No guts, no story, I told myself, and went in.

# = 13 =

I'D HAD A VAGUE MENTAL IMAGE of Bridie's of Donegal. It would be a worn-down pub that had held down its corner of Hollywood with a tattered Hibernian dignity: dark wood and sad songs on the jukebox. What I found, though, was a nearly empty space lit by harsh fluorescent lights. There was no air; the room felt like an airplane with the ventilation system turned off. Until recently, it seemed, the space had belonged to a neighborhood market. Scuffed linoleum bore the ghostly marks of aisles. Empty shelves were shoved into the back against institutional-green walls.

A battered portable bar with six cheap stools had been lined up against one wall, catercorner from two mismatched card tables. There was an old cigarette machine with a small color TV on top. The only new things were some travel posters of Ireland taped up behind the bar, a Harley-Davidson parked in the corner near the door, and a fancy jukebox. CDs rotated in a bubble on the top, playing prisms across the joyless room.

Drew Wilson was sitting at the corner of the bar playing cards with the bartender, smoking a cigar the size of a piano leg. Bills were scattered across the bar between them. Here, Wilson didn't resemble a sensitive young actor or a best-selling novelist. He looked like a junkie, all sunken eyes and facial planes. A cut-off black T-shirt showed off a pair of stringy arms. His hair was split and damaged and in need of a good creme rinse.

Drew Wilson looked as if he was circling the drain.

The bartender shot me a suspicious look. Wilson followed his gaze and tried to focus. "Swede," he said slowly. "Siddown. Get him a glass, Mahaffey."

Mahaffey's flat Irish pan of a face looked as if it belonged on a teenager, but he was built like Broderick Crawford, enormous and bull-necked. Crude tattoos covered his torso. They looked home-made and blurry, as if they'd been done under a prison-issue blanket after lights-out. His biceps looked as if they'd been built by heavy iron instead of a Nautilus machine. Heavy Gothic letters spelled out WHITE POWER on his massive forearms.

"Siddown," Wilson repeated, pouring me a pint from his pitcher. "Play a few hands." Up close, I could see them on Wilson's arms: tiny blue-black specks, tick bites from a needle. They looked fresh.

We played poker for half an hour. Wilson drank three pints to my one while he and Mahaffey reminisced about the good old days: how Mahaffey had constructed a workable knife out of a ballpoint-pen cartridge, and wasn't Little Stevie surprised when they caught him in the shower. Ha-ha-ha. Seven-card stud switched over to jacks-and-deuces wild. No one came in the door. I lost all of the forty-two dollars in my wallet. The smoke from Wilson's cigar hung thick and muzzy in the humid room. I felt as if I'd stepped into a speakeasy, or an opium den.

When I was out of cash, Mahaffey folded his winnings, secured them with a paper clip, and shoved them into his pocket. He still hadn't said a word to me. Wilson went behind the bar and filled a pitcher from an aluminum keg on the floor. He set the pitcher on a tray, added two shot glasses and a bottle of whiskey, and took it over to a table where someone had attempted to even the rickety legs with folded matchbooks. Mahaffey turned on the TV and ignored us. The scene had scared me at first, but now I was getting annoyed. Wilson was trying to intimidate me and all he was doing was pissing me off. I took a slug of beer, ignoring Wilson, and glanced at Mahaffey. He looked like one of those guys from *Deliverance* who'd tell you that you had a pretty mouth. Did they have swamp trash in Ireland?

Wilson yelled over the TV, "Hey, Mahaffey, you know the difference between an Irish wedding and an Irish wake?" Mahaffey didn't know or didn't care. Wilson turned to me.

"One less drunk," I told him.

He haw-hawed a lungful of cigar breath and slapped me on the back. "Isn't this place great? Mahaffey's an old pal of mine from *la pinta*. From *mi vida loca*. From Frank's wild years. I haven't seen him since I left Florida." Wilson poured us two shots of whiskey. "Cheers, queers."

Wilson downed his. I tried to sip at mine. He shook his head angrily and I drank it in two gulps. It singed and soothed my esophagus simultaneously, and Wilson grinned, showing a mouthful of caps that Frank Grassley would be proud of. "You gotta build up your tolerance, Swede. Tolerance is the secret. Not temperance. Remember that. I've put so much shit in this body that this tastes like tap water." He sat back and preened.

I watched him move the cigar between his teeth the way a croupier rolls a chip between his fingers. Wilson didn't need the bullshit facade. He was the real thing, the embodiment of all the bad-boy stuff that so many of the young Hollywood types aspired to: throwing shade in *People* magazine, punching out photographers at movie premieres. Unlike Wilson, though, their stupid brushes with the law always ended with a publicist or an agent picking up their ass and dusting them off. Wilson paid his own debts.

As I said before, sometimes the best way to get information out of someone is to remain blank and have them come to you. I ignored Wilson and watched the soccer match on ESPN. He thrummed out a Krupa beat on the tabletop for a minute and then snapped his fingers. "I brought you something." He unfolded his coat and withdrew a hardback of *The Midnight Hour,* which he inscribed with a few quick strokes of a pen and pushed it across the table toward me.

"What's going to happen with the movie now?"

"I don't know. We were supposed to start shooting a month or two after the Oscars. I don't give a rat's ass, Swede. I got the money and I spent most of it, so it's none of my business either way." He blew a big lazy smoke ring and jetted a smaller one through its center. "Have you read the script?"

"No."

"Read the script, read the script." He laughed. "You gotta read the script, Swede. Then tell me if it was justifiable homicide."

I kept my eyes on ESPN and pitched my voice light. "You killed her?"

Wilson snorted. "I should have. I should have taken her out with my bare hands. Tore her head off her neck and shit down the hole."

Without taking his eyes off the soccer match, Wilson stuck his hand into his jacket. A small white pill appeared in his palm. He popped it into his mouth. He put his hand back in the jacket, opened a vial, and brought it out again. There must have been twenty or thirty pills in it. Keeping his eyes on the match, he brought his hand to his mouth, put in the pills, and washed them down with a swallow of beer.

I watched his eyes close slowly and his jaw go slack. Just as I was about to get Mahaffey, Wilson's eyes opened again and his head bobbed up. "Want one?"

He pulled a box of Tic Tacs out of his jacket.

Right then, the beer and the whiskey I'd been drinking kicked in with a bump, like the moment the carousel music starts and the horse goes down.

I sat there for an hour while Wilson drank and told me stories of his life. The booze cut the edge off his bullyboy attitude and turned him into a bawdy raconteur. I tried to keep my drinking to sips. It was a struggle to keep from getting bleary, but I had to try, because Drew Wilson was a man who spun facts and tall tales simultaneously, weaving reality and lies together so skillfully that I feared I'd never be able to prize them apart.

"Ever since I was twelve years old, I could stay up for three days straight. I'd watch the late movie or sneak out the window, go steal a car, take a ride, be back under the covers in time for my mom to get me up in the morning. Downside was, when I'd crash, I'd crash for thirty-six hours.

"This was still going on after I landed in prison, but I thought it was all the shit I was on. It didn't occur to me that anything else might be wrong. After I got sent up, though, I kicked the shit—but I couldn't kick the *symptoms*." He fixed me with a significant look.

"They thought I was scoring on the inside. They changed my cell assignment twice. But I still couldn't sleep, and when I could sleep, I couldn't wake up. Finally they put me in solitary. But it didn't help. There's no clocks in solitary, no sense of time except when they bring you a tray, and I was still up for three or four days in a row. I was digging at my skin with my fingernails. I was chewing the insides of my cheeks until they got infected. My mouth looked like raw hamburger. My mind was going apeshit."

Mahaffey brought over a new pitcher and took away the empty. Wilson slugged some beer before continuing. "Finally they took me to the house shrink, Peters. He diagnosed me as a severe dysphoric. Manic-depressive to the nth power. Peters got it right away. He knew all about panic disorder and attention-deficit disorder and a bunch of other disorders he diagnosed me with. He started me on a combination of talk therapy and this new psychotropic drug. Percocil. Within a month . . ." Wilson spread his hands. *Safe.* "I was out of isolation and back on the main line, working in the library."

"Percocil did that?"

"Percocil, breakfast of manic-depressive champions. Turned out I'd been manic-depressive since I was a wee lad. Of course, I was also an alcoholic and a drug addict, which made it impossible to diagnose. That stretch in Florida was the first time since I was twelve years old that I wasn't on something."

"So you started working in the library. Is that when you started writing?"

"Yeah," he said, tapping the cover of his book. "I'd never written anything but a bad check before, but Peters started me doing a journal as part of my therapy. He even gave me some books. Frederick Exley, Seth Morgan, *Junky*, *Queer*, all of Burroughs. I wrote a hundred pages and even then I knew it was good. I showed it to Peters and he thought it was good, too. Then I entered it in a few prisoner writing contests. I won the state and I placed in the national. One of the judges was Lynn Farquhar, who's now my agent. She got it to a friend of hers at Black Window Press, and by the time I hit parole, I had a contract and a check waiting for me. I bought a suit, got my teeth fixed—they were rotting out of my head from the smack—and went up to New York."

"How did you hook up with Monica Slezak?"

"Lynn had a bidding war," he said. "Auctioned off the film rights. I spent the whole day in her office, listening on the squawkbox. All of the studios dropped out after the first round, but the Slezaks didn't know that. Lynn kept them strung out all day, and they just kept adding zeroes. I was flying, man. They were so persistent, like they had a personal stake in my book. 'Course they did, but I didn't know what it was at the time."

"You mean Monica's manic-depression."

"Yeah. That and the fact that she wanted to *direct*." He whined the word. "Everybody out here wants to direct. Why is that?"

"I don't know."

"Directors. Real fucking artistes. Shit. Overpaid camera jockeys. Anyway, GMS got the rights for what I thought was a frigging fortune, and Lynn wangled it so I got to write the first draft. Ka-ching. Mo'money mo'money mo'money. I cranked out the first draft in one month. Everybody loved it, just *loved it*," he said bitterly.

"But they wanted some changes."

"How'd you know?"

"They always do."

"Yeah. Well, Monica faxed me some of her 'thoughts.' I read them. And then I went out and got drunk for three days."

Two more men came into Bridie's of Donegal. Both of them wore jeans, hobnailed Doc Martens, heavy black Dickies jackets, and had their hair cut razor-short. More friends of Mahaffey's. They looked at Wilson and me with mild curiosity before going into the back. As Wilson continued, I could hear a faint but persistent scratching and clicking from the back room: a disposable lighter being lit again and again.

"So I came out here to try to work with her. To try to save the project, actually. That was last month." He shook his head. "I gave up after a week and just let her do the second draft herself. I should have just stayed in New York, got drunk for about a year, and forgot about the whole fucking thing."

"Why?"

"She was no different than any dumb-ass English teacher I had in high school. She kept talking about conflict and the arc of the story."

"Why should she have listened to you?"

He shot me an icicle stare. "Because I can *write*. I can also cook smack, and drink you or anyone else into a coma, but writing is the best thing I do. It's the only thing I've ever done that's made me any real money. I've made more off this"—he slammed the book against the table, making me jump—"than I ever did doing anything else."

The two men came out of the back, their eyes glittering like squirrels'. They sat down at the bar and started talking with Mahaffey in a tangled Irish dialect. *Fuck* was the only word I could make out, and they conjugated it endlessly. I tried to keep one eye on them and the other on Drew Wilson, but it was getting hard to focus on more than one thing at a time.

"So when you were working with her, what was she like? Did you ever think that she might be thinking about killing herself?"

Wilson thought about it. "Nah. But, Jesus Christ, you never know. If you've never had manic depression, you just don't know."

"But I thought she was on Percocil, just like you."

"When she bought the book, she was."

"Hmm?"

"When I came out here to work on the rewrite, she wasn't taking it anymore. It's not something you take when you get stressed out, like Valium. Taking a Percocil every once in a while is about as effective as taking the Pill just on the nights you're going to fuck."

"How do you know she wasn't taking Percocil?"

He gave me a shitty grin and poured more whiskey. Christ. I sipped, but he waited until I'd poured it down my throat. It was a sadistic bribe: one shot of whiskey, one more bit of information.

"Okay," I said when my throat stopped burning. "Did she tell you she wasn't taking Percocil?"

"Nah. But I could tell."

"How?"

"Because it's not *holistic*." He sneered. "Because it doesn't have the Suzan Morninglory seal of approval."

"Did she tell you that?"

"She didn't have to." His attention had wandered back to the bar, where Mahaffey and his cronies had started another poker game. After a moment, he added, "It can be bad shit, man."

"What?"

"I've put more crap in this body than Keith Richards." He laughed. "I can eat Percodan or black beauties like they were baby aspirin. But Percocil can be bad news. It giveth and it taketh away. If it's working for you, don't mess with it. 'Cause it'll mess with *you*."

"Do you think going off Percocil, or going on and off Percocil, could make someone kill herself?"

He considered the question for a minute. "Nah. Those Percocil lawsuits were horseshit. That lady who smothered her kids? She was just a nutbar to begin with. Remember, you've got to be pretty fucked up already *before* they put you on Percocil." A ballad began on the jukebox: dulcimer, tin whistle, and a sweet Irish soprano. "What I don't get," he continued, "is why Monica would kill herself right after losing an Academy Award nomination."

"Why doesn't that make sense?"

"Think about it, Swede. She wanted to *direct*. She'd produced pictures before. What she wanted was to be Martin Scorsese. *Martina* Scorsese." Wilson laughed. "Monica thought she was going to knock this town on its fat ass with *The Midnight Hour*. But if she was as bad a director as she was a writer—and she probably was—Monica was going to be in for a surprise. A big surprise, Swede. There would have been a betting pool in the William Morris mailing room over how much money that picture would have lost. Read the script and tell me if I'm wrong," he concluded, a bit angrily.

"I don't have a copy."

"You're a fucking reporter! Get one!"

Wilson's pale-blue eyes were baleful. He'd slopped Jameson on the table. He poured another shot and dosed himself. I got up and went into the back.

The bathroom was tucked away in a corner of the former grocery storeroom. It was filthy, with rust stains all over the toilet and rat droppings behind the bowl. There were postage-stamp-size Ziploc bags and a purple plastic lighter discarded on the floor. A sharp smell hung in the air. The sticker on the stainless-steel mirror reminded employees to wash with soap and hot water before going back to work. I ran water on my wrists, splashed it on my face, and dried myself on a grubby roller towel before going back out.

When I came out, debating whether I was sober enough to drive, Wilson was back at the bar with Mahaffey and company. He shuffled a deck of cards in a fancy steeple fan. "Come on, Swede," he yelled. "I'll stake you."

"I gotta go, Drew."

"My ass. It's not even twelve-thirty." He poured a shot of whiskey big as a glass of iced tea. "Sit down."

"Drew, I've got to get up early—"

*"Shut the fuck up and sit down."*

Everything in the room stopped. Wilson's glare was undiluted venom. Mahaffey and company were grinning evilly at me, hoping, I imagined, for the chance to kick my ass down Western Avenue.

I sat down.

Their expressions didn't change. Wilson's eyes were a challenge. I downed the glass of whiskey, choking as it singed my gullet. For a moment, I thought it would come back out my nose.

"That's it," said Drew, all buddy-buddy again. He pulled a handful of cigars out of his jacket and dealt them around. Macanudos. Not cheap.

Thirty minutes later, I'd gone to that place beyond drunk, where the five senses are one blur and the whiskey tastes like warm water. I was having a pretty good time, working on my second cigar, listening to Mahaffey and the guys joke, joking along with them, feeling the blood in my head throbbing gently in time to the music.

At one forty-five, it was all over. I'd won twenty bucks and lost it again. Wilson disappeared into the bathroom with the taller skinhead while Mahaffey cleared cards and glasses off the bar. Then time muddied, and Wilson was pulling me off the barstool. My copy of the book had materialized in the crook of my elbow.

Wilson hooked his thumbs under my armpits and marionette-walked me to the door. "C'mon, Swede." I tripped over the rubber toes of my Converses, pitching into the door. Wilson caught me and propelled me outside. "You're a mess," he said with satisfaction.

The passing headlights were bright as a carnival and the fresh air sent me reeling. Wilson had to catch me again, holding me up from behind with his arms around my waist. Through the hot fog in my head, one thought emerged. "I can't drive. Oh, God, I can't drive."

"You'll be fine. Just follow me."

A car sluiced by, horn blaring. It startled me and I dropped my copy of his book to the pavement. I reached for it and the world turned upside down. I lay on the sidewalk like a turtle that's been turned over and contemplated not moving again for the rest of my life. When I opened my eyes again, Wilson was down on his haunches beside me.

"Up, Swede."

"Where we going?"

"Koreatown. There's an after-hours party at Warsaw. Lots of girls." Wilson sounded bright and sober.

"I can't." In my temples, I felt the pump of a heartbeat, an ominous sound. I swallowed something thick that kept pooling in the back of my throat.

"Well, you can't stay here." He fixed his eyes on mine expectantly and gave me an encouraging smile, as if I were a kid scared of climbing on the roller coaster. I managed to shake my head, but he just reached into his coat and brought out a waxed-paper bindle.

"Come on, Swede. Come on, me boyo. Do a little crank. You'll be fine."

Another car passed, honking. A voice yelled, "Get up, faggot." Laughter.

I let him lift me to my feet. "You gotta get me home. Please."

He closed off one of my nostrils with his thumb and put the waxed paper to my nose. Inside the waxed paper, something glittered like glass shards.

"Come on, Swede. Come on, baby. Yeah, come on. Yeah." His voice was pitched tight, with a nearly sexual excitement.

I squeezed my eyes shut, trying to focus, trying not to breathe. "I can't drive and I don't have any money," I explained slowly. "I don't have any money and I live in Venice and it's a long way away."

Wilson gave me a disgusted appraisal. Then he disappeared back into Bridie's.

I pressed my back against the wall, my legs splayed out on the sidewalk in front of me, trying to look natural. If he wasn't coming back, I was in big trouble. A car slowed and the occupants peered at me before peeling away. Then Wilson was back, pushing his Harley over the curb and into the gutter.

"Come on," he said. "I ain't gonna carry you, Swede." He flicked on the headlamp, a cyclops with a chrome eye socket, and pivoted the bike so the beam shone in my face.

Trying to shade my eyes, I wove my way to my feet, using the wall for support, and rubber-legged it across the sidewalk to the motorcycle. Its black leather seat gleamed like sucked-on licorice. I plopped my ass on it sidesaddle while he strapped a helmet under my chin and tightened it. My head kept slopping backward; I had to concentrate on a muscle in the very back of my neck and will it to flex. Wilson swung my left leg over the bike, climbed on, and kicked it to life.

"You said you wanted to go home," he said truculently. "We're going home."

We flew.

From the U-turn in front of Bridie's, down Western, past Santa Monica and Melrose and Beverly and all the little streets in between, Wilson lurched between cars, seesawed between lanes, and even drove straight through a nighttime construction crew. In that split second, I saw a ghostly man behind orange cones; his face was a shock mask, illuminated by the acetylene torch spitting sparks in his hand. When Wilson was forced to stop at the Wilshire light, I looked up at the Wiltern Theater, its sea-green Deco blurring through my tears. I grabbed fistfuls of Wilson's leather jacket and screamed into his ear. "I'm gonna be sick."

"Turn your head," he yelled, flooring it through the intersection. We barely missed an El Camino that had run the red.

I clung to his back like a drunken koala, neon signs in Korean slewing past on both sides. When we reached the I-10 overpass, he slowed. "Hang on," he said, and popped the bike into a new gear.

We took the turn at a forty-five-degree angle. I could feel the asphalt rushing past my right kneecap as we went down, and then we were up again, whipping from side to side. Icy air was being blasted into my mouth, pushing my lips away from my teeth in a G-force grimace. Wilson shot between two cars, seeking open pavement. I was helpless, hugging the bike with my legs, burying my face in the back of his jacket, howling in pain and terror, praying for a CHP officer to pull us over, a tire to come off the bike, anything to make this sick ride stop. But it didn't; it just went faster and faster, and over the scream of the wind and the stink of burning gasoline, I could hear the son of a bitch laughing.

An eternity later, I felt the texture of the pavement change, and then we were heading up a gentle grade, slowing, slowing . . .

Stopped.

I looked up. We were in Santa Monica, at the Fourth Street off-ramp. The signal was blinking. Red light, yellow light. Red light, yellow light. I tried to uncurl my fists, but they didn't respond. The knuckles felt bruised and frostbitten. My nose was tender and blasted from sucking up cold freeway air.

Wilson revved his engine. "Left or right?" he yelled.

"Home," I said dully. "I mean left."

The ride had sobered me up a little, but not much. Wilson scissor-walked me up the stairs like a comedy drunk from an old movie and switched on the overhead lamp.

"God, this looks like a place I used to live in in Alphabet City." He unstrapped the helmet from my head and tossed it onto my desk chair. "What's that smell?"

"Old newspapers." I staggered to the bathroom and hung my head over the bowl. Throwing up would have made me felt better, but my stomach wouldn't cooperate, so I sat on the lip of the john and spent some quality time blowing bloody strings of snot into pieces of toilet paper.

When I came out, Wilson had opened the window, letting in a blast of chilly salt air, and was peering out at the boardwalk.

"You throw up?" he asked companionably.

"Couldn't."

"You're gonna feel like shit on toast points in the morning," he said with satisfaction.

I flopped down on the futon and let him pull off my Converses while I studied the whorls in the cottage-cheese ceiling. When he was done, he picked up my copy of *The Midnight Hour* and jotted a number on the flyleaf.

Halfway out the door, he turned.

"Give me a call," he said. "We'll do it again soon."

# = 14 =

I AWOKE ON THE FUTON at eleven o'clock the next morning.
The miracle was that I didn't feel worse than I did. My mouth had a
coating of slime, and the cigars had left my nose hairs feeling as if
they'd been singed with a match, but besides that, I was fairly intact.

Then I sat up and realized I was still drunk.

I dragged myself into the bathroom, ran the shower as hot as I
could stand it, and turned the shower massage until it pulsed sharp
little needles of water. Then I pulled off my clothes, curled up on the
shower floor, and let the needles pelt my body until my skin was red.
I watched the water drip off my arms, imagining the whiskey running out of my pores and down the drain. The lack of pain in my
head was an ominous sign, like when you've cut your finger and it
hasn't started to hurt yet.

I prepared coffee fixings and lay down on the futon to wait. Under
the window, little girls were jumping rope and screaming, sharp
squeals that ricocheted off my four walls and embedded themselves
in my head. The noise activated the pain center of my booze-
numbed brain. By the time the coffee was ready, I had swallowed
two aspirin, two Tylenol, and a multivitamin, even though I realized
it was about as effective as putting up storm windows when a nuclear
blast was in the offing.

One of the little girls hit a soprano note that sent a hot wire
through my lobes. I shut the window, flipped on David Brinkley to
block the noise, and climbed back in the futon with my mug. Drew
Wilson was probably at Hugo's right now, having crepes and mimo-
sas with his latest AMW. For the first time in years, I thought of
Rocky Shattuck.

Rocky Shattuck was the most popular guy in my elementary
school. His specialty was spurring on all the other boys to new and

dangerous levels of stupidity. When you went over to Rocky's to play, you were liable to find yourself making a flamethrower out of wooden fireplace matches and a can of Lysol, or walking on the edge of the roof barefoot with Rocky on the ground shouting encouragement. It was the price of being his friend. Drew Wilson was a lot like Rocky Shattuck—a genial, controlling, sadistic son of a bitch.

Thinking about Bridie's of Donegal sobered me up pretty quickly. I was cautious by nature. I always used two condoms, wore my seat belt before it became law, and refused to use the phone during a thunderstorm because of something I had once read in Ann Landers. The thought of getting drunk in a bad area of Hollywood with a bunch of crackheads gave me a chill that penetrated the flannel sheets on my futon.

Then I remembered my car—still parked on Western Avenue—and I sat bolt upright.

Big mistake.

I lay down again, whimpering, and waited for the whirlies to subside. George Will and Cokie Roberts were dissecting some arcane statute of the free-trade agreement. I tried to focus on their argument while I wondered how I was going to get my car back. I had to be at Cafe Canem at five o'clock. Mahaffey and pals had all my cash. Jeff Brenner was in New York, Pedro was working, and I'd rather abandon the car than ask Claudia for a ride. I was going to have to spring for a taxi.

I zapped the remote control and watched Pat Buchanan disappear into a little dot of light, a satisfying experience in itself. Then I took another shower, this one with soap and a loofah. I pulled on shorts and a sleeveless T-shirt, grabbed my copy of Drew's book, and walked to the ATM on Venice Circle. I took out fifty dollars and stuck the receipt in my back pocket without looking at it. I'd already had enough bad news for one morning.

There was a luxury hotel on Ocean Avenue in Santa Monica that had a cab station. The lead taxi in the cab queue was fastidiously clean. A crucifix and a NO SMOKING sign hung from the rearview. The driver himself was an older black guy whose baseball cap assured me that he was NOT PERFECT, JUST FORGIVEN. Even through the door, I could hear a leather-lunged gospel singer beating a tambourine and proclaiming that "He was Daniel, *stone a-rolling*, and Ezekiel, *wheel a-turning . . .*"

I slid in, enjoying the blast of air-conditioning, and told him, "I'm going to Western and the Hollywood Freeway."

"He was *Moses*, BUSH BURNING! He was SOLOMON! ROSE OF SHARON!"

The cab driver didn't turn around. "I don't do dope runs, son," he said.

Once I had convinced Fred Harvey, part-time cab driver and full-time associate pastor of the First Covenant Bethel Baptist Church of Lynwood, that I was just a hapless motorist whose car had broken down in one of the worst neighborhoods in the city, he relaxed and started the engine. We drove down the Santa Monica Freeway while he listened to KBLH, Southern California's 24-Hour Voice of Comfort and Rejoicing, and I started reading *The Midnight Hour*.

Drew Wilson might have been a bastard, but he was right about one thing. He could write.

The book began with an unnamed narrator huddled under a table in an urban apartment, going through some mix of manic depression and panic disorder. Chemicals recombined in his brain; electrical signals shot through his limbs. Alone, he hallucinated, shook, clawed at himself until blood and bits of flesh hung from his fingernails.

I got to page 40 before the Reverend Fred said, "Lock your doors," and I looked up and saw that we were at the corner of Santa Monica and Western. In daylight, it seemed pretty harmless to me. Salvadorans and Mexicans went about their shopping, carrying plastic net bags of groceries. The crack dealer on the corner was gone. In his place was a heavy woman selling peeled mangoes on sticks, like Popsicles. Children swarmed around her, little dirty-faced ants.

"It's the white car, next block," I said. Fred shot a glance down the street at a gaudy adult bookstore with silhouettes of women painted on its shabby sides. A sign on the door told departing perverts to HAVE AN ADULT DAY! Across the street was the door of Bridie's, now secured by a massive chain and padlock. The shamrock in the window was dark and cold. Fred pulled over in front of my car, admonishing, "You be more careful where your car breaks down, young man."

He watched in the rearview mirror, lips moving in a silent prayer, while I opened the hood of the Buick and pretended to fiddle with some wires. My windows were intact, thank God, but the floor mats were missing and someone had gone through my glove box and dumped out my maps and old gas receipts.

I gave Fred two twenty-dollar bills and told him to keep the change. When I was safely in the car and the motor was running, he waved and pulled away. Once again, I had to wonder at other people's ability to make me feel guilty, even when I hadn't done anything wrong.

I was still queasy, but I needed to eat. I drove down Santa Monica Boulevard to Kiri-Dog, where my remaining ten dollars would buy lunch for two people with change left over.

Kiri-Dog was a burger shack that doubled as a clubhouse for teenage hookers and runaways. It was a fixture on the local news during sweeps month, when all the stations would do their obligatory lurid reports on street prostitution. I parked in front, away from the parking lot in back where chicken hawks in Cadillacs circled their prey. Kiri-Dog's specialty was a foodstuff called the Kosher Burrito: a tortilla filled with scrambled eggs, pastrami, hot dogs, salsa, and cheese, all glued together with orange grease that looked like engine fluid. The Kosher Burrito was better than Lourdes water when it came to clearing up hangovers and banishing the two A.M. munchies. I got extra onion rings and a large Crush and took my tray to a picnic table near the sidewalk, where the smog and the exhaust from passing cars had turned the redwood a dull brown.

God, it was good. Not the burrito, the book. After the grand-mal terror of the first chapter, it switched to flashback, describing a nightmare that read like a collaboration between Jean Genet and Mary Shelley. It had to be autobiographical; no one could make this up. Wilson's words swooped and swaggered. He wrote with a jailhouse strut and a carny barker's flair for language. It was harrowing and profane and, above all, macabrely funny. *The Midnight Hour* was one hell of a book.

How could Monica Slezak turn this into a movie? How could *any-*

*one* turn this into a movie? There was nothing as conventional as a plot; it was just an interior monologue from hell. It would have been impossible to communicate Wilson's images cinematically even if a skilled writer had been able to impose a plot upon it, and from what Wilson told me, Monica was no wordsmith. I had to get hold of Wilson and get that script, even if it meant another night on the wild side. Maybe we could do it in Venice so the cab fare wouldn't bankrupt me.

When the tortilla disintegrated from the orange grease, I picked out the pastrami with my fingers, ate it, and kept going. It was three-thirty when I forced myself to stop. I was due to work at Cafe Canem at five. It gave me just enough time to drive home, take my third shower of the day, and walk over to the coffeehouse with my copy of *The Midnight Hour* stuck into my backpack.

All coffeehouses in Los Angeles have open-mike poetry, but Claudia's readings were unique in that she held them on Sunday afternoons. Weekend afternoons were slow anyway—even coffeehouse denizens like to go to the beach sometime—so by holding poetry readings on Sunday, Claudia managed to pick up a few extra bucks in the process. Those little self-indulgence sessions were why I never went to Cafe Canem on Sunday afternoons. All the world may be a stage, but to a coffeehouse poet, all the world's just a bad installment of "Oprah." I have a low tolerance for clove cigarettes, trust-fund nihilists, and sensitive women who write things like "My boyfriend was gone when I woke up this morning/But he left a dream on the pillow for me. . . ."

By five-thirty, most of the poets had already left, having been interested only in dumping their own angst and going out to dinner. Pedro greeted me with glazed eyes and a sense of relief. He cleared out the cash drawer and did his closing duties while I busied myself washing the scummy residue of foam and siltlike cinnamon out of latte bowls.

At six, the last poet gathered up his composition book and pouted his way into the setting sun, and by six-thirty it was subdued enough to put on a Lionel Hampton CD and get back to *The Midnight Hour*. Even with interruptions for refills and pastry, I got through another substantial chunk of the book. Business started to pick up again around eight-thirty, to my horror, and by nine there was enough of a crowd that I was constantly grinding beans, steaming milk, and emptying ashtrays.

Cafe Canem closed at ten on Sundays, so I made last call for caffeine at nine forty-five and had the joint cleared right on time. I ran a bucketful of hot water, added Top Job, and swabbed around the tables with the Sunday-night news for company. According to Frank Grassley, there had been several "senseless drive-by shootings" over the weekend. As opposed to what? *Sensible* drive-by shootings? By eleven, I was home, having stopped to pick up a pint of ice cream by the way. Since I didn't have to meet Slezak until one o'clock the next afternoon, I planned to stay up as long as it took to finish *The Midnight Hour*.

I made a nest of pillows on the futon and balanced the book and the ice cream on my stomach. Soon I was feeling wonderful: overfed, sticky, and a little dopey, the way you get after an hour or two with junk food and a good book. When the ice cream was gone, I marked my place and went into the kitchen for a drink of water.

Standing at the sink, head under the tap, I had an impulse to call Drew. Was it too late? No; he probably went to bed at dawn and woke up in midafternoon. If anything, he was out on the town. I checked the clock. Almost twelve. The midnight hour. Now, if that wasn't just too much of a coincidence.

Much as I hated to admit it, part of me liked Drew Wilson. I'd been suckered into his vortex, just as the New York literary establishment had. Cautious people, like me, are always fascinated by recklessness. He might have been a sick ticket who couldn't decide whether to destroy himself or the people around him, but Drew Wilson was undeniably magnetic; the air around him crackled with ozone. So did his prose. And while meeting movie stars left me yawning, I was fascinated by anyone who could spin words into gold.

Wilson was in the 213 area code. The exchange was 484, which meant he lived in Silver Lake. The phone burred just as my digital clock flashed to 12:00.

Two rings and then: "Hello?"

Not Drew. A woman.

"Is Drew there?"

*"No."* It was a weird *no*, a *no* that carried an irony I was somehow missing.

"Could I leave a message?"

"Who is this? Paul? Did Digger make you call?"

"My name's Kieran. Who's this?"

*"Vicky,"* she said. "Who the hell are you?"

"Kieran. A friend of Drew's. I saw him last night, and he gave me this number. Could I leave—"

"You were *with Drew* last night?" The woman chortled humorlessly. "Well, whoever you are, Drew is in the hospital."

"In the hospital?"

"Yeah. He got into an accident coming up Hyperion at six in the morning. Wiped out. Totaled the bike. Are you satisfied?"

It sounded like she was.

"Jesus. I'm sorry. Is he all right? What hospital is he at?"

"Oh, yeah. Like I'm going to tell you that. And don't bother calling around, because he's registered under a different name." A baby began crying at Vicky's end of the line, which seemed to sap some of the venom out of her voice. "Aw, *shit*," she moaned, like a little girl.

"Sorry to bother you. My name's Kieran O'Connor. He calls me Swede. If you talk to him, tell him I hope he feels better." I gave Vicky my number, though I doubted she wrote it down before she slammed down the phone.

I tented *The Midnight Hour* on my stomach and laced my fingers behind my head. If Wilson was in the hospital, he was probably at Cedars-Sinai or County USC. He wouldn't be hard to find, even registered under a pseudonym. But who was Vicky? A girlfriend? His *wife?* I decided to call back the next day. Maybe Vicky would be at work, and the message on the machine might give me a few clues.

Before I could start reading, the phone rang again.

"It's Vicky." She sounded embarrassed but defiant. "I'm sorry I hung up on you, but the phone woke up Travis."

" 'S okay."

"Your name is Kieran, right? Look, could you tell me where Drew went last night?" She rushed on. "I'm not trying to bust your balls, but it's important. See, I had breakfast with him at Hugo's on Saturday, and then we were supposed to go to dinner. He never showed up and never called. The next thing I know, I get a call from LAPD at six in the morning. They found drugs in his pocket, and my number in his wallet. I spent my whole weekend waiting around for Drew, and then sitting around with the police, trying to answer a bunch of questions I don't know the answers to. And I am royally pissed." She stopped to take a breath.

"Vicky, I don't even know Drew that well. I'm a reporter, and I was working on a story about Monica Slezak." She didn't react to the name. "I was interviewing him. He called me on Saturday and asked me to meet him at a bar called Bridie's around ten."

"I never heard of it." She didn't believe me.

"Neither had I. It was on Western. Near the Tropicana."

Vicky considered this. "Was anybody else there?"

"Some guys. The only name I got was Mahaffey."

"*Digger*," she said contemptuously. "That asshole."

"I didn't see Drew after two o'clock or so. He said he was going to an after-hours party at Warsaw."

"Oh, Warsaw. Sure." I could almost hear her brain clicking, piecing the facts together, connecting the dots.

"Vicky, are you his girlfriend?"

"One of 'em, I guess. Or I was. Whatever."

"Is he all right?"

"He's fine. No matter what happens, he's always fine. The bike was totaled, but he just got banged up. They had to use a wire brush to get the asphalt out of his knee. I hope it hurt." She sounded distant, as if she'd forgotten I was on the line. "He got busted for DWI and possession. I don't know what the cops are going to do when he gets out."

"Can I do anything to help?"

"Nah. Don't worry about it. Drew's okay. Drew will always be okay." The baby began screeching again. She groaned. "The rest of us I'm not sure about."

# = 15 =

FOOTSTEPS OUTSIDE MY DOOR woke me at five forty-five. It was the paper carrier. I bought a copy from him, made coffee, and flipped through the Metro section. Nothing there about Drew's accident. Apparently the crash wasn't spectacular enough to warrant a story, or even a brief. Or maybe Drew Wilson just wasn't all that famous.

I showered and dressed, putting on an old tweed jacket and a pair of chinos. I decided to stop in Santa Monica for breakfast before heading over to Gregory Slezak's house. There was a 7-Eleven across from the coffee shop, and I went inside to buy fresh batteries for my cassette recorder.

*Variety, Hollywood Reporter,* and *Biz* were all stacked next to the morning newspaper. Only in L.A. does 7-Eleven carry the trades. Neither *Variety* nor *The Hollywood Reporter* had anything of interest beyond the weekend box-office tallies, but *Biz* had a front-page item that caught my attention. I picked up a copy and two packs of AA batteries. A clerk with a garden of pimples on his nose rang it all up.

I walked over to the coffee shop where Claudia and I often ate breakfast, found a seat at the counter, ordered a bacon waffle, and read *Biz*.

## TURNAROUND FOR "MIDNIGHT"

### BY CHUCK RUSSO

It may be curtains for "The Midnight Hour."

"Biz" has learned that Oyster Hill will announce this week that the troubled pic has officially been placed in turn-around. Pic was pacted under a joint deal with Oyster Hill and GMS, the production co. headed by Gregory and the late Monica Slezak. Filming was skedded for May.

Reached Sunday, neither Gregory Slezak nor Oyster Hill prexy Adam Davies would confirm or comment.

The reversal is the latest in a series of mishaps to befall the project, which was to be the directorial debut of Monica Slezak. Even before her death last month, rumors of pre-prod trouble were topic of studio gossip. No lead had been inked. A replacement director had yet to be named, leading to widespread industry speculation that the project would not make its start date in May [CONTINUED, PAGE 12]

Son of a bitch. *The Midnight Hour* was going into turnaround.

Turnaround was an emergency brake, a red light on a previously green-lighted project. In non-Hollywood English, it meant that a script that had gone into pre-production was being canceled. Turn-around was a particularly torturous form of flux, because it was pur-gatory. Any studio or production company that wanted the script could get it by picking up the tab for monies already spent—which could run into the millions. Some projects eventually survived the process—*Splash* and *Risky Business* were two famous examples—but most scripts that went into turnaround disappeared forever.

Sending *The Midnight Hour* into turnaround was a logical deci-sion. Reading between the lines, it seemed clear that the decision stemmed from the script, not Monica's death. Directors are easy to find. Good screenplays are not. If the script was as bad as Drew Wil-son claimed it was—and the fact that they hadn't cast the lead lent credence to his claim—then Oyster Hill had probably pulled the plug before any more money could be sunk into pre-production. There was no reason to expend millions of dollars on a venture that was dicey at best. Hell, even if a decent script of the book could be written, which I doubted, how do you pack a multiplex with the story of a man's nervous breakdown?

My waffle arrived, but I ignored it and got out my backpack. I already had a three-page list of questions for Gregory Slezak. By the end of the breakfast, it had grown by two more.

\* \* \*

Sprinklers chittered in the wind, sending silver sprays across a front lawn that was velvet-green and the size of a small park. An enormous shade oak stood at the edge of the property, stretching its smog-damaged branches halfway across Canon Drive. The perimeter of the lawn was trimmed with camellia bushes and a stand of lemon eucalyptus at the back. The house itself was lovely, a tall two-story with soft red brick facing and black trim. Its unprepossessing exterior was quite a contrast to the houses on either side, which were attempting architectural impersonations of a Swiss ski lodge and a French château. But what ski lodge or château ever had palm trees in the front yard?

I parked on the street—no sense in getting oil all over the flagstone drive—and walked across the lawn. The Slezaks had one of those ubiquitous private security signs planted next to the door: the Beverly Hills equivalent of pink flamingos. A motherly Hispanic maid answered my ring. Through smiles and nods, she indicated that I should follow her.

I'd been in these unassuming Beverly Hills houses before. Sometimes a demure facade disguised a Hearst Castle interior. The inside of this house compared to any I'd ever seen in Beverly Hills, and it was a hell of a lot more tasteful than most. A foyer filled with bouquets of fresh-cut flowers opened on a sunken living room the size and shape of a racquetball court. Whitewashed walls stretched up to a second-story balcony. The floor was terra-cotta, covered with immense tufted carpets. Ivory leather couches formed a conversation group in front of a fireplace. I recognized a Hockney and a de Kooning among the paintings on the wall. What impressed me most, though, was the number of books on the hearth wall: thousands of them, obviously well-read. Many of the Beverly Hills *nouveaux vulgaires* had their decorators buy books by the yard, or install fake leather bindings on their shelves.

The maid led me through the living room toward the back of the house. We passed an office with two desks, a computer station, and more books. It had a large window that opened onto a spacious side yard. Past the office was a kitchen. At the very back of the house was a den; I guessed it was where the Slezaks spent most of their time. It had more comfortable sofas, an electric shiatsu chair, an enormous projection TV, a state-of-the-art music system (complete with DAT player), and still more books. A pinlight shone on a shelf where the Slezaks kept leatherbound copies of the scripts from the films they'd made. Most producers had their scripts bound proudly in leather, as if the contents were Ernest Hemingway instead of *Ernest Goes to Camp*.

The fourth wall of the den was a sliding glass door twenty feet long. We walked outside to a sunny patio brimming with flowers. It terminated in a staircase. The maid pointed me down the stairs and left.

Gregory Slezak was in a lounge chair by the pool, talking on a cellular phone and going through the mail. The pool itself was black-bottomed and large enough to stage a water ballet. A rubber alligator raft bumped against the side. He saw me at the top of the stairs and waved me down. I took the lounge chair next to him, looking off into a copse of citrus trees and trying to act as if I wasn't listening. Among the mail on the table, I noticed, was today's copy of *Biz*.

"Right . . . Let me mull it over . . . Sure, you'll be the first to know . . . Uh-huh . . . Look, Hamish, I've got a reporter here . . . No, absolutely *not* . . . Bye." He flipped the phone closed and smiled at me.

Slezak was a good-looking guy, in the tanned manner of a Beverly Hills feudal baron. He was barefoot, wearing a pair of photogrey aviator frames and a two-piece running outfit made out of some papery material. His hair was wiry and gray, but still full. One corner of his mouth was higher than the other, giving him a bemused expression. He shook my hand, skipping both introductions and small talk.

"If you've brought a tape recorder, go ahead and get it out. I'm afraid I've got even less time today than I thought." He twisted the cap off a bottle of Diet Coke and handed it to me. " 'If you can keep your head when all about you.' Et cetera."

"I read about *The Midnight Hour*," I said, indicating his copy of *Biz*. "Sorry."

"Well . . . there've been bigger things to worry about in the last few weeks." He laughed gently.

"Did you hear about Drew Wilson?" He hadn't, so I filled him in. Slezak didn't seem too surprised. "Motorcycle, huh? Hell of a note."

"Are you good friends with Drew?"

"I don't know him as well as Monie did—she was the one who was working with him on the script. Drew can be a pain in the ass, but he's a good writer. He'd never written for Hollywood before, though. He's not the type who likes rules, and you've got to follow the rules when writing a screenplay. Monie was trying to impose some structure onto the material. I tried to stay out of it as much as possible."

"But you're the producer."

"Yeah," he said slowly, "but I'm also the husband. I think Drew felt like we were ganging up on him. After we had a skirmish or two, I let Monie and Adam handle it."

"His screenplay was that bad?"

He held up his hands. "Don't go putting words in my mouth. The only problem with Drew is that he doesn't understand that a screenplay isn't a novel, it's a blueprint. And a movie isn't a novel, either; it's a collaboration. Drew's a talented fellow, but he's a little combustible."

"Combustible in what way?"

Slezak chewed a cuticle pensively. "Sometimes it makes you sick, the number of young people out here who end up self-destructing. Jimmy Dean. River Phoenix. You get to my age, you start to value life as the precious gift it is." He rubbed his temples and squinted. "I don't know how I got off on that. End of sermon. Anyway, go ahead. Ask whatever you want."

I popped two fresh batteries out of the blister pack, put them in the recorder, and turned it on. "Let's start with the night of the WII awards."

There was a pause. "I don't know where to begin," he said. "Maybe if you ask me some questions. . . ."

For the next hour, we talked. More precisely, I talked and Slezak fumbled.

I had been ready for truculence, sarcasm, even outright hostility. What I wasn't prepared for was an affable, sad man who answered questions in monosyllables. Whenever I asked him about details from their past, Slezak was highly descriptive, but when I pressed him on more recent details, he got morose and taciturn. Three times

I hinted at Monica's suicide; three times he deflected the topic. Once, when he began to talk elliptically about Monica's "moods," I thought I saw an opening.

"How was she doing that last weekend?"

"Fine."

"Was she happy? Sad? Angry? Depressed?"

"She was . . . fine."

I sighed. "All right. Let's reconstruct what the two of you did that weekend. Start with Saturday."

Slezak screwed up his face. "Saturday . . . on Saturday, I got up early and went to the Riviera. Shot nine holes and had lunch. Monica was here working—"

"On *The Midnight Hour?*"

"Yeah. We had a meeting with Adam the next day. Monie had been working around the clock on pre-production, the usual stuff. That Saturday, she was going over the budgets, trying to get some of the costs down. She might have been working on the script, too. I don't know exactly what she was working on. You'd have to ask Alison—you know Monica's assistant, Alison?"

"We've met."

"Well, she was here when I left. Maybe she can fill you in. So. Anyway. I came home and cleaned up about four. I know it was four, because I didn't want to be late and I was checking my watch. I'd planned to surprise Monie with dinner at the Bistro Garden that night. I had it all set up, with seven-thirty reservations, roses at the table, everything."

"Sounds nice. Was there any particular reason?"

Slezak shrugged. "No reason, except we hadn't had a dinner like that in I don't know how long. And she was surprised, believe me."

"How was she when you got back from golf? Was Alison still here?"

"No, Alison had gone out. And Monie was just fine." He blinked. "That's right. She *was* working on the script, because when I came in, she was downstairs in her office on the computer."

"Okay. How was she at the Bistro Garden? Did anything happen there?"

There was a pause. "It's funny you should ask. I've played that evening back in my head several times, looking for . . . I don't know what. But she was just great. I kept the conversation away from business. Both of us can get a little too wrapped up in industry stuff. We had a bottle of wine and just talked about old times. Monie brought up the possibility of the two of us going to Greece this fall. We haven't traveled in a long time."

"So it was nice."

"It was lovely. Wine puts me out, so we left and went to bed early. Like I said, we were having a meeting with Adam the next day. But Saturday night was lovely." He squinted behind his glasses. "Really, really lovely. I'm glad we had it."

"Where was your meeting?"

"Hmm?"

"Where was your meeting with Adam Davies on Sunday?"

"Here. We gave Magdalena Sunday off and made dinner. Monica went to Irvine Ranch in the morning and picked up three gorgeous swordfish steaks. Adam came by about threeish and we barbecued. Monica made a salad and Magdalena made a flan before she left. Right, Magdalena?" he said to the maid, who had arrived with an ice bucket, more Diet Cokes, and a couple of frosted goblets. Magdalena set them down on the table, patted her employer's shoulder, murmured a few words in Spanish, and left again. Slezak popped open another Diet Coke, his third.

"What was the meeting about?"

Slezak shrugged. "General production things. I don't know how much you know about *Midnight Hour,* but we were rushing so we'd be ready to begin shooting in May—"

"Why so soon?"

"To be considered for Oscar nominations, you've got to get it released—even a limited release—by December. Academy rules say that a movie isn't eligible unless it plays in a theater for at least a week before the end of the year. So we were double-timing. As you know, this isn't exactly a summer film."

"Sorry to interrupt."

" 'S okay . . . Where was I?"

He popped his fourth Diet Coke. I began to wonder if he was addicted to the stuff. "Production difficulties."

"Oh, right. There were still some problems to lick."

"You didn't have a lead."

"That wasn't as big a deal as they're making it out. Monica wanted someone, Adam wanted someone else, and Drew was squawking about the whole thing." Slezak leaned into the tape recorder. "And I'm not going to tell you who we were considering, so don't ask. It's a moot point now anyway."

I had started taking notes. "Was that the only hang-up?"

"No. We also discussed ways to shave the budget a bit. Oyster Hill doesn't have the pockets of a Paramount or a Fox. It was imperative to cut costs where we could."

"But you didn't discuss the possibility of going into turnaround?" Slezak shook his head, an emphatic negative. "Did you even get a hint that Davies was considering it?"

He made that face people make when they want to show you they're thinking. "Not a clue. Monica was bending over backwards to accommodate him. She wanted to get this picture done. So did I. Hell, I think we would have found a way to do it for ten bucks if that was what it took. Monie was that determined. She loved the book, she loved the script, and she was determined to direct it. This was her baby." Slezak stretched out his bare feet and cracked his toes, a skill I've never been able to master.

"What happened after Davies left?"

"We went to bed early again. The next morning were the nominations, as you know, and the next evening was the Women in the Industry dinner. It was going to be a long day. Monica got out her dress and tried on some jewelry, I watched '60 Minutes' and read some of the new Michener, and we were in bed by nine-thirty."

"Wait a second, Mr. Slezak—"

"Greg."

"Greg. When did you find out that *The Midnight Hour* was going to go into turnaround, then?"

"Day before yesterday," he said. "Adam called. I argued with him, but there wasn't much I could do. I mean, I saw his point. We couldn't get another director on the project that soon—at least for the kind of money Oyster Hill was paying. Off the record, Monica was going to be working for Guild minimum. If I could have taken over, I would have, but I'm committed to start filming *A Stronger Woman* in June."

"Were you angry?"

"I—wasn't too happy. And Adam wasn't any happier about it than I was, but we're both pragmatists. So we placed a conference call to Chuck Russo at *Biz* and leaked the news ourselves. That's off the record, too," he added. "The part about the leak. The last thing I need is to get *Variety* and *The Hollywood Reporter* on my tail."

"Okay. Tell me about the morning of the Academy Award nominations."

Slezak flinched. "Oh, God." He flexed his toes again, making his feet sound as if they were crushing walnuts. I was fascinated.

"Was she upset?" I prompted.

"Well, no. But—how do I phrase this—I don't know if you know, but my wife had had some stress-related problems."

"I'd heard something about that."

"What had you heard?" His tone was sharp.

"I'd heard that your wife—"

"*Monica.* She has a name. Monica."

"—that *Monica* occasionally suffered from manic depression. And that she occasionally took Zapax and Percocil to combat it."

"Christ," he muttered. "I knew this would happen. This town and rumors."

"Well, go ahead. Now's your chance to dispel them."

He took a deep breath. "My wife wasn't incapacitated. She was diagnosed with clinical depression a few years back, and what they're now calling panic disorder. We used to call it 'soldier's heart.' It meant that she didn't react well to stress, and she had problems driving in heavy traffic, but nothing more than that. Panic disorder's a simple thing to treat, and you treat it with medication, not therapy. It's not a mental illness."

"And she took Zapax for the panic disorder?"

"Does it matter?"

We stared at each other for a minute. Stalemate.

"Kieran, listen to me," Slezak said. "I don't want you to paint this like it was *Valley of the Dolls.* My wife needed medication sometimes, the way a diabetic needs insulin. But my wife was no more a pill popper than a diabetic is a junkie."

"I understand that. But she still had 'stress-related problems,' to use your term—"

"*Occasionally.* Very occasionally. She only had one full-blown episode, the night of the car accident. Ninety-nine percent of the time things were just fine. Just *fine*," he added emphatically. I would have described suicide as another full-blown episode, but I let it go.

"What about the morning of the Academy Award nominations? Would you describe her mood as fine?"

Slezak looked off into the citrus trees. Their shiny leaves rattled with a chilly breeze. Haze was blowing in from the beach, smearing the sky. Slezak sat up and clenched his hands, dangling them between his knees.

"Kieran. Look. I'm doing you a favor by talking to you. You seem like a nice enough fellow. But please. Please don't make this into . . . into something ugly. I invited you over here because I wanted someone to paint an accurate picture of Monica. If you're going to do a responsible job, you can't just write about her death. My wife was a damn good producer—and, frankly, a really nice person. This is all enough of a nightmare without having someone print a bunch of lies and lurid speculation in . . ."

Slezak trailed off, biting his lip. I waited.

"Write what you want to write. Write what you need to write. Just do me one favor, and include this fact: I'm a nice guy, and Monica was a beautiful woman in every way. We loved each other very much."

He began to cry. I can't handle men in tears. Or women, for that matter. I focused on the inflatable alligator, which was bumping against the side of the pool as if it wanted out. Finally he stopped. *"Merde."* Slezak swiped at his nose with his sleeve. "Let's do the rest of this in the house. 'S getting cold out here."

He slipped the cellular phone in his pocket. I followed him up the flagstone steps.

# 16

As I followed Slezak up to the house, my mind was cartwheeling. His story just didn't make sense. The facts themselves seemed to add up, but none of it even began to answer the larger question: Why did Monica Slezak kill herself?

More to the point, what was Gregory Slezak hiding? Not that he wasn't truly grieving; there were too many subtle signals—a sag under his eyes, a slump to his shoulders—that would have been too difficult for an amateur to fake. If he was just telling me the truth, or just lying to me, I would have felt more comfortable, but his story was an evasion worthy of a magician—or a movie director. I knew that he was showing me exactly what he wanted me to see; I just couldn't tell what was going on just outside the frame.

We walked into the carpeted den, where Magdalena was vacuuming. She started to shut off the machine, but Slezak pantomimed that she should finish, and led me up the stairs to the balcony that overlooked the living room. We walked past the master bedroom to a smaller bedroom that had been converted to an office—his, apparently.

This room didn't look as if it belonged in the rest of the house. A desk two sizes too large had been shoehorned under the window that looked out on the front yard. The closet had been filled with several tall filing cabinets, topped with teetering cardboard cartons. An octopus of cords snarled around a large electrical extension box that had been installed under the desk. Slezak's work space was cluttered with scripts, folders, contracts, and loose papers that rivaled any mess I could make. Framed posters for *A Lover's Question* and *The Belgium Diaries* were the only decor. His Best Director nomination certificate for *The Belgium Diaries* hung, off-kilter and lonely, between the posters.

Slezak pulled a director's chair out of the closet, unfolded it, and set it in front of the desk. There was just enough room. "Sorry about the mess," he said. "I don't like Magdalena cleaning up in here. I can never find anything afterward. Anyway. Where were we?"

I switched the recorder back on. "I know it's difficult, but I need to know about the morning of the Academy Award nominations."

Slezak closed his eyes. "Okay. We got up around four, just before the alarm went off. Magdalena doesn't get here until around eight, so we went downstairs and made breakfast ourselves. Monica made an omelette. I had cereal. Grape Nuts. Then, at five, we went into the den and watched the nominations."

"Did your wife say anything significant?"

"Significant?" He rubbed the bridge of his nose, where the aviator glasses had rubbed two angry red marks. "Not that I can remember."

"How would you characterize her mood while she was watching the nominations?"

"Well, she was pretty excited. Bouncing up and down. I remember telling her that she was like a kid on Christmas morning. She laughed."

"Did she think *A Lover's Question* would be nominated for Best Picture?"

"She kept going back and forth, you know? One minute she was sure we would, and the next she thought we didn't have a chance. But when I got nominated for Best Director, I think she got pretty confident." He stopped.

"And then?"

There was a tiny hot plate on the desk, just big enough for a single mug. It had a ring of dried coffee on its surface. Slezak licked his finger and wiped off the coffee ring before he spoke. "That's the part that doesn't make sense. She was okay with it. A little disappointed, sure, but not—*devastated*, you know?" He looked at me helplessly.

"Drew Wilson told me that he thought she was more interested in the next project, because she'd be directing."

He reflected. "That's probably it. *The Midnight Hour* was all that mattered to her those last few . . . it was all that seemed to matter. But she *was* disappointed. I mean, how could you not be?"

"Did she cry? Did she have a panic attack?"

"No, no, no." He dismissed the idea with a wave, though he

didn't look me in the eye. "I gave her a hug, we made a few jokes about next year, and that was it."

"What happened after you watched the nominations?"

"I had a lot of things to do that day, but I stuck around for a while just to make sure she was okay. But everything was fine. I left the house around noonish."

"Okay. Lap dissolve." He made a wiping motion in the air with his right hand. "I had a lunch with Sam Slater to talk about *Stronger Woman*. We went to the Grill. Then I got a trim and a manicure at the Beverly Hilton, went by the cleaner's and picked up my tux, stopped at Jon-Marché and picked Monie up some flowers. Normal, everyday bullshit. I was back around three-thirty and Monie was taking a nap. I had to be at the hotel by six—"

He was going fast. I held up my hand. "Wait. Did Monica take naps every afternoon?"

"Nooo." Slezak paused. "But she'd left me a note, saying that she thought she was coming down with a bug and not to wake her up."

"What kind of a bug?"

"A cold or something, I guess. She didn't say."

The needle on my mental polygraph jerked. I leaned back in the director's chair. "And you didn't think that it might have something to do with losing the nomination."

"No, I didn't," he said crossly. "Everybody in town had a bug right around then. There was something going around. She just wanted to be in good shape for the Women in the Industry dinner."

"Well, if she wasn't upset, why did you buy her flowers, then?"

This had a satisfying effect. Slezak's face went blank as dough. "Because she's my *wife*," he said with some acerbity. "Are you married?"

"No."

"Well, you must have a girlfriend. Don't you ever buy her flowers?"

It was my turn to go blank. I'd never bought Claudia flowers in my life. The most I ever did was cut a few birds-of-paradise from the bush at the foot of her stairs. Had Cathy bought her flowers? Bowers of roses, cascades of hollyhocks? I'd never been half of a normal couple; I had no idea how a normal couple behaved. Slezak slumped in his chair and swiveled back and forth like a sulky child. I waited for him to resume the story, but he just tapped his foot on the electrical box under the desk. Finally I prompted, "So you went to the hotel at six . . ."

"Yeah. And Monie still wasn't awake at five-thirty, so I left her a note, told Magdalena to wake her up in an hour, and went over to the Beverly Hillshire in my own car. The note's still down in Monie's office. You can see it," he added truculently, as if he expected a challenge.

"Okay."

We went downstairs again, past the kitchen where Magdalena was baking something that smelled spicy and delicious, and into the large office I'd glimpsed earlier. This one was bright with afternoon sun and more organized than Slezak's. A Macintosh sat at a computer station, diskettes neatly filed in plastic cases. The smaller desk, which I guessed was Alison Sewell's, was outfitted with secretarial stuff: binders, spare reams of paper, manila folders, Jiffy bags, Post-Its, and a compact copier on an ell. Monica's desk had several large framed photos at its head. A door in the corner of the room was ajar; through it I could see a pedestal sink.

Slezak opened a drawer and began poking around. There were two copies of a script on Monica's desk. Each had the familiar Oyster Hill logo on the front cover, and each was labeled *The Midnight Hour*. I picked one up.

"Can I have this?"

Slezak looked up. "I . . . I'd say yes, Kieran, but I don't even know who owns it now. It's not mine to give away. I wouldn't feel comfortable about it unless Adam gave me permission."

" 'S okay."

He opened another drawer. I moved around the desk to get a better look at the photos. There were a younger Gregory and Monica on a boat, laughing. Gregory in a cable-knit sweater on a breathtaking golf course somewhere—Scotland, I guessed—looking like Heathcliff on the moors. Gregory and Monica with Michael and Shakira Caine at a party.

"Here it is."

He handed me a piece of paper. I stiffened when I saw it. Gray vellum.

*Monie:*

*I've gone over to the hotel. Hope you got some good sleep.*
*These are for you, sweetheart. I can't resist irises.*
*Keep your chin up, kid. ILY.*

XOXOXO—G.

Once he'd found the note, Slezak's gloomy demeanor lifted. "You can have a copy of *this*," he said brightly, as if it were a consolation prize. He took the paper over to the copier and pushed a button just as the cellular phone in his pocket began to ring. He pulled out the phone and flipped it open.

"Greg Slezak . . . Hi, Hamish." He looked at me and held up his index finger—one minute. "Yeah, I've got it. I'm just not sure where it is." He covered the phone. "Will you excuse me for a second, Kieran?"

"Sure. Do you have a bathroom I can use?"

"Right there." He pointed to the door in the corner of the room and left.

I waited until I heard him walking up the stairs before I moved to the computer station and switched on the Mac. While it warmed up, I rooted around in the diskette case. I found what I was looking for in the first partition: a yellow 3.5-inch diskette labeled MIDNIGHT. Working quickly, I put an unlabeled diskette into one drive, the script disk into the other, and punched in a copy command. The process took about ten seconds. The MIDNIGHT disk went back in the case, the newly copied diskette into my shirt pocket.

My heart was beating fast. Slezak still wasn't back, so I went into the bathroom, closed the door, and locked it. I stuck my head under the tap and had a long drink before I looked around.

The room was a half-bath; no shower or tub, just a toilet, sink, and four-line telephone. Perfect for those on-the-bowl conference calls. A small closet was built into one wall. There was a can of air freshener on the back of the john, and above the pedestal sink was a white willow medicine cabinet and a dispenser of miniature Dixie cups. I touched the handle of the medicine cabinet and paused. Once, Pedro had livened up one of his parties by filling his medicine cabinet with marbles, and, naturally, someone had opened it. Since then, I'd been paranoid about peering into anyone's medicine cabinet.

This was silly. The Slezaks weren't setting booby traps for nosy reporters. I yanked it open. No marbles. No nothing. It was empty except for some Benadryl capsules, Advil, and a dusty brown bottle of hydrogen peroxide.

I sat down on the toilet to think. The pills must be upstairs in the master bath, but I couldn't figure out a reasonable excuse for getting in there. Or maybe she kept them in her bedside table, or her purse. I was just about to give up and leave when I noticed a small trash can tucked between the toilet and the sink. Two crumpled paper cups were at the bottom.

Why would Monica Slezak need paper cups in a half-bath? She didn't brush her teeth down here, and the kitchen was right next door if she wanted a glass of water. I would have bet that no one had emptied the trash in here since she died.

I opened the closet. It had four shelves stacked with towels, cleaning supplies, and dozens of rolls of toilet paper. Rich people could afford to buy in bulk. I moved a stack of towels aside.

There were two prescription vials at the back of the shelf—one small, one large.

The small one was Zapax, thirty tabs, 1 mg apiece. A neon-yellow sticker on the side cautioned against taking with alcohol, driving, or operating heavy machinery. It had been filled at a pharmacy in North Hollywood almost seven months ago. I fought with the adult-proof cap, forced it open, and made a quick count. There were seventeen tablets left. When I put the vial back, there were only sixteen.

The second vial was labeled Percocil, fifty tabs, 20 mg apiece. It had been filled in the same place as the Zapax prescription. Even before I opened it, I could tell it was nearly empty. It had been filled on the same date as the Zapax—nearly seven months before. Bad Monica. You gotta keep taking them if you want them to work.

Footsteps outside. Slezak was back.

No time to count. I flushed the toilet and slipped a Percocil into my pocket with the Zapax and the diskette. I'd never stolen anything before, and I was surprised to find it gave me a definite rush.

Was this what kleptomaniacs feel like when they lift a diamond necklace or a package of Top Ramen?

I ran water and shot a blast of Glade Mountain Fresh into the air. When I came out, Slezak was running a piece of floss around his mouth. He had changed into a pair of slacks and a custom-made shirt with his monogram on the sleeve. "I'm going to have to cut this short, Kieran," he said. "That was my lawyer. I've got to head over to his office to sign some things."

"That's okay," I said. "But I've got more questions—mostly about how you and Monica met, stuff like that."

"Sure. I'll call you later this week. If you don't hear from me by the weekend, give me a jingle."

I followed him out of the office and through the kitchen, where Magdalena was cooling *empañadas* on a wire rack and watching a *telenovela* on a countertop TV. The kitchen was decorated in the prevailing Beverly Hills style, which was High-Tech Hotel Restaurant. The refrigerator was an enormous burnished-aluminum box, and the stove had six gas burners and a barbecue grill built into the center. One door in the corner led to a shipshape little maid's quarters. Slezak led me through the other, which opened into an immaculate three-car garage. My whole apartment would have fit into it; Monica Slezak's Cypriot and a chocolate Mercedes took up less than half. Slezak pulled out his keys and punched a button that opened the garage door, letting in the afternoon sunshine.

"I've got one last question for right now."

"Shoot." He was all business.

"What happened backstage at the Women in the Industry dinner?"

He paused and put his keys on top of the Mercedes. "After Monie got sick?"

"Yeah."

"I don't know what to tell you." He focused on a spot somewhere on the garage wall. "I'd barely had a chance to talk to her, because they had me doing some television interviews before dinner. Up on the dais, she was at one end and I was at the other, so we didn't talk during dinner either."

"What happened backstage?"

"It wasn't really a backstage area. It was a corridor to the kitchen.

She had her hands over her face. Addie had already gotten to her, and Suzan—"

"Suzan Morninglory?"

"Yeah."

"Were she and Monica good friends?"

"They had gotten pretty close over the last few months. Monie loved her book. She was the one who had me read it. Monie thought Suzan was really something special."

"You know, she won't talk to me."

"Who? Suzan? I'll put in a call to her." He had his hand on the car door.

"Gee, that would be a big help. Could you do the same thing with Adam Davies if you talk to him?"

"Sure enough." He climbed in the car, which sent off soft *bongs*. Expensive cars even ask you to fasten your seat belt nicely.

"Thanks, Greg. But about the dinner . . ."

"Oh. Right." He was in a hurry now. "Well, Monie had her hands over her face. She was crying, but it didn't last long. I asked her what was wrong and she just shook her head. Then I asked her if she wanted to go home."

"Tell me what you said. Exactly."

Slezak closed his eyes to help himself remember. Directors can never remember anything unless they unspool it in their head like a movie. "I said, 'Are you sick?' and she shook her head no. And then I told her, 'Monie, we can go. Do you want to go?' And she shook her head again and laughed."

"She laughed?"

"Laughed. Not a ha-ha laugh, but a stress reaction."

"Like she was embarrassed?"

"Of course."

"Did you know that she'd taken any medication?"

"Well, I figured it out when she went up to the microphone. All I could think was: Oh, shit. She's having a panic attack."

"Had she been having them lately?"

"No. I told you that. But . . . See, the thing with panic disorder, Kieran, is that it can build up, like an earthquake. Then the stress can get too much, and it all blows. She'd been fine for months, though. Not a single episode. Maybe I should have known that the evening would be too much for her. Maybe I should have told her to stay home. But I guess you can torture yourself with maybes forever, can't you?"

"What happened after she said she didn't want to go home?"

"Not much. Addie went back out to talk to the crowd, and Suzan took Monica away to get her cleaned up. I waited back there for I don't know how long, three or four minutes, and then I went back out to the dinner myself. And that was the last time I saw her." Slezak exhaled sharply.

"Was there anyone else in the corridor? Alison? Drew Wilson?"

"Uh-uh. Nope." He shot his cuff, exposing an oyster Rolex. "I'm late, Kieran. I'll talk to you later."

And he pulled out of the garage, leaving me in a cloud of sweet-smelling Mercedes exhaust fumes.

I sat in the Buick for two minutes and made a few notes on what Gregory Slezak had told me in the garage. Then I started the car and drove down to Santa Monica Boulevard. Traffic was the usual and I was able to catch up to the chocolate Mercedes around Century City, following about two car lengths behind.

Hamish, I figured, was Hamish Dunne, the entertainment lawyer. Dunne, Dunne, and Lambert was in a high-rise at the corner of Wilshire and Westwood Boulevards. I wasn't sure where I expected Slezak to go, but I thought it was worth checking out. Something about his story just didn't sit right.

The Mercedes drove west on Santa Monica, past the Beverly Hilton and Trader Vic's. I kept behind him through Century City into West L.A., where the Mormon temple rose on the north side of the street, looking like a movie set from a D.W. Griffith production. Slezak made a right on Westwood Boulevard. As he made the turn, I caught a glimpse of him gesticulating as he talked into a car phone. He went up Westwood toward UCLA for a few blocks. At the corner of Wilshire, he disappeared into the parking garage of the building where Dunne, Dunne, and Lambert had their offices.

So much for hunches. I made a left on Wilshire and headed back to Santa Monica. All I could think about was the disk in my pocket. My computer was an IBM-compatible that took 5.25-inch floppies. What I needed was a Macintosh, and I didn't have one.

Fortunately, Claudia did.

# = 17 =

I USED MY KEY TO LET MYSELF into Claudia's apartment and opened the windows that looked out onto the street. Claudia had left in a hurry that morning; there were coffee cups and a plate of toast on the counter. Her robe was thrown over an arm of the sofa, and the radio was still on—presumably to discourage that nonexistent sort of burglar who gets intimidated by empty apartments with blaring radios. The message counter on the answering machine was blinking with two messages. Tempting, but I decided against it. Even script thieves have their standards.

Claudia's computer station was next to the window. On it were a Macintosh and a nifty laser printer. We'd spent a whole afternoon trying to put together the computer station, which we bought at one of those unassembled-furniture stores that cater to impoverished urban professionals. I'm maladroit under the best of circumstances; I couldn't even begin to cope with cobbling together sawdust-and-glue boards armed only with a tiny hexagonal screwdriver. We got it together after four hours of banged fingers, hurt feelings, and swearing. Plans to wallpaper the bathroom were quietly aborted.

The only file on the disk was labeled *MIDNITE2*. I booted, retrieved it, and the first page came up.

THE MIDNIGHT HOUR

by
DREW WILSON
and
MONICA SLEZAK

At the bottom was the agent's contact number and the Writers' Guild registration number. This was it. I dropped down a page and started reading.

"THE MIDNIGHT HOUR"

FADE IN ON:

INT. - A DARKENED APARTMENT - SAN FRANCISCO - 3 A.M.

CAMERA PANS SLOWLY

over a SCENE OF CHAOS AND DESTRUCTION. As a counterpoint, JAZZ plays softly on the radio. Clothes are scattered everywhere. Tables, sofas, bookcases are overturned. We are not sure what has happened here. A burglary? Someone looking for something? The jazz trails off into a mournful clarinet. Outside the window, we see THE GOLDEN GATE BRIDGE, swathed in fog.

> ANNOUNCER
> You're listening to KJAZ, your jazz voice in the night . . .

A MOURNFUL FOGHORN sounds. At the sound, a WHIMPER comes from somewhere in the apartment. We PAN back to the sofa, which leans against one wall, creating a lean-to. Now we can see A HUDDLED FIGURE, lying in the fetal position, tucked between sofa and wall. This is TERRY MARKMAN.

> TERRY (voice-over)
> Why won't they just let me die?

A KNOCK at the door, and then another, insistent. Terry's head jerks up. She crawls out of her lean-to and checks herself at the mirror.

TERRY's P.O.V.

Her hair is tangled. Sweat runs down her face.

(CONTINUED)

I stopped reading, astonished. I read the next page, and the next. Terry was a *woman*.

Monica Slezak had rewritten *The Midnight Hour*—and turned Drew Wilson into a woman.

This kind of extreme liberty was unusual, but not exactly unheard of. Hollywood producers always treated books cavalierly when they turned them into movies; transforming Drew Wilson into a woman was child's play for a town that could turn the vampire Lestat into Tom Cruise. "Script doctors" were famous for sucking the juice out of books, leaving behind a husk. Perhaps they had a big-name actress lined up for the part. No, the role hadn't even been cast yet. I tried to think of some other explanation, but there didn't seem to be one.

Unless I was missing something, Monica had arbitrarily changed the lead from a man to a woman.

Well, I thought, if I were Drew Wilson, I would have killed you too.

I mickeyed with the mouse until the file started printing, and then I went into the kitchen. It was after four and I was hungry. I toasted sourdough, smeared it with butter, got out Swiss and ched- dar, sliced a tomato, and browned the whole thing in a pan. This was one of my specialties; in Beverly Hills, they call it a Mixed Grill Aux Fromages Et Tomate and charge you ten bucks. I sat down with a club soda and the first forty-two pages of the script and started to read.

In Monica's defense, I wasn't sure that anyone could have made a movie out of *The Midnight Hour*. It was too internal, and the few external scenes were horrific dreamscapes, brought on by heroin and incarceration and electroshock. Even so, the rest of the script was worse than the first page. Much worse.

After the opening scene, the script flashed back to Terry's previ- ous life. Terry (who was described as having "the fresh face and com- petent mien of a Demi Moore") is a successful lawyer in Manhattan. Her life begins to spiral out of control on page 8 in a crowded sub- way, when she has her first of many panic attacks. By page 30, she has lost her job and flees New York in a fit of manic panic, leaving her husband behind.

Lap dissolve. One year later. Terry is working as a paralegal in San Francisco, finding it increasingly difficult to hide her condition from her co-workers. This section climaxed with the opening scene in the apartment, which lands Terry in the loony bin.

I finished the sandwich, washed the plate, and got the rest of the pages out of the printer. After some *Snake Pit* scenes in the asylum, a sympathetic black doctor ("an Alfre Woodard type") puts Terry on a drug that's a thinly disguised version of Percocil. Terry improves immediately and eventually gets out of the asylum. Her husband wants her back, but she ends up with Aaron, a poor but honest mechanic whom she met when he repaired her car on page 46. In the last scene, she has discovered her true calling—helping other women with manic depression.

Fade out. Credits.

As bad as the story was, the dialogue was worse. And as bad as the dialogue was, the characters were worse—especially the crusading therapist and the *mechanic ex machina*. (He swept Terry away in a white Mustang, which must have been Monica's idea of symbolism.) It was improbable and preposterous and unimaginative—none of which, of course, meant a thing in the movie world. The truly tragic aspect, by Hollywood standards, was that it was unlikely to earn back Xerox costs.

Turnaround, hell. This was dead. And a good thing, too. It had the potential to kill Monica Slezak's fledgling directorial career—and take a few others along for the ride.

When I got home, I changed into a ratty plaid bathrobe, spent some quality time on the futon watching "Action News," and tried to sort through everything Slezak had told me. It was like a knot in a shoelace, and the more I worried it mentally, the tighter it drew. The phone rang at six twenty-five.

"Schmuck. Don't you return your phone calls anymore?"

It was Jeff Brenner, and hearing his voice made me realize how much I missed him. Most of my friends had always been women, and now that Jeff lived in New York, I didn't have any male friends left. He had moved the previous summer to take a job writing about participatory sports at a men's magazine. Participatory sports were the newest thing in the magazine world: stories about canoeing, paragliding, gravity racing. Things that the readers could do themselves—not that I imagined any of them did. Jeff was two years older than I, five times a better writer, and made ten times as much money. As he was my closest male friend, I graciously overlooked these flaws.

Jeff had just gotten back from two weeks of climbing some peak in Alaska, and had lots of stories to tell. For a change, I had one of my own. Monica Slezak's death hadn't gotten significant coverage in the *Anchorage Times*. I filled him in on the facts of the case and told him about my theft of the script.

"How wretched is it?" he wanted to know. "Just plain bad or all-time, *Heaven's Gate*, *Bonfire of the Vanities* bad?"

"Worse than that. The book is a living nightmare; the screenplay is a New Age tale of triumph. It's like adapting *Metamorphosis* by putting Gregor Samsa into Cockroaches Anonymous."

"So who was she? Gregory Slezak's mistress made good?"

"No. She wasn't the bimbo type. She was an okay producer, and she had an eye for a good story. She was just a lousy writer. Listen to this." I read Jeff some of the dialogue. He whistled.

"Well, look at it logically," he said. "Who stands to benefit from the movie not getting made?"

"Wilson. Adam Davies, obviously. I still haven't been able to talk to him. And Slezak. It probably wouldn't derail his career, but it could have been embarrassing."

"What about the assistant?"

"Not really," I said slowly. "Alison was going to get a shot at assistant producer. Even if the picture stiffed, you don't hold the assistant producer responsible. At this point in her career, any producing credit would be better than none."

"Maybe she and Slezak had something going. You said she was attractive."

"It crossed my mind. But something tells me no."

"Why?"

"I don't know," I admitted. "I'm not convinced Slezak was telling me the whole truth, but he did seem to love his wife. You know how Hollywood is; if someone like Greg Slezak had a mistress, I would have heard about it. Besides, you haven't met Alison. She'd consider the time spent having an orgasm to be a waste of time when she could be advancing her career."

"Not that screwing Gregory Slezak wouldn't advance her career," he said, "but never mind. You think Monica could have been sleeping with Wilson? Or Schroeder?"

"Brenner, you've got a dirty mind. I don't think she was sleeping with Schroeder, and I know she wasn't sleeping with Wilson."

"How does the good doctor fit into this whole thing, anyway?"

"I don't know how he fits into this at all," I admitted. "Or Suzan Morninglory, for that matter."

He thought for a moment. "I bet she had a hand in that script."

"Why?"

"Come on. Monica changed the lead character from a man to a woman. A woman who triumphs over adversity by *empowering* herself, whatever that means. Whose fine hand does that suggest to you?"

I hadn't even thought of that. I sighed and rolled over on the futon, propping my feet against the wall. "Jeff, I never thought I'd say it, but I kind of miss the banquet circuit. I'm not an investigative reporter. At least at a party I know when someone's blowing smoke up my ass."

"Speaking of blowing smoke up your ass," he said brightly, "how's Claudia?"

Jeff liked Claudia, but he was of the firm opinion that she was leading me around by the nose. The fact that I *liked* being led around by the nose was lost on him. I informed him that our off-again, on-again romance was on again, at least for the millisecond.

"I saw Claudia's girlfriend last month at a party in the Village. She's quite a piece of work," he informed me dryly.

I wasn't above hearing something nasty about Cathy Bates—not that I'd repeat it to Claudia. "Did you talk to her?"

"I said I *saw* her, not *met* her. She was with—" And he named a young, attractive, Oscar-winning actress whose lesbianism was one of the worst-kept secrets on either coast.

This was interesting. "Was Cathy with her, or *with* her?"

"Just pals, I suppose. If you count making out on the sofa and feeding each other hors d'oeuvres with their fingers to be just pals."

"God, Brenner, you can be catty when you want to be."

"And you, Kieran," he said, "can be a jellyfish."

* * *

Later that night, I was putting my shirt in the laundry basket when I felt something in the pocket. The pills. I'd forgotten about them.

The Percocil was a torpedo-shaped capsule of eggplant purple, the size of a large multivitamin. Next to it, the tiny pale-green oval of Zapax looked cute and harmless, an after-dinner mint for a mouse.

Part of me wanted to take them, but I'm a pharmaceutical coward. Any substance stronger than aspirin or booze gave me the creeps. If I'd been around in the lysergic sixties, I would have been about as hip as David Eisenhower. I rationalized my chickenheartedness by telling myself that these drugs had different effects on different people, anyway. Still . . .

The Percocil was definitely out of the question, but I rolled the tab of Zapax back and forth in my palm, debating. It looked like a toy pill, something out of Barbie's Dream Pharmacy.

Before I could reconsider, I popped the Zapax into my mouth and swallowed.

Nothing happened. I didn't grow a third arm or have an uncontrollable impulse to defenestrate myself. After a while, I forgot about it and lay down to watch television.

At eleven o'clock, I sat up and realized that I'd just watched a two-hour documentary on the history of La Scala without moving once. I shook my head. I wasn't feeling dazed or numb; the closest I could come to describing it was bobbing back to the surface after lying on the bottom of a cool, dark pool.

As I got up to turn off the TV, another wave began to wash over me and I knew that I was going down for the night. I turned off the light, lay down again, and didn't move until ten-thirty the next morning. Even after I woke up and had coffee, I could still feel a heaviness in my body, as if the Zapax had a half-life that was slow to dissipate. My limbs felt as if they were moving through water, and my head had that cottony feeling you get when a cold's coming on.

I still didn't know what effect the pills might have had on Monica, but any mouse that mistook Zapax for an after-dinner mint was resting in rodent Valhalla.

# =18=

GREGORY SLEZAK FOLLOWED THROUGH on his promise. Within two days, I received calls from both Adam Davies and Suzan Morninglory—or, as they say in Hollywood, "their people."

I had stopped at home on my way over to Claudia's and found a message on my answering machine from one of Davies's assistants. She said he was in post-production on his next picture, *The Awakening*, but that if I'd hang tight and be flexible, Davies would be in touch "when he had half a sec." There was also a message from one of the Morninglories, advising me to call back next week. Thank you, Gregory Slezak. I returned both calls and left the second messages in what turned out to be a phone-tag marathon. Other than those messages, all was quiet on the Slezak front.

The Academy Award derby was in full swing now. Hollywood was in its annual Oscar fever. The trade papers were fat with glossy advertisements headlined FOR YOUR CONSIDERATION, and the movie ads in the paper all had tiny print at the bottom, notifying Academy members that their membership cards could get them in to any screening, gratis. Video copies of the Best Picture nominees were being mailed out to the voters at exorbitant studio expense. Bookmakers in Vegas and the agency mailrooms were keeping tabs on the favorites. The tidal wave of stories about who was wearing what, who was coming with whom, who'd been invited to present, was just a week or two away.

And the buzz? *Femme Fatale* and *Beauty and the Bellboy* were, by consensus, two of the Academy's most embarrassing choices of recent years. With two such dumb nominations to atone for, the smart money was tilting toward the serious (and seriously dull) *Country at War*, which had managed to combine two of Hollywood's favorite hobbyhorses *du jour*: homelessness and Vietnam veterans.

The Best Director category was less certain. Some thought that since *A Lover's Question* wasn't even nominated for Best Picture, Slezak didn't have a chance. Others swore that the Academy members, having ignored the picture, would pull a *mea culpa* and name him Best Director. Posthumous Oscars were always very popular, and while Gregory was still alive, his wife was not. Whether or not anyone would admit it, everyone would have loved to see a weeping Gregory at the podium, offering a tribute to his dead wife and partner. Of such artistic considerations are Oscars bestowed. As for Cafe Canem, Pedro was busy with rehearsals and poodle-skirt fittings for *Grease,* and I felt morally and financially obligated to Claudia to work at the coffeehouse as much as possible.

In the middle of one of my twelve-hour shifts, I picked up the phone and found Sally on the other end. She had a couple of assignments for me. The first was the annual Food for Thoughtfulness dinner (a banquet to benefit Third World starvation, traditionally catered by the city's best chefs). There was also the annual Alternative Film Awards, a dinner honoring the best of the year's independent productions. I said yes to both of them.

"While I've got you, we should probably talk about the Oscars," Sally added casually.

"I knew it was coming."

"Only you would complain about a free ticket to the Oscars."

"The price is too high," I told her, and I meant it. I believe that everyone should go to the Oscars once. Once is all you need. Unless you're a nominee, the day has all the *joie de vivre* of a forced march in black tie. Preparations, arrivals, the ceremony itself, and the after-parties all add up to sixteen hours in uncomfortable shoes. The best way to watch the Oscars is the way real people do it—at home, with beer, junk food, a mute button, and a pack of friends to laugh at the fashion felonies and misguided political statements.

"What do you want me to do this year? Backstage interviews? The after-parties around town?"

"Nope. I've got you down for the Governor's Ball."

The Governor's Ball was the Academy's official party. It used to be the party of last resort, since it was held across town, and the big names preferred the more exclusive bashes, like Swifty Lazar's do at Spago. But Swifty's party had passed on when he did, and the Academy had finally hit upon the idea of staging the Governor's Ball ten feet outside the door of the Dorothy Chandler Pavilion, which increased the party's star power by several magnitudes. After four hours of sitting in the auditorium, even the most press-shy celebrities were grateful to stumble into the tent for a while, where they could revive with food and drink before heading elsewhere.

I wondered if I could wrangle Claudia into being my date for one of these affairs. There would be no greater test of her love than asking her to accompany me to something called Food for Thoughtfulness. I doubted she'd have time to go, but anything seemed possible these days. We'd been too busy to talk and too tired to fight. We were spending every night together and our sex life was better than it had ever been—one condom and no diaphragm.

She was home getting some sleep. I called, got the machine, and left a message asking if she wanted to go to the Alternative Film Awards.

While I was at it, I phoned Vicky. Her machine answered with a tinny version of Pachelbel's *Canon*, the preferred choice of middle-brow answering machines everywhere. The message was dignified and careful: "Hello. Victoria and Travis can't take your call right now. Please leave your message after the beep, and someone will get back to you soon. Thank you, and have a nice day." Not a word about Drew Wilson. I left a message anyway, inquiring about Drew and asking her to tell him that I'd read the script.

That afternoon, I tried to push all things Slezak out of my mind. I poured a bucket of ammonia, pulled on a pair of smelly yellow gloves, and gave the Cafe Canem floor a good scrubbing between customers. Without being too Morningloryish about it, I thought that letting my unconscious go to work on the puzzle might yield some results—that I might stop in the middle of steaming a pitcher of milk, stunned at some revelation or epiphany that had taken shape in the back of my brain.

It never happened. My unconscious mind was about as clear as the La Brea Tar Pits. Like the Tar Pits, an occasional bubble would rise to the surface. Still, there was no eureka moment, nothing I could put a name to.

Yet.

\* \* \*

I idled at the guard shack, waiting for the man to find my pass. Ahead, dozens of massive beige soundstages stretched into the distance. Behind them, the Hollywood Hills were draped in crepey brown smog.

After a few more calls, one of Adam Davies's assistants had phoned to suggest that if I was willing to come out to the studio, Davies might have a few minutes to speak to me during scoring sessions for *The Awakening*. Why a producer/director would be sitting in on something as technical as a scoring session, I wasn't sure, but I figured it would give us plenty of time to talk. It was one hundred degrees, and the beach towel I had hung over the back of the driver's seat hadn't worked: my back was covered in sweat.

The guard found my pass and lifted the striped gate arm. I drove carefully through the miniature streets around the soundstages, dodging the little golf carts that ferried workers around the studio. A crowd of extras in lizard suits was drinking Cokes in the shade of a soundstage. My parking pass turned out to be for the farthest lot, and when I finally reached Stage 5A, after a quarter-mile trudge back through the smog and heat, my shirt was soaking wet and the sweat on my forehead felt gritty.

Stage 5A looked like every other building on the lot: a cavernous beige warehouse, with rolling aluminum doors on the sides and one people-sized door tucked into the far corner. The red light over the door was off, meaning that it was all right to enter. Inside, the air-conditioning chilled me instantly, and I coughed. Great, I thought; I'm going to get a cold out of this too.

The scoring stage was the approximate size and shape of an airplane hangar, dominated by a 70mm movie screen at the north end. Acoustic baffles covered the walls, funneling sound into dozens of mikes that hung upside-down from the ceiling like bats. The orchestra was taking a break when I walked in. Most of the musicians sat at their stands, tuning up and flipping through phone-book-sized stacks of sheet music. Others were at a refreshment table, drinking coffee and eating slices of fruit off plastic trays. I recognized Marshall Sparks, corpulent and white-bearded, chatting up a lissome young cellist. Sparks had made millions on his bombastic scores for bombastic action-hero and outer-space sagas. He was what Hollywood referred to as a "classical" composer.

The fourth wall of the room, on the south end, was made of scuffed Plexiglas. Behind it was a raised platform with an amazing array of mixing boards and other electronic gizmos that took up the whole platform, big and clunky as those prehistoric Univac computers. Adam Davies was conferring with some engineers at a mixing board. I pulled open the heavy door to the control room and shivered. You could hang meat in there.

Davies looked up, blinked, and held up two fingers—*just a minute.*

I sat down on a battered, squishy couch that overlooked the orchestra. Sparks had his arms wrapped around the cellist from the back, pushing his pelvis into her rear end while he demonstrated some bow-stroking technique. She looked uncomfortable at being touched by genius. I was waiting to see if she would smack him when Davies sat down beside me.

"Hello," he said. It came out *halloo,* dainty as a dandy. "Would you like some tea? Pat, if you'd be so good—two cups of tea."

Davies's head came up to my shoulder; I put him at five-three or five-four. His hair was thin, but not thinning, and no particular color at all. He wore a tailored pale-blue shirt with the sleeves rolled up. Over his breast was a small monogram in thread of the same color as the shirt. Suspenders, navy slacks, and black loafers completed the outfit. Despite his loosened collar, he was still the most dapper figure on the soundstage; even the older musicians were in T-shirts and jams.

Davies coughed, pulled a tin of hard candies out of his pocket, and offered me one. "I'm afraid I've got a bit of a cold," he said in his plummy accent. Everyone in Hollywood was a sucker for British accents. It didn't matter if the speaker was a viscount or a no-account; English accents meant class, which is why there were so many Alison Sewells answering the phones at the agencies and the studios.

"Thanks for seeing me," I said, accepting a blackberry pastille.

"We're way behind schedule, but they must be given a break every hour. Union rules." He nodded toward the big window, behind which the orchestra was taking ten, and coughed again. "Not to be unfriendly, Mr. O'Connor, but I've got exactly eight minutes. What can I help you with?"

"I wanted to talk about the script for *Midnight Hour.*"

A birdlike look. "Have you read it, Mr. O'Connor?"

Something in his voice made me say, "No."

Pat (who looked like Whitney Houston with a pair of zeppelins docked in her brassiere) arrived with a tray containing steaming cups of water. Two fat Celestial Seasonings tea bags floated on the surface of the cups. I was disappointed; I'd rather expected Adam Davies to have a tea service with bone-china cups and an infuser. "Well, I can't get you a copy, if that was what you wanted," he said, lifting his tea bag out with his fingers and laying the wet little pillow on the tray.

"People are saying that the project went into turnaround because of the script."

He shrugged unconcernedly. "If I paid attention to everything that people said, I wouldn't be making movies like *The Awakening*. As you know, my films are hardly the sort of projects that make studio chiefs get out their checkbooks."

I poked my tea bag, which sent out a cloud of lemon-smelling ink, and waited. Davies cleared his throat.

"It needed work, Mr. O'Connor. Most scripts do. Drew Wilson is a very powerful novelist, but he'd never written for the screen. Neither had Monica Slezak. But it was nothing that couldn't be fixed in the pinks." He fixed me with a thin-blue eye, the color of skim milk. "You know what a fix in the pinks is?"

"No," I said, the dumb American.

"The pink pages. Script rewrites are done on pink pages."

"Oh."

"We were discussing rewrites with several writers. Then Monica killed herself, and there was no way to rebound, to regroup, that quickly. Perhaps if Gregory had been available to direct, but he was not, so . . . there you are." Davies held the cup under his nose, breathing in the steam.

Another pair of large breasts approached. These were attached to another attractive black woman. I had a feeling I knew where Davies's sexual preferences lay. "Adam," she said in a soft Jamaican accent, proffering a cellular phone, "Marty's on the line. From London."

Davies took the phone and stuck out his hand, which I didn't shake. "Was that all you wanted? The script?"

"I had a few more questions."

The door to the orchestra hangar opened and closed; Marshall Sparks's sweater-clad stomach passed by my nose. Through the window, I saw the orchestra back in their chairs, the conductor flipping pages at his stand.

"Well, you'll have to wait an hour until the next break. You can sit here and watch if you like." He uncovered the receiver. "Marty? Davies here."

"Thanks," I told him, but he was off the couch and gone, climbing the stairs to the elevated platform, murmuring into the phone. I sat back and sipped my tea. Thanks to the Plexiglas, I could see the orchestra as well as the reflections of Sparks, Davies, and the engineers behind me.

The control room and the orchestra room were soundproof, linked through an intercom system. Sparks murmured "25D through 25F" into a microphone, and the orchestra members opened their music to the proper places.

The screen at the far end of the hangar lit up with a scene of a fancy turn-of-the-century dinner party. The camera passed lovingly over old silver and heavy damask, roasted birds and fresh flowers, while the orchestra played a thirty-second piece of music. It sounded fine to me, but Sparks and one of the engineers immediately began kibitzing.

"Too hot. Too bright." "There was a sharp in the horns somewhere." "We can take that out later." "Tell the glock not to come in so strong." "Softly, softly." "Play back the horns." For the next hour, it went on like that: music filtering over the intercom in dribs and drabs while snippets of *The Awakening* played on the screen. I finished my tea and made half-moons on the edge of the Styrofoam cup with my thumbnail.

When the clock reached fifteen minutes after the hour, Davies told the conductor, "All right. That's a ten." He dismounted from the platform and sat down beside me again. One of his assistants brought him more tea. While he watched her caboose sashay away, I picked up my notepad.

"I didn't know you sat in on orchestra sessions. I thought you left that to the composer."

"Most producers don't. But I'm a bit of a perfectionist. Besides, today's the last day of sound recording, and it's costing thousands of dollars a minute. We have the orchestra until exactly two-thirty. You can't make an authentic period drama on the sorts of budgets that I have without keeping an eye on every phase of the production. In Hollywood, time *is*, quite literally, money."

He looked at me significantly, as if he was considering presenting me with a bill.

"And I appreciate your taking the time to talk to me. What I'm looking for is anything you might be able to tell me that would put Monica Slezak's suicide into perspective."

Davies was barely paying attention. "You mean why she would do such a thing? Well, the Academy Award nomination, obviously."

"Do you think that really could have made her so depressed she would have killed herself?"

With a pointed look at my notepad: "I couldn't even speculate on that, Mr. O'Connor."

"Gregory Slezak said that you'd come over to their house the night before for a production meeting. Did you see any signs? Anything unusual, anything that would have taken on significance in retrospect?"

"Nothing at all," Davies said. He rolled down his sleeves, pressing the creases down flat with the heel of his hand. "You must remember that I'd only known Monica Slezak from meetings. We'd never worked together before. Ours was a business relationship. I didn't see anything in her behavior that would have been considered unusual."

"You saw her again the next night, at the Women in the Industry dinner."

"We barely spoke. You know Hollywood. Kiss-kiss, you look marvelous. Love you, mean it, bye."

I smiled. "Do you know who her friends were?"

"Mr. O'Connor, I just told you that I didn't know her that well. She never talked to me about anything except *The Midnight Hour*."

"Did she ever mention Suzan Morninglory?"

He stared at me. The British have a peculiar talent for making you feel like an idiot even as they're being faultlessly polite.

"I have been here, on and off, for twelve years," he said slowly. "I have eaten at your restaurants. I have gone to your meetings. I have fucked some of your women.

"I can tell you how a studio works. I can tell you how to get a script read at CAA. I can even tell you how to get a table at Morton's on Monday night at eight. But please"—and here he held up a hand—"*please* don't ask me to decipher the social relationships in this town."

Davies coughed up some phlegm, ruining what had been, to that point, a rather dramatic little speech.

"Despite what anyone says about the English class system, at least it makes social situations clear-cut."

He picked up my hand from my lap, shook it, and walked into the orchestra room with a little flourish.

# =19=

TWO NIGHTS LATER, I WAS on another soundstage, sitting on a straw mat and eating gluey rice out of a communal bowl with several hundred of Hollywood's filthiest, guiltiest rich.

The Food for Thoughtfulness banquet had undergone some changes. At last year's dinner, the irony of celebrities raising money for starving children by snarfing down duck-and-goat-cheese pizza might have been lost on the organizers—but not on the media, which had gotten a week's worth of stories and commentary out of the spectacle. Rush Limbaugh had even staged a little radio pageant called "Let Them Eat Brioche." Withering under the attack and muttering darkly about misunderstood intentions, the organizers had decided to make a modification or two, which I didn't find out about until I arrived.

A volunteer at the press table directed me and Marilyn Amsterdam to a line where the other guests were queued up to draw a marble out of a burlap bag. Those who drew red marbles were led to one corner of the soundstage, where Michel Patoix, the noted *saucier* and owner of Couchon, was preparing an elegant dinner. The rest of us—the black-marble crowd—were given trenchers, gourds of water, wooden spoons, and bowls of rice, which we were to eat while seated on mats at the elegantly shod feet of the red-marblers. This, according to the Food for Thoughtfulness press release, was supposed to dramatize the "outrageous inequality in the world's food distribution."

I spooned some rice glumly and said a silent prayer of thanks that Claudia wasn't here to see this massive spasm of liberal guilt. We had struck a deal: she had agreed to go to the Alternative Film Awards and the Oscars with me on the condition that I leave her out of this one. Besides, I'd seen Cathy Bates drawing a red marble out of one of the bags. If Claudia had been there, she'd probably have gotten a red marble, too, and I would have spent the evening humped up at their feet.

I hadn't eaten a thing all day. My stomach was making noises like a cat in a sack. After fifteen minutes of chewing rice and listening to the emcee, Roger Dahlgren, I'd had enough. I got up, brushing straw from my butt, and began to wander the room in search of some quotes. I was already planning to despoil the planet by stopping at In-N-Out for a burger on the way home.

"Kieran!"

The voice came from a mat two pallets over. I turned around and saw Dr. Schroeder grinning up at me, waving his wooden spoon like a semaphore. He patted the square foot of mat next to him. I sat down like an obedient puppy.

"Here," he said, reaching into the pocket of his surgeon's scrubs and handing me a tablet. It was dark-green and shiny, like a piece of varnished seaweed.

"What is it? A vitamin?"

"It's my newest life supplement—*schroederbalance.*"

He handed me his water gourd. I hesitated. "What's in it?"

"That's still a secret. I'm having a party next month at the Four Seasons to launch the new *schroederbalance* line. You'll have to come."

"Try it, darling, it's wonderful," said the woman to my left. She was wearing a one-piece parachute suit drawn in at the waist with a Gucci belt.

Everyone in the little rice circle was smiling at me expectantly. There was nothing to do but down the tablet. Schroeder patted my knee. Good puppy, Kieran.

"How's your story coming?" he asked sotto voce.

"It's on hold."

"Really? How come?"

"I've had a couple of other deadlines land in my lap," I lied.

"Well, if you need to talk to me again, you've got my number," he said, ever the genial solipsist, before returning to his conversation.

Conversation, hell; lecture was the word. Schroeder was rhapsodizing about his latest discovery, "food combining"—the practice of eating two different foods together to increase the nutritional benefit of each. Everyone on our little straw-mat island seemed to find the subject fascinating, but my mind was wandering from boredom and hunger. The only foods I wanted to combine were a Jumbo Jack and a bag of onion rings.

When Schroeder began to enthuse eloquent about the digestive value of combining legumes with citrus, I caught Marilyn Amsterdam's eye and waved at her. With a please-don't-let-*me*-interrupt pat on his shoulder, I left the good doctor in the midst of a scintillating monologue about the miracles of eating lentils with your grapefruit.

Over by the front door, one of the blow-dried talking heads from Channel 9 was doing a live remote. I checked her out for a while. Sometimes I wondered if my newscaster fetish was getting out of control, but there's just something about a woman in a business suit holding a microphone with a windscreen. I was so absorbed watching the Barbie doll in banker drag that it took me a minute to register the identity of the woman who pushed past me and disappeared out the door of the soundstage.

Maria Tankovich.

I darted outside, hoping to catch her before she got into her car, but she was leaning against the building, pulling on a Benson & Hedges with such satisfaction that I found myself wishing I smoked.

Maria was barely five feet tall, even in stiletto heels. Her hair was half-spiked, half-bobbed, and she wore a man's button-down shirt, untucked, with the sleeves rolled up. It was hard to imagine this punky gamine as the woman whose book had shorted out half the pacemakers in Hollywood.

While I was trying to think of a way to introduce myself, she looked over and said, "Hello."

I gave her my name. She nodded, but didn't reciprocate. I guess the Maria Tankoviches of this world assume that people know who they are. She offered me her pack of cigarettes and withdrew it again before I could take one. "No, you don't smoke."

"How do you know?"

"It's a guess. But I'm a good guesser." She stuck her hand back into her purse. This time she pulled out a red-and-white bag. Mrs. Fields' Cookies.

"White-chocolate macadamia. Try one, they're fabulous."

I hesitated, momentarily nonplussed by a woman who would bring gourmet cookies to a hunger benefit.

"Oh, come on. They're delicious." She popped one into her mouth. "You can go back inside and be bored and eat rice, or you can stand out here and be entertained by me while you eat this cookie. It's not going to make one bit of difference to the Flies-on-the-Children Foundation."

I took a cookie. She put the bag back in her purse and grinned.

Applause floated out through the open door, and the stentorian voice of Roger Dahlgren began to recite some suspiciously round statistics about how many acres of grain it takes to produce one hamburger. Dahlgren was a fixture at these left-leaning dinners. He'd begun his career playing a teddy-bear romantic lead, and had spent the next two decades trying to reinvent himself as the conscience of Hollywood. Though he was only in his mid-forties, he came off like John Houseman without the sense of humor.

"*That's* why I came out here," Maria said. "I don't have the stomach to be lectured to by that pompous ass. Our families grew up next door to each other. My father used to produce his father's pictures, those awful things with pirates swinging from chandeliers. Some swashbuckler; more like a *swishbuckler*, if you ask me. Anyway, little Rog used to come over to play in my sandbox and try to get into my pants. Once a lech, always a lech." She lit another cigarette and exhaled dismissively. "I kicked him in the balls when I was seven."

"Really? What happened?"

"Nothing. His mother's housekeeper came over to yell at my mother's housekeeper. Just another day on Camden Drive. My mother was upstairs, marinating in Smirnoff, and missed the whole brouhaha."

Maria was the child of "Tank" Tankovich, the Russian émigré producer, and Carmel Day, the musical-comedy star who spent her ingenuedom waltzing with Fred Astaire in Technicolor and tippy-tapping with Gene Kelly in CinemaScope. Tank, his arteries clogged with red meat and Scotch, had gone on to the big Romanoff's in the sky several years ago; but Carmel was still rattling around the ancestral home, accepting daily deliveries from Beverly Glen Liquor and doing occasional duty on the few game shows that were left. Her most recent venture had been a late-night infomercial for

The Carmel Day Psychic Assistance Network. Maria had quite a lineage.

"Not that I've got a right to criticize a drunk, even if said drunk is my own mother." She held her cigarette between her thumb and index finger and examined it sternly. "I've eliminated all those things that kill me quickly, but I haven't been able to get rid of the ones that kill me slowly."

Marilyn Amsterdam emerged from the soundstage, loading lenses back into her bag. We waved good-bye to each other. Maria watched, bemused.

"What are you possibly going to write about this?" she wondered.

"The truth. They came, they saw, they ate, they talked."

"That's not the truth. If you ever wrote the truth, you'd never get invited back to any of these parties."

"So what's the truth?"

"The truth is: If all these people had spent the evening ladling out food at the Union Rescue Mission, they would have made a real difference in who goes to bed hungry tonight. Not a big difference, maybe, but a real one. And you may quote me on that, if you clean up the grammar first."

I smiled at her. "So if you tell the truth, how do you get invited back?"

" 'Cause I've been around longer than any of 'em. I'm the child of *Hollywood royalty*." She did a grotesque Shirley Temple, lewdly lifting an imaginary pinafore and sticking a middle finger into her cheek. "Seriously, I'd rather go through peritonitis than a Hollywood benefit. But it's like a tune-up to do it every so often—and I do enjoy watching these people run from me when I walk in the door. Being seen with Maria Tankovich can be hazardous to your professional health." She lit another cigarette and brushed ashes off her shirt. "In this town, they treat the truth like a fart in church."

"You really into the truth?"

"You didn't read my book?"

"Sure I did."

"Okay, then."

"Okay, then. Tell me about Monica Slezak."

Maria caught her breath for a moment, then studied me with new interest. "Monica Slezak," she said softly. "Poor little bird. I worked with her on *White Ice*. Why do you want to know about Monica Slezak?"

I told her about my article. She shrugged.

"Well, we didn't keep in contact after *White Ice*," she said. "She and Gregory weren't the types for the party circuit. They kept to themselves. I always had the impression that she wasn't comfortable in Hollywood. She was an English teacher. From *Nebraska* or some such place."

I smiled politely. Industry types can be terribly patronizing when it comes to anyone who doesn't live in L.A. or New York. They call them "flyovers"—the people they fly over on their way to the other coast. The irony, of course, is that most of the people in the industry came from somewhere else themselves. As soon as they make their pile, they're off to live on a farm in Montana or Virginia, complaining about the "hollow values" of Hollywood and how hard it is to raise children there.

"How was she as a producer?"

Maria shrugged. "She was okay. She picked things up quickly. Greg and I helped her out. It was only her second movie, and the first one was some piece of shit about flamenco dancers."

"So Gregory Slezak ran things on the set."

"No, not really." She pressed her hand to her forehead. "How do I explain it? He kept his eye on the big stuff—the director, the actors, the studio execs—and Monica dealt with the littler things. But don't get me wrong. She pulled her weight. When things got slow on the set, we used to talk about books. You know how many people actually read books out here. Not many. I mean, she was the one who had gotten the rights to *White Ice*, back when no one had ever heard of it. By the time it hit the best-seller list, we were already in pre-production. She got the rights to that dirt-cheap."

"Monica bought the rights to *White Ice?*"

More applause drifted out the door, ghostly handclaps that floated away on the light Santa Ana winds. I should have been back inside, working, but something was beginning to prickle at the back of my neck.

Maria snorted. "The only thing Greg Slezak reads is scripts. He would never have heard of *White Ice*."

I remembered the thousands of books on the Slezaks' shelves.

"You know, she bought the rights to *The Midnight Hour*, too."

"She bought the rights for all their pictures. *Dark at the End of the Tunnel* and *The Belgium Diaries* and that memoir of Suzan Morninglory's."

"What?"

"You know who I mean," she said impatiently. "That sow. The Kathryn Kuhlman of the HIV set. What the hell was that book called—"

I remembered the name from Monica's obituary.

*"That Which Makes Me Stronger?"*

"Yeah. What are they calling the movie? Greg Slezak's shooting it now, or he's about to start. What the hell is it called?" She pounded her temple. "This happens to me all the time. I never forget a name, but I swear, I've got Title Alzheimer's—"

*"A Stronger Woman."*

"That's the one."

We talked for a while after that, but I don't remember much of it.

An hour later, I was waiting for my car. I was hungry, and there was a story to be written when I got home, but I couldn't even think about food or work.

*A Stronger Woman* was the film adaptation of *That Which Makes Me Stronger*—

—which was a vapid self-help book that had surprised everyone when it became a best-seller.

When did Monica Slezak buy it?

How much did she pay?

How much money was Suzan Morninglory losing?

And why hadn't Monica wanted to direct it herself?

I was distracted by the sight of a willowy blond valet getting out of a luxury sedan: an AMW in a BMW. The parkers at this event were all college women. The agency, which only hired Penthouse Pet material to park cars, called itself Valet Girls.

"Hello, Kieran."

I turned around.

It was Cathy Bates.

She had cropped her hair razor-close and was wearing an unconstructed leather jacket that gave her a Grace Jones aspect. She seemed to be staring at me oddly, but maybe it was just the severity of her new style. It seemed a little over-the-top to me.

"How was your trip to New York?" I said, still startled.

"Fine."

"Getting everything set for your next picture?"

"Mm-hm."

"How's it coming?"

"Fine."

It wasn't my imagination; she was staring at me balefully, as if she wanted to push me into the line of oncoming cars. I wondered if I'd said something wrong, and then I knew what it was.

Cathy Bates wasn't nearly as gracious in defeat as she was in triumph.

A black limousine left a line of its brothers and pulled up to the curb in front of us. Cathy opened the door herself, not waiting for the chauffeur.

"See you around," I said.

"See you around," she repeated, shutting the door and leaving me to look at my own face in the reflective glass.

The limo pulled into the stream of traffic, a shiny black fish rejoining its school, and was gone.

# =20=

SPINNING TIN WINDMILLS, hundreds of them, sprouted up and down the scorched brown rocks on either side of Interstate 10.

"What are those for?" I asked.

"Energy production, I imagine," Claudia said. She was trying to tie a pink tulle scarf around her head, a difficult job in a speeding convertible.

"But how do they work?"

"Search me. You want some 7-Up?"

"Yeah."

She guided the can to my mouth, and I tasted her lipstick on the end of the straw.

We were almost there. After the giant plaster dinosaurs at the Cabazon truck stop, the weird fields of windmills were the last landmark on the road from Los Angeles to Palm Springs. It had become a tradition: whenever Claudia and I were feeling particularly wrung out, we'd rent a car, drive out to the desert, and splurge on a motel room. I usually lounged around the pool, reading Pushkin and mulling over what the hell I intended to do with my life. Claudia slept. Still, the excursions usually put a little zing back into our sex life; Palm Springs was the place where we'd attempted the Bathtub Incident.

Claudia was looking less stressed already: her hair was blowing in the breeze and she was wearing the pair of white-rimmed shades that I thought of as her *La Dolce Vita* glasses. I took another slug of 7-Up and floored the gas pedal, humming the theme to *A Man and a Woman*.

When we got to Highway 111, I turned off the interstate and drove through the crags that led to the city. At the edge of town, we pulled into a huge liquor store with tartan carpeting and took six-packs of Dr Pepper and Heineken from the refrigerator case. A leathery desert matron with purple eye shadow and a condominium of peroxided hair rang us up. We were back.

In the 1940s, Palm Springs was a getaway for Hollywood stars, a place where they could misbehave, an orgy of boozing and wenching unobserved by studio chiefs and gossip columnists. Today, it was a tourist destination: poky in the summer, busy with snowbirds and sun-seekers in the winter. The year-round residents were mostly retirees and gay yuppies, many of whom had purchased the old movie-star compounds and converted them to clothing-optional guest houses.

We puttered through the traffic on Palm Canyon Drive, where the shop windows displayed white bucks, white belts, and polyester jackets with epaulets. To the left, there was nothing but sand and scrub; to the right, rugged peaks scraped a flat blue sky. It was a warm day, but there was still a light chill in the air as a reminder of how cold the desert could be at night. Cirrus feather clouds, paintbrush-perfect, finished the picture.

Claudia pointed toward a hill where a flying-saucer house was perched amid the rocks. "Look," she said. "Bob Hope's place." Back in the early sixties, Hope's hideaway must have been a space-age vision. Today it was quaint, one of those Houses of the Future you see in photographs of the World's Fair. Most of Hollywood had deserted the desert, and the hoary old ones who were left had streets named after them: Bob Hope Drive, Gerald Ford Drive, Gene Autry Trail. If there was a real celebrity in town, he or she was probably at the Betty Ford Center, drying out and making deals.

I swung off the boulevard and pulled under the thatched carport of our usual stopping point, the Hanailea Motor Court. The Hanailea was one of the last Eisenhower-era motels on the strip, a two-story horseshoe of rooms that encircled a large pool and tiny Jacuzzi. We liked it because it was decrepit and it was cheap. Hotel designers hadn't swooped down to rip out the crumbling Polynesian decor and install their horrid Santa Fe pastels. Nuclear families would drive up in their Ford Explorers, take one look at the peeling orange paint and Easter Island heads around the pool, and drive out again in search of a decent Motel 6.

We paid sixty-two dollars at the office, which got us two days' ownership of a rusty room key attached to a rubber pool float. Claudia turned the air conditioner on high and unpacked our bags while I pulled a pair of trunks over my spare tire. The pool was abandoned. We found a pair of chaise longues under a huge tiki and Claudia smeared sunblock all over the both of us before she went to sleep. I swam a few laps, drank a couple of Heinekens, and watched the white ball of desert sun chase the clouds across the sky until it got dark.

Claudia was quiet that night when we walked down the road to the nearby steak house. I knew when she was decompressing from work and I didn't press it. She had a chef's salad and I busted my diet with creamed spinach and a slab of prime rib. I chewed each bite thirty-two times and watched the Perry Como set gather around the piano bar, where a mummified guy in a tux held court behind a brandy snifter of bills.

By the time he got to a Bacharach medley, everyone was singing along, and Claudia was pressed up against me in the banquette, her fingertips resting on the inside of my thigh, her head on my shoulder. I wound a piece of her hair around my finger. It smelled like chlorine and hot desert sun. We sat like that, not moving, not talking, through "Volare," "Georgy Girl," and "Love Is Blue."

Back at the hotel, Claudia undressed and sprawled across the bedspread, arms and legs out in an X shape. I climbed into the lower half of the X and laid my head on the inside of her thigh, tickling her crotch with my nose.

"How're you doing?" she asked.

"Good."

"You're thinking about Monica Slezak again, aren't you?"

"Nope."

"What are you thinking about?"

"Right now I'm thinking, gee, your hair smells terrific."

She cuffed the top of my head. "You're bad."

"I know."

"You having fun?"

"Yeah. Are you?"

"Yeah."

"Anything you want to talk about?"

"Yeah," she said. "But not now. Tomorrow."

"It's a date," I said, scooting my head northward as Claudia scissor-locked her legs around my neck like a vise.

An hour later, she was asleep.

I put on my still-damp bathing suit, picked up my backpack with the Slezak files, and went down to the pool. No one was around. The only sound came from a few faint TVs in the distance. The sky was a cereal bowl of stars.

I ripped the plastic off a new legal pad, printed MONICA at the top of the page, drew a line under it, and made a list.

> Gregory Slezak
> Alison Sewell
> Drew Wilson
> Suzan Morninglory
> Adam Davies
> Eric Schroeder
> ?????
> Suicide

That was a big help. I turned the page and began jotting down notes, letting myself free-associate.

Say Gregory Slezak killed his wife. What would his motive have been? You don't kill your wife just to get a picture scratched. Still, something about his story had been nagging at me ever since that day at his house: the flowers. I couldn't believe he'd buy irises for Monica unless she was upset about losing the nomination. Or was she upset about something else?

I wrote down Alison Sewell's name and circled it. She was at the banquet; she could have followed Monica into the bathroom, shot her, and arranged the scene to look like a suicide. That didn't explain the note, of course, but there was a bigger question: What would Alison have to gain? On the contrary, it seemed to me, she had a lot to lose. If there was a motive there, I was missing it. I put a question mark in Alison's circle.

Suzan Morninglory and Adam Davies got their own circles, connected with a thick line. Both of them were at the Women in the

Industry dinner. Forget about fixing the script in the pinks; Davies stood to lose millions if *The Midnight Hour* flopped as a movie, and he certainly knew that if Monica was out of the way, the project was on ice. As for Morninglory, she could have shot her for revenge, or to try to regain control of the property. I drew dollar signs around both of their names, but it didn't seem to fit. Davies could have put the picture into turnaround with Monica alive or dead. Morninglory didn't get the rights to her book reverted just because the purchaser died. The movie was still on.

I gave Schroeder his own satellite, far from the other names. He was still a cipher.

I looked at my little chart. The more I looked, the less it made sense. A real detective might have seen some pattern to it, but I wasn't a real detective; I was just a professional canapé-eater.

To hell with it. I was bloated and sun-drunk and tired.

I tried to shove the legal pad into the backpack, but it wouldn't fit. My backpack, once a sleek leather package, now looked like it did back in college during a particularly horrible eighteen-credit semester. I dumped the pack out on the chaise longue to sort through some of the detritus.

There was the faxed suicide note . . . Monica's obituaries . . . my notes from the Alison Sewell interview . . . the transcripts from Slezak, Schroeder, and Davies . . . Stan Nyman's folder . . . the schroederfoods press kit . . . the Slezak clippings from the Academy library . . . Slezak's note to Monica . . . Wilson's book . . . Monica's script of Wilson's book . . . the copy of *Biz* . . . and several Pee-Chees that I had stupidly labeled MISCELLANEOUS.

I opened one of them and discovered "Nice Guys Finish First," the Gregory Slezak profile, as well as a story on the Film Futures Foundation, the fledgling-director program that the Slezaks had founded at USC. I wadded them up and tossed them at the nearest trash can. Two points. The schroederfoods press kit was too big to wad up and slam-dunk, so I opened it. Nothing there but Schroeder's artfully airbrushed eight-by-ten, a typed biography, and a bunch of third-generation Xeroxes from *People* and *The Wall Street Journal.*

The *People* article had several photos, including one of Schroeder at a party with Meg Campbell and—surprise—Monica. The caption read: *Meg Campbell and producer Monica Slezak ("A Lover's Question") do some nutritional networking with bad-boy-turned-good-doctor Erich Schroeder. Schroeder's client list includes many Tinseltown glitterati.*

I studied the photo, which was muddy from the photocopying. Schroeder was telling the actress something that must have been a real scream; her mouth was a rictus of caps. Monica was in the background, half-hidden by Schroeder's shoulder, smiling demurely and somewhat nervously. I checked the date (one year ago), and then I glanced at the caption again.

It spelled Schroeder's first name with a *ch*, not a *c*.

A warm sirocco came off the desert, guttering the gas flames in the tiki lights. Something akin to déjà vu prickled at the back of my neck. A quick scrabble through the folders, and there it was, in the clipping from *Le Hills*: Monica and Gregory with Schroeder. *Erich* Schroeder.

Just to be sure, I rechecked the suicide note, but I already knew: Monica had spelled Erich with a *c*.

I read Schroeder's own typed biography. It was *ch* all the way through. Erich Schroeder.

I scratched my sunburned back. Had Monica simply misspelled his name? You're not likely to misspell the name of someone you know well enough to include in a suicide note. Maybe Monica was stoned on Zapax, or maybe her spelling was as lousy as her screenplay. But the handwriting had been Palmer-method perfect, and Monica *had* been an English teacher.

There was another possibility, one that hadn't occurred to me until that moment. Maybe Erich Schroeder didn't *seem* to fit into this puzzle—because he really *didn't* fit at all.

The light in the pool shut off abruptly, turning the water from shimmering blue to ink.

I slipped into my flip-flops and padded back to Room 23. Claudia was curled into the fetal position, asleep. I slipped off the bathing suit and climbed in bed behind her, my chest against her back. She stirred lightly and pressed her backside against my crotch. It was a long time before I dropped off to sleep.

\* \* \*

The next morning we woke up late, spent an hour cuddling and making use of the gym bag, and decided to drive out to Indio to get breakfast. On the way back, we passed a huge road stand. "Date shakes," Claudia said. "Let's stop."

The stand was one of those roadside-America places that sold all kinds of date baskets and gift packs, wrapped up with amber cellophane. In the back was a little theater where they showed a campy old filmstrip called *The Sex Life of the Date*. We took our shakes into the cool darkness and watched faded images of field hands pollinating date trees and 1950s housewives performing culinary magic with fat medjools and date crystals. The shakes were so good we stopped on the way out and bought two more from a sullen teenager who had an eggplant-colored bob and an eight-gauge ring in her nose.

Back in the convertible, Claudia shook her head. "That girl looked like any kid you'd see on Melrose," she said. "Ever since MTV, there's no underground culture anymore."

"Trends make it out to the desert, too."

"Yeah, but there used to be a lag time. Now everything is happening everywhere, simultaneously. Even out here, in the yuccas and the dust."

We drove another mile or two. Chewy pieces of date kept getting stuck in my straw. An emerald golf course rose from the parched sand on our left, brought to life by God knows how many thousands of gallons of water.

Eric/Erich was heavy on my mind, as it had been all morning. I was tired of thinking about it.

"You said you had something to talk about," I reminded her.

Claudia slid over on the seat and laid her head on my shoulder. "I'm thinking of selling Cafe Canem."

"And do what?"

"I don't know. Move back to New Orleans. Rent a little shop in the Quarter. Maybe open up another coffeehouse there."

I sucked on my straw and said nothing.

"All I wanted was a place where people could write and talk," she said. "Someplace I could fix up myself. Make it a little bit unique, a little bit underground. A place that was . . . kind of a secret, I guess.

And what do I have? Canem is a movie set half the time. And when it's not, it's a yuppie hangout."

"A yuppie hangout that's kept you from having to get a day job."

"I know." Claudia slumped in her seat like a little girl. "I feel like one of those punk bands that sell a million records and then spend the rest of their lives trying to get rid of their fans."

I kept my voice impassive. "What brought all this on?"

"The copy shop next door is going out of business. The realtor called and wanted to know if I'd be interested in knocking out the west wall and expanding. So I called my lawyer and my accountant and they told me that it would make sense."

"Well, it does make sense."

Claudia groaned. "I've got an *accountant*. And a *lawyer*. That's why I'm thinking of giving it up."

I sucked the last of the shake through the straw and threw the empty cup in the backseat. "You're a moron, Claude."

"I know," she said in a soft voice.

"No, you don't. You don't have any idea. It's a *business*, Claudia, not a literary salon. It's none of your business if people would rather read Danielle Steel instead of Proust. Or write bad poetry. Or pick each other up."

"Why are you so steamed?"

"Because! You climb all over my ass for blowing *my* life? You've actually built something out of nothing, and all you can think of doing is shutting it down—"

"Slow down."

"I'm not finished. Don't tell me to slow down."

"No," she said quietly. "Slow down."

I looked at the speedometer. Seventy-five.

I took my foot off the gas and cruised into the right lane. We passed the golf course and got back on the tacky strip of El Pollo Locos and Taco Bells. Claudia fiddled with the strap on her purse and didn't utter a word.

"New Orleans," I finally said. "That's great. You work hard, build something, and you want to cut and run back home."

"It's not your business, Kieran."

"Claudia, you just can't commit to anything."

"You're not talking about New Orleans. You're talking about us."

"Yeah, well, when you're right, you're right."

I pulled across a couple of lanes of traffic and swung left with a screech of brakes, scraping the undercarriage of the car on the macadam of the Hanailea.

"Would you be a little careful? It's a rent-a-car," she said, irritated for the first time.

I pulled into our space, got out, and slammed the door. "That's the good part about rentals, Claude. You can always turn them in when you wear them out. Or when you get tired of them."

"Kieran," she said, but I was halfway up the stairs to our room.

# THREE

# =21=

"HELLO, PEACHES." It was Jocelyn, sounding dangerously chipper. I pulled up the covers on the futon and checked the clock: 6:25 A.M., Left Coast time. In the background, I heard car horns blaring. "Where are you calling from?" I said groggily.

"Central Park West. We're stopped for a motorcade. *Get away from this car or I will kill you,*" she said.

"Jocelyn? Are you all right?"

"I'm fine. There was a filthy man with a squeegee approaching. It's not important. Listen, peaches, I just had a lovely breakfast with Suzanne Christie at Sandcastle Press. She's looking for someone to do a quickie paperback biography of Courtney Menzies. Forty thousand words, two weeks."

"Wow," I said. Courtney Menzies was the thirty-two-year-old star of a nighttime soap opera about Malibu high school students with overactive libidos. As for my own libido, I'd been spending my nights alone on the futon ever since Claudia and I got back from Palm Springs.

Our drive back had been unrancorous and dangerously cordial, like a pair of divorced parents with joint custody forced to make a car trip together. Since we'd been back, she had engineered the schedule at Cafe Canem so we worked different shifts and didn't see each other for more than a few minutes a day. I hadn't asked her if she was planning to expand the coffeehouse or move back to Louisiana; I didn't dare and I didn't much care. Cathy Bates could have her, and to hell with them.

"It's four thousand," Jocelyn said. "The split is two up front, two on delivery. Shall I call her back and tell her we're interested?"

"Four thousand? That's only ten cents a word, Jocelyn."

"I know, and the royalties are nonexistent. But I think I can push her to five if we can get the contract signed ASAP."

"Meaning before Courtney hits menopause."

"You're a regular David Letterman in the morning. Are we interested?"

"No. Well, maybe. Look, it's six-thirty, Jocelyn. I don't know anything at six-thirty."

"You're still working on the Monica Slezak thing."

"Yes, I am still working on that *thing.*"

"Oh, Kieran. Put it aside. I'm offering you the easiest four thousand dollars you'll ever make. It won't take you more than two weeks. Don't think of it as ten cents a word; think of it as two thousand dollars a week. Less fifteen percent, of course."

"Of course."

I rolled over and picked at a piece of kapok peeking out of the futon. It *would* be an easy four thousand: a few photocopy sessions at the Academy library and a couple of all-nighters would finish it off. These quickie biographies were more like term papers than books, and about as original. Still, the idea was loathsome.

"Let me sleep on it for a few days."

She chose to miss the sarcasm. "Kieran, if you want my advice, take this book. It's the best we can do right now."

"No."

A shower of white noise came through the line. I realized that I'd never said no to Jocelyn before. When the line cleared, she said, "What?"

"I said . . . I don't know."

She sighed. "My poor ambivalent Kieran. All right. Do what you need to do. But let me know within the week."

"Two weeks."

"*One* week. I'll tell Suzanne you're swamped with Oscar coverage, but I can't keep her hanging on much—"

There was an odd pause. "Are you there?" I asked.

"Yes. I'm getting a fax. Call me next week, peaches."

That afternoon, I drove north on the Pacific Coast Highway toward Malibu. It was a beautiful March day, perfect as a soft-drink commercial. To the left of the highway stretched the Santa Monica Bay; to the right, the cliffs and canyons honeycombed with quaint little million-dollar cottages. A few empty foundations still stood in some knolls where residents had fled the fires of '93. Here and there a brick chimney or a stone skeleton poked from the underbrush in a Modigliani vertical line. The Thelma Todd house was at the next light, a dilapidated old *Sunset Boulevard* place where, decades before, a silent film queen had been found murdered in her garage. Death-styles of the rich and famous. Seagulls wheeled above the highway, flying home from a morning of feasting on trash in the lunch court at Palisades High.

The interview had been a bitch to set up. A man who called himself "J.R., Ms. Morninglory's assistant for press relations," had been my adversary in a marathon phone duel for two weeks. By the fourth call, I recognized a brush-off. Morninglory thought that if she threw enough roadblocks in my way, my deadline would expire, or I'd just give up and quit calling.

Wrong. I phoned Gregory Slezak, made small talk for a few minutes, assumed wounded puzzlement at Morninglory's busy schedule, and counted on him to do the rest. Within a day, J.R. called to say that a hole had opened in Ms. Morninglory's calendar. Could I come up to the office the next day at one o'clock?

You bet your amethysts I could, Suzan Morninglory.

I reached the Topanga Canyon intersection and swung right. As I drove into the scrubby hills, I grinned. Aimee Semple McPherson had had her headquarters up here, too.

The Morning's Glory compound—for *compound* was the first word that came to mind—was a bunker of lilac-colored concrete built against the side of a hill, fireproof and impervious to the elements. A couple of smaller buildings ran down the slope in a series of terraces. The whole spread was the shade of the jacaranda blossoms that littered the rutted road leading from Topanga Canyon Drive. I pulled the Buick under a copse of jacaranda trees, between a brand-new Viper and a Ford Explorer whose bumper sticker chirped MIRACLES HAPPEN.

So does shit, I thought, strolling up to the entrance.

The lobby was an airy glass box with blond parquet floors. Home-made patchwork quilts hung in wooden frames, the squares of cloth all in different shades of purple. A languid young man behind the desk stopped playing with his hair long enough to take my name. While I waited, I sat down and flipped through a pile of publications: *Whole Life Times, Frontiers, Women's Wellness,* and something called *Positively Alive!*, a life-style magazine for HIV-positives.

I was reading recipes for hi-cal entrees guarnateed to pack on the pounds when another functionary materialized. Like the receptionist, he wore a turtleneck with an enameled red-ribbon pin over the breast. He introduced himself as J.R. and invited me to come along.

I followed J.R. down a long, cool passageway that reminded me of the grand hall in Schroeder's office. Other employees glided past. Though they were different ages and sizes, they were all somehow like J.R.: calm and bland, talking in murmurs. All of the Morning's Glory disciples seemed to have the same casual, unruffled demeanor. Pedro called them the Stepford Fags.

J.R. led me into a long, low office at the end of the hall. One whole wall was glass; it overlooked the hills and the whitecapped ocean. Against the other wall, Herself was seated on the floor, in the midst of several enormous batik pillows meant to take the place of a sofa. In front of her was an amethyst marble table, with a steaming mug of blood-red tea and a white plastic box that emitted sounds of the surf. Morninglory was an imposing figure even in repose, clad in her usual diaphanous caftan with a beeper clipped to the bodice. I felt as if I'd been granted an audience with the Pope, or—considering her girth—a rather impatient Buddha.

J.R. closed the door and glided over to another pillow at Morninglory's side. Apparently he wasn't going to leave. Normally I object when publicists sit in on interviews, but I decided to let it pass. As he sat down, I realized that J.R. was the man who had followed me out to my car the night of the Morning's Glory meeting in West Hollywood.

I perched on a stack of pillows across from Morninglory. She took the beeper from her bosom, pushed a few buttons, and set it on the table between us. It wasn't a beeper after all; it was a kitchen timer. Subtle.

"Gregory Slezak told me to cooperate with you in any way possible," she said, by way of greeting.

"And I appreciate it. Shall we start?"

She waved her hand imperiously. No time for niceties. I got out my notepad and tape recorder and began with the purchase of the film rights to *That Which Makes Me Stronger*. She nodded impatiently. "What did you want to know?"

"When did the Slezaks buy the film rights?"

"I don't remember the exact date. It was about a year ago. Monica read it before it was published, back when it was still in galleys."

"Did Monica buy it because she wanted to direct it?"

"No. She wanted to produce it. Gregory was going to direct it."

"I don't understand. Monica wanted to get out of producing. She was adapting and directing Drew Wilson's book. Didn't she ever indicate an interest in doing that with your book?"

"Never. We both thought the material would be better served with Monica as a producer. No studio would have come up with the money to have a first-time director take on what they consider a risky project. And they do consider it risky, which is why they got someone as experienced as Sam Slater to adapt it. After all, you can't insert a car chase or a gun battle, so there will always be people who assume the public isn't ready for it. Monica never thought of it as a risky project, which is why I knew she was the woman I wanted to shape the material and oversee the production."

The pillows were uncomfortable. I humped my butt around as unobtrusively as I could. "I know the contributions you've made to Women in the Industry, so I guess I'm a little surprised that *A Stronger Woman* is going to be written and directed by men."

"You're questioning Gregory Slezak's ability?" she said lightly.

"Not at all. It's just that the theme of your book is women claiming their inner power, and it's not like there aren't qualified women directors. Look at Jane Campion, Martha Coolidge, Penelope Spheeris—"

"There's power and then there's *power*. You know how much power women have in Hollywood. Writers have even less. How many writers in Hollywood have creative control? If they won't give it to Tom Clancy, they won't give it to me. The book was optioned by Monica and Gregory, two people I like and respect. After that, I was out of the decision-making loop." She gave me a gentle, winning smile. This woman was cool as melon soup. "You write about Hollywood. You know that a lot of books get optioned, and very few of them get made. And I wanted this movie made."

"So the Slezaks decided who would direct."

"We all decided—or, rather, there was nothing to decide. It was an obvious decision. Gregory would direct, and both he and Monica would produce. I'm the technical adviser and associate producer."

I pretended to shuffle through my notes. "I'm sorry, but you said they optioned the book when?"

"A year ago."

"About, say, six months before it was published?"

"More or less."

"So I suppose that they got the rights for a bargain."

She pressed her fingers together in some isometric position. "Why would you say that?"

"Number one, you were a first-time author. Number two, it didn't become a best-seller until later. Number three, it's a book on spirituality. How much were the rights?"

"I can't tell you that," she said reprovingly, as if I were a very naughty reporter indeed.

"Ballpark, then." I took a deep breath and conjured a number. "My sources told me six figures. Very low six figures."

Morninglory sipped her tea placidly and said nothing, but J.R. stirred. "Next question."

"Excuse me?"

"You heard me. That's not appropriate. Next question."

*O-kay.* I shifted on my pillows again to keep them from toppling, and realized that they had been stacked that way on purpose. Winning through intimidation, New Age style.

"I suppose I'll have to go with what my sources tell me," I said, pretending to make a note. "So how's the pre-production coming?"

Morninglory smiled and put on her best "Entertainment Tonight" voice. "I'm delighted. Obviously you have to omit a lot when you're condensing a three-hundred-page book into a two-hour movie, but Sam Slater wrote a wonderful script. Gregory understands the book. Meg Campbell's been around a few times to observe me and work on her character. Just yesterday, we got permission to film at some sacred sites in Tibet and Chile. It looks *auspicious.*" She went on a five-minute jag that was half stump speech, half press release. Politicians may be the champs at obfuscation, but no one can touch Hollywood types when it comes to spitting out cheery pabulum.

When she was done speechifying, there was silence, broken only by the sound of wind chimes tinkling in the central air-conditioning. I took a deep breath and sneaked a glance at the timer, which sat on the table between us like the Wicked Witch's hourglass in *The Wizard of Oz*.

"Well. Great. I think we have enough about the film. Now I'd like to talk about Monica herself. How long had you known her?"

If J.R. was a dog, he would have bristled, but Morninglory was unflappable. "I'd never met her before she bought the rights to my book."

"But you knew who she was?"

"Oh, of course."

"Gregory said that you were a great comfort to her emotionally."

"That's nice to know."

"Did she see you professionally, or was it more of a casual relationship?"

Morninglory looked out at the ocean. "Without divulging any confidences, I can tell you that we discussed some problems that she had been having, just as any friends would, and I tried to show her some approaches to working *within* them."

"So you were counseling her for manic depression."

"That's not a term I use."

"What isn't a term you'd use? Counseling or manic depression?"

"Neither, really. But I was speaking of so-called manic depression."

"What would your term be?"

Suzan Morninglory exhaled softly, a weight-of-the-world sigh, and got up with a great clanking of bracelets. She crossed to a low bookshelf, removed a lavender plastic slipcase, and brought it back to me. Large purple letters proclaimed it THE MORNING'S GLORY PLAN FOR STRONGER SELFHOOD.

I opened it. Inside were three cassettes, one videotape, and a paperback with the same title. The topic might have been self-help, but it looked for all the world like one of those make-a-fortune-in-real-estate packages they sell on late-night TV.

"Interesting. Can I take this with me?"

"We're running short, but I'll have J.R. send you one. Look. This is really what I wanted you to see." She thumbed through the paperback to Chapter 7, "The Fallacy of Diagnosis."

"What is the opposite of a diagnosis?" she asked.

"A misdiagnosis?"

"No, no, no. The dictionary defines *diagnosis* as 'the act of defining a disease or problem from known symptoms.' So the opposite of a diagnosis would be—"

I flashed back to my interview with Dr. Schroeder. *"Not* defining a disease."

"Precisely. Monica Slezak was in pain—spiritual pain as well as physical pain. Rather than take away the physical pain with drugs, I was working with her to eliminate the metaphysical pain—the true source of her problems."

"Which was?"

"Which was confidential."

"I'm not asking you to divulge a confidence. I just want to know what the treatment program was."

"It's all in this course. I encourage people to spend at least as much time on *metaphysical* fitness as they do on *physical* fitness—"

I was getting impatient with this semantic gobbledygook. "And just how do you do that?"

"We start with outlining goals—targeting the problem, writing it down, tallying strengths and weaknesses. If you're strong in one area, you don't need to work on it. If you're weak, you concentrate on that."

"Kind of like a spiritual pentathlete."

If she noticed the snottiness, she gave no sign. "Precisely. And to do that, we use a whole variety of things. Counseling. Daily affirmations. Letters to yourself. Creative visualizations. Journeys."

"Journeys? Where?"

"Not real journeys. Journeys are what we call journals. After all, what is a journal but a written record of the journey of the self?"

"I see." And I did. Like Dr. Schroeder, Suzan Morninglory wasn't selling snake oil or lies, but pure common sense, tarted up in wipe-clean plastic slipcases and marketed as something new. Successful film-industry people have always needed someone to reassure them that they're decent and moral folk, and Morninglory was the right woman in the right place at the right time. She hawked Cosmic Wisdom the way Wolfgang Puck sold frozen pizzas, and with the same success.

"But how would you characterize what you were doing for her if it wasn't a therapy relationship?"

"Why are you so hung up on these terms?"

"Bear with me. Were you her therapist, or her friend?"

"Off the record?" She waited for my assent. "Somewhere between a therapist and a friend."

"Can you tell me if what she was working through could have had any relation to her suicide?"

"No. Not that I could see. What happened to Monica is as much a mystery to me as it is a tragedy."

"In retrospect, can you see any signs that she was—"

"I've thought about it and thought about it. I've even gone back through my notes, and there's not a one. What happened to Monica is as much a mystery as a tragedy," she repeated. I had a feeling she'd rehearsed the line.

This was going nowhere. Morninglory had me outfoxed, and she knew it. "Well, could you give me any personal anecdotes?"

"Anecdotes?"

"Speaking as one friend about another. The human side."

Morninglory nodded and spaded up a few meaningless Monica stories for me while I glanced at the timer. Time was running out. I chanced an interruption.

"By the way, in her suicide note, she had mentioned someone named Eric. Do you know who that was?"

The guru shrugged. "No."

"Could it have been Erich Schroeder? The nutritionist? Monica stopped seeing him just before she began seeing you."

The beeper on the table went off. She rose immediately. "It's possible," she said, extending her hand. "But I don't even know the man."

I wished Suzan Morninglory luck with *A Stronger Woman*, allowed J.R. to escort me back to my car, and sat there for a moment, thinking. The jacaranda tree had shed purple blooms all over my windshield.

Something was taking shape. I still couldn't make out its form. But a buzz had been droning in my head ever since I'd asked her about Eric, a buzz insistent and persistent as a car alarm.

*She knows. She knows. And she knows I don't know.*

I was getting close to something.

But what?

I drove down the hill, drumming my fingers on the steering wheel. The purple jacaranda flowers fluttered from my windshield all the way down Topanga Canyon, and by the time I turned back onto traffic-clogged PCH, they were gone.

# =22=

IF I HADN'T STOPPED TO DROP off my phone bill on the way home, if I hadn't spent an hour dawdling at the newsstand, if I hadn't grabbed a late-afternoon BLT at Callahan's . . . then I might have been home by six o'clock. But I wasn't, and I missed Vicky's call by ten minutes.

"Hello? Hello? Okay. I guess you're not home screening your calls or anything. This is Vicky. Andrew Wilson's girlfriend." She cleared her throat. Some people can't talk to answering machines; I usually prefer to. "Shoot. I've gotta leave for work now, but I probably won't be there till seven, so . . . Okay. Maybe you can leave a message for me at work and I'll try to call you on my break. Okay." She left a work number in the 818 area code and hung up. 818. The San Fernando Valley.

I jotted down the number, trying to suss out whether this meant Vicky had heard from Drew. Probably not. She would have mentioned it if he'd been in contact. I played the message again, but the only thing of significance I gleaned was that she called him Andrew instead of Drew, which meant she was either younger than I'd thought, or she was in love. Jeff Brenner once had a twenty-year-old girlfriend who consistently referred to him as "Jeffrey." Nauseating stuff.

On the off chance Vicky would still be home, I called her house. The Vicky-and-Travis message came on. I hung up and dialed the Valley number.

At first I thought I'd gotten the number wrong. It sounded like a party; I heard televised football and Van Halen. Through the din, a man yelled, "Fenders."

I disconnected and chewed on the phone antenna thoughtfully.

\* \* \*

The parking lot of Fenders was packed with cars, most of which were decorated with bumper stickers delineating the driver's favorite radio station (KKAS, Kick-Ass Rock) and preferred country of residence (USA Kicks Butt). Butt-kicking seemed to be very big among these people. Fenders itself was a squat cinderblock building half a block long, with several spiny satellite dishes on the roof and neon beer signs on the facade. Aerosmith poured from the open door. Even from the edge of the parking lot, I could smell the stink of buffalo wings and spilled beer and testosterone with no place to go.

Fenders didn't have a maître d' station, but there was a gift kiosk inside the door. T-shirts, key rings, and more bumper stickers were displayed in a glass counter. A cashier sat behind the counter on a high stool. She had on a pair of pre-shredded cutoffs that fit her like body paint and the halter top that all the employees wore, with the word FENDERS stretched across her tits in chrome lettering like the logo on a Coupe de Ville. Her hair was a fried blond tornado. What hath Farrah wrought.

I asked for Vicky. The woman parked a wad of fluorescent Bubble Yum between cheek and gum and said, "Blond Vicky or brunette Vicky?"

"Vicky from Silver Lake." It worked. The blond bombshelter told me in flawless Valleyspeak that the next time Vicky came by, she'd send her over to the bar. Slouching through the room, scuffing my way through peanut shells and crumpled serviettes, I kept my head down, hoping that no one would be seized with a sudden urge to kick *my* butt.

Fenders had been built as a roller disco, remodeled as a country bar during the urban-cowboy fad, switched back to disco in the eighties, back to country during the achy-breaky craze, and now it was—well, Fenders. The long bar was made of corrugated metal, decorated with license plates and other remnants from classic cruisers. Stick shifts took the place of tap handles, and the front of a Ford Skyliner had been hung by wires to make it appear to be crashing through the wall. The only thing that didn't look as if it came from a chop shop was a hairdresser's sink, complete with molded headrest, built into the middle of the bar. A hairdresser's sink? It was beyond me.

I squeezed into an empty stool and found myself sandwiched between two groups of soft non-forms dressed in California doofwear. With their billowing "muscle pants," fanny packs, and tank tops exposing gelatinous forearms, they looked like overgrown babies who had flown their cribs. The fattest one dipped a chicken wing into blue cheese and washed it down with a mugful of suds. These guys had never heard of the women's movement. Or cholesterol. Or Mothers Against Drunk Driving.

"Anchor Steam," I said to the bartender, who wore a referee's striped jersey.

"You got it, Holmes."

*Holmes.*

I accepted the cold bottle and swiveled to check out the room. Seven projection TVs hung from the ceiling, each broadcasting a different sports match, each louder than the next. On the ceiling, speakers the size of file cabinets reverberated with electric guitar, which ricocheted off the bare ceiling and made the corrugated tin vibrate. Drunken blue-collar dudes were everywhere, drinking draft beer, pawing passing waitresses, and slapping at each other like third-graders on a sugar buzz. It was the modern version of the old Playboy Club: a Chuck E. Cheese for twentynothing morons.

Behind the bar hung a gag calendar with a picture of a nude five-hundred-pound woman on it. One of the wits next to me was pummeling my ribs with an adipose elbow, allowing as to how he wouldn't fuck her with *my* dick, when a waitress materialized from the crowd. Like the other servers, she wore a tight halter top and cutoffs, with a beeper clipped to her waistband.

"Kieran?"

"Hi."

Her eyes lashed the room nervously. "I told you to call me, not to come down here. You could get my ass fired."

She was twenty-three or twenty-four, with long black hair and a pair of lapis eyes that didn't need makeup. She folded her arms across her chest and scowled. The halter top articulated her nipples as if they were gumdrops.

"I'm here now," was all I could manage.

"Yeah, well, no shit."

"I can leave."

Vicky thought about it before grabbing a passing waitress. "Doria, I'm going on break. Watch my tables for me."

Vicky led me to a small glass-topped table in the quietest part of the bar, near the gift kiosk. I sat down and watched her apply lip gloss. She used a napkin dispenser as a makeup mirror.

"Andrew called me this morning," she said.

"Where is he?"

"Like I know. He wouldn't say where he was calling from. The phone rang at eight-thirty, and there he was."

"That's pretty early in the morning for Drew."

"More like late from the night before." She blotted the goop from her lips on a napkin.

"So he's out of the hospital?"

"He was only there for two days. They released him on the condition that he would go check into this treatment facility in Century City. But the asshole skipped town."

"You sound mad," I said blandly. Active listening—a trick used by reporters and psychologists. Acknowledge someone's mood, and she or he will usually amplify upon it.

"It's their own fault. They should have had cops or doctors or somebody escort him over there. But no. He skips town, and the police came out to my house again and ask me a bunch of questions. And scare the crap out of my son. So, yeah. I'm mad. I'm real fuckin' mad." She screwed her lip gloss closed with a vicious twist. "If I ever see him again, I'm gonna tear off his head and shit down the hole."

I suppressed a smile. This was Drew Wilson's girlfriend, all right.

The little box clipped to her cutoffs beeped. "Ah, shit. There's an order of potato skins I forgot about. Hang on. I'll be back in a minute."

Vicky stood, tugging the denim out of her crotch, and disappeared into the crowd. I examined the table. It had a glass top, and people had shoved business cards under it. Nothing too impressive. Swimming-pool service. Restaurant supply. A company called Dyna-Magic Enterprises, makers of the Dyna-Carpet Shampooer. Some wit had stuck a tenth-generation fax joke under the glass: *The Top*

*10 Reasons a Beer Is Better Than a Woman.* Claudia would have been apoplectic.

How did Vicky hook up with Drew Wilson? She seemed like nothing more than a run-of-the-mill hardscrabble Valley girl. Probably ditched class to smoke weed with her girlfriends, probably lost it at the old Chatsworth Drive-In when she was fourteen, probably a single mother by the age of twenty. Just another product of the Southern California suburbs, weaned on malls and smog and single-parent tract houses. I knew Drew didn't go for Susan Sontag types, but I wouldn't have thought he went for Fenders girls.

I glanced over at the bar. A kid in a UCLA sweatshirt had his head back in the hairdresser's sink. The bartender was pouring tequila straight out of the bottle into the kid's open mouth while his buddies barked encouragement. Thin yellow liquid ran out of the sides of his mouth. It looked as if he was getting a golden shower. I shuddered.

Fortunately, Vicky came back. She had brought another Anchor Steam for me and a cigarette and cola for herself.

"Vicky," I said, as tactfully as I could, "where did you and Drew meet? Here?"

If there was a thought balloon over her head, it would have had one word in it: *duh.* "Andrew would never come out to a place like this. I met him when I worked in the bar across the street from the Chateau Marmont. On the Strip, in West Hollywood."

"Was Drew living at the Marmont, or was he living with you?"

"He was living there when he first came to town, but then he was living with me and Travis. Well, sort of," she amended. "He stayed at my place sometimes, along with a few other places. He kind of moved around."

"Where?"

"He stayed at Digger's a couple of times, I guess. I don't know. I really didn't know much about his business."

"But you knew he was a writer."

"Oh, yeah. He came out to L.A. to work on a screenplay. But he didn't talk about it. He didn't like to talk about work at all—at least to me. I don't know anything about that stuff." She sounded defensive. "I mean, I read *Premiere*, but I don't know anything about the movie industry."

It was refreshing to meet an Angeleno whose only knowledge of the industry came from *Premiere*, and I smiled. "I'm sorry he cut out on you."

"I'm *glad* he's gone," she said, with a viciousness that caught me off-guard. "He was always staying out all night, coming in and waking Travis up, borrowing money."

"He borrowed money from you?"

"He used to borrow money from me something terrible. I thought screenwriters were supposed to make a lot of money. Maybe they do, but I never saw any of it."

I wasn't sure if she was telling the truth, or larding the tale so I would be on her side. "Drew borrowed a lot of money from you?"

"Not a lot. Ten here, twenty there. Tip money. But it adds up. Especially when you got a kid." She pulled a maraschino cherry from her glass with one curved talon and chewed the stem nervously. Under all the Mary Kay, she looked about fifteen years old. "What are you askin' all these questions about *me* for?"

"No reason. Drew just never mentioned you, that's all."

"Yeah, well, he never mentioned you, either. He never mentioned much. Unless he wanted something."

"What did he say when you talked to him?"

"Huh?"

"This morning. When you talked to him."

"Oh. This morning." A get-ready-for-*this* look. "Well, the phone rings at eight-thirty, and I'm like, 'Hello?' And then he says . . . 'Hey, it's me. Any messages?'"

"'*Any messages?*'" I thought it was funny, but Vicky must have read my reaction as outrage. She nodded and pursed her glossed lips into a he-done-me-wrong pout.

"Yeah. After just cutting out and disappearing, not even calling to say hello, he has the nerve to call up and the first words out of his lying, shitty mouth are, 'Any messages?'"

"What did you say?"

"So I'm like, 'Where the fuck have *you* been?' Then he says he's gone back to New York. Which I know is a lie."

"Why?"

" 'Cause his agent called twice this week looking for him. She was a bitch, too. She accused me of hiding him out. I told her, 'Listen, lady—"

There was a scream and a crash from across the room. Doria the waitress was splayed on the sawdust floor in a puddle of beer, broken mugs all around her. Some joker started applauding. The rest of the room joined in. Vicky looked alarmed, and then she just looked tired.

"I've gotta get back to work," she muttered. She stubbed out her cigarette, mashing the white filter into a trayful of butts.

"Why did you call me, Vicky?"

"Huh?"

"You wanted to talk to me about something."

She slumped back in her seat. "I guess I just wanted to know if you had any idea where I could find Andrew. I want my money back. I'm so sick of his shit I could puke," she added, but there was a flicker in her eye, and I knew better. She still loved him.

"Did you tell him I called?"

"Yeah. He didn't remember who you were at first, which I thought was another fake-out. But I got your name wrong. I thought you said it was Sweet. He told me it was Swede."

"Did he say anything else?"

"Not much. I asked him who you were, and he said you were a reporter, doing an article on some woman he used to work for. Some woman who was having an affair or something."

"An affair?"

"Or something. I don't remember exactly what it was." She got up, tugging at her crotch where the denim bit into her labia.

"Vicky, this is important. What did he say exactly?"

"I don't know! It was like ten seconds, okay? He said something about the woman he worked for was having an affair, and he wanted to know if you had figured out who—"

"Did he say the woman's name?"

"I don't—"

I grabbed her wrist. "Think. Was it Monica? Monica Slezak? Did he say who the affair was with? Did he say any names at all?"

Nervous now, she licked her lips and looked around. "No. He didn't say a name."

A guy in a pearl-gray double-breasted suit and too much hair gel came over and put his hand on Vicky's shoulder.

"Break's over, Vic." He gave me a once-over.

"I gotta go."

I threw a ten on the table. "Vicky, please, just a minute—"

"I don't want to lose my job!" This was delivered to me, but it was for the benefit of the guy in the suit, who hadn't taken his hand off her shoulder. Vicky allowed him to steer her back into the crowd. Just as they were almost gone, she turned around, and through the smoke and the noise I heard her say:

*"He said she wrote about it. But you hadn't read it yet."*

# = 23 =

WHEN I ARRIVED AT CAFE CANEM the next morning, the coffeehouse was dark. Pedro was just pulling up on his Harley. There were a dozen people standing outside, all looking grouchy and undercaffeinated. So did Pedro; his hair wasn't combed and one flannel shirttail poked out of the fly of his 501s.

"XYZ," I said cheerfully.

"You're late."

"So are you. Hey, where's Claudia? I thought she and I were opening up this morning." It would have been the first time we'd worked together since Palm Springs.

"She called an hour ago and switched our shifts."

He fumbled with the keys, not looking at me. I was suspicious. "Why?"

"I don't know. I was asleep. She said she'd be in after two."

"What's going on, Pedro?"

He opened the door and flipped on the lights. "I don't *know*, Kieran. Look, there's a box of bagels and muffins on the back of my bike. Would you just grab it and get in here, please?"

We spent the next hour jump-starting customers with caffeine and sugar. Pedro was sullen, not saying a word except to take orders, make change, and order me to get more sipper lids out of the storeroom. Around nine-thirty, when there was a lull, I broached the subject again. "Come on, Pedro. What's going on?"

"My name is Paul, and that's between y'all," he muttered.

A kid in a bowling shirt came up to the counter. Pedro tried to move around me, but I blocked the cash register with my body. "Give it up, you goombah."

Pedro groaned. "Kieran, I don't know what happened in Palm Springs, and I don't want to know. Rehearsal wasn't over until three

A.M., and coming to work on three hours' sleep is bad enough without you playing Arlene Francis."

"Who's Arlene Francis?" asked the bowling shirt.

" 'What's My Line,' " Pedro told him. "Before your time. 'Family Feud' with blindfolds. What can I get you?"

"Can I get a double decaf latte?"

"Latte deuce, no-fun, coming up." Pedro turned around. "Amscray, Kieran. Outta my way."

I followed him to the steamer. "Where was she calling from?"

Pedro's eyes became slits. "Take a break. Pour yourself a cup of coffee. Read the paper. Just get out of my damn face."

Fine. I made myself a depth charge—coffee with a shotglass of espresso sunk to the bottom—and found an empty table where I could drink and brood. I tried to concentrate on Vicky's words: *He said she wrote about it. But you hadn't read it yet.* Problem was, all I could think about was Claudia.

Why not? Why not take Jeff Brenner's advice and excommunicate myself from Claudia forever? She and Cathy were both angry with me, and it didn't take a Stan Nyman to figure out that the two of them were probably holed up at Cathy's place in the Hollywood Hills. Our relationship was over, despite the fact that neither one of us had the guts, the grace, nor the good sense to pull the plug.

And speaking of pulling the plug . . . maybe Jocelyn was as right as Jeff. Investigating Monica Slezak's suicide was nothing but a series of time-consuming dead ends. It wasn't too late to bag the whole thing and start chronicling the life of Courtney Menzies. With a check for four thousand dollars, I could quit Cafe Canem, pay back Claudia, get out of her life for good, take care of some bills, and buy a new dinner jacket. That would put me back to where I was before Monica Slezak entered my life: single, poor, back on the banquet circuit, soon to be on the wrong side of thirty with no health insurance and nothing in the bank.

*He said she wrote about it. But you hadn't read it yet.*

Last night, I thought it was a significant clue. Today it just felt like the final dead end. So Monica was having an affair, probably with Eric. So she wrote about it in her journals. So what? Gregory Slezak wasn't going to let me read his wife's journals. The only other

— 210 —

person who might have access to them was Alison Sewell. I was sure Alison wouldn't let me read Monica's journals even if she liked me, which she didn't. And if the journals were in Suzan Morninglory's hands, they were as good as lost.

Damn Drew Wilson. He must have known that Vicky would give me that message, and that it would drive me out of my tree. The words clung to me like a burr in my brain: *He said she wrote about it. But you hadn't read it yet.*

*Damn* Drew Wilson. Even from points unknown, he was still playing mind games with me.

Now thoroughly morose, I went behind the counter, but Pedro was studying the latest issue of *Hothead Paisan* and pointedly ignoring me. I hooked a cinnamon-raisin bagel, picked up my backpack, went into Claudia's office, and closed the door. The office was really a large broom closet, but she'd outfitted it with a table, a chair, and a clunky black dial phone that looked as if it belonged on Sergeant Joe Friday's desk. I dialed Manhattan information, got the number for *Aspect* ("The Active Magazine for Today's Active Man"), and called Jeff Brenner.

"Hey, I was just about to call you," he said. "What would you say to doing a book review? We're doing a summer wrap-up of the new workout books for men."

"I'd say it was a nice try. You don't have to throw assignments at me, Brenner. Especially on topics for which I am eminently unsuitable."

"Let me just send the book out before you say no." I heard his door close. "What's going on in California?"

"Nothing. Nada. Zip. Zero."

"Come on. You sound like death warmed over a hot plate."

There was a box of plastic panty hose eggs under the desk—another one of Claudia's swap-meet treasures. I bounced one off the wall idly.

"I think I'm taking your advice for a change, Brenner."

"What advice?"

"I'm breaking up with Claudia."

We talked for half an hour. Once I'd made the decision, it seemed Jeff was going to do everything he could to talk me out of it. He poked and prodded my psyche thoroughly before announcing his verdict:

"If that's what you want to do."

"Forget about what I want to do. Don't be a shrink, be a pal. Just tell me if it's the right thing to do."

"Can't. Won't. Wouldn't even if I could. Just make sure that whatever you do, you think about it." Someone came into the room on his end. "There's my two-o'clock meeting. By the way, anything new on the Slezak front?"

I told Jeff about meeting Vicky, and what Drew Wilson had said. He crowed. "Come on, Kieran, that's helpful. That's a real break."

"It's a pain in my big butt, is what it is. I don't even know if it's true. How the hell am I supposed to read her diaries? Break into her house?"

"What makes you think it's in her diaries? Wilson wouldn't have told you that if he didn't expect you to find it." He was making paper-shuffling noises, getting ready to leave. "Look, do whatever you think is right about Claudia, but don't give up on this story just yet. I'll Fed-Ex you the galleys of the workout book this afternoon and give you a call this weekend."

I grunted good-bye and swiveled around in the chair, tossing the egg off the door and catching it in my lap. It made a lousy tennis ball.

*He said she wrote about it. But you hadn't read it yet.*

I gave the egg a harder toss, nicking the doorframe and sending it against the wall. It caromed off the doorframe and into the trash can, where it broke open.

*He said she wrote about it. But—*

And, all of a sudden, I knew.

I sat agape for a moment. Then I dug out the Yellow Pages and dialed a number in Beverly Hills. The man who answered the phone gave me another number to try, and an address on Cabazon Street, just off Lankershim in North Hollywood. I dialed. Someone picked up on the second ring. I heard a speed drill squealing in the background.

"Is Eric there?"

"Yeah. Hang on."

I disconnected, pocketed the piece of paper with the address, and went back into the café.

It was eleven o'clock. The lunch crowd would be in soon, but at the moment there were only two people in the place, dawdling over cappuccinos. Pedro was still reading his comic book. He glanced up when I took his keys and his helmet from the hook, but he didn't start bawling until I was out the door, on his motorcycle, strapping the helmet on my head.

"What the hell are you doing on my bike?" he yelled. "Where are you going?"

"I'll be back in two hours."

"It's lunchtime, Kieran!"

"Two hours. I promise. I owe you big, Pedro." I revved the motor and looked over my shoulder.

"What am I supposed to tell Claudia?"

"I'll be back before she gets here. Thanks for the loan of the bike. I'll fill it up."

He was still standing on the sidewalk, furious, as I merged with the traffic, pulled an illegal U, and peeled down Abbot Kinney Boulevard toward the freeway, making my second Valley run in twenty-four hours.

I switched freeways twice, missed getting creamed by a semi once, and got off in North Hollywood on an industrial section of Lankershim Boulevard. Forlorn buildings with earthquake cracks sat abandoned on both sides of the street. A once-proud movie theater in the middle of the block had been lassoed with chain-link fence and razor wire. The theater was my landmark; I remembered seeing Cabazon Street around here somewhere.

There it was, at a corner where a gas station had been converted into a minimall: nail salon, doughnut shop, Video-2-Go, and a small drugstore. Two shifty-looking men were sharing a forty-ouncer of malt liquor in the parking lot. As I idled at the light, another piece of the puzzle fit into place: this was the pharmacy where Monica had filled her Zapax and Percocil prescriptions. I hadn't questioned it at the time, but why would a woman in Beverly Hills drive to North Hollywood to get a prescription filled?

Cabazon Street was a dingy cul-de-sac, bifurcated by railroad tracks and festooned with the kind of malevolent high-tension wires that make me think of increased cancer rates and mutant children. There were only two buildings. The first was a trophy company. The second was a warehouse, fenced off with chain-link fence, razor wire, and security cameras. A sign on the fence identified it as Cypriot Motor Repair. I hopped the bike over a low curb and into the lot, drawing a curious stare from a worker smoking a cigarette outside the office.

In contrast to the outside of the building, the mechanic bay was as spotless and high-tech as the bridge on *Star Trek*. Half a dozen gleaming cars hung above the floor on hydraulic hoists, each meticulously restored, each worth a fortune. One man was steam-cleaning the undercarriage of a burnished-caramel Cypriot, making the metal gleam. Other men in coveralls worked on Cypriots of various vintages, doing body work with earsplitting power tools.

I went into the office and was directed outside, where the man who had stared at me was picking grease out of his cuticles. He was short, with thick sandy hair and craggy cheekbones like a Harlequin romance cover boy. The embroidered badge on his coveralls spelled out the name ERIC COFFIELD.

"Eric?" I said.

He nodded without looking up.

"You own a white Mustang?"

"It's not for sale."

"I don't want to buy your car. I want to talk about Monica Slezak."

No immediate reaction. He glanced from side to side before flipping away his cigarette with one grease-stained thumbnail. When he spoke, it was in a lilting Liverpudlian accent.

"Who the hell are you?"

I told him to take an early lunch.


We drove Coffield's '65 Mustang down Victory Boulevard into Van Nuys, where he pulled over in front of a small pub called the Crowninshield. I followed him inside without a word. It wasn't yet noon, but the bar was packed. Tables the size of Scrabble boards were scattered through the room. Coffield picked one near the darts lanes.

I sat down while he went to wash up. It was a little early in the day to be hanging out in a bar, but a couple dozen expatriate Brits were downing pints in various corners of the room. The number of Brits in Monica Slezak's life seemed too large to be a coincidence, even in a town as Anglophilic as Hollywood: Alison Sewell, Adam Davies, and now Eric Coffield.

When Coffield came back, he had combed his hair and gotten most of the grease from under his nails. A waitress in a corny polyester barmaid's uniform came by and greeted him by name. He asked for a black-and-tan and something called a Scotch egg. Feeling outnumbered among so many Brits, I decided on an Irish coffee.

When the waitress was gone, Coffield pulled cigarettes out of his shirt pocket and lit one. "Are you a cop?"

"A reporter."

He didn't look terribly relieved. "Who told you about this?"

"Nobody. I figured it out. Monica mentioned your name in her suicide note."

He blanched. "Well, why haven't the cops been out to see me?"

"Not your whole name. Just Eric. I figured out the rest on my own. It's a long story, but she had written a screenplay. It was an adaptation of a book, but there was one character that didn't fit . . ." I gave up. "She made up a character based on you. A mechanic. She wrote you into a film script."

"There're a lot of mechanics in L.A., man. Some of them are even named Eric."

"But there aren't a lot of repair shops that work on Cypriots. I admit it, it was a guess. But I guessed right."

He nodded, pulled on his cigarette, and blew the smoke out thoughtfully. "She put me in a movie, eh?"

"In a script."

"Huh." Coffield couldn't hide his pleasure. He watched a dart match as the barmaid returned with our drinks and a strange object that looked like a breaded pterodactyl dropping.

As he dug into his lunch, I reappraised Eric Coffield. Back at the repair shop, all I'd seen was a short man with thick sandy hair, a prominent beak, and a mouthful of teeth that was a testament to the failings of the British dental system. Degreased, with his hair combed and his mouth shut, Coffield was a striking-looking man—if you like the dockworker genus. His hair verged on pompadour status without being too poofy, and his prominent nose lent him an aquiline profile. Handsome but not pretty, well-built but not gym-toned, he was the antithesis of a Hollywood film executive; with his cheap clothes and broad hands, he had an unself-conscious sexuality that it was easy to imagine appealing to a woman like Monica Slezak.

Fork tucked into his left paw, Coffield cut into the dactyl dropping and took a huge sloppy bite. From what I could tell, a Scotch egg was a hard-boiled egg encased in sausage, breaded, and deep-fried. Lovely.

"Eric, I know the two of you were having an affair—"

"Bullshit."

"I've seen her diaries." Bullshit it was, but it got his attention. He paused in mid-chew, exposing a mouthful of gray sausage and grayer egg. "Look. I'm not out to get you in trouble. I'm just trying to put together the pieces of why Monica killed herself. I'll make you a deal. You tell me everything you know about her. In exchange, you'll be a background source. I won't use your name. I won't write anything about your affair. And I won't tell her husband."

The minute I said it, I saw my mistake; if I had read the diaries, why wouldn't Gregory Slezak have read them also? Fortunately, Eric Coffield's deductive powers seemed limited to faulty carburetors and transmissions. "You think I'm balmy?" he said belligerently. "Why should I trust you?"

"Because you're out of options, Coffield."

He swallowed with one huge bob of his Adam's apple and took a reflective sip of his beer.

"I didn't know who she was. I didn't know she made motion pictures. I didn't know she was married. I didn't know anything except she'd banged up her car real good. I didn't know who she was. We only did it three times. I swear, only three times." It came out *free toimes*.

"Okay. I don't have any reason not to believe you."

"I'd just moved down here. I don't know anything about the motion picture industry. And then she dies, and I read in the paper that she makes movies with Adam fucking Davies and half the people in Hollywood. I swear, I thought she was just some rich housewife. I see half a dozen of them come into the shop every day." He polished off the rest of his black-and-tan with one gulp and signaled for another.

"So you met when she brought in her car for repairs."

"Yeah. It was a bloody wreck. She says she wants to restore it, make it better than new. I says, you bashed it up pretty good, that could take a month or two. She says, fine. So I think, oh, I get it. Here's another one taking advantage of her insurance company. I get paid either way, right? And then she starts coming out to the shop. Just to check up on the progress, she says."

"Is that unusual?"

He took a huge chomp of Scotch egg and pressed the tines of his fork in the saucer to get the crumbs. "Yeah. I guess. But you tell me what's usual and what's unusual when you're dealing with a woman, you know?" He horse-laughed. "She'd drive up in her Mercedes, hang around, ask a bunch of silly questions about engines and such. Then, around the third visit, say, it begins to dawn on me that she was just looking for an excuse to talk to me." He held up his palm. Scout's honor. "I swear it. I wasn't the only one who noticed. The guys in the shop were teasing me. Gerry, him with the red hair, he bet me ten bucks that I wouldn't ask her out for a drink. So I did."

"You picked her up at her house?"

"No! I never even knew where she lived. She came to the shop when we were closing, and then we came here. We had to, so the guys could see—so I could win the bet. You know what I mean." His face colored.

"Sure."

"We had a few drinks, and then a few more—I'm not even believing this myself at the time, mind—and then we went back to my apartment."

"You had sex."

"Yeah."

The Scotch egg was history. Coffield lit another cigarette. I cursed myself for leaving my tape recorder back in Venice.

"So you got together again."

"Well, why not? I'm separated, she told me that she was divorced. I knew her name was Monica Slezak, but I dunno Monica Slezak from the Queen Mother, you know?"

"Was she wearing a wedding ring?"

"Yeah, sure she was. A big one, with diamonds all over it." He scoffed. "Of course not."

"And she said she was divorced. Not separated or estranged, but divorced."

"That's what she said."

"Come on, Eric. You didn't really believe that."

He started to look wounded, and then decided it wasn't worth the trouble. "Aw, I knew she was married after that first night. I just didn't *want* to know. I figured if she didn't care, I didn't either. All the signs were there, you know? After that first night, the only time we could get together was in the afternoon, on my days off. She never gave me her phone number. Put it all together, I'm not stupid."

"Did she act . . . strange in any ways?"

"You tell *me* what's strange when you're talking about a woman," he said with a surprising amount of rancor. He sipped and wiped foam from his lips. "You have a girlfriend?"

This caught me by surprise. "Right at the moment, you mean? I, well . . . I honestly don't know."

"See? They're out of their bloody minds, every one of 'em."

I thought it best to get off the topic of women in general and back to Monica in particular. "Did she act like she was on drugs?"

It would have been an easy out, if he had chosen to take it, but Coffield shook his head. "No. Actually, I thought she was going through change of life. Very emotional. Laughing one minute and crying the next. Or laughing and crying at the same time." He paused. "I suppose there are drugs that can do that to you, yeah? Not like crank or coke, but . . . *rich people's drugs*. God only know what those sods in Beverly Hills are taking, right? And movie people, they take a lot of drugs, right?"

"Some of them do, I suppose."

"So old Monica was on drugs," he said, as if he enjoyed the notion. "Isn't that a piss."

"I don't know that for sure."

"Yeah. Yeah," he repeated, as if he'd just figured something out. "It makes sense. Especially after what happened later."

"Go on."

Coffield paused and chose his words carefully. "I finally broke it off. But Monica wouldn't leave me alone. She'd call me at home in the middle of the night, crying. It got so bad I finally bought an answering machine to screen my calls."

I kept a poker face. "How often did this go on?"

"Every day. Every day for three weeks. I was trying to patch things up with my wife, and I really didn't need it, you know? Then she started phoning me at work—which didn't go over very well with my boss, I don't mind telling you. It was like . . ." He thought. "You ever seen that movie with Michael Douglas? The one where the crazy bitch boils the rabbit?"

I studied Coffield. He seemed sincere, but I couldn't imagine Monica Slezak, drugged or not, as a stalker. It was *possible*, particularly if she was taking enough drugs to crash her car. It was equally probable, though, that this Englishman was blackmailing her.

As if he knew I didn't quite believe him, Coffield flushed and turned away. I sipped my Irish coffee. It was cold, and the aerosol whipped cream had melted into an oily pool of scum.

"Of course," I said slowly, "you don't have any proof for any of this."

Coffield's face went flinty. He pulled out his wallet, drew out a well-worn business card, and handed it to me. It was from a Burbank fajitas restaurant notorious for its singles action.

"You've been to Casa del Sueño. So?"

"The other side."

I turned it over. There was a license number scrawled in ballpoint pen, along with the words "brown Mercedes" and a date. The first week of January. Almost two months ago, exactly.

"That's her license number. I told her to bugger off way last fall. I thought I wouldn't hear from her again. Then I come home from work one day and see her car parked across the street."

"Did you talk to her?"

"I didn't even stop. She wasn't in the car, so I figured she was inside my apartment building. I just kept driving. Stayed the night at a friend's place. Check with him. Gerry Trudgill."

The hair on my arms prickled. Coffield wasn't bright enough to make this up. "Eric, why did you write this down?"

He shrugged. "I dunno why. Just in case anything happened."

"Well, why didn't you call the police?"

"The police! What am I gonna say? Hey, I'm a mechanic who makes three hundred a week, and I'm being stalked by some rich broad from Beverly Hills?" He took back the card and tucked it in his billfold. "I'm not over here legally. They'd send me home in a leaky boat. I'm trying to tell you, man, I was stuck. I couldn't even call the police if she took a *shot* at me. It was fuckin' scary, I don't mind telling you."

Coffield shook his head and lit another cigarette. He got up and went over to the dartboard, palming a handful of darts from the pitted felt. "You know how to play?"

"Sure, if you show me how," I replied, realizing as I said it how idiotic it sounded.

He handed me the darts and I threw. Five. Double seventeen. The wall.

"How many times was she waiting for you when you came home from work?"

"Just once, as far as I know." He sighted down his nose and threw three graceful underhands: two bull's-eyes and eighteen. "After that, I didn't hear from her for a month. I thought she'd given up. But she called one night—"

"What did she say?"

He retrieved his darts and threw again. "Said she was sorry. Said she'd started seeing someone and realized her mistake—"

"She was seeing another man?"

"Nah. A shrink. It was a woman, 'cause she said *she*. Said she was trying to make amends, hoped I'd forgive her. I knew what she wanted; she wanted me to forget about the whole thing. Fine by me. So I says, hey, it happens, no hard feelings, you know?" He circled a forefinger in the vicinity of his temple. "Then she wished me luck, I wished her luck, and that was the end of it. It was pretty clear that we wouldn't be talking anymore."

"But you heard from her again?"

"Nah. Never did. I kind of forgot about it until recently. I was watching the news and they were at some fancy hotel where this woman producer had shot herself dead, and it turns out to be Monica. Jesus, I don't know what surprised me more: that she was dead or that she was a big movie producer. She worked with *Adam*

*Davies,*" he added, in the awed tones that an American might reserve for God or Steven Spielberg.

Coffield threw three bull's-eyes with his practiced underhand and checked his watch. "That's all she wrote," he said. "Hey, I gotta get back to work."

The interior of Coffield's Mustang was pristine white leather, free of candy wrappers and cigarette butts. Despite his Marlboro habit, the ashtray was clean, filled with Tootsie Pops that must have been his highway substitute for nicotine. Once we were in the car and the interview was over, Coffield treated me like a buddy. He asked me several questions about newspaper reporting. Like a lot of people, he seemed to think it was a glamorous job, as if reporters spent weeks nosing around stories before banging out a few hundred words, collecting an award, and jetting off to Gstaad for the weekend. I ran across this misconception frequently and blamed it on "Lou Grant."

Coffield was blathering about *All the President's Men.* I stared out the window. It was hot and hazy. A bank clock gave the time as 12:57 and the temperature as 95. Half a mile in the distance, someone had hit a fire hydrant, shearing off the top. A geyser of water was arcing over the eastbound lanes of Victory.

"Send me a copy of your story when you're done," Coffield said jovially. "You said you wouldn't use my name, right?"

I selected a cherry Tootsie Pop and unwrapped it. "That's not quite true, Eric."

"Huh?"

"I said that I wouldn't use your name if you told me the whole truth."

"I did!"

I sucked my Tootsie Pop and watched the water jet into the sky. "You heard from Monica again."

"Bollocks, man."

"You heard from her right before she died."

"Bollocks."

"She mentioned you in the suicide note," I reminded him. "I think you heard from her again. Right before she died."

The sooty ass of an RTD bus cut us off, plunging the car into shadow. The Mustang came to a stop. Coffield leaned across me and opened the passenger door. "It's only another mile. You can walk."

"What did she say, Eric?"

"Get out."

"Tell it to me or tell it to the police, Eric."

He considered for a moment before slamming the door again.

"Fuck you," he muttered, dumping the transmission into drive. The traffic began moving forward at fifteen miles an hour.

I sighed, rolling down my window. The bus pulled over to disgorge its sweaty and rumpled passengers. Somewhere behind us, a lowrider was pumping out rap music. Ahead, Victory Boulevard stretched into the distance: all traffic, asphalt, and billboards. The sunlight itself looked gritty. Hundreds of gallons of water were overflowing the gutter and lapping across the sidewalk. I couldn't remember if we were in a drought this year or not.

I was tired of this. Tired of the lies, tired of people concealing the truth, tired of outright lies and obfuscations and roadblocks thrown up in my way just as I was getting somewhere. I was tired of parties, of Claudia, of my ten-year-old car, of the prospect of churning out a celebrity biography for a check that wouldn't do a thing to change my poverty level. I was tired of living like a teenage adult.

I was tired of my life.

Ahead, a light turned green and I saw red.

"I don't want to get you in trouble, Eric. But I have spent the last month being jacked around by everyone who ever knew Monica Slezak. I've been lied to by her husband, her assistant, her shrink, and half of Hollywood. And the worst part is that I don't even know what they have to lie about.

"You know why you've gotten off the hook so far? Everyone assumed that the Eric in her suicide note was her goddamned nutritionist. Right now, I'm the only one who knows better. So listen up. If you don't tell me the truth, I'm going straight to the Beverly Hills Police Department and tell them just what you just told me. So if you've got a good reason—a real good reason—why I shouldn't do that, start talking."

We pulled through the geyser, getting a quick car wash, and drove in silence for a mile. When we reached the Lankershim intersection, he went straight through the light.

"You missed the turn," I said.

"No, I didn't."

"Where are we going?"

He didn't answer. We passed Tujunga, then Vineland, and then we were in Burbank.

"Where the hell are we going?" I said.

Coffield didn't look at me. When he spoke, his voice was sullen. "My place."

# =24=

ERIC COFFIELD LIVED ON A LONG block of dreary stucco apartment buildings with names like EL PATIO and LANAI WEST. These cheap structures with their suburbo-Spanish names are to the San Fernando Valley what gingerbread Victorians are to Haight-Ashbury. Coffield pulled the Mustang into the carport of a particularly depressing building: two stories of crumbly all-season weathercoat that circled a swimming pool full of leaves and newspapers. The landscaping was dusty lantania bushes and bottle brush. On the front, cursive letters spelled out VILLA CONTENTO. Coffield took the stairs two at a time, leading me past other apartments where window-box fans blew dirty air into the dark interiors. The place smelled of hot lard and dryer exhaust. Inside one apartment, a blue light flickered and a talk-show host asked, "So when did your daughter start turning tricks?"

Coffield stopped at number 18, where he unlocked the door, flipped on an overhead fixture, and grunted at me to sit down before disappearing into the bedroom.

His place was cheerless, even by furnished-apartment standards. An avocado-green refrigerator sat next to a harvest-gold stove. The living-room couch and chair were covered in nubby orange fabric that made me wonder if they made *fake* Naugahyde. Blinds covered the front windows; the slats that weren't missing were filthy. The ell where the kitchen table should have been was occupied by a weight bench with cracked red plastic seats. The only personal objects in the living room were a large Hitachi television, a boom box, and two framed poster maps: one of England and one of San Francisco. Atop the coffee table were the TV book from the Sunday paper and a cheap glass ashtray suffocating in butts. A half-smoked roach sat in one of the lip depressions of the ashtray. I don't know what I had expected—perhaps a Lalique vase with a gift tag, TO ERIC WITH LOVE FROM MONICA—but it wasn't this. I couldn't imagine Monica Slezak coming to this end of the Valley, much less to this apartment.

Coffield emerged from the bedroom with a Ziploc bag. In it were two cassettes. He sat beside me on the couch, lit the roach, took a deep hit, and offered it to me. I declined.

"I couldn't call the police," he said, holding in lungfuls of smoke, "but I finally got an answering machine to screen my calls. I figured if things got real bad, I could always threaten to play the messages for her husband. But like I said, she stopped calling. I did get her on tape a couple of times, though." He exhaled noisily, picked up the Ziploc bag and the roach, and went back into the bedroom. I followed.

That room was even more depressing than the living room. Sickly yellow light filtered in through jalousie windows, and wall-to-wall dirty clothes covered the wall-to-wall dirty shag carpet. The closet doors had been taken off their sliders and propped against the wall. An unmade mattress and a plastic parson's table were the only furniture. The table was stacked with a hodgepodge of crap: a brown ginger-jar lamp, a dish of pocket change, a roach clip, a couple of gold-coin condoms, a Westclox alarm clock, an empty Sprite bottle, and a fancy telephone/answering machine unit. Under the table was a stack of *Penthouse* magazines and a crusty hand towel, which I politely ignored.

Had this guy really seduced one of Hollywood's most powerful producers in this grungy bedroom?

I cleared a space on the floor with the tip of my shoe and sat down. Coffield flipped open the top of the answering machine, removed the incoming message cassette, and replaced it with one of the tapes from the plastic bag.

"This was the first one."

He pushed PLAYBACK. A mechanical voice announced that message one had been left several months before, on a Wednesday night at eight-nineteen. There was a beep.

"Eric? Eric, if you're there, please pick up."

There was an electronic clumping sound. I heard Sting singing "Wrapped Around Your Finger," and then Eric's voice.

"Yeah."

"It's Monica."

"Yeah."

"How are you?"

There was the kind of pause you might hear in the voice of a father whose child has just asked for her umpteenth glass of water at bedtime.

"Okay."

"Good." She cleared her throat. "Can you turn that down, please?"

Sting disappeared from the soundtrack. Coffield was sitting on the edge of the mattress, head down, eyes closed. It was damned eerie, sitting in that darkened bedroom listening to the voice of a woman who didn't know she was about to die.

"Thank you . . . How are you, Eric?"

"What do you want, Monica?"

"I just wanted to tell you that . . . the car's running fine." A nervous laugh.

"Good-bye, Monica—"

"Wait! Don't hang up."

"Tell me what you want."

"I want to apologize."

"For what? Calling me in the middle of the night? Calling me at work? Following me—"

Her voice regained a little dignity. "I haven't called you in over a month, and I'm not going to call you again." Silence. "This is very embarrassing—"

"Get to the point."

"—but I'm seeing a therapist now. She's helping me with my problems, and I'm feeling much better. I'm just embarrassed about . . . what happened."

"Why are you calling, Monica?"

She sighed, and spoke as if she was reading from a script. "My therapist says that in order for me to move forward, I have to make amends with the people that I've hurt." A line straight out of the Morninglory *oeuvre*, I guessed, probably adapted from the Twelve Steps.

"You haven't hurt me. You've been a real pain in the ass."

Softly: "I know."

"Don't call here anymore. Don't call me at all, okay?"

"I'm not going to. That's why I'm calling, if that makes any sense. To tell you that I'm not going to be calling anymore." She breathed. "This is very hard."

"You want to help? Just leave me alone, Monica."

"Oh, that's what I intend to do." Her laugh was desperate, gas escaping from a balloon. "I'd like to explain more. Apologize more . . . but like you said, I think you'd rather be left alone."

"Yeah."

"All right. Very well. I guess this is good-bye, then."

"Bye, Monica." There was a click, but I couldn't tell who had hung up on whom.

Coffield stopped the tape and waggled his eyebrows at me. I nodded my head noncommittally.

"Then I got this call." He changed cassettes and pushed PLAY-BACK. The mechanical voice gave the time as 10:52 P.M., and the date as a Sunday, the night before the Women in the Industry dinner. The night before the Academy Award nominations. The night before Monica died.

"Hey. Hey, Eric. Are you there?"

It was Monica, all right—but a different woman from the embarrassed Monica that had left the earlier message. Her voice was dragged-out, murky-sounding. I guessed she was on Zapax. Or several Zapax. Or Zapax and Percocil.

Coffield picked up the line. "Yeah."

"How are you?" The question trailed off in a ghostly *ooooo*.

"What the fuck do you want?"

"Don't be like that. Don't be like that, Eric. How are you?"

"Asleep," he said rudely. "Didn't you say you weren't going to call here anymore?"

"I need to talk to somebody. I don't have anyone to talk to." Her voice was more languid than desperate. I could picture her in bed, all cuddled up, ready for a long comfy conversation.

"I'm asleep. Talk to your husband."

A hollow laugh. "Oh, I don't think that would work."

"You're drunk."

"No. No-o-o."

"You sure sound like it. Listen, Monica, I'm sick of these games. If you call me one more time, I'll find your husband and I'll tell him everything. You got that?"

"You can't help me," she said dreamily. "No one can help me."

"Don't call here again. I mean it."

"Bye-bye, Eric. Bye-bye."

Click.

Coffield relit the end of the joint. A seed popped in the darkness. He pinched the twisted butt in the roach clip and took a deep hit. He looked embarrassed, as if I'd just listened to a tape of him and Monica having sex. "Was it like I told you?"

"Yeah."

"Did I tell you everything?"

"Seems like it. But I want copies of both of those tapes."

"No way."

"Just for my personal use. You'll get them back when I'm done with the article."

"I don't have any blank cassettes, man."

"We'll figure something out."

The boom box in the living room had a dubbing deck. I showed him how to fit cellophane tape over the lugs in a pre-recorded cassette, and we dubbed both phone conversations over an old Eagles tape.

Ten minutes later, I was on the Ventura Freeway, heading back to Venice with a dead woman's voice in my pocket.

I stopped at an Arco in Santa Monica to fill the tank in Pedro's bike. By the time I pulled up in front of Cafe Canem, it was two forty-five. I was almost two hours late. Except for two regulars dawdling over a game of chess, the place was empty. Claudia was behind the counter, wearing a peasant dress with a Brooklyn Dodgers jacket over it.

"Pedro in the back?"

She didn't even glance up from her book. "Pedro went home. He needed some sleep, so I loaned him my car. He wants you to drive the bike over and switch it for the car after you get off."

"Okay," I said cautiously, unstrapping the helmet and hanging it up. Claudia was terrible at hiding her emotions; I had expected fire-

— 228 —

works, or sullen rage, but she seemed more pensive than anything else. I was flummoxed.

It took a minute for something else to register: Claudia had cut her hair again. This time she'd done something to it that made it shine. She had also applied makeup, something she rarely bothered with anymore. This was all too strange. I felt uneasy and uncertain, like Lassie used to when stupid Timmy got pinned under a log. If Claudia would have called me a terminal screwup or thrown a latte bowl at my head, it would have been a relief, but she just sat there reading her book as if I went on a four-hour break every afternoon.

"You look nice," I ventured.

"Thanks. I had an impromptu makeover. It's a long story." She swept her hair behind her ears. "You really like it?"

"I do."

"Did you eat lunch?"

"No."

"Neither did I. Let's go to Jody Maroni's." She took the key out of the register and addressed the chess players. "Hey, Mikey, Kyle, we're closing for a while."

"It's only three o'clock," whined Kyle.

"Yeah, and you've been sitting here since noon with that same cup of coffee. Leave your pieces where they are and come back after six. I'll buy you a cappuccino." Claudia picked up her purse and headed for the door. I was in an amazed paralysis; Claudia never closed the shop on a whim. There was a whole case of pastries if she was really hungry.

She shooed Mikey and Kyle outside, flipped the OPEN sign to CLOSED, and held the door open. "Kieran, don't bother turning off the machines; we won't be gone that long."

I followed her out to the sidewalk like a kid about to get a whipping.

We bought sausage sandwiches and Cokes at a stand on Ocean Front Walk and went down to the waterline to eat. It was a sunny afternoon, but there was a chill coming off the water. Claudia was still inscrutable. I followed her, scrunching my way across the beach, until she plopped down near the wreck of an abandoned and water-logged sand castle.

"First of all," she began, unwrapping a sandwich and passing it to me, "I'm in a good mood and I don't want to spoil it, so please don't tell me where you went this afternoon. I don't want to know. Let me tell you where I was last night."

It was a GET OUT OF JAIL FREE card, and I didn't question it. I took a bite of sausage and watched a dreadlocked white kid in a Charles Manson shirt skimboard along the water's edge.

"I got a call yesterday from a high school friend. More of an acquaintance, really. Mindy Kane. She was in town for a cosmetology convention out at the airport, and they'd put her up at a hotel in the Marina. She looked me up in the phone book and wanted to have dinner. I hadn't seen her in ten years—I hadn't even *thought* of her—but I figured what the hey."

"Mindy Kane?" I couldn't picture Claudia being friends with a Mindy Kane.

"Yes, and she has a twin sister named Candy. It's tragic, really. Anyway, we went to T.G.I. Fridays—her choice—and caught up on things. After dinner, I brought her over to Canem for coffee, and then we went back to her hotel and ended up ordering too much chardonnay from room service. It was fun, actually."

"So what's Mindy up to?"

"Pretty much what I expected. She got married right after high school and popped out three kids by the time she was twenty-five. She lives out in Metairie—that's what we have in New Orleans instead of the Valley—and has a salon out on Airline Highway. We stayed up until four, getting plotzed on white wine and talking. We finally had them bring up a rollaway. I ended up liking her more than I thought I would. Respecting her, really."

"What were you talking about?"

"Everything. Mindy just opened up about her life. She's tired of her husband, tired of the kids, tired of cutting hair. She'd been looking forward to this trip for a year and a half. Isn't that sad? A weekend at a convention out at LAX has been keeping her going for a year and a half."

Claudia dug in her purse, found her *La Dolce Vita* glasses, and put them on. I pulled off my shoes and socks and dumped out two little clouds of sand.

"So what did you talk about?"

"You. Me. Cathy. She took *that* one better than I thought she would. But around one in the morning, while she was cutting my hair and we were into our second bottle of wine, I told her I was thinking of moving back to New Orleans and selling the shop." Claudia took a bite of sandwich and wiped her mouth on her sleeve. "Hand me a napkin."

"And what did Mindy say?"

"The same thing you told me in Palm Springs—that I was crazy. Out of my mind. When I heard her say it, I realized that she was right. And so was Pedro. And so were you."

Creamy curls of surf bubbled at the water's edge where the water receded. I dug my toes into the sand and waited.

"I went out to Chez Jay with Pedro and Dagny last weekend, and we ended up reminiscing about what Canem was like when I first opened. Remember? A coffeemaker and a bunch of mismatched mugs. Some tables and chairs from Saint Vincent de Paul. I didn't even have the money to get a pastry case, so we used Dagny's old aquarium. And now it's . . . *something*. I can't just sell it or throw it away, any more than Mindy could ditch her salon and her husband and her three spawn. No matter how much I might want to sometimes."

I squinted at the horizon, where Catalina Island lay twenty-six miles across the sea, shrouded by smog and sunset haze. "Face it, Claude: you get to a certain age, and you find that you've put down some roots. Whether you like it or not, that's just the way it is."

Claudia smiled. "I know. But I grew up reading Kerouac and Cassady and Kesey and all that crap. It's not crap, really. It's just *history*. The 1960s are just as dead as the 1860s. No matter what the people in charge try to tell us." She drained her Coke and peered at me over her sunglasses. "There's got to be a middle line somewhere, Kieran. Somewhere between Mindy Kane and just . . . drifting. 'Cause both of them are damn hard work."

A wave hit the sand castle. It melted like a Popsicle. "So what *are* you going to do?"

"I'm going to expand. Knock out the wall and put in a little stage. Pedro's hot on this idea of booking a lecture series, and it occurred to me that we might be able to dump the bad poetry amateur hour and get some decent people in to read."

"That'll go over real well with the regulars."

"It'll piss off a few of them, but they're the ones who never buy anything anyway. Besides, if they come to hear some real writers read their stuff, they might stop their public masturbation and learn something."

"Good for you, Claude."

"Now." She folded her arms and stared at me. "The second thing. As long as I'm clearing out the deadwood, I want to get rid of some things in this relationship."

My hands and feet tingled.

"I don't mean you, Kieran. I mean this off-again, on-again stuff. It's exhausting. I get exhausted just *thinking* about it. We're not sixteen anymore, no matter how much I'd like to be sixteen. No matter how much we act like it. So what I propose is this." Claudia lost some of her brio; she began molding damp sand around my feet. "We start fresh. If we don't make it, we say good-bye and move on. Lightning round. Sudden death. What do you think?"

I clasped my hands behind my head and fell back in the sand.

"What do you think?" she repeated.

"I don't know. What about Cathy?"

"Cathy's gone. I told you that."

"That's been over before, too."

"Believe me. She called a couple of weeks ago, and I burned that bridge. I burned that sucker and threw gasoline on it. I told her to buzz off for good. Not in those words, exactly." She laughed hoarsely. "It didn't go very well. Cathy enjoys playing like she's some street-smart underdog, but she's really just a spoiled yuppie. Her parents put her through Vassar and USC film school with cash—no student loans. She's very pampered and used to getting her own way. What we had going was never great, but it had really turned into something ugly."

"You don't need to explain if you don't want to."

"I don't care." Claudia had interred my feet and was starting on the ankles. "She'd been sleeping with someone else for months. It made sense. I mean, we'd go for days without even talking to each other, but our schedules were so crazy that it took me a long time to figure out what was going on."

A Frisbee landed nearby, but I ignored it. First Eric Coffield, then the Monica tape, and now a reconciliation with Claudia. It was a little much to process in one afternoon.

"Geez, Claude. Are you okay?"

"Oh, yeah. I got my ya-yas out about this a long time ago." She picked up the Frisbee and flung it fifty yards down the sand. A golden retriever leaped high into the air and caught it. *"C'est la vie. Or la guerre. C'est la* whatever."

She looked so sad that I reached over and tugged on the back of her Dodgers jacket. "Come here."

"Kieran, you don't need to—"

"Just shut up and come here for a minute."

Claudia lay down beside me. I wrapped my arms around her and felt her burrow into my chest. It was four-fifteen.

We lay there, not moving, as the rest of the people on the beach left in singles and pairs. When I checked my watch again, it was past five o'clock, and beach fleas were dancing among the hairs on my legs.

I started to get up, but the sand on my feet had hardened, and it would have required some serious digging to get me out, so I watched the sun sink behind the line of the horizon, listening to the hiss of the waves and the soft breathing of Claudia lying beside me.

# = 25 =

THE ALTERNATIVE FILM AWARDS is the kind of event at
which Hollywood excels: a purportedly social occasion where everyone is there to take maximum advantage of everyone else. The honorees—young directors whose independent films have shown
promise—show up to make business contacts and snarf down a free
dinner. The agents come to work the room the way a horny swinger
works a singles' bar. And the studio heads show up to convince
themselves that they're really Medicis instead of Milkens. It makes
for a great column. Luckily, this year's ceremony was being held at
the St. Monica Shores, a beachfront hotel near Claudia's apartment.
I picked her up at six-thirty and we were there in five minutes.

The AFA steering committee traditionally landed a big director
to dole out the statuettes. This year's catch was Dick Cannon, the
action-movie star who had used his box-office muscles to wangle a
job directing *Darrow's Arrow*, a self-penned, three-hour epic about
the Scopes trial. Response at the studio level had been lukewarm
until Cannon also agreed to play the title character, at which point
the suits called it "high concept" and gave him thirty million dollars
and a green light. Detractors (and there were plenty) snickered that
Cannon could do a better job as the monkey, but he managed to
turn in one of those performances that gets nominated for an Oscar
simply because it wasn't *quite* as embarrassing as it could have been. I
hoped that Cannon would pull an upset and win on Oscar night,
because I had a feeling he'd thank his Nautilus instructor.

Cannon was tucked away in a secluded but highly visible corner
of the cocktail reception, chewing an unlit Havana and schmoozing
with Chep Orlovsky, the head of InterCreative Talent. Cannon had
gotten his start as Orlovsky's kung fu instructor. Susan D'Andrea,
Cannon's publicist, factotum, and harridan-at-large, was circling the

big guy like an agitated wasp, shrieking at partygoers to leave him alone. She noticed my notebook and gave me a glare that could chip ice.

Claudia wasn't impressed. "He looks like a child's action figure," she pronounced, snagging a pair of champagne flutes from a passing waiter. She gave me one and sipped hers. "Ecch. The cheap stuff."

"This isn't the Oscars," I reminded her. "The AFA isn't going to waste the good stuff on a bunch of film students who aren't old enough to drink in the first place."

I caught a glimpse of us in a mirror. Dressing down for the AFA was *de rigueur*—conspicuous inconsumption, a sign of starving-artist seriousness—so I had worn jeans and my houndstooth jacket. Claudia had opted for a black pantsuit and platforms. I thought we looked rather dashing. But Claudia was looking in the same mirror, and she saw something I didn't.

"The ice-cream man cometh," she murmured.

I turned around. Adam Davies was making a grand entrance, his lockstep parting a gaggle of awed baby directors. He was wearing his usual out-and-about outfit, a white double-breasted suit accessorized with spats.

"That's Adam Davies," I told her. "The one who directs all those adaptations of Anthony Trollope. I interviewed him for the Slezak story."

"I thought so," was Claudia's only comment, but she continued to inspect Davies as if through a lorgnette.

"He's a little bit affected, but he's not that bad. Hey, there's Deb Takasugi. She made that documentary on the Swedish karaoke bars that you thought was so great. Let's go meet her."

Deb Takasugi turned out to be a brilliant, inarticulate twenty-year-old in a kilt whose ten-minute student film had earned her a three-picture deal in the seven figures. Unfortunately, Deb was tongue-tied to the point of aphasia; the more praise Claudia heaped at her Mary Janes, the more painful the conversation got. After five minutes, four of which were awkward pauses, I closed my notebook and told Deb it was nice to meet her.

"When will this be in the paper?" she whispered.

"Day after tomorrow."

"Gee, thanks. Nice to meet you. You too, ma'am."

Claudia was vibrating after Deb slunk away. *"Ma'am?!"*

"She was just being polite."

"Some polite. She wasn't being that polite to *you*."

I rolled my eyes. "Come on, Claude. I've got work to do. If you're hungry, you can grab some food while I do a couple of interviews."

But Claudia wasn't listening. She was standing stock-still, frozen at the sight of Davies conferring with someone at the other end of the room. I craned my neck to see who it was.

Cathy Bates.

Damn. It was the AFA that had given Cathy her big break the year before. Of course she would be here. I turned to Claudia, expecting her to be furious, but she only looked pale and shaken.

"I've got all the quotes I need," I told her. "Let's go sit down for dinner."

We had a great table right in front of the dais, unlike at the Women in the Industry banquet. The AFA had more to gain by sucking up to the press. Almost everyone else was still at the reception, so we took the two best seats at the table and poured ourselves some almost-generic wine from the bottle in the centerpiece. If I hadn't seen the cork, I would have sworn there was a screw top back in the kitchen. William Schilling, the wine critic down at the paper, would have swooned.

"I'm sorry," I told her. "It didn't even occur to me that Cathy might show up."

"That makes two of us." Claudia drained her wine, and an eager cater waiter bobbed up to refill it. "Eh, it doesn't matter," she added, more to herself than to me.

I discovered that I had been toying nervously with my food. It looked as if a hamster had been doing the twist in my salad. Something had been nagging at me ever since we saw Cathy.

"You know what you said yesterday on the beach about starting fresh? I need to tell you something. Please don't get mad, because this happened when we weren't speaking, but . . . Jeff Brenner called me from New York a couple weeks ago—"

"Oh, Jeff. How does he like it at *Aspect?*"

"Great. He's Mr. Frequent Flyer. But he went to a party in the

Village recently, and he saw Cathy there. With . . ." I named the actress Jeff had told me about.

Claudia tilted her head impassively. I crunched iceberg and took a sudden interest in the chandelier. *When will you learn to keep your mouth shut, O'Connor?*

"I knew about that," she said slowly. "They used to go out a couple of years ago."

"Brenner *saw* them, Claudia. Just last month."

"Oh." She processed this. "Well, I wouldn't put it past her. But I wasn't talking about that. I was talking about Adam Davies."

For a minute, it didn't compute.

"Cathy . . . is sleeping with Adam Davies?"

"She certainly is."

"Wait a minute. Cathy is . . ."

"Of course she is. Why do you think she didn't want anyone to know? The biggest out lesbian in Hollywood sleeping with a man? She'd lose every gay and lesbian fan she ever had. They'd think she was a hypocrite—and they'd be right."

"But . . ." I couldn't think of anything to say. "How do you know?"

Claudia took a deep breath. "Dagny was watching Cathy's dogs while Cathy was in New York. She went over to feed them one morning, and she saw Cathy's car in the driveway. She figured that Cathy had gotten back a couple of days early, so she went around back to let herself in and drop off the keys. They were in bed together. They didn't see Dagny, so she left."

A couple arrived at our table. Claudia broke off the story while we introduced ourselves. Once they were settled, she continued in a lower voice. "Dagny didn't know what to do, so she told Pedro that night at rehearsal. They decided that Pedro should tell me. I sat on it for a day or so, then, when Cathy finally called me, I confronted her without telling her how I knew. She denied the whole thing for a minute, and then she gave up and admitted it."

I remembered Adam Davies's coterie of assistants—all black, beautiful, and top-heavy. Cathy *was* his type. "But she's a *lesbian*," I said weakly. "Not a bisexual. Right?"

"Kieran, you can be dense sometimes. Of course she is. She told me that this is strictly business. I think she thought that that would make everything okay between us, if you can believe that."

A cater waiter replaced my salad with a chicken breast I thought I recognized from my last airplane trip. "When did this happen?"

"Right before we went to Palm Springs. I almost told you then. Remember how much I slept?"

I started to ask another question, but four young film students arrived at our table at once. Three of them were chattering and laughing. The fourth was Deb Takasugi, who sat down as if she were assuming the electric chair.

The guy sitting next to me introduced himself as Tim Zinsser and said that he was up for Best Director. Tim was a dead ringer for a teenage Bobby Darin, and once he found out I was a reporter he wouldn't shut up. I made the please-rescue-me eye signal to Claudia, but she was trapped by the woman sitting next to her.

"You must get to go to a lot of parties," Tim said enthusiastically.

"I've had this dinner many times."

"Really?" He inspected his plate with undisguised pleasure. "What's it called?"

"Chicken à la hotel." I excused myself to go to the bathroom, but the lights went down and Chep Orlovsky took the mike just as I pushed out my chair. Stuck.

Chep kicked things off with a windy speech about how the men and women in this room were the future of the motion picture industry. He also listed all the Establishment directors who had gotten their start with an AFA award—a not unimpressive roster. Then the mike went to Dick Cannon, who had a lot to say about pulling oneself up by the bootstraps. Of course, it's a lot easier to reach those bootstraps when a studio is throwing thirty million at you, but I noted his comments and hoped my readers would catch the irony. When Cannon finished pontificating, there was polite applause, and then Mary Lasater, the slappably perky host of "Hollywood Today!", assumed the podium to introduce a program of selections from the year's best independent films. A video screen dropped from the ceiling and the room went dark. A banquet wasn't a banquet these days without a multimedia presentation.

"Back in two minutes. Write down anything important that happens," I whispered to Claudia. I slipped her my notebook and went out to the lobby.

Though it was only a couple of years old, the St. Monica had a seventies feel. Glass elevators ferried guests up to plant-covered terraces overlooking the lobby, and enormous chrome supports held up unfinished concrete walls striped with Mylar. The signs were made of that silvery Broadway-style lettering that always reminds me of *A Chorus Line*. Low planters separated the lobby into quasi-spaces of different functions: cocktail lounge, café, sitting area. The place was deserted.

A porter directed me to a short staircase tucked away in a corner. At the foot of the stairs were two bathrooms separated by a green felt couch and a bank of telephones. I strolled into the men's room and peed. The bathroom looked as if it had never been used. I guessed the St. Monica wasn't going to be around much longer. I rinsed my hands perfunctorily and walked back into the lounge area drying them on a paper towel.

"How are you, Kieran?"

I whipped around, startled.

Cathy Bates was sitting on the couch, hanging up a phone. She had been using the one installed at wheelchair level. Were there laws against using the handicapped phone, like parking in the handicapped space? Cathy wore a pair of thick black glasses with heavy frames and a mid-calf skirt. Her legs were crossed at the knees, and one foot was tapping in the air, giving her the mien of a intellectual fashion model with a grudge.

A wave of déjà vu washed over me. The hotel, the hall, the bathroom . . .

I grunted at her. Between her snub at the Food for Thoughtfulness dinner and her maltreatment of Claudia, I wasn't in the mood.

"Do you know what time it is?" she asked. "I'm supposed to be presenting the Best Director award to Deb Takasugi at nine."

"I thought no one was supposed to know who won."

"They gave me the envelope. I peeked. So sue me."

"Why aren't you upstairs, then?"

"I'm waiting for a callback." She tilted her head. "Sit down for a minute. Talk to me."

"I've got to work. See you later." I started for the stairs.

"Claudia told you that I was having an affair with Adam Davies, didn't she?"

I stopped. "What do you care, Cathy?"

"Because it's not true. I've been meeting with him because I want him to produce my next picture. You know how rumors get started in this town. Just because a man and a woman are working together doesn't mean they're sleeping together." Cathy stretched one long arm across the back of the sofa, a gesture which I tried very hard not to find irritating. "I think Claudia was just looking for a reason not to commit. You know what problems she has in the commitment department."

"You always take your meetings in bed?"

"What are you talking about?"

"Come off it, Cathy. Dagny Weiss saw you."

Cathy couldn't hide the surprise on her face. Game and set for O'Connor.

Cathy processed this information for a moment, weighing the possibility of another lie, and decided against it. She shrugged and smiled. I felt angry and uncomfortable and a little bit sad, as if on the way to the bathroom I'd stepped into the Twilight Zone and met Roy Cohn. Cathy Bates was talented, bright, poised, and beautiful. There was no reason in the world for her to sleep with anyone to get ahead in Hollywood, much less a man, but she had done it with such ease that I knew she wasn't betraying her principles. She simply didn't have any.

Several different remarks popped into my head, but I didn't have the energy for any of them. I settled for "See you later," and started back for the stairs.

"Good luck with Claudia," Cathy added, and laughed.

I whipped around. "What are you talking about?"

"Claudia," she said calmly. "You're not a bad guy, Kieran, but it's just the way she is."

"The way *what* is?"

"It's not your fault. She likes you a lot, but she prefers women."

"You are so full of—"

"She told me that she couldn't even have sex with you without a condom, a diaphragm, and a few other things."

My throat went tight. Game, set, and match for Bates. I felt something in my chest go stiff, and a hot white light swam in my eyes.

I had always accepted Claudia's bisexuality as a natural part of her being, as organic as her green eyes or her left-handedness. God knows I don't understand sex, much less sexuality, but from what I could gather, Claudia's bisexuality was no different from the fact that I liked both blondes and brunettes. But I didn't prefer one to the other—and I didn't need both to make me happy.

Did Claudia?

Cathy smiled. "Ask her about it. You'll see."

The pay phone rang. I jumped. In the stillness of the lounge, it sounded like a Klaxon.

Cathy reached over and picked up the receiver. With her other hand, she opened her purse, a palm-sized gold scallop, and took out a tiny notepad and pencil. She pushed the black glasses higher on her nose and began to write something down.

I stared at her for a moment, and then the white light in my eyes fizzed and popped like a filament burning up, and when the light cleared, I knew who had killed Monica Slezak.

# ═26═

"WHERE ARE WE GOING?"

"I'll tell you when we get there." The light at Olympic and Sepulveda went from green to amber. I floored the gas pedal. The cheapo low-octane fuel in the tank made the Buick cough and buck, throwing Claudia's purse to the floor.

"Kieran, I'm getting out right here if you don't—"

"Dammit, Claude, trust me. Just sit tight."

She folded her arms and glared out the window, her lips set in a thin line. We left West L.A. and neared the glass monoliths of Century City.

It occurred to me belatedly that arriving unannounced at Gregory Slezak's house wasn't the best idea—especially at nine-thirty at night. For all I knew, he wasn't home, and some busybody neighbor might call the cops. Some of those Beverly Hills people would sic a Doberman on an Avon lady.

There was an all-night gas station and minimart coming up on the right. A bank of pay phones stood near the sidewalk. I pulled in with a sharp jerk of the wheel, making the car cough again. I hopped out, checking my pockets. No change. Swell.

Inside the fluorescent-lit box there was a painfully slow line of gas buyers. The place smelled like hot coffee and burned hot dogs. My heart was beating fast, and I was rubbing my hands together anxiously. The woman behind me stepped back a few paces, as if I might be a speed freak come to toss the Arco. The attendant refused to make change without a purchase, so I slammed a candy bar on the counter, exchanged a bill for coins, and ran back out to the phones, one of which actually worked. Luckily, I had memorized Slezak's home number. The last four digits were 1847—the year of the potato famine. Sometimes it pays to be Irish.

Slezak sounded surprised, but something in my voice must have convinced him it was an emergency. He told me to come on over.

I flipped the candy bar in Claudia's lap and pulled back onto Olympic. We crested the hill at Century City, and then we were in the Beverly Hills flats, south of Wilshire. Schroeder's offices were just two blocks away.

Claudia hadn't said a word. As we idled at the Wilshire light, she held up the candy bar.

"Pay Day," she said dryly. "My favorite."

As impressive as Canon Drive was during the day, it was night that brought out its true luxury. Just a few hundred yards to the north and south, Sunset and Santa Monica Boulevards seethed with traffic, but Canon was as quiet as Mayberry. There was only one automobile parked at the curb; the rest were in gated driveways or tucked away in garages large enough to stable Clydesdales. Not a soul walked the block. Beverly Hills cops were legendary for stopping pedestrians after dark and inquiring about their business. The inability to take an evening stroll was the price you paid for safety and security. The neighborhood breathed with a certain smugness about itself.

A cricket in the ivy ceased his chirring when I slammed the door of the Buick. Claudia came up to my side, took my hand, and looked at the house quizzically.

"Gregory Slezak's," I told her. "Come on."

Automatic floodlights came on as we crossed the damp lawn. We rang the bell and waited. When Slezak answered the door, he was wearing another one of his papery athletic suits and a pair of loafers. He looked tired and sallow in the porch light. I introduced Claudia, and he invited us in.

The living room was dark. Slezak led us down the hall past the kitchen to the den at the back of the house. He had been working. A light was on over one of the couches, and there was a yellow legal pad and a sweating bottle of Diet Coke on the table. Outside the sliding glass doors, the black-bottomed pool was lit from within, floating in the night. His zillion-dollar stereo system was ablaze with LED readouts and lighted bar graphs that hopped and pulsed to the music. It was tuned to one of those soft-hits stations that I associate with a bib around my neck and a drill in my mouth. Old-style Muzak may be dead, but damned if I could figure out the big difference between The 101 Strings and Phil Collins.

Claudia and I sat down on the opposite sofa while Slezak fussed at a minibar and brought out more Diet Cokes. "It's a beautiful house," said Claudia. Her usual poise had returned, and she accepted the drink as if Slezak were a neighbor who had invited us over for cocktails.

"It is, isn't it? My wife did most of it." Slezak sat down and twisted the cap off his drink. The white plastic band that remained around the neck had little sharp points on it, like the jawbone of a piranha.

Both of them stared at me pleasantly but expectantly. I realized that I hadn't thought out how to begin. "Sorry to interrupt," I said, stalling for time.

"That's all right. I was just working on a speech I have to deliver at the Director's Guild. We're having a symposium next month on colorization." He smiled at me. The man had a terrific smile, made even warmer by its lopsidedness. "Now, there's a story you should write. I'd be happy to get you a pair of tickets and hook you up with some interviews if you're interested. I think Woody Allen may even fly out for this one."

"I'm in favor of colorization," I blurted. Claudia shot me a disapproving look.

Slezak cocked his head and laughed. "Really? Can I ask why?"

"I'm not in favor of it aesthetically," I amended. "But I think the real reason most people in the film industry are opposed to colorization is that they're not the ones making money off it."

"That's pretty cynical," he said, but his voice was still friendly. "So if you buy a Van Gogh, you should be able to paint over it?"

"Not necessarily. I think a better analogy would be a book. If you own a book, the publisher doesn't tell you that you can't write in it."

"So if somebody got hold of, say, *Manhattan*, they should be able to colorize it? Even if it significantly altered what Woody was trying to do?"

"If they owned it, yeah. I mean, he bought a Japanese movie and took off the soundtrack and turned it into *What's Up, Tiger Lily?* He didn't have a problem with that. What's the difference?"

Claudia sighed. "Oh, Kieran."

"It's just that whenever Hollywood buys a book, they justify rip-ping it to shreds by saying that they own it and they can do whatever they want with it. I just don't see how Hollywood can defend movies as art, and then call it a business when they buy a book and destroy the source material when they make it into a movie." I stopped in embarrassment, realizing that I had just described *The Midnight Hour*. "Sorry."

"Hey, I'm not offended. It's not an invalid point. Maybe we should get you up on the panel. But I'm sure you and Claudia here didn't come over to debate colorization."

"No. We didn't." I picked at the label on my soda. "Actually, Mr. Slezak—"

"Greg."

"Greg . . . I think I've figured out something about your wife's death."

Claudia gave me an alarmed look, but Slezak's face was gentle, inquisitive. "But I need you to tell me something before I can be sure that I'm right. So . . . please be honest with me."

His expression didn't change. "Shoot."

I lost my nerve. I picked up an LP that was leaning against the sofa. Nope, not an LP; the laser disc of *The Belgium Diaries*. It looked like a cross between a compact disc and a pizza.

"When I was here before, you told me that you and your wife had Adam Davies over for a barbecue the night before the Women in the Industry dinner. You told me that it was just a regular pre-pro-duction meeting, that you were talking about budgets and casting."

"And?"

"I don't think that was what happened. I think that was the night that *The Midnight Hour* went into turnaround. I think Adam Davies told the two of you that Sunday. Then your wife died the next night, and the two of you decided to wait a couple of weeks before leaking the information to *Biz*."

Slezak raised his eyebrows noncommittally and looked out at the swimming pool.

"This is way off the record," I added. "This doesn't even have anything to do with my story. I'm not trying to catch you in a lie. It's just that I've got a theory about what happened at the Women in the Industry banquet. I don't understand it all myself, but if Adam Davies didn't tell you about turnaround at the barbecue, then my theory doesn't make any sense."

Slezak folded his hands across his stomach. "Well, Kieran, you're partially right," he said slowly. "But Adam had told me the day before the barbecue. On Saturday. I had an appointment with him after I played golf."

"He told you on Saturday?"

"That's right. We're way off the record now, remember. He met me at the Riviera for a drink. There was some concern about the script, and Adam wanted to talk to me about it. Believe me, the script wasn't unfixable, but the book was a complex property. Drew had been raising hell about some of Monie's changes, and Adam had some serious difficulties of his own."

"Your wife had changed the lead to a woman."

"How the hell—" He stopped himself.

"I can't tell you that."

Slezak crossed and recrossed his legs, making the papery warm-up suit crinkle. "We thought we had Meg Campbell," he said quietly. "But her agent talked her out of it. She decided to do *A Stronger Woman* instead."

"And she couldn't do two pictures at the same time."

"Adam and I weren't colluding, if that's what you're thinking," he said. "Adam knew about Monie's problems and he didn't want to upset her any more than necessary. As a matter of fact, the two of us came up with the idea of a barbecue so we could talk to her about it."

"Davies was pulling out on the financial end."

"Yeah."

"Because of the script."

"Yeah."

"You didn't try to talk him out of it."

"No. He had every right."

"And your wife didn't take it very well."

He pinched the bridge of his nose. "No. No, she did not. To be honest, one of the reasons I wanted to tell her Sunday night was because I was sure that *Lover's Question* was going to get nominated for Best Picture the next morning. I thought that might take away some of the sting. But *Lover's Question* didn't get nominated, and things got . . . worse." His voice trailed off.

"And she took Zapax Sunday night. Or was it Percocil?"

"She took something to go to sleep. I don't know what it was."

"And she also took something the next morning."

"And she also took something the next morning," he repeated. His voice was dead and airless. "First time in months."

Claudia couldn't have looked more amazed if I had sat down at the piano and played a Chopin étude. Slezak cupped his chin in his hand and looked at me. "Now you know. May I ask why any of this is significant?"

"Greg, I . . . I copied your wife's suicide note." I explained briefly about finding the letter next to Monica's body, how I had picked it up with toilet paper and faxed it to myself before replacing it in the bathroom. "I read it and reread it. I kept thinking there was a clue in the note. There was a clue. But I was the only one who knew about it."

"A clue? A clue to what?"

"Suzan Morninglory said that she had encouraged Monica to keep a journal. A 'journey,' she called it—"

"I don't know anything that Monie talked to Suzan about. But Monica did start keeping a journal last year. It's in her office drawer. Locked," he added. "And I don't know where she kept the key."

"You didn't tell the police about it?"

"Why?" he said. "You think I want the police to go through my wife's diaries? Her personal thoughts? She's dead, for Christ's sake. That would be . . . I don't know. The final violation, I suppose." He blanched. "The police. Good God. I wouldn't even read them myself."

"The note in the bathroom wasn't a suicide note," I told him. "I think it was written Sunday night, after she found out *The Midnight Hour* was going into turnaround. Read it again. When your wife wrote that she was going to sleep, I think she meant it literally. She had taken some pills and was going to go to sleep for the night."

Slezak looked baffled. There was an uncomfortable pause, filled with the syrupy tones of Christopher Cross detailing what might happen if you get caught between the moon and New York City.

The diodes on the stereo pulsed in the dark room.

"She wrote the note, but she didn't kill herself. If you're making a point, I'm afraid I don't get it. I'm just a movie producer, Kieran. Help me out here." Slezak put on his photogrey glasses, as if that might help him comprehend. His face was the color of dust. He wasn't in his early fifties, as I had guessed. More like sixty.

"The note that was with your wife's body was written on gray vellum, the same kind of paper that was in her office. You used a sheet of it to write the love note to her on Monday—"

"Sure. That was Monica's stationery, and her handwriting. No one else in the world writes like that. I verified it for the police when they showed me the note." He looked at Claudia, and then me. "Even if you're right and she had written it in her journal, I don't get your point. She brought it to the hotel with her—"

"She couldn't have."

"Why?" Slezak and Claudia asked the question simultaneously.

"When I saw her that night, she was carrying a tiny purse. It was shaped like a gold scallop."

"Yes. I gave her that purse for Christmas. She folded up the note and put it in there with the gun."

"She couldn't have, Greg. I folded it. I folded it when I took it out of the bathroom to copy it. When I found it, it was folded just once, down the middle."

"Kieran—"

"I *saw* your wife get out of her car and arrive at the banquet. There was no place she could have carried it. Someone else brought it, along with the gun."

"Kieran, it's too far-fetched. I can't play these games with you. I don't know how she brought it, but—"

"Greg, listen to me for a second—"

"Kieran," Claudia said softly.

"Greg. Please. Hear me out. I've got one more question. Do you remember where your wife was during the first week of January?"

"How do you expect—" He stopped himself short, surprised. "Yes. As a matter of fact, I do. We had gone to Washington the first week of January. We were meeting with some members of the House of Representatives on a colorization bill."

"Right. I read a news clipping about it. But you were there all week? Together? She didn't come back early?"

"No."

"You didn't loan your car to anyone while you were in Washington?"

"Of course not. What are you—"

"Your Mercedes was spotted in the Valley," I told him. "Someone was driving your car that week. The same person who had access to your wife's office. The same person who killed her."

"Someone . . ." Slezak's face was a mask of willful incomprehension. In a minute, it was going to crack. I couldn't look at him.

"I think Alison Sewell killed your wife. She used your cars before. In fact, she used one of them the day she met me in Venice. She had access to your wife's office. She was at the dinner. And on the night of the banquet, she was carrying a portfolio case big enough to hold the note—and a gun."

Slezak's face had turned to oak. I reached across the table and took his wrist gently.

"I might be wrong, Greg. It's just a theory. But can you think of any reason that Alison—"

"We've got to get out of here."

"Greg—"

"Hurry up." He shook my hand off his arm and headed for the living room, his Santoni loafers leaving little moccasin tracks in the deep pile.

Claudia and I looked at each other and shrugged in unison, a glance that managed to cover puzzlement, resignation, and amusement in one shoulder twitch. Sometimes the intimacy of our non-verbal communication scares me. We're getting to be too much of an old married couple.

Slezak was grabbing keys and a wallet from a hall table. The only illumination came from a dim light in the kitchen.

"Mr. Slezak," Claudia began, but he disappeared into the kitchen. We rounded the corner and bumped into his back.

Alison was standing in the middle of the kitchen, blocking the exit to the garage. An open container of yogurt and a book, spine up, sat on the counter next to her. She was wearing a maroon USC sweatshirt, jeans, pink leg warmers, Doc Martens, and a pair of gold-rimmed spectacles. She looked like a college student who had been cramming for finals, except for the gun in her hand.

"My God." Gregory sounded less afraid than disgusted.

Alison poked the pistol at us wordlessly, advancing. I kept my eye on the gun barrel for further instructions. Unlike Monica's, this gun didn't look like a toy. It was black with a matte finish, and the barrel looked thick as a sink pipe. For a moment, I thought I saw a bullet winking inside, a snake in its lair.

I looked at the open door to the maid's quarters. Slezak had told me that Magdalena lived out, that she didn't come to the house until eight. Yet I had seen the maid's room on my last visit to the house. A lot of these big producers had live-in assistants. Some of them, apparently, also had live-in assassins.

We backed into the hall, Goldilocks holding the Three Bears hostage. Alison moved us a few feet back toward the den. None of us turned around. I forced myself to concentrate. There were the sliding glass doors. It was a potential escape—out the doors, onto the terrace, down the steps to the swimming pool. But the backyard was dark, and I wasn't sure—

"Come on, Allie. Please." Slezak's face was petrified wood. He turned up the corner of his mouth, attempting to smile, but all he could muster was a grimace.

The light from the den reflected off Alison's glasses, obscuring her eyes. She wasn't moving. Somewhere in her head, a gear had jammed. His eyes locked on hers, not the gun, Slezak put a hand out. Alison still didn't move. Slezak took one step forward, and then another, and she fired.

Something in the living room shattered. I smelled gunpowder and burning guncotton. Slezak was paralyzed, his hand still outstretched. He brought it down to his side slowly and stepped back. Above the stink of the gunpowder, I smelled something new: Claudia's pheromones. The sight of Monica Slezak's body came back to me in a flood, and I had to will my knees to lock to keep from falling.

The gunshot brought Alison out of her trance. She snapped the barrel at us. Not at us—at me. Something deep in my body clenched and wouldn't relax.

"Into the office."

We obeyed: Claudia first, then me, then Slezak. Monica's office was dark. Blinds were drawn across the window, and the only light came from a halogen desk lamp with a banker's green glass shade. I glanced around the room, looking for a weapon, but the office was immaculate. Maybe someone had heard the gunshot and called BHPD, but I doubted it. The Slezak house was on a long lot, flanked by trees on either side. The nearest house was several hundred yards away. We would have to get out of this ourselves. My hands hung empty at my side, damp and useless.

"On the floor. Face down. Don't look at me."

Alison was breathing hard. Pant-pant. In-out.

I dropped to my knees and spread out, prone. Claudia's right hand was next to my left, her head turned away from me. I took her hand. She squeezed back. There it was; something in my hand. That felt better. Gregory Slezak was out of my line of vision. There was no way to see him unless I turned my head, and I didn't think that was such a hot idea.

When you live in Venice, you spend time thinking about being held at gunpoint. You build these fantasies about your attacker letting his guard down for a moment. You see yourself wrestling him to the ground or kicking the weapon out of his hand. It's about revenge more than survival; it's about seizing control, giving back better than you get, making him know what it feels like. You imagine pressing the gun against the hard bone of his temple, reaching down into the pit of his soul, exorcising the blackness and terror he has implanted in you. Making him take it back.

In real life, of course, you do what you're told. It's a moment you feel in your throat and your gut: terror and banality and a stopped clock. It's being in the moment like never before and somehow separate from the reality of the situation, watching yourself from a point on the ceiling.

In real life, you lie on the goddamn carpet. And you wait.

I listened to Alison Sewell breathe as if she'd just run a four-minute mile, and I knew she was crazy.

"Lite hits. Ten in a row, the way you like them. And we never talk over the beginning or ending of your favorite songs," said the radio in the next room. Michael Bolton began to sing about time, love, and tenderness.

No one moved. No one said a word. Alison's breathing was getting choppy, and I realized that she didn't know what to do any more than we did.

"The keys to the Mercedes are in my pocket. Take them." Greg Slezak's voice came from somewhere to my right.

"Shut up."

"There's some money upstairs in my office—" His voice was cut off by a thump and a sharp cry of pain. She had kicked him.

"Your wife—" Alison stopped to breathe. "Your wife was fucking my husband."

He couldn't know what she was talking about. I did.

Some of the pieces were still missing, but it made sense. Monica's car had been in an accident, and Alison had recommended the services of her husband—or was he her ex-husband? She had found out when she read the diaries—or had he told her? She had taken the Slezaks' Mercedes to the Valley to confront him, or perhaps search the apartment, or . . .

I felt the gun at the back of my neck, a cold O of steel pressed against the muscle. Adrenaline spattered through my limbs like iced syrup. I bit down on the inside of my cheek.

"Don't do it," Slezak said softly. "I'll go with you if you want. We can lock them in the bathroom. The door locks from the outside. We can lock them in there, and then I can go with you and get some money. Whatever you want."

"There's a *phone* in that bathroom," Alison said with disgust.

My thought exactly. The gun shifted a few millimeters to the left, but the pressure was steady. Now the barrel was resting on a vein or an artery, fat with blood. It pulsed against the now-warm steel, and I couldn't think of anything at all.

"Get up, Gregory. Go into the bathroom. Don't come close to me. Take the phone out of the wall and put it on Monica's desk."

I saw Slezak's loafers disappear into the bathroom just behind Claudia's head. There was the snick of a telephone clip being taken out of the wall, and his feet reappeared in the bathroom door. I saw a beige cord spiraling to the floor.

"Don't do it, Alison." His voice was soothing, cajoling, the tone a cop would use with a jumper. She held the gun firm against my neck, as if she were a nurse and I was about to get an injection.

"Put your hands against the wall, Gregory." Alison was panting so hard that I hoped she might hyperventilate and pass out.

Slezak's feet moved past my nose slowly. The toes of his loafers pressed against the baseboard two feet from the bathroom door.

Alison jerked the gun, never easing the pressure against my neck. "Let go of her hand. When I tell you, get up slowly. Both of you. I've got a gun to the back of his head," she told Claudia, butting me with it again. "Tell her."

"She does, Claude."

Claudia and I rose slowly, eyes locked, as if playing a mirror game. My legs felt like wrung-out towels. How long had we been lying on the carpet? Alison kept the gun pressed against my neck so firmly that a tendon squirted to the side under the force of the barrel. The half-bath in front of us was windowless; the pedestal sink made a darker hump in the darkness within. I tried to remember what was in that bathroom, tried to come up with something that could help us.

Tried, and came up empty.

"Stop. Turn around."

Claudia and I stopped in the doorway. When we turned around, I saw Slezak, his palms spread helplessly against the pastel-flowered wallpaper, pinned to the wall like a butterfly. Claudia began to cry, something that was so unlike her that it momentarily distracted me.

"Shut up." Alison wasn't wheezing anymore; her voice was sharp and strong. Her lips were slick and unnaturally wet, but what really scared me were the pupils of her eyes, two black circles, flat and opaque as holes punched out of carbon paper. Slezak looked at me helplessly. Claudia was sobbing openly now, her head shaking, her fists pressed to her eyes.

*"Bitch!"*

Claudia's fist sliced. The gun went off, electrically charging the air and assaulting my nose with the stink of burned feathers and a thousand sulphur matches. It sailed wildly across the room, hitting the desk, sending diskettes cascading to the floor. Slezak's elbow caught me in the chest as he tackled. He struck her at an oblique angle, taking her down to the carpet in a stagger dance. Alison fought him with the mad strength of a PCP addict, screeching, a blur of limbs striking at his head, kneeing him in the balls with enough force that I heard him gasp. I kicked wildly at them, catching Alison's boot, and then aimed my second kick at her kidneys. My shoe hit midway between rib and pelvis. Under the flesh was something both soft and hard, like a kidney, and Alison recoiled, howling.

Slezak half-carried, half-threw her into the bathroom and scrabbled back out across her writhing body. He pulled the door shut, popped the lock, and jumped back, as though Alison's fury might propel her through the door.

Claudia had landed to the side of the desk, her elbow twisted oddly under her chest. I fell to my knees beside her and tried to turn her over. She moaned and clutched at my wrist, crying for real now, her nails digging into the tender flesh at my wrists. Then I saw the stain, dark as oil against her black pantsuit, and I watched as it spread from a ragged place under her arm.

Lights flew by the tiny back window in jagged blurs like a time-lapse film of the city at night. One image, sharp as a photograph: a new high-rise condominium, illuminated by flat ballpark lights. A billboard admonished, IF YOU LIVED HERE, YOU'D BE HOME BY NOW.

I sat on a leatherette bunk between two paramedics, knees hugged to my chest. Claudia lay on a gurney in front of me. A limp plastic bag and IV hung from the ceiling, dripping thick clear liquid into her arm. On the opposite wall were built-in metal shelves like the ones in a flight attendant's galley. Instead of chicken dinners, these racks held bandages and blankets, bottles with rubber stoppers and long medical names.

I held Claudia's hand in mine. Her fingers were warm, but there was no response in pressure. Her eyes were closed and her mouth was open, covered with a hard plastic cup.

"Going into shock," said the person who had loaded Claudia into the ambulance. She was a black woman in a white jacket.

"Check the systolic," said another voice.

The woman wrapped a Velcro cuff around my arm.

They were talking about me. I smelled exhaust and rubbing alcohol.

Suddenly, I was tired, as tired as I'd ever been in my life.

I tried to lie down next to Claudia, but there wasn't room on the narrow gurney, so I wrapped my arms around her stomach and listened to her breathing.

It was shallow and irregular, like that of an animal who's been hit by a car.

# =27=

ON TV, THE ENTRANCE TO THE Academy Awards looks enormous and exciting. Exciting it may be, but enormous it ain't. Arrivals only have to walk thirty feet or so from their car to the auditorium, a trek for which most of them, inexplicably, don sunglasses.

I had avoided the limo jam by parking at the paper and walking the three blocks up First Street to the entrance. The streets around the Music Center were a parking lot of police cars, satellite trucks, LAPD blockades, and limos of varying stretchiness. Helicopters circled like vultures, filming the arrivals as they climbed out of their limousines. Knots of protesters were behind the blockades on Hope Street, all competing to get their picket signs on worldwide TV. TURN TO JESUS (JOHN 4:16). MAINTENANCE WORKERS UNION LOCAL 818. REAL STARS DON'T WEAR FUR. PROMOTE QUEER VISIBILITY. U.S. OUT OF ISRAEL. CHOOSY WOMEN CHOOSE CHOICE. ABORTED CHILDREN *NEVER* HAVE A NICE DAY.

"You'd think," Claudia shouted over the helicopters, "that somebody would be out here demonstrating for better movies."

A biplane flew over, trailing a banner: "WORLD'S FUNNYEST SCREENPLAY. CALL ___-____."

"Or better spelling," I told her.

We were at the entrance. I could see Frank Grassley on the red carpet, holding a microphone and bouncing around like a puppy with a bladder control problem. To the right was the Dorothy Chandler Pavilion, a stately battleship of a building. It had been built in the 1960s and therefore qualified as a historic structure by Los Angeles standards. Directly outside the front door was a block-long tent where the Governors' Ball would be held.

Guards with Armani suits and squiggly cords in their ears checked ducats at the entrance to the plaza. Bleachers flanked the red carpet, filled with fans and their ice chests, beach chairs, blankets, binoculars, and cameras. They shouted at each arrival with a ferocious idolatry that made me cringe. Past them, the credentialed press and photographers strained and jostled behind steel barricades. Marilyn Amsterdam caught my eye and gave me the finger. Half the reporters were screaming questions at the arrivals, and the other half were yelling into cellular phones, one finger jammed in their ears. I knew from experience that individual interviews were impossible when you were trapped behind the barricades, but the media were putting up a good battle. Mary Lasater from "Hollywood Today!" was waving a sign that begged WHO DESIGNED YOUR BEAUTIFUL DRESS?

"That woman needs to be slapped," Claudia said cheerfully, hoisting her own beautiful dress with her good hand. "Wait a sec. Let me check my lipstick before we go in."

Her left arm was still in a sling, but you could barely see the gauze bandage in her armpit. The stitches weren't supposed to come out for another week, but her doctor had told us there was no reason she shouldn't go to the Oscars. She had bought an ice-blue sheath of some shimmering material and her hair was twisted into a simple chignon. She caught me grinning at her in her compact.

"You look like Kim Novak," I told her, kissing her cheek.

"I feel like Tippi Hedren. After the birds," she grumbled, but she was smiling. "You don't look too bad yourself. Almost like a real adult."

"Have tux. Will travel."

I glanced at the reporters seething like a koi pond behind the barricades, and tried to hide a shudder. For the first time in my life, I'd been on the other side of those poking microphones, and I hadn't enjoyed the experience.

Once Alison had been installed at the Sybil Brand Institute to await trial and the first cloud of dust from the Action/Eyewitness/Real News crews had cleared, there had been dozens of reporters sniffing around, trying to get their hooks into the players. I felt like someone who had discovered a meteor in his backyard, only to have NASA swoop down and spirit it away. Of course, I had been in a position to scoop them all, but it could never happen now. By any reasonable journalistic yardstick, I was no longer a reporter; I had become part of the story. Any hopes that I'd had for writing a book or an article on Monica Slezak were gone.

I refused almost all the interview requests, which did nothing for my bank account but earned me the profuse thanks of Gregory Slezak. He understood when I told him I felt obligated to cooperate with Catherine Camminger, the reporter from my own paper. She took me to Cormorant-at-the-Shore. We ate a two-hour, three-dessert lunch that we charged to the paper, and I went home, eager to get back to my usual underpaid obscurity.

A week later, though, Slezak called again. He had a favor to ask.

A sleazebag from a tabloid–TV show had gotten both of our home phone numbers and been hounding us for days. The show had been airing a series of exclusive interviews with Eric Coffield, whose publicity-shyness had disappeared the minute a checkbook was opened. Slezak wanted to know if I would consent to an interview, just to put Monica in a more sympathetic light. The next morning, I drove to a studio in West L.A., where they smeared gunk on my face, shone hot lights in my eyes, and spent two hours trying to get me to say nasty things about a dead woman I'd never met. I never took the bait, so my comments were limited to five seconds on that night's broadcast.

For my participation, though, I received a cashier's check in the amount of several thousand dollars. Jocelyn had brokered the appearance for me, so once fifteen percent had been subtracted, I had enough left over to take care of my outstanding debts and put a little in the bank. My sole bit of extravagance was dropping $472.35 on a beautiful new tuxedo—which came back from the alteration shop the very morning of the Academy Awards.

We staked out a spot by the front door of the Dorothy Chandler, where we watched the arrivals, critiqued the clothes, eavesdropped on a few conversations, and got a few quotes. Every nominee told me the same thing ("I'm so excited to be here. It's an honor just to be *nominated*")—which might have been true but made for lousy copy. By the magic hour of six, everyone was inside. This wasn't a real celebration; it was a TV taping. No glamorous, fashionably late entrances at the Academy Awards.

Since my job was to cover the party, not the award ceremony, the Academy had provided me with passes for the party only. This meant Claudia and I had to wait outside the Chandler for three hours—or more, depending on the gusts of windbaggery to which the more "socially conscious" presenters were inspired tonight. I killed a few minutes by borrowing Marilyn Amsterdam's cellular phone and calling in my quotes to the copy desk, where an editor would boil them down for the next day's edition.

By seven, a stiff breeze was sweeping down Hope Street, sending newspapers and other garbage rattling against the barricades. The reporters and photographers had dispersed, moving on to the various Oscar parties around town, and the grand entrance—watched by one billion people around the world just an hour before—was an abandoned set. The red carpet was dirty and worn, held down at the edges with potted plants and fraying black tape. The bleachers where the fans had camped out all weekend were now empty of everything but food wrappers and a discarded Igloo cooler. The only impressive things were the two giant gold statues of Oscar, and even *they* looked a little shabby in person. *Ozymandias*, as imagined by Steven Spielberg.

We killed another hour by hanging around the back of the tent, where dozens of caterers were scuttling around a makeshift outdoor kitchen. The women all had buzz cuts; the men, ponytails. It looked like a M*A*S*H unit staffed by MTV. A friendly cater waiter slipped us some smoked duck and brownies. Claudia and I found a bench on the Hope Street side of the Pavilion and sat down with our food.

It was eight-fifteen, well into the middle portion of the show, the long hammock between the opening number and the big awards. Several dozen people had drifted outside, chattering, lighting up cigarettes. Across from us, standing next to a pillar, were Dick Cannon and his latest AMW. She looked as if she should have a staple through her navel and a list of turn-ons and turn-offs printed on her backside. They weren't talking. With no one in the vicinity to interview or photograph them, Cannon and the woman seemed to have shut down, as lifelike and lifeless as Disney's Mr. Lincoln.

I gazed up to the tops of the trucks that ringed the Music Center. Satellite dishes turned their faces toward the heavens, beaming images to Europe, South America, Africa, and, for all I knew, Antarctica. Even Drew Wilson was probably watching, wherever he was.

The whole world cared about the Academy Awards—cared about them deeply—but it would take a better detective than I to figure out why, or what relation it had to their lives. After all, I was there, and I was damned if I knew what it had to do with mine.

Claudia elbowed me in the ribs with her sling. "Hello?"

"Sorry."

"What are you thinking about?"

"Something someone told me once. That Oliver North can commit treason and no one cares, but Oliver Stone lights a fart and the world stops to listen."

"That's not your fault."

I murmured something noncommittal.

"And you know something else?"

"What?"

"Get over it."

We munched the last strips of duck in silence.

"I'm still hungry," Claudia said.

"Me too."

"I'm cold."

"Me too."

"It *is* better on TV."

"I told you."

A man in an shawl-collared Armani tux walked toward us, shouting into a cellular phone and gesticulating as if he were closing a three-picture deal. "No, no, no. I said *no*, Joshua. No more *Aladdin.*" As he got closer, his voice dropped. "If Margreet already let you watch *Aladdin*, then it's time for bed *right now*, Joshua."

Claudia shook her head. "There must be a hundred people out here. How come you never see any empty seats on TV?"

"The Academy hires seat-sitters. Professional mannequins in tuxedos and evening gowns. If Dick Cannon gets up to take a whiz, a seat-sitter grabs his chair until he comes back."

"And just how does one get a job as a seat-sitter?"

"That's one of the great mysteries of Hollywood. The Academy won't say, and the seat-sitters can lose their jobs if they talk about it. Personally, I think they're androids. At the end of the night, they put them in a truck and send them back to a warehouse at Industrial Light and Magic."

Claudia laughed. "I used to want a stand-in for my life. Or a stunt double. Now that I'm getting older, I'd settle for a seat-sitter."

She put her arm around my waist companionably, and her fingers prodded something in my pocket. "What's this?"

"Something I was going to show you later."

"Why later? Show me now. It'll give us something to do for thirty seconds."

"Help yourself."

She pulled out a box two inches square, covered in blue velvet. "Can I open it?"

"If you like."

Inside were two silver rings of the same design: a heart, cupped with hands, topped with a crown. Claudia pulled one out of its satiny nest and inspected it. A question mark formed between her eyebrows like a cloud.

"It's called a claddagh." I took a deep breath. "An Irish wedding band."

She gave me a look that I couldn't quite interpret.

"It doesn't have to be a wedding band. It could be an engagement ring, or a friendship ring, or just a plain old ring ring." I studied the shine on my new shoes. "I picked them out. I thought I'd let you decide what they mean."

Claudia's look was blank as an egg. Then something inside peeked through like the beak of a chick, and her smile was full of tenderness.

"I think . . ." she said slowly, and stopped.

"Yes?"

"I think . . . we should wear these for a while and then see what they mean."

I discovered that I had been holding my breath. It came out with a whoosh. "Good answer," I said. "Now let's change the subject."

"Let's."

Claudia put on the ring—right hand, second finger, perfect fit. I did the same with the other one, making sure the point of the heart was turned inward. She twined her hand in mine and squeezed. I squeezed back.

If we never got married, we could never get divorced. If we never came together, nothing could ever tear us apart.

The wind came up again, strong enough to shake the giant Oscars, so we huddled together on the bench, trying not to mess up our dress-up clothes, waiting for the fantasy inside the auditorium to end and the real-life portion of the evening to begin.